THE SILVER FALCON

'Don't talk,' Isabel soothed him. 'Stay quiet, darling, don't tire yourself . . .'

'I've left you everything,' he said. 'The stud, the horses, everything. You're the best thing that ever happened to me . . . I want you to have it all. And the Falcon—' He made an effort to raise himself and failed. She could see that every word was a tremendous effort, and she tried to quiet him, but he went on, driving himself by the force of an indomitable will.

'The Falcon . . . he'll win the Derby. I want you to race him for me. I want you to promise me—promise me you'll send him over. Carry my colours . . . even if I don't see it. Promise me!'

'I promise,' Isabel said. 'I promise you, darling. I'll do just what you want.'

He sighed as if a burden had been lifted from him; for a moment his eyes closed. Isabel knew that death was very near; she held him close and tight against her.

'Richard . . .' She could hardly hear him. It was a hoarse, slow whisper.

'Don't have him round after I've gone. Don't ever trust him . . . he'll try and stop you running the Falcon . . . he knows how much it means. . .'

Also in Arrow by Evelyn Anthony

The Defector
The Grave of Truth
The Return
The Avenue of the Dead
The Occupying Power
The Assassin
The Poellenburg Inheritance
The Rendezvous
The Legend
The Company of Saints
The Malaspiga Exit
Voices on the Wind
Albatross
No Enemy But Time

THE SILVER FALCON

FALCON

Evelyn Anthony

ARROW BOOKS

Arrow Books Limited
62–65 Chandos Place, London WC2N 4NW

An imprint of Century Hutchinson Limited

London Melbourne Sydney Auckland
Johannesburg and agencies throughout
the world

First published by
Hutchinson & Co. (Publishers) Ltd 1977
Arrow edition 1988

© Anthony Enterprises (UK) Ltd 1977

Printed and bound in Great Britain by
Anchor Brendon Limited, Tiptree, Essex

ISBN 0 09 955070 9

To Pat Redford with my love

With grateful thanks to Simon Parker-Bowles,
John de Burgh, Peter O'Sullevan and the staff
of BBC 'Grandstand' for their kind help and
advice

I

Autumn was the most beautiful time of the year at Beaumont. In late October the leaves had not finished falling, and the massive beech trees round the house were still in full colour. When Isabel Cunningham came to work as Charles Schriber's secretary three years earlier, it had been in the middle of a blazing Kentucky summer. By the time September came, she was his wife.

It was four o'clock and she had been out walking with her husband's favourite terrier; they had gone through the wood at the north side of the grounds. The little dog had scampered through the leaves, barking and bustling round, looking for rabbit holes, Isabel following slowly after him. The wood was dim and peaceful, with lovely paths which in April were full of spring flowers. The sunlight filtered through the trees, making bright patterns at her feet. Charles loved to walk there with her, and to go on and inspect the rolling paddocks where the mares and foals were out at grass. It was too late to see them that afternoon; they would have been brought in for the night. She called the dog and came out into the sunlight, taking the way round through the large formal gardens at the rear of the house. Her husband hadn't been interested in the gardens; he was content to have a neat, conventional frame for his house, and the house itself was the centre of the all-important stud. Isabel had taken charge of the gardens, planting out beds in the front to provide colour against the stark Georgian white of Beaumont itself and the harsh brilliance of the rolling green paddocks that surrounded it.

It was a beautiful house, built in the late 1780s by a wealthy merchant whose family had emigrated from England; the style was semi-classical, with a central block supported by massive white pillars and two wings that curved outwards. She came round to the front and saw Andrew Graham's car. The terrier was walking quietly at her side; he stopped as she did, and looked up at her, with the bright intelligence of his breed. He seemed to sense that there was something wrong.

She hadn't expected Andrew to come round. He had promised to telephone the results. The fact that he had come in person could only mean one thing. She hurried to the front door, always left open in Kentucky fashion, and glanced up quickly at the first-floor windows.

It was two months since Charles Schriber became ill. The summer cold had turned into an ugly cough, the cough into a persistent chest infection which did not respond satisfactorily to drugs. For the past two weeks he had been too ill to come downstairs. He was a big man, as tough mentally as he was strong physically. He had a profound contempt for illness and a disregard of his own health. It often seemed strange to Isabel, that a man so lustily alive should choose his doctor as his greatest friend. His resistance to suggestions that he should call in Andrew Graham at the beginning of his illness, coupled with his refusal to rest or go to bed, had delayed proper diagnosis. Summer colds were always hell in the hot weather, he insisted, while the cough went on and on and the temperature refused to settle. By the time she over-ruled him and sent for Andrew he was already very ill.

She found the doctor in the study; it was Charles's favourite room, panelled in the original pine, one whole wall covered in his racing trophies. Andrew got up as she came in; he was the physical opposite of Charles. Of medium height, rather slightly built, with receding sandy hair and a diffident manner. He walked with a horseman's gait; he had been a gifted amateur jockey in his youth. He was a typical Kentuckian, courteous, somewhat old-fashioned, ultra conservative, slow to give his trust. It had taken a long time before she felt he had accepted

8

her after the marriage. He came and held out his hand and took both of hers.

'Andrew?' she couldn't keep her voice quite steady.

'Sit down, Isabel,' he said. She did so and he placed himself beside her. 'I've had the X-ray results,' he said. 'I'm afraid it's very bad news. The left lung has been completely invaded and there are signs that the cancer has gotten a hold generally.'

'Oh God – ' She didn't cry; there was a sick, empty feeling that increased as he talked. He used technical terms which she didn't really understand, trying to explain that the condition was inoperable; the dreadful tentacles had crept too far and surgery would release more. There was nothing to be done for Charles, but keep the pain at bay and wait with him till the end came.

'He won't accept it,' Isabel said slowly. 'He keeps threatening to get up. He won't take the medicines – you know he's living for going to England next year. Isn't there any hope even of that – '

'None,' Andrew shook his head. 'He'll last a month or so, if he stays bedridden. He'll be too weak to do anything else.' He turned away and she saw there were tears in his eyes.

'It's a bastard,' he said. 'He's the best man I know. It shouldn't happen to him, Isabel.' He blew his nose and cleared his throat.

'I'm not going to tell him,' Isabel said slowly. 'He's not to know. We'll go upstairs and see him together, and you can tell him the X-ray showed something trivial like an infection. I'm going to go on as if nothing was wrong.' She looked at the doctor, and her own tears fell. 'I've loved him so much,' she said. 'I'm going to lie to him now and I want you to do the same.'

Graham glanced at her, and shook his head.

'He knows,' he said. 'He wanted me to keep the truth from you. Charles has never ducked out of anything. He won't be afraid of this. He told me so. We've talked about it, Isabel. I've already been up to see him.'

She didn't know what to say to him. There was his twenty

years of friendship and his medical position, ranged alongside her three-year marriage. He hadn't consulted her. At this the crucial moment in Charles Schriber's life, he had acted as if she were not there.

She got up, and after a moment he did the same. She stood facing him.

'You had no right to do that, Andrew. You had no right to tell Charles without first talking to me.'

'I'm sorry,' he said quietly. 'But all along he's been worried about the effect this would have on you. He told me to give him the results first. I had to do as he asked.'

She turned away from him then, but he went on talking, explaining patiently. 'You mustn't feel shut out, Isabel. Charles wanted to keep it from you. I wouldn't agree. I persuaded him you ought to know the truth. He's upstairs waiting for you, and he's very cheerful. Don't let him see you crying. It won't help him. I'll get you a drink.'

He went to the trolley by the sofa, and poured out a measure of Scotch for her, and one for himself. He came up and made her take it.

'Come on now,' he said. 'This is doctor's orders. Drink this and take a good pull on yourself. Think of him.'

She did as he suggested; she drank the whisky and forced herself to be calm, to suppress the agony that wanted to express itself in a torrent of crying in a private place. Three years. Three years of being happy, of living with a man she loved and upon whom she totally relied. Strong and safe and indestructible. And now dying of a loathsome creeping illness that was eating away at his strength, wasting the powerful body, frustrating the courageous will. He had known all along that he was mortally ill. His only thought had been to save her pain. Andrew Graham was right. This was no time for petty feelings, for personal quibblings between the people he loved.

'Thanks,' she said. 'I'm better now. I'm sorry I said that, Andrew. I didn't mean it. I was just so shocked – '

He smiled at her and patted her shoulder. 'I know,' he said. 'I know.'

'What about Richard?'

She saw him stiffen. His shoulders went back and his head turned quickly, at the mention of Charles Schriber's son.

'Richard – what about Richard?'

'He ought to know,' Isabel said. 'His father's dying and he ought to be told.' He relaxed as visibly as he had tensed up. He shook his head, slowly, with an air of patience. It made her feel like a child instead of a woman of twenty-seven. With a husband thirty years older than she was.

'Charles wouldn't want it,' he said carefully, his tone the slow explanatory one she knew so well. 'It wouldn't be in his best interests at this moment. You don't want to upset him, Isabel. They never did get along.'

'I know,' she said, 'or at least I don't know, because Charles never wanted to talk about it, but this is different. This is the time to end a quarrel! Surely Richard should be given the chance. . . .'

'I wouldn't advise it,' he said. 'I'll talk to Charles about it if you like, but I know he won't want any part – '

'No thank you,' she said. 'I'll talk to him. It's my job to make peace between them, if I can. I'll go up and see him now. You'll see yourself out, Andrew?'

'Of course. I'll call by tomorrow and see him. Tell him that.'

She went out of the room and across the spacious marble floored hall to the sweeping staircase that led to the two upper storeys, paused for a moment to collect herself, and heard the study door open behind her and the doctor walking out to the front door as she began to go up the steps to her bedroom and her husband.

It was one of the biggest rooms in the house, built above the drawing room, with magnificent views over the paddocks. Charles was propped up in the double bed on a throne of pillows. He loved to look out during the day and see his beloved mares and foals. It was weeks since he had been well enough to go down and visit them. He turned as she came in; his thick hair, so full of life, was visibly whiter, and there was a faint sheen of sweat over his forehead and the ridge of cheek-bone, which now stood out from loss of weight. It was a distinctive face, handsome in a rough-cut way, with dark eyes that were always penetrating. He smiled as soon as he saw her, and held out his hand.

The voice was deep, with the Kentucky drawl very pronounced. It was the first thing that had attracted her, that beautiful male voice, full of power.

'Come here, my darling. I've been waiting for you. Where's Andy?'

'Gone,' she said. She came and sat with him; their hands clasped tight.

'I should have been here,' she said. 'I took Sam for a walk.'

'Damn little dog,' he said and smiled. 'Sits by the bed here and as good as says to me, come on you lazy old bastard, get up and take me out – did he catch anything?'

'No. We went through the woods and he raced around looking. It was lovely today. We both missed you.'

'I guess Andy's told you,' he said.

She faced him without hesitating. 'Yes, darling. He did.' She felt him shrug beside her; the grip of her hand increased for a moment.

'It wasn't any surprise to me,' he said. 'I didn't need any damned X-rays. I could've told them what they'd find. It doesn't bother me, Isabel. I want you to know that. I'm not scared.'

'I know,' she said gently. 'That's what Andrew said. And you needn't be, darling. They could even be wrong. It's happened before.'

'No chance,' he said. 'I want you to face that. No chance at all. Do you have any idea how much I love you?'

It was dangerous for her to answer. She only shook her head.

'I was saying to Andy,' he said. 'I've done two things in my life that I'm really proud of – I bred the Falcon and I had the good sense to run you off your feet and marry you. I've had three very wonderful years with you, Isabel. You made me young again.'

She put her arms round him and kissed him; her cheeks were wet and there was nothing she could do. He whispered to her.

'It was good with us, wasn't it – the age didn't make a damned bit of difference. . . .'

'It was wonderful,' she said. 'I wish I'd had a child. I wanted so much to give you something – you'd given me so much.'

'I didn't want children,' he said. 'I told you that, right at the start. Just you and me. Kiss me, Isabel.'

He leaned his head back against the pillows. He was holding her hand in both of his. The room was very still.

'I'm going to miss the Derby,' he said suddenly. 'That really cuts me up. If I could buy time I'd give a million dollars to last out till June – I know he'll win.' He turned and looked at her. 'To win every major Classic in the States – but never an English Derby. I've planned and worked towards this for the last four years. And now I'm not going to live to see the god-damned race. That hurts, Isabel. That really hurts.'

'You might,' she started to say, and then stopped. There was no hope of deceiving him. Nobody had ever fooled Charles Schriber. And it was typical of him that his only regret in the face of death was that he would miss the race which he had set his heart on winning. He had bred the colt himself, and from the day it was foaled, it became an obsession with him. He was one of the best known breeders in the world, a millionaire many times over who had built up a famous stud in the thirty years he had been at Beaumont. He was an owner breeder, keeping what he considered the best stock to race for himself. A man of power and influence in his community and in the international world of racing.

Isabel's meeting with him had been pure chance. In three short years he had changed her outlook, her interests and her life. Sitting beside him, watching him in the moments when he closed his eyes and rested, it seemed impossible to believe that he was going to die. The personality, even in sickness, was still so strong, the willpower like a current, touching the nerve endings of anyone in contact with him. Isabel had only felt its beneficial influence; protecting, guiding, spoiling her. But it was known that he was a dangerous man to cross, a tough businessman, and an exacting employer. There were no second-raters at Beaumont. They didn't last more than a day or two before he found them out. Isabel had never been afraid of him, but a lot of people were.

'Darling,' she said. 'Shouldn't I let Richard know about this?'
He opened his eyes slowly; there was no expression in them.
'No.'
'Why not,' she persisted. 'He's your son. He has a right to know.'
'He has no rights so far as I'm concerned. The day I die he'll throw a party.'
'Why did you fall out?' Isabel asked him. 'I've never asked you because it was obvious that you didn't want to talk about it, but how can you feel so bitter – what's he done to you, darling? If you could tell me, I might be able to understand.'
He squeezed her hand and let it go. 'There's no mystery,' he said. 'I didn't want to talk about him because there wasn't a good word I could say. He was a trouble as soon as he could walk. His mother spoiled him rotten, and when he inherited her money he took off. He's dragged my name in the dirt. Drink, women, gambling; never a day's work. You talk about having children. One was enough for me. Forget it, sweetheart. The last person in the world I want standing round my bed is Richard.'
He smiled at her; he looked drawn and very tired. 'Now you put it out of your head. Put a call through to Tim and tell him to come on up here. I want a report on the horses.'
'It'll tire you out,' she protested. 'He can come in tomorrow.'
'I want him tonight,' her husband said. 'Make the call, sweetheart. And don't fuss over me. If I'm dying, I'm going to do it in my own damned way.'
Tim Ryan arrived some twenty minutes later; she went downstairs, leaving them together. Charles liked to talk over the day's progress without any interruption. She went back to the study and waited for Tim to come down. He had been one of her first friends when she came to Beaumont. He was in his

thirties, and he had held the post of racing manager to the Schriber stable for almost five years.

She lit a cigarette and smoked it slowly; she felt a sense of profound unreality. It seemed impossible that the conversation with Andrew had taken place. The room was full of her husband's presence; his armchair loomed opposite to her, a chair where no one else ever sat, even when he wasn't in the room. The picture above the fireplace was his Christmas present to her, a magnificent Stubbs of a grey stallion. He had bought it because he said it reminded him of his colt, the Silver Falcon. The wall of silver trophies glittered in the lamplight; he refused to lock them away in spite of the insurance company's protests. What the hell was the good of keeping something in the bank; they were made to look at and to remember their significance. Life, as he said forcefully, was for living. The capacity to extract the maximum out of every moment, good or bad, was part of his magnetism; she had never met anyone like him in England or even in the States, where personal dynamism was far more common. And now that singular spirit was going to be extinguished. A matter of a few weeks, two months at the most; that was the verdict. Christmas. She closed her eyes, fighting the tears. Christmas at Beaumont was the highlight of their year; Charles loved entertaining, and he kept open house for the week before and over the holiday. There were presents for every member of the staff and a huge Christmas tree which they decorated themselves. Neighbours dropped in to see them in a constant stream, bringing presents, children and friends. It had been the greatest imaginable contrast to the austere university festivities of her own home. The polite sherry parties and compulsory attendances at the glorious services were no preparation for the roaring hospitality of Beaumont, presided over by Charles. Their first Christmas, soon after their marriage, he had given her a mink coat wrapped up in a gigantic tinsel cracker. In three years he had given her more furs and jewellery, the Stubbs painting, a custom-made Rolls-Royce and a dress allowance that she couldn't begin to spend. But he knew every item in the household accounts and nobody got away with overcharging him a cent. It seemed to please him to spoil and indulge her as if she were more like a daughter than a wife; and then the mood would change and he would be a man, wanting her urgently in his bed.

When they first married, Isabel had tried to become as much a partner as a wife; her attempts to share his early life had been skilfully frustrated, her questions turned aside. The subject of his first wife was never mentioned. Remembering his reaction to her the one time she asked him about Frances, chilled her even now. He was a very private man in some ways, as secretive and resentful of intrusion as he was open-handed and extroverted in the normal way. There was a hint of despotism in his relationship with her which she had resolutely ignored.

Then immediately he would do something loving and generous, so that she felt ashamed, and anxious to make up for the fleeting criticism. And it was fleeting. Now, sadly for such a powerful man, his dependence in the last stages of the fatal illness had reversed the roles. It had made her deeply grateful for the chance to give him back the love he had so lavishly given to her.

She heard the door open and sat up quickly. Tim Ryan came in. She touched the sofa seat beside her. 'Get us both a drink, Tim, and sit down.'

He sat holding the glass in his hand, making the ice float from side to side. 'He was in great spirits,' he said. 'Full of plans for next season. He seemed to get tired, though. How is he, Isabel?'

And then she told him. He looked down for a moment, not saying anything. He had a narrow, Celtic face, with deeply set blue eyes, and thick dark hair.

'I'm so sorry,' he said slowly. 'He's a grand man. I'm going to miss him. Is there anything I can do for you – you know if there's anything at all – '

'Just keep him happy,' Isabel said. 'Come and see him every night, just as usual and cheer him up. He's very fond of you.'

'We've always got along,' Tim said. 'Right from the start. And he's been very good to me. Does he know?'

'Yes,' she said. 'He may tell you himself when he's ready. I can't believe it, Tim. I can't imagine life without him.'

He reached over and took her hand. 'Don't think about it,' he said. 'Close your mind. And when the time comes I want you to know something. I'll be right with you. We all will.'

He had been in love with her since she first arrived to work for Charles as a temporary secretary. He had liked the quiet young English girl immediately and set out to gain her confidence. Tim knew as much about women as he did about horses, and this was not the type to be rushed. She had quality, and quality was worth waiting for. But he hadn't calculated on his employer. Charles Schriber had adopted a very different technique. Not for him the patient pursuit of a shy quarry. She hadn't been at Beaumont more than a fortnight before he set out to rush her off her feet. Tim had stood aside, reluctantly and in silence. One hint of competition and he would lose his job. Charles Schriber didn't give away anything he wanted. And he wanted Isabel Cunningham.

Tim had stood by at the wedding, toasted them along with the hundreds of guests, listened to the whispers among the neighbours about how much younger she was, and seen his employer, proud as an old stallion, standing beside his new wife, slim and dark, in a long cream dress. And now it was ending. Sooner, much sooner than he could ever have expected. Or hoped. He went on holding Isabel's hand.

'We'll see him through it,' he said. 'He was fretting because he couldn't get down to the yard and see the Falcon. I told him I'd bring the box up here and unload him in front. If he can be moved to the window he'll be able to see him from upstairs.'

Isabel turned to him. 'Thank you, Tim – that would really please him! I know how much he loves the colt. He was saying to me tonight that he minded missing the Derby more than anything. If only he could have lived till June!'

'As far as I'm concerned,' Tim Ryan said, 'I'm going to act as if he will.'

'Would you do me a favour?' she asked him.

He nodded. 'Anything.'

'Stay and have dinner with me tonight. We can go up and sit with him afterwards. He sleeps very early. I don't want to be alone. Do you mind – '

He was careful not to look at her.

'I'd be happy to stay,' he said.

The next weeks went by very quickly. It seemed to Isabel and everyone in the house and on the stud that the days of Charles Schriber's life were flying past. Nothing changed outwardly. The great occasion was the morning Tim Ryan kept his promise and brought the Silver Falcon up to the front of Beaumont in a horse box. Isabel, Rogers the coloured butler, and the nurse lifted Charles out of bed and into a wheelchair. He was brought to the window, and the colt was unloaded and walked up and down below where he could see it.

Everyone from the youngest stable lad, to Geoffrey Oliver the stud manager, turned up to see it, and when the horse walked down the ramp, and Charles was seen at the window, there was a spontaneous cheer.

Isabel was beside him; he caught hold of her in his excitement and his grip was surprisingly strong.

'Look at him – doesn't he look great! Look at that walk – and the quarters he's got on him! He's better than ever, my darling. He'll murder them. . . .' He had looked at her, and his haggard face was flushed with excitement; the flash of fire was in his sunken eyes. For a moment, watching his horse circle below him, Charles Schriber seemed ready to hold death at bay. Then the coughing began, rending him in a brutal spasm that robbed him of all strength. He had been taken back to bed, exhausted and almost too weak to speak. It was a whisper as Isabel bent over him, terrified by the effect of the outburst.

'He'll win . . . even if I can't live to see him . . . he'll win the Derby for me. . . .' He had lost consciousness then, and when Andrew Graham was sent for he said that there had been a serious deterioration. He hadn't blamed Tim or Isabel; he asked, in his slow, measured way, what had brought on the attack and then looked at both of them.

'He wanted to see him,' Isabel had heard herself excusing what they had done. 'He fretted about the colt. Tim and I thought it would make him happy.'

'I'm sure you had the best of motives,' Andrew said. 'But you should have asked me. The excitement has been too much for him. I hate to say this – ' he was looking at Isabel as he spoke – 'but you may have hastened his end.'

Since she told Tim about Charles's illness they had drawn very close. He seemed to understand and to respect her grief. She transferred some of her dependence upon her dying husband to the young and healthy man who seemed so eager to support her. And he loved Charles; Isabel never doubted that. And because she trusted him and had learned to rely on him, she said something when Andrew had gone that she had hardly said to herself.

'It was cruel of him to say that! He knows I wouldn't do anything to shorten Charles's time by a single second and yet he tried to blame me.' She looked up at him. 'He's never liked me. He's hidden it in front of Charles but I can feel it!'

'Don't take any notice,' Tim said. 'He's just emotional himself and taking it out on you. Forget it. If you ask me, he's too involved with Charles to doctor him. You should have called in someone else. He was damned near breaking down when he came in today.'

She had sounded more bitter than she realized.

'Call someone else – you don't know Charles! He and Andrew are like twins – he's always calling here. They play golf together, they go off to town together, they shut themselves up in the study for hours. I've always felt that Andrew criticized me. He makes me feel I've got to justify myself; whatever I do where Charles is concerned, it's somehow wrong. I'm too young, I don't understand, it's always done *this* way – Charles wouldn't like it! He goes on, sounding so damned reasonable and trying to be kind, when I feel underneath he hated it when Charles married me!'

'Maybe,' Tim was soothing; 'Maybe he's jealous.' He was more concerned with calming the overwrought emotions than with analysing Andrew Graham. 'Maybe, but don't let it rile you. He's possessive of an old friend, and he can't save him; that probably means he's suffering a lot in his own way. And he isn't hostile to you, Isabel. I'm sure of that. He's a pedantic old bastard and a bit of a mule, but no more than that. Don't let anything he said upset you. You go up and lie down now. I'll call round after evening stables and see how you are. Charles will be all right. And you can believe this.' He lifted her face and made her look at him.

'If he died tonight you did the right thing. He'd rather go thinking about the Falcon winning at Epsom than any other way. Go on upstairs now. I'll tell Rogers you're not to be disturbed.'

The next morning Charles had rallied; he seemed cheerful and alert, but talking tired him; Isabel sat beside him and read the newspapers aloud. Often he fell asleep, and then she laid the paper aside and just sat quietly with him. He didn't sleep that morning; his eyes were open and he moved in sudden restlessness. He touched her on the arm.

'No more – ' it was said with an effort. 'Don't read any more.' She bent over him in alarm. His colour had changed; there was a blue shade round his mouth.

The dark eyes looked up at her, intelligence and determination still made them burn.

'Get Andy, darling. Right away.'

She never stayed in the bedroom when he was being examined; Charles didn't like her watching. She waited downstairs, and it seemed as if Andrew Graham was upstairs with him for hours. She lit a cigarette and then another and wondered whether to call for Tim. She didn't want to see Andrew Graham alone. She waited close to the door and when she heard him coming down the stairs she stepped out into the hall. His face was solemn; he started when she came up to him.

'Andrew? Is he worse – '

Andrew Graham nodded. She saw that his mouth was

quivering slightly. As Tim had said, he was too emotionally involved with this particular patient. He must have seen countless patients die, many of them friends. But there was no hiding the extent of his personal grief for Charles Schriber.

'I'm afraid so. You must be ready, Isabel. He'll go at any moment. I've given him something and he'll sleep. I've told the nurse to stay with him till he wakes and then call you. I'll be back this afternoon.' He walked on down the hall, his shoulders sagging, his head bent. Isabel hurried after him. There was something unbearably forlorn about him as he left the house. She caught him by the arm.

'Andy – you've done everything you could – please – try not to be so upset.'

He shook his head. 'I didn't do enough. If I'd known earlier maybe we could have operated. . . . You should have called me, Isabel. Whatever he said, you should have called me at the first sign.' He walked away from her, and slowly got into his car and drove away.

Isabel went back inside. Rogers the butler met her in the hall. He was a tall, dignified Negro, who had worked at Beaumont for twenty years, and he had taken some months to accept her after the marriage. She had won first his respect and then his loyalty. He would know, through the strange telegraph that operated among Negro servants, that his master was close to death.

'Ah saw Doctor Graham come runnin', Mis Schriber – Ah hope nuthin's gone worse with Mista Schriber – '

'I'm afraid he's dying, Rogers,' Isabel said. 'Doctor Graham says it can be any time. But he's not in any pain.'

'Is there anythin' yuh want – anythin' Ah can do for yuh?'

Isabel shook her head. 'Nothing, thank you, Rogers. We just have to wait with him, that's all. Will you tell the staff for me – I'll be in the study if I'm wanted. Thank you.'

She closed the door, and went over to her husband's desk. There was a big leather address book, and she began to read through it under the letter S. Schriber, Richard. The address was in London. Isabel closed the book and sat still for some time.

Charles had refused to see his son. Andrew Graham had advised her against contacting him. He was never mentioned in the house; there wasn't a photograph of him or evidence of his existence anywhere at Beaumont. Nor of his mother. There was a half-length portrait of Charles in the dining room on one side of the fireplace. On the other was a superb Herring of hunters and a groom. It was obvious that it had replaced the companion portrait of Frances Schriber. She had only asked him about his first wife once. It was the day before their wedding, which was to take place at Beaumont. Her parents had been flown over at his expense, and her mother had expressed surprise that Isabel knew so little about her predecessor. 'Hasn't he ever talked about her – how very odd. Why don't you ask him, dear? It seems so unnatural not to mention a first wife at all – it's not as if she ran off or anything. The poor thing only died. . . .'

And so Isabel had asked Charles about Frances. She could remember the incident very clearly, because it was the first time she had seen him angry, and with his anger there had been a sharp withdrawal from her. They were in the drawing room, all gold and white and banked with masses of yellow and white flowers. Charles had decided to get married in his own home, rather than the Episcopalian church, and to throw the house open for a huge reception afterwards.

'Tell me something, darling,' Isabel had asked him. 'Were you unhappy with Frances? You never mention her.'

He had stiffened; his arm had been round her shoulders and they were standing together looking at the setting for the ceremony that was to unite them for life. His arm had slipped away.

'There's nothing to mention,' he said. 'Why ask about her tonight – it's not exactly appropriate before our wedding.'

Isabel persisted. 'Yes it is. I'm just about to take her place. I'd like to know something about her. If you were unhappy with her, then I want to know what she did wrong. It might be a help to me.'

'She did everything wrong,' he said abruptly. 'And you've

got nothing to learn from her. I don't know why the hell you suddenly turn curious. You've never talked about her before.'

'I didn't want to pry,' Isabel said. 'But there were hints in the newspapers about a tragic death. I hoped you'd tell me yourself.'

There had been widespread coverage of their engagement. Not all the comments had been kind. There were snide references to the difference in their ages. And one New York columnist had used exactly those words about the first Mrs Schriber. A tragic death. 'How did she die?' Isabel asked. He had stepped back from her, and there was an expression on his face that shocked her. Not just angry, but cold and hostile, as if she had stepped over a forbidden line.

'She killed herself,' he said. 'It was the last thing she could do to try and wreck my life. So now you know, and don't ever ask me about her again. I hope your curiosity is satisfied.' He had turned and walked out of the room. When he came to her room before dinner he brought her a diamond heart-shaped pendant on a platinum chain.

'My wedding present,' he had said, and taken her in his arms. It was also his way of apologizing. Isabel felt such a sense of guilt for having opened an old wound that she had never mentioned his first wife again.

He had been equally reticent about his son. A trouble from the start. No damned good for anything. There had been a paternity suit in New York, with an internationally famous model claiming that Richard Schriber was the father of her baby daughter, which Isabel remembered reading about, before she ever came to Beaumont. The suit had been dismissed, but it exposed an unattractive lifestyle in which money and sex played the main parts. Richard was a disappointment, and a waster. But he was still Charles Schriber's only son.

Isabel was also an only child; her circumstances couldn't have been less similar, except that her parents were disappointed in her, and in their way, equally distant. Her father was a remote, but pleasant man, so immersed in his academic life that he scarcely noticed his daughter; her mother was equally absorbed by the university, its politics, its staff and its students. She had more time to spare for some shy first-year student than for Isabel. Intellectually she had been their inferior; intelligent without being academic, she was less interesting to her parents than other people's clever children. She had grown up shy, but independent, sensing that she was tolerated rather than loved. Even her first love affair, with a young don in her father's college, had gone unnoticed by either of them. They had seen her married to Charles, whom they didn't pretend to understand, and hurried back to Oxford to live their own lives. An occasional duty letter and a present at Christmas was all the contact Isabel had had with them since. And yet if she had been ignored in a time of crisis, much less mortal illness, she could imagine her own sense of personal hurt. It was easy for Andrew Graham, who obviously disliked the younger man, to dismiss Richard Schriber as having no right to know about his father's illness.

Less understandable but excusable for Charles himself to reject him; Isabel knew him well enough to suspect that pride could play a major role in his decision not to see his son. There was no possible excuse for her to listen to either of them and deprive Charles's son of the chance to make peace with his father before he died.

She picked up the telephone and sent the cable to the London address. Very short and direct. 'Your father is dying. Please come immediately. Your stepmother, Isabel.'

She decided not to tell anyone, not even Tim Ryan, what she had done. The hours passed; Andrew Graham came again. They stood by Charles's bed and the nurse reported that he hadn't woken since the morning. Andrew didn't disturb him.

'He's sleeping peacefully,' he said. 'There's nothing to be gained by rousing him. This may be the way he'll go.' He went downstairs and Isabel took over the nurse's vigil. She sent a message to Tim Ryan not to come up that night. She wanted to be alone with Charles.

She had decided to leave England after her second love affair. Her father cultivated writers. It was one of his friends,

24

a self-important intellectual nearing forty, who persuaded Isabel at twenty-two, that what she needed to make life interesting was a mature lover like himself. The relationship had been as bogus as the writer's books. Isabel had gone to America, less to escape than to find some direction in her life. She had worked in New York for six months and then drifted southwards with a girl she had met. The job as a temporary secretary to Charles Schriber came through an agency in Freemont.

She had never seen a stud before; the thriving business side was fascinating enough, but from the beginning her employer had involved her with the horses. Isabel hadn't learned to ride as a child; her parents despised the purely physical activities and had no rapport with animals. It was Charles's suggestion that she should learn, and one of his lads was given the job of teaching her. She had worked very hard for him in the first weeks, but it didn't seem to matter how many hours she stayed in the office, because he took her with him round the stud, came to watch her riding lessons, criticized and praised her when she began to make real progress and inexorably involved her with every aspect of his horses. Isabel discovered two things about herself in those first weeks at Beaumont. She was physically brave and she was more at home in the new world of men and horses than she had ever been in the cloisters of Oxford.

People seemed to like her; she responded to the friendliness of the staff at the stud. She wasn't sure when Charles's courtship actually began. She was invited to sit in with Tim and Geoffrey Oliver, who managed the stud, in the evening drinking session, and found herself playing hostess to his friends. There was no suggestion that he was fatherly towards her; no greater contrast to her own desiccated parent could be imagined than the dynamic, powerful, older man, with his exuberant masculinity. When he asked her to marry him she had been at Beaumont for less than three months. For a man of such personal pride that it bordered on arrogance, his proposal had been touching. If she could accept someone so much older, and trust him to make her happy, he would spend the rest of his life in doing exactly that. When he kissed her, the two men who had come and gone in her life were less substantial than shadows. She loved him and she felt in the most poignant way that she had found her home.

Three happy years. Marred perhaps by twinges of uncertainty, because there was so much about him that she didn't know, and there was a sense of disappointment which she suppressed because he didn't want her to have children. It was soon sublimated in her devotion to him. It was a warm, secure world, presided over by her husband. She moved her chair closer to his bed, and took his hand in hers. It had wasted like his body; the veins stood out like cords above the pallid skin; his hands were the epitome of him. Large and strong, with a thick powerful wrist: they could be gentle with her and at the same time hold the strongest horse. She stayed by his bedside in the chair, from the evening through the night, sleeping in fits, but mostly awake and quietly waiting. Although he didn't show any sign of consciousness, she felt that he knew she was near.

She saw the dawn come up, creeping above the grey window panes, turning the glass rosy until the pink became suffused with gold as the sun rose. She had left the curtains open; it was Charles's habit to sleep like that. He disliked the dark; he liked to wake to the sight of his own green fields. Isabel felt stiff and tired; she went into the big marble bathroom which led off their bedroom, and washed in cold water. Her reflection looked hollow-eyed and weary. It was six thirty; the household would be stirring soon. As she turned to come back into the bedroom she saw that Charles Schriber was awake.

She stroked his forehead; it was cold, as cold as his cheek when she kissed him. 'I'll get the nurse, darling,' she whispered. 'She'll help me make you comfortable.' Slowly he shook his head. He was breathing with slow, laboured breaths and he caught at her with his hand, drawing her down to him.

'No nurse . . . I want you, Isabel. Only you. Stay with me.' The eyes were dull, the hand fell away, slack and powerless to keep hold of her.

'I'm here,' she whispered. 'Don't worry. I'm with you.' She put her arms around him, resting his head against her breast.

'You've been here all night,' he said. 'I felt you.'

'Don't talk,' Isabel soothed him. 'Stay quiet, darling, don't tire yourself. . . .'

'I've left you everything,' he said. 'The stud, the horses, everything. You're the best thing that ever happened to me. . . . I want you to have it all. And the Falcon – ' He made an effort to raise himself and failed. She could see that every word was a tremendous effort, and she tried to quiet him, but he went on, driving himself by the force of an indomitable will.

'The Falcon . . . he'll win the Derby. I want you to race him for me. I want you to promise me – promise me you'll send him over. Carry my colours . . . even if I don't see it. Promise me!'

'I promise,' Isabel said. 'I promise you, darling. I'll do just what you want.'

'I wanted to win that damned race. . . .' For a moment his voice sank to a mumble, repeating the words again and again. 'I bred him for it. Just for the Derby. He'll do it. I know he will . . . you do this for me, Isabel. The last thing . . .'

'Nothing will stop me,' she said. 'I give you my promise.' He sighed as if a burden had been lifted from him; for a moment his eyes closed. Isabel knew that death was very near; she held him close and tight against her.

'Richard . . .' She could hardly hear him. It was a hoarse, slow whisper.

'Don't have him round after I've gone. Don't ever trust him . . . he'll try and stop you running the Falcon . . . he knows how much it means. . . . Don't let him near you, Isabel. . . . I won't be here to take care . . .' He didn't finish the sentence; his breathing deepened, a harsh choking sound came in his throat. She knew its significance, and her tears fell. She was holding him against her like a child when a few minutes later he died.

There were no arrangements for Isabel to make; Charles had thought of everything. He had planned his funeral; he wanted a service in the Episcopalian church and a private burial in the grounds of his home, near his beloved horses. He had left a list specifying the close friends who were to be invited to the final ceremony.

The day of his death passed in a curious blur for Isabel. From the time she left his bedroom the sense of unreality grew stronger. It couldn't have happened. It wasn't possible that the long sad weeks of waiting had culminated that morning. She saw Rogers, who gathered the old black cook, weeping copiously, the three indoor maids and a young boy who had run general errands round the house, into the drawing room, and told them that Charles was dead. There was a silence, broken by the butler clearing his throat; there were tears in his eyes.

'He was a fine man, Mis Schriber. We're surely going to miss him. We want yuh to know we'll do anythin' we can for you. Just like it was for him.'

She thanked them; when they went out, closing the door, she was alone in the room where she had been married. She had never felt more lonely in her life, nor more determined not to fail him in the smallest detail.

And the most important was five miles away in his private trainer's yard. His last wish, wrung from his sinking body with such effort, was for the grey colt, Silver Falcon. Promise me . . . the words whispered again in her mind, and then the others followed them. Richard . . . don't ever trust him. . . . She shut them out. To be so implacable even in the moment before death – and now it was too late. She hadn't sent the cable in time. There would be no reconciliation now.

She went round to the back of the house; the hours had fled by and it was late afternoon. She took the Range Rover out of the garage and drove round to the back gates.

A few minutes later she drove through the entrance to the training yard, and pulled up outside Tim Ryan's bungalow.

The stables for Charles's two- and three-year-olds were part of a handsome complex, and included the bungalows occupied by Harry Grogan and his wife, and Tim Ryan. Each was bordered by a low white paling fence, with a small well-kept garden. The staff quarters were a modern, brick-built building, backing on to the two-year-old fillies' yard, which was sheltered on three sides to protect the more delicate female stock.

Tim opened the door as she got out. He came towards her, and she knew that he had heard the news. He held out his hand and took both of hers.

'Andy telephoned,' he said. 'I'm terribly sorry. He was a grand man. Come inside.'

'No,' Isabel said. 'I'd like to see the Falcon first. It'll help me, Tim.'

'If you say so, of course. We'll walk round. Do you want me to get Grogan?'

She shook her head. Grogan was a talkative, tough professional; she had never got on to close terms with him or his wife.

'No, I'd rather see him with you,' she said. They walked down towards the rectangular yard where the horses' boxes stood. It was a clear evening, but chill with the approach of winter. The unmistakable odour of horseflesh was stronger than usual. As soon as they approached the first line of boxes a security guard approached them; he held a German Shepherd dog on a chain leash. When he saw Ryan and Isabel he saluted and went back to his post.

Ever since a neighbour had lost three valuable two-year-olds, every stud and private stable had its nightwatchman, some of them armed or with guard dogs. The three colts had been found with their front tendons cut, and had to be destroyed. It was never proved, but there was a rumour that their trainer had resisted pressure to pull an odds-on favourite in a five-furlong race at Saratoga. The bookmaking syndicate had taken their revenge. As Charles told Isabel, soon after she arrived there were aspects of racing which had nothing to do with sport.

Tim Ryan stopped at a big box situated at the end of the line, close to the covered school, where the horses were exercised in bad weather. He switched on the outside light, unlatched the top door and Isabel came up beside him. The horse was resting. He stood in one corner, near the bulging haynet, his off hind leg at rest; when the light came on he turned his head and looked at them. His ears had gone flat back.

'I'll go in first,' Ryan said. 'You don't come in till I've got hold of him.'

The colt watched him come across the straw; there was a malevolent look in the big bold eye. Ryan was talking to him; he had a way with horses, especially with the more difficult ones, and he was a genius with fillies. Even the most temperamental responded to him. He slipped a head collar over the colt's neck and buckled it on. He hooked his fingers in the strap, and called to Isabel.

'Come on in; mind you don't get too near his quarters. He's been a real bastard today. I'll tie him up and then strip him off for you.' He attached the head collar to a piece of twine, which was fastened in turn to a chain hooked into a ring in the wall. It was just strong enough to let the animal know he was tethered, but a sudden backward jerk would break it without damage to the horse's neck muscles. Isabel stood some feet away, near to the colt's head. Ryan, still murmuring and patting his neck, unbuckled the surcingle that held his rugs in place, and slipped them off.

'There,' he said. 'Doesn't he look great?'

The dark, iron-grey coat was gleaming with health, and the loins and quarters were broad and tight with muscle. He stood all of sixteen-two hands high, his mane and tail were black. He had a proud head set on a magnificent full neck. Isabel stood watching him in silence. The living result of Charles Schriber's years of careful planning, a horse bred with one specific prize in mind. The most prestigious of them all. The Epsom Derby.

He had explained it all to her one night, tracing the cross breeding to the great Derby winner Hyperion and Nearco on the male line and the Phalaris blood from the dam's side. The dam, Silvia, had won two American Classics for Charles; she was a beautiful, sweet-natured filly who went on to become a very successful brood mare. He had mated her with his best Classic stallion Silver Dancer. Her first two foals were fillies. The final result of that third mating stood in front of her, the embodiment of one man's ambition. A superb, beautifully bred Classic colt. He had raced as a two-year-old, winning the Champagne Stakes at Belmont by three lengths and the Futurity at Laurel Park, again by a comfortable margin. He turned his eye to look at her; a rim of white showed round it. His dam had loved being handled and trusted human beings. She hadn't passed the characteristics on to her son. From the time he was foaled, he had resented being touched by anyone. His temper was notorious; his ferocity with the stable lads made him unpopular, but by contrast it seemed to amuse Charles.

'Just high spirited, that's all he is – won't stand any god-damned messing around – ' she could remember him saying it and laughing. He had almost taken pride in the colt's tempera-ment; he spoke of it as if it were in a way an extension of him-self. And he refused to approach him with caution, as Tim and Grogan advised. He would march up to him in his box, grab him by the head collar to restrain the colt from snapping at him, pat him on the neck and exult out loud.

Isabel looked at Tim.

'He looks marvellous. Thank you, Tim.'

'I'll rug him up again; we don't want him catching cold.' She left the box as he slipped off the colt's head collar. He swung round and came towards them as Tim shut and fastened both upper and lower doors. Tim switched out the light. It was quite dark outside. He did something he had never done before. He put his arm round her.

'It may sound funny,' he said, 'but I felt he was in there with us.'

'So did I,' Isabel said. 'And I believe he was.'

'I'm going to take you back to the bungalow and get a brandy inside you,' Tim said. 'And then I'm going to make us both something to eat. You're not going up to that house tonight until you step into your bed.'

He grilled two steaks and made a salad; she wasn't allowed

to help. And she hadn't realized that she was hungry; he had given her a brandy and followed it with a full-bodied red wine. Some of the raw sensibilities were dulled and she found herself at peace, sitting opposite to him. And then she told him what Charles had said.

'He's left me the stud,' she said. 'And he wants me to carry on exactly as he did. More than anything, he wants the Falcon to run in the Derby next year. I promised him I'd go ahead with all his plans. And I'm going to keep that promise. I hope you'll help me, Tim.'

'You know I will. I'll be right behind you, every step of the way. And I'm glad, Isabel – I'm glad you're going to carry on. We have a great tradition here. Nobody's said anything around the place, because they all trusted Charles to take care of them, but they're going to be very relieved you're taking it on. And you'll make a success of it. We'll all see to that.'

'It won't be easy,' she said. She sipped the wine. 'In a way I'm scared of the responsibility. But in another way I'm glad of it. I'm glad he gave it to me. I've got something to work for. And I'm going to win that race for him. Carrying his colours.'

'He loved that colt,' Tim said. 'I've never known a man so obsessed as he was. You remember the night he was foaled?'

'I'd just arrived,' she said. 'He took me along to watch.'

'When it looked as if the mare was in difficulties, I had to hold him back from going in to her – remember that? And then the little fellow came through and he was beside himself, he was so excited. He was determined she'd have a colt, and there it was. After two matings, both producing fillies by the Dancer, she'd given him his Derby colt. God, we got through the champagne that night!'

Isabel didn't need to be reminded. It had almost been her introduction to life at Beaumont, that night when she was rung through on the house telephone and told to come downstairs because Mr Schriber wanted to show her something important. It was two in the morning. The viewing box, filled with Grogan, Tim Ryan, Geoffrey Oliver and Charles, a fire burning to keep out the cold, a table with whisky and glasses, everyone peering through the window into the foaling box, where the mare was in labour. The anxiety, Charles swearing and arguing with the vet when things looked complicated, and then the moment when the little foal was thrown, and Charles had dragged her forward to the window to look. A leggy, wet, bedraggled little creature, struggling to get up, slipping and stumbling and then finally straddled on his four feet.

'There he is – ' Charles had hugged her. 'Look at him, Miss Cunningham – that's my Derby winner!' They had gone back to the house and drunk champagne, until she slipped away to her room, leaving them to celebrate till the morning.

'You've brought me luck,' he told her that day. 'We'll get through these letters and then we'll go look at the little fellow. And damn it, Miss Cunningham's too much of a mouthful. I'm going to call you Isabel.' It had all begun after that.

It was eleven o'clock when she got up to go.

'You're sure you'll be all right? You can stay here if you don't want to sleep at Beaumont tonight,' Tim suggested. 'I can go over there and leave you the bungalow.'

'No thanks, Tim. I'm very tired. I don't mind going home now. I feel so much better, you've been a great help.'

He saw her into the Range Rover. 'Any time,' he said quietly. 'I'll come up tomorrow. And don't worry about anything.'

'I won't,' she said. 'Good night.'

There was no sign of what he was thinking as he waved her out of sight. It was a popular misconception that the Irish showed their feelings. They could be very secretive and very patient. Tim Ryan had never admitted to himself that since he knew Charles Schriber had cancer he had been quietly waiting for him to die. He went back into his bungalow and poured himself another drink. It was a luxurious open-plan room, furnished to his own choice. And the style betrayed the background of gentility which he preferred to hide. The family were old and, like so many of the Irish upper classes, beset by lack of money. The Georgian mansion where he had been born was empty and for sale; his father, with an unmarried sister and his grandmother, who was ninety and senile, lived in a modest house on the estate. There was no money and no prospect of any. At twenty-seven, Tim had found himself a well-known amateur jockey with a host of well-connected friends, but without a penny to his name. It was chance that introduced him to Charles Schriber. They met at Punchestown races, where a mutual friend brought them together. He mentioned to Tim before the meeting that he was entertaining a very rich American who needed a racing manager, having sacked the previous incumbent.

'There's a chance for some lucky fellow. He's a tough nut, but he's got more money than he knows what to do with, and some of the best horses in the States.'

By six o'clock that evening, Tim had got himself the job. He couldn't and wouldn't have worked for an ignorant or vulgar man whose only interest was making money. There had to be something more. He respected Charles more than he liked him; he had seen men who showed up well so long as they were in the winner's enclosure, but Charles Schriber knew how to accept defeat with equal grace. He was a hard man, who knew what he wanted and made certain that he got it, but he was generous and completely fair. Breeding top-quality horses was not just his hobby, but a highly successful business, netting him millions of dollars a year.

He had been just as shrewd in choosing his second wife. She was a rare woman, Isabel Schriber. It couldn't have been easy to be his secretary then his wife, inside a year. Tim had seen her gradually overcome the suspicion of her husband's friends and the reserve of his staff, who were ready to resent the slightest show of arrogance from someone who had so recently been one of themselves. She had acquitted herself with modesty and dignity; she hadn't fawned on local society in order to be accepted. She filled her role as Charles's wife and left public opinion to decide for itself. He wondered how so much money and the power that went with it would affect her. Most women would be frightened, casting about for support. She had asked him to help her carry out her husband's wishes. But he felt sure she would have gone on whatever his answer had been.

34

As Isabel drove up to the house she was surprised to see the lights burning in the study window. Instinctively she glanced up to the first floor. Her bedroom was shuttered and dark. Charles was resting there overnight. Rogers had told the maid to get a guest room ready for her. She had slept in her husband's dressing room since he became seriously ill.

She knew that Andrew Graham had been waiting for her; even before he opened the study door and came out, she sensed his presence in the house.

'Isabel? Where have you been – I came along after dinner and nobody knew where you were?'

'I went down to see Tim,' she said. 'Rogers knew that perfectly well.'

'I didn't think you'd have stayed on so late,' the slow voice reproached her. 'I thought maybe you'd gone calling somewhere else.'

Isabel came into the room; she didn't sit down. The feeling of calm had gone; she was on the defensive and she didn't know how he had managed to put her there. She remembered Tim's remark. 'Andy telephoned.' He had usurped her role yet again, and given the news of Charles's death without reference to her.

'I brought you these,' Andrew said. 'I thought you ought to have a proper night's sleep. It's been a rough day for you.'

It was a plastic phial, full of tablets.

'You should take two of them,' he said. He sounded very tired himself. 'They don't leave any hangover in the morning. If you wake in the night you can take two more. Jane has one occasionally.'

'No thank you,' Isabel said. 'I've never taken a sleeping pill in my life. Charles hated anything like that. It's very kind of you, but I don't need anything.'

The eyes were sad, and ringed with fatigue. He looked much older than she had realized. 'Please take my advice. You'll have more of a reaction to all this than you expect. You'll have a lot to cope with now.'

She felt suddenly guilty; there had been no need for him to

come or wait so long, except that he was trying to help her. She had been hostile and rude. She took his arm and walked with him to the door. 'Andrew,' she said. 'I want to thank you for all you did for Charles. You've been the most wonderful friend. You meant a great deal to him.'

'We saw some good times together,' he said quietly. 'And some bad. I can't believe he's gone. I hope you'll feel you can come to me, Isabel. If ever you need advice or help – and don't be bullheaded about those pills – get some sleep – '

'I will,' Isabel said. She held out her hand and he took it. 'I won't forget.' She closed the door behind him, outside she heard his car start up. It must have been parked at an angle in the courtyard. She hadn't seen it when she drove up from the yard. The house was heavy, silent. He had left the sleeping pills on the hall table. Charles had been obsessive in his dislike of any kind of drug. Listening to his angry denunciation of their friends for taking tranquillizers or appetite suppressants, she had wondered whether Frances Schriber had chosen that way to take her life. She didn't touch the plastic phial. She went upstairs to the guest room.

The funeral was due to take place at ten thirty in the morning, two days later. Isabel woke early. She had been sleeping very badly, waking at intervals during the night. Andrew Graham's sleeping pills had been left in the bathroom by the maid Ellie. Isabel had meant to throw them away and then forgotten. If she were patient and emptied her mind, sleep would come. When it did, it was so deep that it took Ellie some minutes to wake her. She had drawn the curtains and the room was full of the morning sunshine. She had put a breakfast tray beside the bed, and was standing by it. There was an anxious look on her face.

'Mis Schriber? Mis Schriber it's past nine o'clock.'

Isabel sat up. 'Oh, thank you, Ellie – ' She pushed her hair back, dragged up her pillows behind her and reached for the cup of coffee which the maid had poured out. 'It's a beautiful day. I'm glad. Run the bath, will you please?'

There was something about the way the girl was waiting,

twisting her hands in front of her, the look of anxiety still on her black face.

'Ellie? What is it – what's the matter?'

'Mis Schriber – downstairs in de study – Mista Richard is here! He says to tell yuh he's come for de funeral. Man, whatever would Mista Charles say!'

Isabel threw back the bedcovers. I'll run the bath, Ellie. You go and tell Mister Richard I'll be down in a few minutes.'

It didn't take her long to bathe and dress. At the study door she hesitated. Almost the last words Charles said before he lost consciousness were a warning to her. 'Don't trust him, Isabel. Don't ever trust him.' Her hand was on the door handle and she still hesitated. Then she turned it and walked in. He had his back to her; he was standing by the window looking out over the lush green pastures. He turned round, and she saw that he was holding a glass full of whisky. It was a little past nine thirty.

He walked towards her and held out the hand which was free.

'You must be Isabel. I'm Richard, the prodigal son.'

He had red hair and blue eyes; he didn't resemble his father. His voice was gentle, with only a trace of American accent. He was the most striking man she had seen in her life.

2

The Church of St John the Evangelist was the principal Episcopalian church in the town. Charles Schriber had been a generous patron although he wasn't a regular attendant at the services. Isabel was driven up in her husband's large grey Cadillac. Her stepson was beside her. They didn't speak during the drive from Beaumont. She glanced at him; he was looking out of the window. He seemed perfectly relaxed. Ellie had sewn a black armband round the left sleeve of his grey jacket. He wore no hat, and his hair gleamed dark red in the sunshine. They turned into the main road. The streets were crowded, and the traffic slowed them down. The silence began to grate on her. He had declined breakfast or even coffee; in spite of the second glass of whisky which he had taken before they drove off, he seemed perfectly sober.

'I'm so glad you came,' she said. 'I'm dreading this service.'

'You needn't,' he looked round at her. 'My father was very popular with everyone. They'll all be your friends today. Where do you want me to sit?'

'With me, of course,' she stared at him. 'Where else – you're his son!'

'Thank you,' he said. 'You're being very nice.'

'I'm not being nice at all,' Isabel said. 'Please don't say that. I want you to take your rightful place.'

'The congregation won't appreciate it,' he said. 'But I'd like you to know that I do.' The car drew up outside the church, and the chauffeur jumped out to open the door for her. As she came into the church her stepson took her arm. It was a bright building, whitewashed and colourful with flowers and great sprays of evergreen foliage. For a moment the altar seemed a long distance away, the figure of the minister a blur. There was a discreet voluntary being played on the organ. And then she noticed it. There was a murmur that followed them as they walked slowly down towards the front pew. People were whispering to each other. She could feel them staring as she walked, her hand lightly resting on Richard Schriber's right arm. She saw the Grahams, his wife wearing deep black, in the pew immediately behind the first row. She saw the expression on both their faces, and Joan Graham turn to whisper agitatedly to her husband. She took her place and her stepson sat beside her. The music changed for the opening hymn and they stood up. Several times her eyes filled with tears. There was a horrible feeling of being stared at, which was not connected with being Charles's widow. It was because of the man at her side. He stood for the hymns but he didn't sing. He knelt for the prayers but he made no pretence of praying. He showed no emotion at all. The body of the church was full of people. The senator had flown in; she saw him on the opposite side, with his wife and son.

The minister gave an address. He had released the text to the newspapers and in the corner of the nave a television camera turned. He spoke of Charles Schriber as a man of honour and generosity of heart; he called him a great sportsman, a good neighbour and a faithful friend. He praised his courage, using a phrase that struck at Isabel. In time of personal trial her husband had never faltered. He had been an example to them all. She felt Richard Schriber stir beside her; she glanced at him but he showed nothing. The remark about personal trial could only refer to his first wife's suicide. She thought it an odd way to describe a tragedy. People in the congregation were weeping. There were men blowing their noses and women wiping their eyes. The minister addressed himself to the TV camera as he finished his address. A fine man and a great Kentuckian; the world no less than the bloodstock industry, would be a poorer place without him. Behind them Andrew Graham paused to kneel for a moment when the service was over. Isabel had always been headstrong, resenting his advice; it was inconceivable that she had ignored his warning and sent a message to Richard: but there was no other explanation. It was incredible that he should parade himself, escorting his stepmother into the church before everyone in Freemont. Without a trace of shame. By the time they left the church Andrew was shaking with anger. Charles had spoiled Isabel, that was the trouble. Her obstinate and ignorant action had made a public mockery of her husband's memorial service.

He set out to follow the Cadillac back to Beaumont; beside him, Joan Graham said nothing. She had seen the grim expression and the tight line of his jaw. She knew that this was not the moment to comment; she laid a hand on his knee to comfort him as they turned into the gates.

The burial was a simple service, carried out according to Charles's wishes. His body had been cremated early that morning; the small casket was buried in a consecrated plot close to the paddock west of the house. Sunshine patterned the ground through the branches of trees overhead.

Isabel stood apart from the small group of mourners. It was a private moment, a farewell which belonged only to her. She didn't need comfort or support; she stood very straight as her husband's ashes were lowered into the grave. He had left her the responsibility for what he had loved most; the stud and his horses. However difficult the task ahead might be, she promised at his graveside not to fail him.

She turned to the minister and shook hands. Then she spoke to the group of mourners. Her stepson was standing a little apart from them.

'Thank you all for coming,' she said. 'You were dear friends of Charles. I hope you'll join me for lunch back at the house.' She came up to Richard. His isolation had not escaped her. 'Drive up with me,' she said. They walked back to the car together. He offered her a cigarette.

'I won't,' she said. 'They taste of nothing at the moment.'

'You don't mind if I do? I thought you were very brave back there.'

Isabel looked at him. 'It's what your father would have wanted. He hated fuss. I'm very glad you came, Richard. I'm just so sorry it was too late to see him.'

He had a curious smile, which she saw for the first time. There was a cynical twist to it. 'I wouldn't worry about that,' he said. 'I don't think he'd have been pleased to see me. But it was a nice thought. I want you to know I appreciate it.'

They had arrived at the house; the chauffeur opened the door and he got out first. He gave his hand to Isabel and helped her out. They walked up the steps to the entrance together.

By mid afternoon the lunch was over; the buffet was cleared away, Rogers served liqueurs and cigars on a massive silver tray, and people began to say goodbye. Isabel found herself having to talk to her stepson. He wasn't ignored; Charles's friends wouldn't commit a breach of manners, but nobody stayed to talk for long. Andrew and Joan Graham didn't speak to him at all. He didn't seem to mind; he helped himself to food and drink. He stood alone without self-consciousness. Harry Grogan spent some time talking about his father. He had drunk too much and he was becoming maudlin. The disquieting little smile was on Richard Schriber's mouth again as he listened.

Tim Ryan made Isabel sit down. 'I'm all right,' she said. 'These are all Charles's old friends. He wouldn't want them hurried away. I can rest after they've gone. Come in and have dinner with us tonight.'

Us. He noticed the word. He didn't know anything about Richard Schriber except that he was a forbidden subject at Beaumont, and if Charles had cast him off, then Tim assumed he had good reason. A man like that would have rejoiced in a good son.

'Is he staying then?' He looked towards Richard. Grogan was leaning near him, talking hard.

'Yes,' Isabel said. 'He flew all the way from England. I've asked him to spend the night. It's the least I can do. You've met him, haven't you – I saw you talking.' She didn't ask him what he thought; he answered the unspoken question.

'I had a few words with him. He's an odd fellow. Nothing

41

soft about him. I expected some kind of lounge lizard – I don't know what to make of him.'

'He came as soon as he got my cable,' Isabel said. 'It should have been sent much earlier. That was my fault, listening to Andy. He had no right to interfere; they might have come together.'

'Whatever he's feeling,' Tim said, watching him, 'he isn't showing it. I'll go and get Grogan away from him; he's boring drunk and he ought to go home.'

She went to the front door and said goodbye to the last of the guests; there were emotional embraces and offers of help and friendship. Isabel went back to them. Richard Schriber had a fresh drink in his hand.

'Tim's joining us for dinner,' she said. 'I told Rogers to get your old bedroom ready, Richard. I hope you'll find everything comfortable.' He lifted the glass to her in salute.

'I know I shall,' he said. 'I was saying to Mr Ryan here, I haven't been made so welcome in my old home for a very long time. In fact I can't remember when. Sleep well.'

She went upstairs and kicked off her shoes; she was suddenly mentally and physically exhausted. The sense of anti-climax after the drama of death and burial made the silence seem oppressive. As oppressive as the atmosphere in the church when she appeared with Richard Schriber. She couldn't get rid of the image of him, standing apart among that group downstairs, a background figure, watching and aloof on his own account, contemptuous of their attempts to make him feel unwelcome. That was what she had sensed in him, and what disturbed her. Contempt. There was arrogance and contempt for them all. But not for her. He was curious about her. She had felt that from the moment she walked into the study that morning.

He hadn't made up his mind how he felt about the stepmother who had taken his own mother's place. And he hadn't given any indication why he had answered that cable by flying all the way from England. To be reconciled with his father – to attend the funeral. Or to see her. Isabel didn't know.

It was the sound of a car on the gravel outside that woke her. She got up and looked through the window. Andrew Graham's blue convertible was parked square outside the front door. She hadn't invited him to call that night. If he had come to lecture her or to embarrass Richard Schriber, then she was going to be very angry. And anger was the last thing she wanted that night. It was a time to try and heal old wounds.

She dressed quickly in a plain black dress which had been one of her husband's favourites, and fastened his anniversary present of three matched rows of pearls round her neck. As she came down the stairs to the hall, she could hear voices coming from the study. Angry voices.

'Just because your father's gone you think you can walk back here and get away with it! Well you've made one mighty big mistake – ' Andrew Graham stood facing Richard Schriber; his face was scarlet and his fists were clenched. He looked ready to hit him. 'You rotten son-of-a-bitch, coming here, walking into that church. You've no right to show your face at Beaumont! Just because that fool woman doesn't know the truth!'

Richard looked at him over a glass full of whisky. 'Why don't you tell her? But you're too loyal, aren't you – too much the good friend to dirty the image. . . . You can go ahead and yell your head off. I'm here and there's damned well nothing you can do about it.'

'Oh yes there is,' Andrew shouted at him. 'I've written off to Charles's lawyer and Isabel can get an injunction forbidding you the house! You're not coming back here to start any more trouble – '

'I got the trouble,' Richard Schriber said. 'Maybe it's time I made some for you and a few other people around here.'

'You bastard,' Andrew said, his voice had dropped. 'One day somebody's going to beat the hell out of you!'

'Not any more,' Richard said. 'The last time my loving father laid into me I was sixteen – I told him I'd kill him. He never tried it again.'

'He didn't do it enough,' the doctor snarled at him. 'He couldn't make anything of you, whatever he did. And you turned on him when he needed you most. . . . What kind of a man are you, that you could show up at his grave today! Get out of Beaumont! There's no place for you here, and there's enough of us who loved your father to run you out – don't push us, Richard. You just might get hurt!'

'You know something – I think you're scared.' He actually smiled as he said it. 'I'll tell you – I've come out of curiosity. I wanted to meet my stepmother, and I'm going to stay around and get to know her. She seems all right; I'd like to know what she saw in that old bastard apart from his money. . . .'

'I'll tell her that,' Andrew threatened. 'I'll go right upstairs and tell her what you've said. She'll throw you out – '

'I don't think she'll listen to you,' Richard said calmly. 'She's a woman with a mind of her own. She thinks I've had a rough deal. She wants me to feel at home. If she tells me to go, I'll go. It's her house now.'

He turned as he spoke and Isabel was standing in the doorway. Andrew saw her and started forward.

'Now see here, Isabel,' he began, his voice rising, but she held up a hand.

'Just a moment, Andrew. I must ask you not to shout. I didn't invite you here, you asked yourself. I'm not very happy to hear angry voices in my house tonight. What's been happening – why are you and Richard arguing?'

'He wants me to leave,' Richard said. 'He thinks I've forced myself on you.'

'That isn't true,' Isabel said quickly. 'I asked Richard to come and I asked him to stay. This is his home as much as mine, Andrew. As far as I'm concerned he's welcome to stay for as long as he likes. You have no right to come here and interfere.'

'I was your husband's oldest friend,' Andrew said. 'You're a fool, Isabel. Charles warned you about him – ' he gestured angrily at Richard.

'I am the best judge of that,' she said. Richard came up to her.

'I can drive down to Kellway and catch a plane to New York. I don't want to upset things here, Isabel. It'd be better if I went.'

'No,' she said. 'It would be better if Andrew went. I want you to stay. Good night, Andrew.'

Graham didn't answer; he hesitated for a moment, glaring at Richard and then he turned and hurried out of the room. The door didn't close quietly behind him.

Richard went and poured a drink; he gave it to Isabel.

'I'm very sorry about all this,' he said. 'I should never have come back.'

'Why not?' she turned to him. 'Why shouldn't you come to see your own father before he dies? Why shouldn't you go to his funeral and stay in your own home! I don't understand any of this – I know things went wrong between you and Charles. But I don't want to be a part of it. I think it's horrible, and I'm only upset because Andrew attacked you like that.... How dare he do it!'

'He's held a very privileged position in this family,' he answered. 'Old habits die hard.'

'I shan't have him here again unless he apologizes,' she said. She sipped the drink and tried to calm herself. The scene had sickened her. She looked up at Richard Schriber. 'Please forget what happened. There's Tim – ' She got up as the door opened. He and Ryan shook hands.

While Isabel gave them a drink, Richard watched the Irishman. He couldn't hide his proprietary attitude to Isabel. She might be his employer, but that wasn't how Tim Ryan saw her. They dined in the huge dining room, gathered round one end of the fifteen-foot table that shone with silver and gold plate.

His stepmother looked very attractive by candlelight; he had a connoisseur's eye for beautiful women, and while she didn't stand comparison with the starlets and models who had trooped through his bedroom in the last few years, she was still very attractive. She was cool and self-contained, which interested him. She made no conscious effort to attract, and he wondered if she even realized that Ryan was in love with her. They were talking about horses; mentally he cut off. Beaumont hadn't changed. He couldn't remember a single occasion, even as a child, when the topic round that dining table had been anything else. The portrait of his father was behind him. His mother's portrait used to hang opposite. She had been very beautiful. She was always associated in his mind with scent and lace and chiffon, except when she was hunting, when she seemed most frail and vulnerable in the elegant dark blue riding habit. She had been brought up to ride side-saddle. He had a permanent memory of her sitting on a big chestnut hunter, whom she once confessed she found a terrifying ride. When he asked her why she did it, she had smiled her nervous smile and said it was because she had to. His father expected it.

'Richard – ' He turned to Isabel.

'I'm sorry,' he said. 'I was miles away. You were talking about Father's horses – '

'Silver Dancer's colt; Silver Falcon,' Ryan was explaining. 'He's the best two-year-old we've got.'

'I know,' Richard said. 'He won the Champagne Stakes and the Futurity this year.'

'Charles believed he was the best colt he'd ever bred. I can't tell you how he loved that horse.' Isabel leaned towards him.

'I can imagine,' her stepson said.

'I helped choose his name,' she said. 'The Silver Falcon. He was almost impossible to break; in the end Tim had to do it. Nobody else could get the roller on him. And Charles couldn't have been more pleased!'

'He loved spirit,' his son said. 'In horses.'

'He believed Falcon would win the Derby,' Ryan said. 'He's proved he can stay a mile and a quarter with plenty in hand. And we were bloody careful. He hasn't been overdone.' He leaned back and helped himself from the decanter of port, passing it left-handed to Isabel. 'I know the tendency here is to race two-year-olds hell for leather, and I believe it's ruined more good horses than we'll ever know. I had some pretty tough arguments with your father about it.'

'I can imagine,' Richard said. 'Don't tell me you won?'

'He did,' Isabel said. 'He persuaded Charles to give Falcon a training run in April, and then the two races only. And he was right. Falcon won the Champagne by three lengths and the Futurity by a length and a half.'

'Instead of being wrecked, he was improved. His strength hadn't been overtaxed, and he'd enjoyed himself. At that stage in a horse's career it's vital he should associate racing with having a good time. Frank Gill rode him; he was told not to touch him with the whip and he never needed to; he just asked the question of him in the final furlong and that was quite enough. He's a hell of a good horse.'

'And does all this mean you're going to run him in the Derby, Isabel?' Richard looked at her, his eyebrows slightly raised. 'You realize you're talking to a compulsive punter, don't you – after all this, you'll get very short ante-post odds.'

'I never bet,' she said. 'And I'm not going to do it for myself. It means taking the horse to England and putting him into training there. That was your father's wish. He wanted to win the Derby more than any race in the world. He was living for next June, and then he started to be ill. . . . And he knew he'd never see it. I promised him I'd run the horse, and I'm going to keep that promise. And he'll run in Charles's colours.'

'So he gets what he wants even after death?'

'That's not what Isabel means,' Ryan said sharply. 'It's in his memory.'

'I know what she means,' Richard answered. 'Pass me the port, will you, Isabel – thanks. You want to do something for father, carry out his dying wish, and the rest of it. You're not interested in the glory or the money from your own point of view. Right?'

'Yes. Absolutely right,' Isabel said. 'What I hoped is that you would think it was a good idea. I hoped you'd share my feeling about it.'

'If it will make you happy,' Richard Schriber shrugged, 'then I think it's great.' He looked across at Tim Ryan.

'My father and I weren't exactly buddy buddies,' he said. 'In fact we didn't speak for the last ten years. Isabel tried to bring

47

us together and I guess I was ready to be reconciled if he was. It was unlucky that I came too late. But don't expect me to feel the same about him as she does, or you do. All right, he wanted to win the Derby. He always wanted to win; not only with horses. But if she wants to go ahead, then I wish her all the luck in the world. Here's to the Silver Falcon.' He raised his port glass. Isabel did the same and after a second's hesitation, so did Tim Ryan.

'After all,' Richard said, smiling at both of them. 'Why shouldn't my old man win – he always did!'

There was no formal reading of the will. Charles's lawyer, Henry Winter, came over from Kellway, and lunched privately with Isabel. She had asked Richard to join them, but he had refused. 'I don't think it's going to concern me,' he said. 'And please believe me, I don't give a damn. I'm going to take off for the day; you can tell me all about it this evening.'

After lunch the lawyer cleared his throat and wiped his lips with his napkin.

'I have to talk to you about the will, Mrs Schriber. And one other matter.'

She got up from the table. 'Then let's go and talk about it over some coffee,' she said. 'And we can go through our business at the same time.'

'I think,' Henry Winter said, 'that it would be better if I give you the copy of your husband's will first. I don't think you'll find it complicated, but I'll just explain the important points before you come to them. As I am sure you know, you are the beneficiary.'

Isabel poured the coffee. 'So he told me. But that's all I know. I imagine it's on trust.'

'No,' he said. 'No, it's not. I must confess we advised him to set up a series of trusts for you, because that is the normal way when there's such a large estate involved, but he wouldn't agree. He has left you everything without restriction. Except one clause. Beaumont is yours, the stud, the bloodstock; his stock holdings, chattels, art collection, everything.' He paused. 'I estimate the value of the whole estate at something like twenty million dollars.'

She drank some of the coffee and then put the cup down; a little of it spilled into the saucer. Twenty million dollars. Even when they were married she had never regarded herself as rich. It was his money. Twenty million.

'I don't think I can cope with that, Mr Winter,' she said. 'It's too much money. I don't need it.'

'I should read the will,' he suggested. He drank his coffee and grimaced. He liked it decaffeinated.

Isabel had forgotten him. She was reading slowly. It was not so much a legal document as a testament of Charles Schriber's love for her and his gratitude for what he described as three years of perfect happiness, and the most tender devotion in the last months of his life. The words were very clear and free from legal jargon. 'I give and bequeath to my beloved wife Isabel Jane, the house known as Beaumont House, with all its parks and amenities, the stud and all bloodstock therein, all chattels inside and outside the said house, to include my collection of sporting pictures and trophies; I also give and bequeath to the said Isabel Jane my racehorses and the following stock holdings and investments herein designated. . . .' There followed a long list of shares and Blue Chip investments. And then the clause the solicitor had mentioned. In the event of her remarriage, the estate reverted to a central trust fund in favour of any children she might have, the income to be hers for life. If she died unmarried within a period of two years from the date of the will, Beaumont with its stud and bloodstock was bequeathed to Dr Andrew Graham, his stock holdings to be held on trust for the Graham child who was his godson during his minority. His collection of sporting art was left to the Kellway Museum. There was a codicil, added a week before he died, in which there was a bequest of two hundred and fifty thousand dollars to Timothy Robert Ryan in the event of the Derby being won by Silver Falcon, and the said Timothy Robert Ryan being still in his widow's employment. The will stated that no bequest had been made to his son Richard Anthony, since adequate provision had been made for him under his mother's will. Isabel put the paper down and looked at Henry Winter.

'I can't accept this,' she said. 'He's left his only son without a dollar. I think it's dreadful.'

'Richard Schriber was left two million in a trust fund by his mother,' the lawyer said. 'I have copies of her will with me. I can assure you, Mrs Schriber; I know your stepson's financial circumstances and there is certainly no hardship.' He gave a brief smile which she didn't like. 'He's an extremely rich young man. Which considering his mode of life is probably a pity. He was a great disappointment to Mr Schriber, and your husband had us draw up this will in such terms that if his son did decide to contest it, he wouldn't have a chance of winning. Your husband made his wishes and his devotion to you very clear. I don't think you need feel any embarrassment.'

'Embarrassment is not the word,' she said. 'I feel bewildered. I can't believe my husband could dismiss his son like that. Not a word of affection, not a personal token. All right so his mother left him everything. It doesn't justify treating him like this! What am I going to say to him – '

'Well,' Henry Winter said. 'That brings me to the other matter. I received a letter from Dr Graham. I know the doctor and I must say straight away, I have a great respect for his opinion. He asked me to prepare an application for an injunction, to prevent Richard Schriber from coming to Beaumont. I wonder if you'd consider signing it?'

'No I certainly would not!' Isabel snapped. 'My husband is dead. I live here now and I shall say who comes to visit and who doesn't. How dare Dr Graham do such a thing – I've never heard of such a disgraceful suggestion!'

'Mrs Schriber,' the lawyer said. 'Please. Consider your husband's wishes. And I assure you, the doctor is only acting in your best interests. He's trying to protect you!'

'From what?' she demanded. 'I'm not criticizing my husband, Mr Winter. He took a certain attitude towards his son and nothing I could say could change it. But I don't have to follow on. I shall tell Dr Graham myself what I think of his writing to you behind my back!'

Henry Winter stood up. 'Very well, Mrs Schriber. As you please. There will be certain formalities until the will is probated but that shouldn't present any problem. If there is anything we can do for you, please don't hesitate to call.'

Isabel shook hands with him. 'I won't,' she said. 'Thank you for coming.' She went to the door with him and called Rogers to see him to his car. She went back into the study. Twenty million. The magnificent house and the stud, all his bloodstock. She didn't begin to understand the significance of that list of shares. She didn't feel elated; it suddenly seemed a crushing responsibility. She could do what she liked, travel anywhere, buy anything. And she didn't want it like that. It gave her the most awful sensation of loneliness. She went out to the hall and the entrance and walked down the steps onto the yellow gravel. It was a bitterly cold, grey day and she shivered. It was all hers. Just three and a half years ago she had come to Beaumont to work for a few weeks, and now it belonged to her. She turned back into the house. And she had made up her mind what must be done.

'You really mean it, don't you?' Richard said. The inevitable glass of whisky was in his hand; he stood in front of the fireplace, warming himself. She had gone to find him as soon as Rogers told her he had returned. He seemed in a mischievous mood, mocking and casual; he had lifted her face by the chin and looked at her. 'You're looking mighty grave,' he said. 'Lawyers don't agree with you.'

'I don't know how to tell you this,' Isabel had said. 'In fact I can't. You'd better read the will for yourself.' She watched him carefully, searching for signs of hurt or anger on his face. It was unnaturally smooth and expressionless; not a flicker in the blue eyes or round the mouth. He put the will down and looked at her. There was a slight smile on his lips.

'There's nothing I didn't expect. What's wrong, Isabel – you look unhappy. You ought to be flattered. It's quite a testimonial. I never knew he had it in him to love anyone.'

'I am unhappy,' she said. 'It's a dreadful will. He had no right to cut you out like that. I don't want the money.'

Her stepson actually laughed. It was a strange sound. 'It was his money. He had the right to do what he liked with it. I tell you, if he hadn't married you he'd have left it to the local dogs' home before he gave anything to me. Or he'd have given it to our pal Andrew Graham. They were such close friends.' He drained the whisky down and went to re-fill the glass.

'I wish you wouldn't drink like that,' Isabel said. 'I know you're hurt whatever you pretend. You're his son; he could have given you something as a token, said something affectionate. It's not the money that matters.'

'Just the sentiment,' Richard said. 'I see. Well the only sentiment he had for me was pure gut loathing. He couldn't put that in the will.'

'I want you to have half the estate,' Isabel said quietly. 'I was thinking about it this afternoon. And that's what I want to do. The money isn't entailed in any way – the lawyer said so. I can do what I like with it. I'm going to make over half to you.'

And that was when he said it. 'You really mean it, don't you?' He was rocking slightly in the way men have when they're standing on a curb in front of a fire, with a full glass in their hand.

'You'd give me ten million dollars, just like that. Because you think my father wasn't fair to me?'

'Yes,' she said. 'I'm going to call Winter tomorrow and tell him that as soon as the will is probated, I want to transfer half the value to you. Will you take it in stock holdings and maybe some of the pictures? I don't know exactly what everything is worth.'

'I don't know,' he said slowly. He frowned, looking into the whisky. 'I'd have to take advice.'

'Of course you would,' Isabel said. She came up and put one hand on his arm. 'Richard, I'm so very glad. Take whatever you want. I feel so much happier.'

'You know I'm not exactly short of money?' he asked. 'My mother left me a couple of million, my grandmother left me half her estate; oddly enough I've invested very well. It's worth almost double. You still want to give me the money? You might change your mind tomorrow – '

'I never change my mind,' she said. 'When I make it up, that's the end of it.'

He finished his drink and lit a cigarette.

'Don't be a damned fool, Isabel. I wouldn't take a cent of the money. I never asked for anything when he was alive and I wouldn't touch it with a twenty-foot pole now. But I appreciate the offer. It's not often I meet someone who wants to give me ten million dollars.'

'Richard please,' she began, but he stopped her.

'Don't mention the goddamned money again,' he said. 'But there is something I would like to have. There was a portrait of my mother used to hang in the dining room. Where the Herring is, opposite the picture of my father. I'd like to have it.'

'Of course,' Isabel said. 'I don't know where it is, I've never seen a picture of her anywhere – not even a photograph.'

'He got rid of them all after she died,' Richard said. 'But she was painted by an expensive artist. Father didn't like wasting anything; I'll bet it's put away somewhere. Ask Rogers; he'll know.'

They went up to the attic floor together; Rogers showed the way. The top floor was used for storage; there were rooms full of cases and furniture shrouded in dust sheets. The butler picked his way through and stopped before a stack of pictures standing against the wall. He didn't look at Richard.

'Ah think the picture's here, Mis Schriber,' he said. 'Ah'll get it out for yuh – '

'No,' Richard said abruptly. 'I'll do it.' She knew that he didn't want the butler to stay; there was an atmosphere of hostility between them. 'Thank you, Rogers.' He went out, and Richard glanced after him. 'When I was a kid,' he said, 'I caught that bastard screwing one of the maids. She was only

53

sixteen; if they didn't lie down for him he got them fired. Here it is.'

It had been covered by a green cloth; there was no dust on it. It was a big picture, the companion to the three-quarter-length portrait of Charles Schriber downstairs. He turned it round to the light.

'She was beautiful,' Isabel said. 'She had your colouring.'

'Yes,' Richard said. He propped the picture upright. 'Red hair ran in the family. They were all good-looking. She was said to be one of the most beautiful girls in Carolina.'

The woman in the picture was in a white dress, cut low and showing a pair of sloping shoulders. She carried a posy of spring flowers on her lap. The face was a true oval, framed in long red hair styled in the fashion of thirty-odd years ago. The eyes were large and blue and they gazed at Isabel with a strange mixture of innocence and apprehension.

It was a bad picture. Dated and unreal, a typical portrait of a pretty socialite of the early forties. And yet in spite of the artist's ineptitude, something disturbing had come out in the canvas. Something sad and vaguely frightened.

'How old was your mother when this was done?' Isabel asked. He didn't answer for a moment. He looked grim and distant, as if his mind were somewhere far from the attic room.

'Twenty-two,' he said. 'She'd just married my father. I'd like to have this, Isabel.'

'Of course,' she said. The silence was awkward. He seemed tense and odd; he kept staring at the picture.

'You loved her very much, didn't you,' she said quietly.

'I guess I did.'

'Charles told me she committed suicide,' Isabel said. 'What a terrible thing. He'd never talk to me about it.'

'No,' Richard said. 'I guess he wouldn't. Let's go down. I feel like a drink.' He draped the green cloth over the picture. 'Thanks. It's the only thing in the house I really wanted. If you don't mind I'll get it crated up and sent to England.'

They spent the evening quietly; Tim phoned to say that one of Charles's most valuable two-year-olds had colic and he didn't want to leave the yard. Richard watched the television and Isabel read. It was a best-selling novel concerned with the sex life of Washington senators, and she had been enjoying it. That night she couldn't concentrate. The wistful, lovely face of the dead woman kept blurring the page. Suicide. Instability, emotional or mental breakdown. The seeds of tragedy were sown when she sat for that picture, even at twenty-two.

She glanced up and saw Richard Schriber's face. He wasn't watching the screen or even aware of the programme. The same look of grim intensity was there that she had seen in the attic. Charles wouldn't discuss what had happened and nor would he. The dead woman had been buried and the portrait banished out of sight. She wished she hadn't gone to find it with him.

When Joan Graham was indignant her neck broke out in red blotches. As a girl, facing the ordeal of dates and dances, she was embarrassed by the ugly nervous patches on her throat. She was very angry that December day.

'Three weeks after the funeral,' she said, 'and he's still there! It's the talk of the neighbourhood! How could she, Andy? Hasn't she any idea how people round here feel?'

'I don't think she cares,' her husband said.

'And look at the way she's treated you! It makes me boiling mad – after all you did for that family – '

'She doesn't know about that,' he answered.

'Why didn't you tell her?' his wife said. He looked up at her sharply.

'Don't be a damned fool. She isn't one of us. She's the last person in the world I'd want to know. You shouldn't even talk about it.'

'But I think about it,' Joan Graham said. She came and sat beside him. She loved him and admired him. In her view he was always coming to the rescue of people far less worthwhile than he was. He worked very hard, and he made do with so much less than everyone else, with their big houses and cars and money behind them. Her damnfool father-in-law had gambled till there was very little left for his family. By comparison with most of their friends the Grahams were poor. 'I think about what you did for Charles, and whatever you say, he should have made it up to you!'

'You don't put a price on friendship,' her husband said.

'Deep down,' Joan said, 'I never really trusted her. She took all of you men in with that English way, but she didn't fool me. I said to myself when I heard he was going to marry her, he's making a fool of himself over a young girl. Old enough to be her father, and she took advantage of his vanity – I know, I know,' she lifted her hand as he started to protest. 'You won't have me say he was vain, but you know he was vain as a peacock! Having a young wife to show around was just his ticket – it's the only time Charles's judgement failed him: when it came to women. First Frances and then this one. My, Andrew Graham, when I think of that will!'

He didn't answer her. What she said was true. His old friend had indulged his vanity the second time around; it was fortunate for him that he hadn't lived long enough to see Isabel's true worth.

Only she had been clever enough to disguise her feelings while Charles was alive. Now her real colours were flying. Richard Schriber stayed on at Beaumont, while he, Charles's greatest friend, was forbidden the house.

'I don't know why you bother yourself,' his wife said. 'Let her go ahead – she'll find out what Richard Schriber's really like. If you ask me, they're probably sleeping together!'

The remark jarred on him. He looked up at her irritably. 'Don't say a thing like that!' he said. 'She's just being bullheaded, keeping him around. He'll go in time. . . .'

'Maybe,' Joan Graham said. 'But it's mightly funny him hanging round this long. They're about the same age; she's been tied to an old sick man for almost eight months. I wouldn't be surprised what they were up to!'

'He hated his father,' Andrew said slowly. 'Hated him enough to do anything to get back at him. Even now. If you're right, Joan, and you may be, then it will be a kind of judgment on her. And since she won't see me, I can't warn her.'

'No,' his wife said flatly. 'You can't. And don't you fret. You forget about those Schribers and think of yourself for a change.' She got up, and for a moment her hand stroked his hair. 'You look tired, Andy. I'm going to make you a cup of milk with a little Comfort in it. It'll do you good.'

Downstairs in the office, Richard Schriber was going through his father's desk. He sat down and began methodically, opening each drawer and reading through every paper. In the bottom drawer there was a flat cardboard file. The name of his father's attorneys was on it. He took it out and began to read through the letters. When he found the copy of Charles's will, he leaned back in the chair, tipping it slightly. He put the letters back, replaced the will in the end of the file and closed up the desk. He moved the chair away to its place against the wall. He went back to the study and sat in the big leather chair which Charles used, and lit a cigarette. His father's library of racing books and references were either side of the fireplace. The Plazzotta bronze of his favourite brood mare, Silvia, with her foal at foot, stood on a table by his elbow. Richard reached out and ran his finger down the mare's back. Horses. All his life he had lived with horses; seen them, smelt them, been put up to ride as soon as he could walk across the nursery floor. Hunting, breeding, racing. Men with legs slightly bowed, as distinctive in their profession as boxers or footballers. He had always thought that there was a horseman's face; several varieties indeed. The long, lean huntsman, the narrow foreshortened jockey with his monkey stature, the stable man and the amateur with features slightly bruised and coarsened. Always the talk of horses, the phrases that were part of a language unintelligible to outsiders. The mystique, perpetuated by people involved in what was essentially a tough and money-making industry. His father, surrounded by the sentimental paraphernalia – photographs in silver frames, that solid wall of trophies, paintings and sculptures, reminders at every turn in the house that

57

Beaumont and everyone in it owed their existence to the horse. He had always hated them. As a child he had been terrified.

He had hunted, the only one among the crowd of local children tearing their way across country who thought the ritual death of the fox was a cruel and disgusting climax to hours of danger and discomfort. He remembered his mother being brought home unconscious after a fall out hunting; he was only nine and he had cried all night because he thought she was going to die. As he grew older, he lost his fear and became as good a horseman as anyone on the place. But it was done with an object in view. At the age of twelve, when he was at home on holiday, he told his father that he would never ride again. It had given him a moment of soaring satisfaction to stand in front of his father and say in his English accent, acquired at a Swiss private school which he detested, that he wouldn't get on a horse again his in life because he loathed the animals. What he was saying, and which he felt sure was understood, was that he loathed his father.

He lit a cigarette, got up, mixed himself a whisky from the drinks tray, and sat back in Charles's chair. He thought about his stepmother Isabel. The news of the marriage had reached him in Paris. He had rented an apartment on the Rue Constantin and was living there with a beautiful French actress. It had amused him one night to give her politician friend some competition; he had been drunk at the time. He couldn't believe it at first. But there was a photograph of his father in *Le Monde*, under the heading 'Millionaire to wed secretary'. His reaction was instinctive. He got out of bed, pulled the bedclothes off the actress and yelled at her to get up.

For a moment her perfect, nude body had enraged and disgusted him. With the paper crumpled in his hand he had told her to get dressed and get out. So his father was going to re-marry. After ten years as a widower, the object of many ambitious women's attentions, he had chosen an English girl thirty years younger than himself, and blazoned his romance with her across the newspapers. He had formed a mental picture of Isabel Cunningham. She was described as the daughter of a university professor; she had come to work at Beaumont as his father's secretary. He had spent that day in the flat alone. He drank but without getting drunk. When the first reporter called for his reaction, he said he hadn't met the bride-to-be, and only wished his father happiness. Then he took his phone off the hook. It was so close to his mother's anniversary; just ten years ago she had been buried privately in Freemont, with the minimum of ceremony. He had torn up the newspapers, one by one. When the actress arrived at the apartment to collect her clothes and indulge in a dramatic scene, which might, she hoped, end in a reconciliation, Richard had slammed the front door in her face.

Now, just a week before Christmas he was leaving Beaumont. Isabel had asked him to stay; he sensed, with irony, that she was dreading the holiday period, in contrast to Tim Ryan, who could only see it as another opportunity to comfort the widow. It amused Richard, who knew more about the pursuit of women than the Irishman would learn in the rest of his life, to watch him make his moves. Very carefully, with great regard for the proprieties. A gentleman dealing with a lady. He was so obviously in love with her that she must be blind not to see it. Richard believed that Isabel, unlike most women, did not equate herself and her relationships with people in terms of personal gain or simple vanity.

She was an unusual woman; in some ways over simple, in others complex and obdurate. A generous spirit and a strong will. It was strange to him to find these qualities in her, rather than the ones he had been expecting. The cable had warned him not to pre-judge too quickly. The first impression of her confirmed his suspicion that his father hadn't chosen a clever little fortune-hunter as his second wife. He was no fool; he judged human beings as he did horses. The only standard was their usefulness to him. He had found a rarity in Isabel Cunningham, and added her to his possessions. And then he had succeeded, after three years of failure, in breeding his colt by the dam immortalized in bronze. He got his Derby prospect after all. The only justice was in the cancer that killed him before he could see it win. And even that he was determined to thwart. He pushed the chair back and got up from the desk. He thought of the terms of that will, and a smile flitted briefly across his face. The terms were unbreakable. Isabel, or her children if she remarried, inherited everything. Unless she died within two years. He went to the door and opened it quietly. He looked out; the passage leading into the main hall was empty. Isabel had gone into Freemont; the servants were in their rooms for the afternoon. He closed the office door very quietly and sprang lightly up the stairs. Nobody heard him; he reached his own room and shut himself inside. When Isabel returned he came down to meet her smiling, and took her parcels. He mentioned that he had taken his father's terrier for a walk in the woods. And then he had finished his packing.

Isabel went to the airport to see him off. It was freezing cold; she was wrapped in a fur coat and hat. They said goodbye in the departure lounge. There was a sad, empty feeling which she couldn't explain. She hadn't wanted him to leave. A part of Charles was with her while he stayed at Beaumont. Tears were quite near as he shook hands.

'I'm not very good at saying thank you,' Richard said. 'So I've thought of something to do it for me. Happy Christmas.' He put a small package into her hand. And then he bent and kissed her on the cheek. 'From a grateful stepson,' he said. Then he turned, waved once and walked through to catch his plane. Isabel opened the parcel in the car on her way back to Beaumont. There was a flat gold box, with her initials on it in diamonds. Inside it was a letter.

'To remind you of the prodigal. To say thank you for the fatted calf, and the enclosed is to make sure I see you again. I've included Ryan in case he makes you go to England with him and his damned horse instead. I can promise you'll enjoy it. Richard.' Inside the letter were two air tickets to Barbados, dated the first week in January.

Christmas was bearable because of the efforts made by Tim

Ryan and the staff at Beaumont. It was his suggestion to carry on Charles's tradition; to have the huge tree with its load of presents, to keep open house for their friends. It had worked because everyone close to her was determined that it should. A lot of old faces presented themselves; people sent flowers or personal presents, but there were exceptions. Andrew Graham, his wife and children, and some of their intimates did not appear, although Isabel had sent the Graham family a corporate message, asking them to call and see her. She was going to the West Indies for a holiday and then on to England, where the Silver Falcon was going into training for the coming season.

The festival came and passed; she survived the Communion Service, sitting in the pew reserved for Charles, which he had occupied only at Christmas and Easter out of consideration for the minister. It was painful and yet it heartened her. She felt that he was very close during that time; the friendship and good wishes of their neighbours were a comfort. And there was Tim Ryan, solicitous, reliable, never obtrusive but always at hand. With the first biting January days, she prepared for the trip to Barbados. At first she had hesitated; it was Tim who insisted that she should go. The holiday would do her good; they could spend a lazy three weeks in the sun, while the Falcon settled into his new quarters at Lambourn. He was going to Nigel Foster, top of the Flat trainers' league for the third year running, an old friend of Charles, and responsible for his string in England. The Derby was the objective; everything was being carried out exactly as if Charles Schriber were alive and in command. As the winter gripped them, and the anti-climax of Christmas made her feel even lonelier, the prospect of escape into the Caribbean became ever more attractive.

Three days before they left, a cable arrived from Richard. He had cancelled their reservations at the Sandy Lane Hotel. They were staying with him at the house of an amusing friend, Roy Farrant. The name was familiar, and Ryan filled in the details. 'Farrant,' Tim said. 'He's quite a figure in English racing. I'm surprised you haven't met him.'

'I may have done,' she said. 'But there were always such

crowds of people when Charles and I were over. Doesn't he own Rocket Man?'

'He does,' Harry Grogan said. 'And Trembler and Harrabin. He's one of the most successful owners in England. But he's a bit *persona non grata*, if you know what I mean. They don't like them larger than life in the Jockey Club.' Grogan didn't like the English racing establishment and he never missed an opportunity to criticize.

'He had a Derby hope last year,' Tim said. 'As usual. He's been trying to win the race for years. It's as big an obsession with him as it was with Charles. He's spent a fortune trying. And he's going to lose to us this time!'

'Funny Richard being such a friend,' Grogan remarked. He hadn't forgiven Charles's son for telling him how much he disliked racing. 'Considering he hates horses.'

'I'll be interested to meet him,' Tim remarked. 'I've heard a story or two about him . . . they say he's a real character.' He smiled at Isabel. 'I bet he's anxious to meet you too,' he said. 'And find out all he can about the Falcon. I think we're going to enjoy ourselves.' Isabel smiled back at him.

'You can talk horses to your heart's content. I'm going to swim and lie in the sun. And I'm sure he's nice, or Richard wouldn't have invited us to stay with him.'

She had put the gold box in her bedroom; the room where Charles had died was kept shut up and she had moved permanently into the green room suite. His letter was folded up inside it. 'To say thank you for the fatted calf. And to make sure I see you again.' To lie in the sun, to swim in the warm West Indian sea, to live for a while in a different environment, where there was no Beaumont, no role to fill as Charles's widow. No feeling of guilt because she was beginning to feel stifled. She hadn't admitted to herself until that night, sitting with Tim and the Grogans, talking about the Falcon and Roy Farrant, just how much she was looking forward to seeing Richard Schriber again.

3

'God, it's hot!' Patsy Farrant dipped her feet into the swimming pool and splashed the blue water. Just behind her, stretched out on a canvas bed, her husband opened his eyes.

'What do you expect, for Christ's sake? Snow?' He had long accepted the fact that when she wasn't making love to him, his wife was the most irritating and stupid human being he knew. Behind his dark glasses he looked with dislike at the perfect shape of her brown back, narrowing into hips and buttocks like a pair of peaches. She had a marvellous body; it had brought her into the top-earning bracket as an international model, and she had a face of such exquisite beauty that he supposed it was asking too much to expect her to have intelligence as well. He had married her after living with her for two years, and two years was a very long time for Roy Farrant to remain interested in any woman. But she had a God-given talent for sex, and she bore his rudeness and irritability with smiling calm. He had married her because another rich man was sniffing round, and he knew Patsy well enough to realize that she would simply move out on him and move on.

Four years later he was still as dependent upon her sexually; when he had been particularly unpleasant to her, he gave her an expensive piece of jewellery or a new fur coat. She accepted the presents and the bullying with equal calm. When he first moved her into his Eaton Square flat, she had been sent to an elocution teacher to remove a grating Cockney accent. The same woman had smoothed away his broad Yorkshire vowels into the classless diction known as Middle English by those disposed to be unkind. He had no real social pretensions, but he refused to be laughed at by people he regarded as quite inferior in intellect and achievement, just because they went to certain public schools and had a different background.

Roy had grown up in Barnsley, where his father kept a pub. He had worked hard at school and got himself to university, where he took a degree in economics. An academic career, or a job in the Civil Service was his expected choice, but he had borrowed five hundred pounds from his parents and made a down payment on a local ironmonger's shop that was going broke. Within two months he had sold off the stock and the lease for three times the purchasing price. He was twenty-three and he had made himself a working capital of five thousand pounds. By the time he was forty, and sunning himself by his swimming pool in one of the most expensive residential areas in the West Indies, he was the chairman of Farrant Investment Brokers, the major stock-holder in a company owning a chain of luxury hotels, and his estimated fortune topped eighteen million pounds. He had also netted another million out of racing since he took it up ten years before. Everything he touched made money; he knew this himself, and in all his business calculations, he left a place for luck.

It was a glorious morning, and in spite of hearing Patsy make the same remark about the heat, every day for the past three weeks, he felt in a good mood. After a time inactivity bored him; he couldn't help doing business even when he was supposed to be on holiday. He kept in constant touch by telephone and cable with his investment brokers, and he flew his trainers and his jockeys out to make their plans for the coming Flat season. That was another thing that annoyed him about his wife. She didn't like horses, and in spite of living in constant touch with the racing community since she first met him, she had never quite mastered the simplest facts connected with running a horse in a Flat race. He had fallen into the habit of discussing some of his most delicate business and gambling propositions in front of her, on the assumption that if she heard him plotting murder, she was too stupid to understand.

His trainer Gerry Garvin was staying with them. He had a young and pretty wife, who got on well with everybody. She was ideal for the job, and Roy liked her. She could contribute something sensible to the discussion about his various horses, but didn't push herself.

Patsy turned round from the pool; she had taken off her bikini top and her breasts were a beautiful golden brown.

'Come in the pool, darling,' she said.

'No,' Roy answered. 'Gerry'll be down in a minute. Cover your boobs up for Christ's sake!'

She giggled. 'All right. Hook me up at the back, will you, please?' She always said please and thank you, like a polite child. The elocutionist had struggled hard to stop her saying, 'Ta'. Very occasionally it still slipped out.

'What time are they coming?'

'I told you. Lunchtime.' He sat up and clasped his legs round the knees. He had muscular arms and a broad, hairy chest. He wore a gold chain round his neck with his Zodiac sign on it. Scorpio. Patsy had given it to him one Christmas. He had been very touched, although he knew she had charged it to his account at the best jeweller's in London. Nobody gave him anything. He was the one who did the giving. And the paying. He never took the medal off. 'I wonder how the hell he's brought it off,' he said.

'Brought off what?' she asked. She had long silky dark hair; she tossed it back over her shoulder.

'Getting her to come out here,' he said. 'He must have worked pretty fast! For ten bloody years he's not allowed inside the place – I always said if he got an inch he'd grab a mile!'

'I wonder what she's like,' Patsy said. 'Some old bag, I suppose.'

'Oh Jesus,' Roy got up. 'Don't you ever read a newspaper? She's younger than Richard. She married the old man for his money – she's no bag! If she was clever enough to hook Schriber, Richard'll have his work cut out.'

'Not necessarily, darling,' his wife said. Her deep blue eyes were wide and innocent. 'If she's been tied to an old goat for all this time she's probably dying for a good bang. Why is she coming over otherwise?'

He reached out and pulled a strand of her hair. 'Sometimes,' he said, 'you almost make sense. Hullo there, Gerry. Slept well?' Gerry Garvin was in his middle thirties. He had a 108 horses in training in his Newmarket yard, and twenty-two of them belonged to Roy Farrant. He was a keen, ambitious man, a fine horsemaster and one of the most astute trainers in the business. He had a reputation for gambling heavily on his own horses.

'Slept like the dead,' he said. 'What a gorgeous morning – Susan is still asleep. I'm going to have a swim.'

'I'll join you,' Farrant said. They dived together into the pool. They swam a length at some speed, and then slowed down, swimming together. Farrant turned on his back.

'Do you want me to come and meet Isabel Schriber with you?' Garvin asked.

'No,' Roy answered. 'Richard's coming with me. I don't want Patsy opening her big mouth as soon as they arrive. I want to get a good look at her first. Get a line on her.'

'I must say,' Garvin slipped round onto his back and floated. 'It's going to be a fascinating visit. But I don't see exactly how it's going to help us.'

'I don't either,' Farrant admitted. 'But I'll bet Richard does. He's persuaded her to bring the bloody racing manager as well.'

'Well,' Gerry Garvin said, climbing onto the edge of the pool. 'Mrs Schriber won't need an enemy if she has Richard as a friend.'

'I want to make them very welcome,' Roy Farrant said. 'I want her and this fellow Ryan to enjoy themselves and feel they're right at home. Whatever you think about Richard, Gerry, you'd better hide it!'

'Don't worry, Roy.' The trainer shrugged. 'I'm as anxious to take full advantage as you are. Susan and I will play along.' He picked up a towel, threw it round his shoulders and went back to the terrace to eat his breakfast. Whatever Roy Farrant and his friend Richard Schriber were planning, it was none of his business. In his two-year association with Farrant, he had learned not to ask questions.

'It's not as beautiful as Jamaica,' Isabel said. She had spent a holiday there with Charles. 'But it's more serene; there's a lovely, gentle atmosphere.' She turned to Tim Ryan. 'I'm so glad we came. I want you to enjoy it too.'

'It's a real busman's holiday,' he grinned at her. 'Farrant and the Garvins. He tells me Barry Lawrence is coming out the day after tomorrow.' Lawrence was one of the most successful jockeys in the world; he was a personal friend of Roy Farrant's and often rode for him.

'I've only seen him on the track,' she said.

'I knew him in Ireland,' Tim said. 'He's full of charm and one of the biggest shits in racing. I wouldn't trust him an inch.'

They were sitting on the terrace above the swimming pool; it was dusk but no one else had come down from their afternoon rest. It had become uncomfortably hot during the afternoon, and after a long lunch with endless bottles of champagne appearing, Farrant had led his guests upstairs. Isabel had tried to sleep, but she was too hot and she passed the hours lying on her back, watching the big electric fan turning above her head, trying to sort out her impressions of the day. It had been a stimulating but exhausting day, the culmination of a short flight from Kentucky to Kennedy airport, and then the long trip to Bridgetown. Farrant had met them at the airport, driving a huge open Rolls-Royce. Richard had brought her forward by the arm and said solemnly, 'This is my stepmother, Isabel.' Farrant had shaken hands with her. 'Some stepmother!' They all started to laugh and hurried into the gleaming, car to drive up the coastline to Sandy Lane.

She thought Roy Farrant was a good-looking man, full of vitality; tough and obviously self-made, but his welcome disarmed criticism and she was determined not to make any. The house was faultless; a long white bungalow built round a small central courtyard; in the middle a glorious jacaranda tree grew up between the four blocks of the building. The effect was like living in a garden. There was nothing in poor taste; it was luxurious and yet simple. She wondered whether his wife or a decorator were responsible. Tim had relaxed as soon as he arrived. There was an instant camaraderie between the racing professionals. He was soon deep in discussion with Gerry Garvin.

Richard seemed very much at home, stretching himself in the hot sun. He talked to Roy Farrant about things and people unknown to her, and then suddenly threw a question at Patsy, who responded with a beautiful vacant stare. It was amusing, but unkind. He had this trick of disconcerting people; but to her he was solicitous and charming; once he leaned across the table where they were lunching in the shade and raised his glass to her. She saw Farrant watching them. 'As Roy said, with his usual tact – you're some stepmother!' There was nothing she could do but raise hers in reply. When she came downstairs there was no sign of him. She had found Tim sitting on the terrace. They watched the sun set together. It was an impressive view; the terrace was built out from the first floor, and it overlooked the island down to the sea. As it grew dark and the sun began slipping lower towards the level of the ocean, lights were coming on like fireflies in the distance. The evening air was soft and full of tropical scents, unrecognizable but distinctive. Jamaica had been the same; the same smooth transition from the burning heat to the caressing warmth of the night. It made her think of Charles. A steward in a white linen jacket had offered them a choice of drinks. Ryan had chosen a planter's punch and so had she.

'Tim,' she said suddenly. 'Do you think Charles would mind me doing this – coming away and staying with people so soon after he died? I keep remembering the time we went to Jamaica together.' She turned round to face him. 'I wouldn't want anyone to think I'd forgotten him. Or that I didn't really care.'

'Nobody thinks that,' Ryan said gently. 'You went through hell for those six months. Everyone knew how you looked after him. You need this break, Isabel. He was a grand person and there wasn't a mean thing in him. He loved you and he'd want you to be happy. You know he would.'

'But not like this; not staying with Richard's friends. There's something that worries me, Tim. Why did they hate each other so much? Why did he tell me not to trust Richard, just before he died! What's at the back of it all?'

Ryan looked at her. 'I didn't know that,' he said. 'I knew he didn't like Richard and he always spoke of him as a waster. That bothers me, Isabel. I wish you'd told me before.'

'Everyone seemed to be against him,' she said slowly. 'Andrew bursting in the night of the funeral and telling him to go. Trying to turn me against him. It didn't seem fair. He'd been shut out for so long, and he did come back to make it up with his father. Right up to now I felt I was doing absolutely the right thing. Now I wonder whether I'm being disloyal to Charles.' She looked at him unhappily. 'Tell me the truth, Tim. What do you think?'

He stretched out and took her hand. She didn't pull away.

'I don't know,' he said. 'But I think you should ask him what really went wrong between him and his father. You've come in for criticism at home for having him at Beaumont. There'll be more of it because you've gone on this trip. That's one of the reasons I came with you. People can hardly talk if there are three of us. But you have a right to know the truth. I'm surprised Charles didn't tell you.'

'He never told me anything,' she said. 'I did ask him once, about Richard's mother, and he wouldn't discuss it at all. I felt too proud to go on asking if he didn't want to tell me. It was his business. All I knew was that they weren't happy and that she killed herself. It must have been horrible for him and I didn't want to pry. The same with Richard. He wouldn't talk about him. He just said the same thing to me as he did to you. He's a waster and no good. And never trust him. He said he'd try and stop me running the Falcon. . . .'

'He must have been wandering in his mind,' Tim said. 'Richard doesn't give a good goddamn about the horse. I know that. He just joins in to please you. I wouldn't take that seriously.'

He sat on quietly, holding her hand. There were lights set

among the palm trees in the garden and below them the pool shimmered pale blue from underwater floodlighting. She was wearing loose silk beach pyjamas and a long gold chain with her initials in diamonds set onto a crystal heart. He came very close in those few moments to telling her he was in love with her. But instinctively he knew that it was premature. She needed time to find herself again. Proximity was nine-tenths of the game. He didn't intend to be far away. It was a perfect night, with a vast swollen moon riding the sky, the lights of the houses and hotel below them glittering in the darkness. But in spite of the beguiling peace of the villa garden, and the quiet presence of the woman he loved beside him, Ryan was suddenly uneasy. There was nothing logical about the feeling – a dying man's suspicion of his son, a family feud that had its origins long years before he even came to America. It was all in the past and he shouldn't have been disturbed by what Isabel had told him. But he was.

'Hullo,' the voice of Patsy Farrant came from behind them. 'Sorry you've been left all alone.' She came round and stood beside them, one hand balanced on her left hip. She wore a white one-piece trouser suit, slit to the navel, and a mass of gold chains round her neck. 'I suppose Roy's talking business with Richard,' she said. She took the chair beside Tim Ryan and stretched out on it, her beautiful thighs extended. 'That's the second thing he lives for,' she said. She gave a slow sensual smile and tapped Ryan's arm. 'Go and find that lazy nigger, will you, please? I want a glass of champagne. They're never about when you want them.' She watched Tim move into the room behind them. Then she turned to Isabel.

'He's delicious,' she said. 'I saw you two holding hands. I'm glad so glad it's him, dear. I nearly had a heart attack thinking you'd picked Richard. Your Irishman's lovely. I like him.' She twisted round to watch him come back. He was carrying her drink himself. As he gave it to her she brushed his hand with her fingers. The big blue eyes were turned on him like search-lights. At that moment Roy Farrant, followed by Richard, came to join them.

In the bedroom, Susan Garvin turned to her husband. 'Hook this up for me, darling.' He came and fastened the silk blouse at the back of her neck. They had known each other since they were children. It was a very happy and successful marriage; she hoped to become pregnant while they were staying with the Farrants, but she hadn't told him this. He didn't feel enthusiastic about children; he liked her to come racing with him and he didn't want their bed life disturbed by sickness and a swelling abdomen. She wasn't worried; he was the kind of man who would be wild about a child when it was a reality.

'Gerry – what's going on with Roy and Richard?'

'I don't know.' He did the tiny hooks up one by one. It was all very well to buy couture clothes but it was presupposed you had a ladies' maid to get you in and out of them.

'Why has he brought Mrs Schriber over here – there must be something behind it.'

'Maybe he thinks I'll learn something from them, or from Tim Ryan. If that's the idea he's made a bloody great mistake. I tried pumping Ryan about their horse and I got nowhere. Not a hint of anything.'

He had finished negotiating the hooks and eyes. Susan Garvin turned round to him. 'You be careful,' she said. 'Don't let Roy get you involved in anything. Never mind about the Derby – he doesn't care what he does so long as he wins this time. His reputation stinks anyway. But you look out for yourself!'

'Don't worry, I've thought of that,' her husband said. 'I'd trust Richard Schriber as far as I could kick a grand piano. And they're certainly up to something. Farrant would commit a murder to win with Rocket Man, but he knows where I stand. I want to win as much as anyone – more. We've never had a Derby winner. But I'm not risking my reputation or my licence. He can do his own dirty work so long as I don't know anything about it.'

She came and put her arms round his neck. 'You promise me? You're the only trainer he's had who hasn't been asked to pull horses and all the rest of the big betting stuff. Everybody knows it too. I'd rather you didn't win the Derby if stooping to his level is the price.'

Susan had never liked Roy Farrant; she was friendly and frank by nature. Farrant made her uncomfortable. She didn't trust his bonhomie and she thought his wife a mentally retarded nymphomaniac; she often wished he would take his horses away from her husband. Gerry was successful enough not to need them. Perhaps if they won the Derby, then she could persuade him. . . .

'You be a good girl now,' Gerry Garvin said. He kissed her. 'Don't worry about me; I promise you I won't be drawn into anything and Roy knows bloody well I won't. But you've got to be nice to the Schriber woman and chat up Ryan. Roy wants us all to be one big happy family. And for God's sake don't turn your nose up at Richard!'

'There's something funny about that man,' she said. 'I've never believed in that business of being a playboy – drunk at nine in the morning and never doing a day's work – I don't think he's really like that at all!'

'That's exactly what he is, my sweet. A rich bastard with nothing to do but get himself into trouble. Especially with women. I happen to know Roy's bailed him out a couple of times. And Roy never lets anyone forget a favour. I'd say the time has come for Richard to pay up.'

'I watched him this afternoon,' Susan said slowly. 'He's getting round that woman and she doesn't even know it. I feel really sorry for her.'

'We can't afford to be,' Gerry said. 'There's a lot at stake for us too. Come on, darling, nice bright smile – let's get outside some of Roy's champagne.'

'How good is the Falcon?' Roy Farrant asked. He and Richard had gone off to play golf at the exclusive course adjoining the housing estate. They had driven off with golf clubs in the little buggy the Farrants kept for running round the island. When they got to the golf course, they left the clubs in the buggy and went straight into the club house. Farrant ordered iced coffee and Richard asked for rum. They chose a table on the verandah far from the few people having an early morning drink. Farrant's eyes were hard and narrowed; he looked much older when he wasn't smiling. Richard swallowed hard at his drink.

'Very good,' he said. 'But you ought to know that; you know what his performance was last season.'

'Yes of course I bloody know that,' Farrant interrupted angrily. 'He won two Grade I races. But there's all the difference in the world between a top-class two-year-old and a Classic winner! Is he going to train on? And is he going to be as good as he was?'

'Better,' Richard said. 'He's grown on since last year; he was very lightly raced because Ryan doesn't believe in overdoing two-year-olds. He's a big, powerful colt and he hasn't been stretched at all. Ryan said he got a mile and a quarter without any trouble. He's confident he'll get the distance for the Derby. From the look of him and what I picked up out there, he'll slaughter Rocket Man.'

'Christ,' Farrant said. 'There's nothing else in England that can beat us. Nothing!'

'It's been a bad year for English two-year-olds,' Richard remarked slyly.

Farrant glared at him. 'Keep your bloody cracks to yourself,' he said. 'You know Rocket Man is a certain winner this year. Everybody knows it. There's only one Frenchman to reckon with and we can fix him. I'm not worried about that.'

'If you want me to tell you that Silver Falcon doesn't look the better horse, then okay, I will. But it isn't the truth. If I were you I wouldn't plunge on Rocket Man. My money goes on the Falcon.' He got up and went to the bar. He came back with another glass of rum. Farrant looked up at him and scowled.

'You must have bloody hollow legs,' he said. Richard played with the glass, making the ice tinkle. He didn't say anything. After a few minutes Roy Farrant looked up.

'I have plunged,' he said slowly. 'I've laid thirty thousand on him. But it isn't the money. I want that race!'

'You sound like my father,' Richard said. 'He was a glory hunter too.'

'It's definite she's going to run him?' Farrant asked.

'No question; she promised my father on his death bed. The old bastard couldn't even let up when he was dying. Falcon'll run.'

'Unless something happens to him,' Farrant muttered.

Richard Schriber shook his head. 'I wouldn't rely on it,' he said. 'Nigel Foster'll guard him like the gold in Fort Knox. He's never broken down a horse in his life in training. And you won't get within a mile of him before the race. There's nothing you can do about it.'

'When Schriber died I thought we were home and dry,' Farrant said. 'All the papers were full of it. You've never read such a lot of crap in your life about the great American sports-man and how tragic he didn't live to see his great hope run in the Derby. You wouldn't believe it! I went out and laid another ten grand on my fellow – everything was just great, till you phoned from Beaumont and told me the bloody news!'

'Forewarned,' Richard Schriber said, 'is forearmed.'

Farrant looked up at him. 'What do you mean? You said you had an idea when you suggested bringing her out here. I've been trying to talk to you ever since you came out and all you say is you're thinking about it! For Christ's sake, Richard, you know how much this means to me – if you've got a scheme, then I want to hear it!'

'You said you weren't interested in the money,' Richard said. 'I don't know what price you got on Rocket Man but I don't suppose it was less than sixes at this stage. That's a hundred and eighty grand if he wins. Syndication value for stud between a million and a half and two million, depending on how decisive the victory. But if you say money isn't important to you, then I believe you.' He finished the rum. 'Thousands wouldn't.'

'Get to the point,' Farrant said. 'You've got something up your sleeve and you're holding out on me.' He spoke slowly, leaning forward across the table. 'I did you a favour not so long ago. I reckon you owe me something. Morris's boys would have spoiled you for life if I hadn't squared him!'

'I don't pay gambling debts on a crooked wheel,' Richard Schriber said. 'And if I laid his daughter so did half London. But I'm still grateful to you, Roy. And I'm going to prove it. The Falcon won't run at Epsom.'

Farrant looked at him. 'If I can't stop it, how can you?'

'That's my business. Just take it on trust.'

Farrant suddenly leaned back. 'All right,' he said. 'I'm on. How much do you want?'

Richard Schriber smiled. He ran his hand over his red hair and tipped the chair slightly backwards.

'Nothing,' he said. 'Nothing you could give me, Roy. Not money, certainly. Just let's say I'm paying back the favour you mentioned.'

'You can name your price,' Farrant said. 'Don't frig about – '

'I'll settle for another rum,' he said. He pushed his glass over to Farrant. 'Don't worry about it. I'd like to see you win the Derby. I'd get a real kick out of seeing your face. You just fix the Frenchman when the time comes and leave the Silver Falcon to me.'

'You've got a reason,' Farrant said. 'Why don't you trust me – '

'Because my reasons are none of your business,' Richard said gently. 'Let's have that drink and then I'll beat the hell out of you in eighteen holes.'

It was Richard who suggested they went deep-sea fishing. Tim had arranged to play golf with Farrant, and the Garvins had gone off to spend the day at the Farrants' beach cabin.

'I don't know anything about ordinary fishing, let alone deep sea,' Isabel protested.

'You don't have to know. I'll fish and you can watch if you don't want to try it. We can hire a boat and they take you right out. It's great fun. Come on, let's go.'

She took a picnic in the buggy and they drove down to St

Peter's, where the boats were hired out. Richard picked a neat motor cruiser with a single crewman. He was an elderly Negro, his hair bleached white under a faded cap with the peak turned up; he helped her into the boat and she settled in the bows as they cast off, and the engines started up. Isabel had never liked the sea. She could swim moderately, in the simple style of someone who spent occasional holidays on the English coast, but she had never felt at home in the water. She disliked the sense of isolation in a small boat surrounded by ocean and sky. But the morning was beautiful and as they left the coast there was a pleasant breeze. Richard was standing with the skipper; he took a turn at the wheel. He looked experienced and relaxed, his legs braced against the pitch of the boat. He called to her over his shoulder.

'Are you all right? Enjoying it?'

'Yes,' she called back. 'It's lovely. I'm glad we came.'

'Wait till you hook a nice big marlin! Then we'll see some fun – '

The skipper took over for the last quarter of a mile. He throttled back and very slowly drifted into neutral. Richard helped him drop the anchor. Isabel watched the chain playing out; it seemed to go on for a long time. They were in very deep water. He came back and dropped into the little canvas chair beside her. He fished in the picnic basket. 'Let's have a drink,' he said. 'I asked Patsy to put something special in for us.' He brought out a large metal cold box; inside it was a bottle of Saran Nature, perfectly chilled. 'I love this stuff in the morning,' Richard said. 'Get the glasses out while I open it.' He poured a small tumbler full of the still champagne. It was one of the most expensive wines in the world. 'Ah,' he sipped it and leaned back closing his eyes against the sun. 'This is the life – sun, sea, good wine and a beautiful stepmother beside me. Who could want anything more?'

He looked round at her and smiled. 'You're an attractive woman, Isabel. It's all very well living at Beaumont with my old man's shadow over the place. But how much of this is really you? Have you ever faced that? You should.'

'I love Beaumont,' she said. 'And I don't feel any shadow. I'm looking forward to my life.'

'Racing my father's horses,' he said. He filled their glasses again. 'Living with the Grogans and good old Tim. He forced you into it, Isabel. Whether you realize it or not, he committed you to his kind of life regardless of whether it suited you. Tell me the truth – do you really want to go to England and go through this Derby performance? Wouldn't you rather take time off, travel a bit, find out exactly what you want to do with your life?'

She shook her head. 'I can't do that. I promised him. I've got no other objective. You talk about travel – it wouldn't be much fun on my own. I've never been close to my family; all my friends are at Beaumont. I'll admit, I did feel strange at first – even overshadowed if you like. But it's my background now, my home. I love the horses; I want to make a success of it. And I'm going to try and win that race.'

'He certainly got his hooks into you, didn't he?' Richard said.

'He was very good to me,' Isabel said. 'And I promised. It's a funny thing; he said you'd try and persuade me not to run the horse. That's what you're doing, aren't you?'

'I suppose I am,' he said. 'Let's finish the bottle. But not because I want to spite him or thwart his dying wish. Simply because I've got very fond of you. And I hate to see him pulling the strings on people. I'm frightened you'll end up as just another leathery lady, probably married to Tim and knee-deep in manure for the rest of your life. You're worth more than that.'

'Wait till after the Derby,' Isabel answered. 'And please don't start marrying me off to Tim.'

'Okay,' he said. He stretched. 'If you're quite certain that's what you want. I won't say another word.'

'I am certain,' Isabel said. 'And nothing is going to change me.' He shook his head and smiled at her.

'Very determined lady, aren't you – let's go and swim, it's getting very hot.'

He stripped off his shorts and sweat shirt. He was powerfully built with muscled legs and arms. The back of his neck and shoulders was freckled by the sun. He dived off the side. When he surfaced he shouted up to her. 'It's great – come on in!'

She climbed down the ladder at the side and slid into the water. The cold was a shock that took her breath away. It was as black as ink when she looked down. The boat idled above them; the anchor chain was upright as a stick in the water, its hook lost somewhere in the darkness below. She swam lazily, keeping close to the boat; Richard circled it, swimming powerfully. He came up to her and turned on his back.

'Swim underneath with me.'

'I can't swim underwater,' she said.

'It's easy, I'll show you. Give me your hand.' He gripped very tightly; she couldn't have pulled away from him. He was drawing her towards the hull of the boat.

'No,' she said. 'No, I don't want to – ' The sudden sense of panic was so strong that she began to struggle. 'Please Richard, let go. . . .'

But her hand was in a vice. 'Hold your breath,' he shouted, and then she was pulled under. The water closed over her head so suddenly that she swallowed some. Instinctively she closed her eyes; she was being dragged down and along by him, when she opened them she saw nothing for a second or two, then his pale reflection swimming a little ahead of her, towing her down and under the boat. Isabel had never panicked completely in her life, but she did so then. Her lungs were bursting; there was a hot pain in her chest. All she could see was a dark void around her with the black shadow of the hull above her head. The effect was totally claustrophobic. She began to kick out and thresh wildly with her free arm. The force drawing her forward checked. She could see his body close beside her. She gave a violent wrench to loose his grip on her. The next moment her hand was free. Her body shot upwards through the water. The pressure on her lungs was beyond control. She opened her mouth to gasp for air, and as her head cracked into the hull above her, she began to drown.

4

The first person she saw was Tim Ryan. She had a headache of such intensity that she could hardly focus on him.

'Where am I?'

'St Patrick's Hospital,' Tim said. 'You were nearly drowned.'

She gripped his hand in remembered terror. 'I was swimming – it was all black and I couldn't breathe – '

'Apparently you hit the hull,' Tim said. 'Richard and the skipper pulled you out. Richard gave you mouth-to-mouth resuscitation. He saved your life.' Isabel closed her eyes; the headache was excruciating. She remembered the water and the blind, horrible panic of fighting to breathe. Something had been stopping her, holding her back.

'I'm muddled,' she whispered. 'I can't remember how it happened. . . .'

'You're concussed,' Tim told her. 'You hit the hull with a hell of a crack. Don't talk any more. You'll be home by tomorrow. They just want you to stay in here tonight for observation. Richard was in a terrible state when he brought you in. Roy and Patsy send their love. He's coming to fetch you out tomorrow.'

'Who's coming?' she asked. She felt sore and battered round the ribs. Breathing hurt her.

'Richard,' Tim said. 'He keeps saying it was his fault.'

'He made me swim,' she said slowly. 'I didn't want to. . . . I don't like the sea. . . .' He was alarmed to see tears rolling down her face. He beckoned the coloured nurse.

'It's just a bit of a shock,' she whispered. 'I'll give her something to make her sleep and she'll be fine by the morning.'

'I'm going now,' he said. 'Thank God you're all right. My heart bloody nearly stopped for good when Richard telephoned. Sleep well.' He moved aside for the nurse; she was soothing Isabel, and straightening the pillows. She looked at him over her shoulder and smiled.

'Don't worry about her,' she said. 'She's a very lucky lady. All she needs is a good long sleep.'

Andrew Graham didn't tell his wife he was going to New York. He timed the trip to coincide with one that she wanted to make to her sister in Southport; she left home believing he was spending two days with friends in nearby Alvis. His partner could look after the practice; the change would do them both good. Andrew disliked the North and especially New York, he found it brash and confusing, its inhabitants rude and alien. It had taken him some time to decide to go there; the temptation to seek help nearer home had to be resisted. New York was anonymous; the sort of assistance he needed was best found there. He landed at Kennedy and took a taxicab direct to an office block on West 68th. The driver was surly and grabbed at the tip without a word of thanks. For a moment Andrew hesitated. He looked up at the tall building with its rows of gleaming sunlit windows. It was going to cost money, but he had accepted that. It was wise to get the best. The office was on the seventeenth floor. He was surprised to find that it consisted of only two rooms. An outer office, presided over by a secretary who was answering the telephone when he came in, and an inner room with the lettering, F. MacNeil, in black on the glass.

The girl put down the receiver and smiled at him. She had beautiful teeth and was skilfully made up.

'My name's Graham,' he said. 'I have an appointment with Mr MacNeil.'

She glanced at the diary open in front of her, and ticked something off. 'That's right. Twelve fifteen. I'll buzz him.' She did so and spoke into the intercom. 'Dr Graham to see you,

Mr MacNeil.' She looked up and gave him the toothpaste smile.

'Go right in please.'

He didn't know what to expect. His imagination had nothing but old Bogart movies to draw on. He was subconsciously prepared for a seedy office and a shabby figure lounging behind the desk with a bottle in front of him. Frank MacNeil was in his late thirties; he wore a smart blue worsted suit with buttondown shirt and a discreet red and blue tie. His brown hair was slicked down and neatly barbered. He looked like a Madison Avenue executive. He got up, held out his hand to Graham. He had a flat New York accent. 'Dr Graham. Sit down, won't you. Cigarette?'

'No thanks, I don't.' Andrew took a comfortable Swedish leather chair and wondered how to open the subject.

MacNeil smiled. He made an arch with his fingers.

'Now,' he said. 'What can I do for you? I take it this is personal business. And remember – this office is like the confessional. We hear everything and say nothing. We only have one interest and that is to satisfy our clients. With the maximum of discretion. Now, what exactly do you want investigated?'

Andrew took a piece of newspaper out of his wallet. It was a cutting from the *Kellway Gazette*. He gave it to the private detective. 'This,' he said. He watched MacNeil read it; his lips moved silently.

It was a Reuters news item, and it had made minor headlines in the Kentucky paper.

'Isabel Schriber escapes death'. It gave an account of the accident in Barbados, describing it as near fatal; it took place while Mrs Schriber was out deep-sea fishing and she was rescued by her stepson. They were guests of the wealthy English racehorse owner Roy Farrant. Mrs Schriber was recovering in hospital. MacNeil read it twice.

His tone was brisk. He had dropped the fancy manner.

'Is this woman a relative?'

'No,' Andrew said. 'She's the widow of my greatest friend.

81

I've been very worried since I saw that clipping. Especially since it happened when she was with her stepson.'

'What do you suspect, Dr Graham?'

Andrew shifted in his seat. 'I don't know,' he said. 'I'm just uneasy. I want you to get all the details, find out what really happened on that boat.'

'Hmm,' MacNeil leaned back in his chair. He said, 'I'll keep this clipping for the file. And now, if you want me to take the case, you've got to give me the full story. Everything you know about the woman, the stepson, the family background – everything. Because, if I'm reading your mind, you think this could have been an attempted murder.'

'Yes,' Andrew said slowly. 'I think it could.'

He wondered whether MacNeil approximated enough to his fictional counterparts to keep a drink in his office. It was almost telepathic; the detective got up, went to a cupboard near the door and it opened out into a well-stocked bar. He was used to clients like the doctor; the more respectable they were the more difficult they found it to rattle skeletons.

'What'll you have?'

'Scotch,' Andrew said. 'With a splash.'

'Ice?'

'No ice.'

They drank and looked at each other over their glasses.

'It's not a nice story,' Andrew Graham said at last.

'They never are,' MacNeil answered. He began to make notes while Graham talked.

Tim was a light sleeper. He woke instantly when the door to his bedroom opened. The curtains were open and the big West Indian moon shone into the room like a searchlight. He stayed quiet, watching the woman come across the floor. She came to the bed and stood, looking down at him. She wore a silk dressing gown. It was Patsy Farrant. She didn't speak; she pulled the tie round her waist and the gown fell open. She slipped it off and stood naked for a moment. Then she sat on the edge of the bed, ran her hands over his chest and shoulders and began to kiss him. She pulled back the cover and lay on him, her body moving. He submitted for a few moments, holding himself in check against the slow, rhythmic assault. Then he turned, pulling her over and underneath him. She gave a gasp of pleasure. 'What the hell are you doing,' he said.

'I'm fucking,' she giggled, heaving against him. 'Silly old Roy got pissed tonight. I think you're delicious.' She bit him on the chest. Tim pulled her arms up and held them over her head. He let his full weight come down on her and she was forced to lie still. She managed to caress his legs with her foot.

'Supposing he's not that pissed?' he said. 'What happens if he wakes up – ?'

She giggled again. Her eyes were bright and she stuck out her tongue at him like a provocative child. 'He won't. He's pissed as an owl. Don't be so nasty, darling. You're hurting me. . . .' She giggled again and nipped him on the side of the neck. 'I love it,' she said. 'Come on, Timmy, bang me! Bang me hard – '

'Sorry, sweetheart, anything to please a lady but not this time.' Ryan rolled away from her and got up.

She sat up in bed, her arms above her head; even the angle of her breasts could not excite him. He genuinely wanted to get rid of her.

'For Christ's sake,' he said. 'Get back to your own room. He'll wake up and find you gone.'

'Not with half a bottle of brandy inside him,' she said. 'Stop worrying, darling Timmy. I know what I'm doing. I never get caught.'

'I'm glad to hear it,' Tim said.

'He'll be in a filthy mood today,' Patsy said. She pouted at him.

'He'll take it out on me,' she went on. 'He thought she was dead, when Richard first called.' Ryan had gone to the door, holding it open; suddenly he slammed it shut.

'What the hell do you mean?'

'I told you,' she protested. 'He got pissed out of his mind tonight. He'll yell at me all day tomorrow. You see!'

'He thought who was dead,' Tim said very quietly. 'Isabel?'
She shrugged; instinct told her to withdraw.

'Oh I didn't mean that – he was just disappointed I suppose. After all your horse wouldn't have run against us, would it?'

'No,' Ryan said. He looked into the vacant eyes and stopped himself from hitting her. 'No, it wouldn't. Not if anything happened to Isabel.'

He moved away from the naked body lying on the bed. He felt chilled and sickened with himself. What kind of people were these? Big, jovial Roy Farrant with his string of successful horses and his dubious reputation. Racing was full of men like that. Crooks and sharpers, ready to grab an advantage. He could understand those. But not this; not the cold obscenity of that one word. Disappointed. Disappointed that Isabel hadn't drowned out there in the black sea, so his horse could win the Derby. He reached down and pulled Patsy off the bed.

'Get out,' he said. 'Go back to your husband. I'm going to sleep.' But he couldn't get back to sleep. Instead he showered and dressed and went down through the silent bungalow. The dirty glasses and ashtrays hadn't been cleared away. There was a staleness in the air. He opened the sliding doors and stepped out onto the terrace. The sun was coming up over the palm trees. A red and purple sky with gold at the centre; the tropical birds were shrilling excitedly in the trees.

Farrant had thought she was dead. His distress over the accident, the anxious offer to help in any way – it had all been an act, masking the murderous disappointment that fate had so nearly intervened on his behalf. If that was how much winning the race meant to him, the sooner he got Isabel off the island the better. He had been completely taken in and so had Isabel. And Richard, who spoke of Farrant as his friend. If it hadn't been for Richard's knowledge of artificial respiration, she would have died on the trip back to the mainland.

He telephoned the airport and found out that there was a British Airways flight to England the following morning. He reserved two seats. He heard them coming out onto the terrace; Farrant's voice was raised, angrily abusing the servants. Tim disappeared into the garden. He couldn't trust himself to meet Farrant face to face. He came back in time to see Richard easing the big white Rolls out of the garage.

'I'm going to bring Isabel back,' he called. 'Roy thought this would be more comfortable for her.'

Tim came up and opened the passenger door. He swung himself in beside Richard. 'Like hell he did,' he snapped. 'I'm coming with you. I've got something to tell you about your friend.'

It took twenty minutes to get to the hospital. Richard didn't say anything until they were almost there. He drew the big car through the entrance and parked in front of the bungalow buildings.

'I don't believe Roy really meant it,' he said. 'She was exaggerating; he'd never want anything to happen to Isabel.'

'Listen,' Tim said angrily. 'You're embarrassed because he's a friend of yours. All right, he's pretty sharp and he doesn't much care how he wins, but this is different. A man who wants something that badly might get really rough. I'm not leaving Isabel here; we've got tickets on the Thursday flight and we're going to be on it. You can stay on with the Farrants if you like, but she's getting out of here!'

There was a celebration lunch for Isabel at the villa. Farrant and Patsy, flanked by Gerry and Susan Garvin were waiting to welcome her. Already the incident was in perspective in her mind. She had panicked under water and cracked her head on the hull. If she hadn't been fighting against Richard, they would have swum clear and surfaced in a few seconds.

Tim Ryan was in a curious mood. She noticed that he didn't talk to Farrant; his announcement that he had got them on a flight back to England seemed peremptory. To her surprise Richard supported him.

'I think Tim's right,' he said at lunch. 'Isabel ought to get settled in. She's got to look for a house. And she might as well get a check-up in London, just to make sure everything's okay.'

'What a shame,' Patsy Farrant said. 'We had some super parties planned for you, didn't we, Roy?'

'Yes, but it can't be helped. I'd got a barbecue organized for

Friday. About twenty people. And Barry Lawrence is flying out.' He mentioned the great jockey and Richard glanced up. 'Is he riding for you this season?'

'As much as he rides for anyone,' Farrant shrugged. 'You know Barry – if he likes the horse he'll ride it, and if he changes his mind the day of the race he'll let you down and ride your biggest bloody rival.'

Tim Ryan looked at him. 'I wouldn't put that crook up on a donkey,' he said. 'As for chopping and changing his rides, there's only one man big enough to get away with that, and Lawrence is no Lester Piggott. He'll never come within a hundred miles of him, whatever the gutter press says.' He pushed back his chair. 'Isabel, I think you ought to lie down before it gets too hot. You've just come out of hospital.'

Isabel hesitated. Tim's attitude was creating an awkward atmosphere. She decided that it was just as well to break up the lunch party. Susan Garvin came to her room with her.

'Are you really feeling all right?' she said.

'Yes, I'm fine, thanks. I'm afraid it's all been a big fuss about nothing. I behaved like an idiot.'

Susan came inside and closed the door.

'What actually happened,' she said. 'Can't you swim?'

'Oh – up to a point. I'm not a strong swimmer, and I'm not very keen on the sea anyway. Richard took me underwater and I panicked and hit my head.'

'I thought you dived off and hit yourself coming up,' Susan Garvin said slowly. She came and sat on the bed. Isabel could see that she wanted to talk and didn't know how to begin. She was frowning.

'Why did he take you underwater if you're not a good swimmer?'

'I don't think he realized,' Isabel said.

'What a bloody stupid thing to do,' Susan Garvin said suddenly. 'I hope you won't be offended or anything, but I should be a bit careful of Richard if I were you. I've never liked him: I do like you.' She looked at Isabel. 'You are annoyed, aren't you? I can see it.'

'I'm fond of Richard,' Isabel said. 'I don't like innuendos, Mrs Garvin.'

The girl stood up. 'Then I won't make any. I don't like Roy Farrant either, although he has horses with my husband. They're as thick as thieves those two. Roy punts like a lunatic, so does Richard. And they're not too particular about how they win. Gerry's never done anything crooked and never will, but the other trainers do it, and Barry Lawrence is in it with them. Just be careful, Mrs Schriber. You're not on home ground any more.' She went out and closed the door.

Isabel agreed to give a press conference after she arrived in London. Tim and Richard sat on either side of her in a private room at the Savoy Hotel where Tim had booked them. She posed for photographs, and a reporter from the *Daily Express* put the first questions. Was it true that she had come to England to carry out her husband's dying wish and win the Derby? She said it had been her husband's greatest ambition to win the race and she intended to do what he would have done had he lived. Any questions concerned with the Silver Falcon, she referred to Tim. At the back of the room, a neatly dressed man, with slicked-down brown hair and a smooth, well-barbered face, made notes in a small pad, and watched her carefully.

She wore a dark blue dress and a matching turban; she was tanned from her trip to Barbados and he considered her to be a very attractive woman. The red-haired man beside her interested him even more than she did. He had found out a lot about Richard Schriber apart from what Graham had told him; a big gambler, with a dubious reputation and a circle of unsavoury friends. His name had been linked with a lot of women on the periphery of respectable society. His ultra-conservative father couldn't have been very happy with what the New York tabloids made of the famous paternity case and the model girl. It hardly tied in with the image of the aristocratic Southern sportsman and breeder, living in gracious

Beaumont in the heart of the Blue grass. MacNeil had got in on a fake press card from the *New York Daily News*. He had no intention of calling himself to the notice of either Isabel or Richard Schriber by asking a question. He was just forming his own impressions. After what Andrew Graham had told him in his office that day, he had decided that the case was too big to be left to a subordinate. He had assigned himself. Someone had asked Isabel about the swimming accident. She paid a handsome tribute to her stepson for saving her life. MacNeil allowed himself a sour grin. He had long lost his capacity to be cynical, for cynicism presupposed some sense of disillusion. He had none left. He believed in all sincerity, that the human race stank. In his twenty years as a high-class private detective, nothing had happened to modify his opinion. MacNeil made notes. They helped him concentrate when he was fitting pieces together in a particular puzzle. And this was a very interesting puzzle which looked as if it would become more complicated as he tried to solve it. He thought of the gentlemanly doctor from Kentucky, and how he had squirmed and sweated when he told the real story of Richard Schriber and his father to MacNeil in New York. He had said it was the real story, but MacNeil didn't believe him. Clients always held something back. He was sure that Andrew Graham was the same as all the rest. He had a man working on it now, ferreting round the sacred precincts of Kentucky society. Turning the horse shit over, as MacNeil privately described it.

He watched Isabel, his eyes narrow. Twenty million dollars on the hoof. He wondered how much she knew about her late husband and his first wife. And his son. Graham had insisted she knew nothing. Charles Schriber had buried his past as effectively as his dead wife. He remembered Graham's suppressed emotion as he came to the climax of the story; in MacNeil's view he was a little too emotional on just one Scotch.

He half listened to the racing manager Ryan talking about the Silver Falcon; he didn't know much about racing and the subject bored him. He concentrated on Richard Schriber. He looked relaxed, sitting at ease beside his absurdly young step-mother. Very good-looking if you could take the colouring, which MacNeil personally disliked. Red-heads smelt like foxes. Someone had told him that years ago when he was a boy and the revulsion stayed with him. A smooth, cool customer; the kind of self-proclaimed shit that would have women flocking to find out if he was as bad as he was supposed to be. It was a technique with whiskers. There was an animal quality about him which MacNeil's trained instincts detected; something coiled and watchful, carefully covered by the lazy arrogance and the reputation of the international playboy with a taste for low life. Graham suspected him of trying to murder Isabel Schriber. MacNeil judged him quite capable of it. The conference was breaking up; Isabel smiled and thanked the press. He could see she had made a good impression. She left the room flanked by Ryan and her stepson. If Richard Schriber was planning another attempt it wouldn't be too soon. She was probably safe enough until she had rented a house. Accidents were always happening in the home. He went out at the tail of the group of reporters and slipped away.

5

Tim Ryan was still asleep when the bedside telephone rang. He was in the habit of waking very early, a habit common to anyone working with horses, but that morning he slept so deeply that the ringing took a full minute to penetrate. He grabbed the receiver; a voice was shouting down the other end.

'Ryan – Ryan are you there?'

'Yes, speaking. Who's that – ' He was yawning as he spoke. Sunlight was cutting through a gap in the curtains. Christ, he thought, I wonder what time it is –

'Ryan, this is Nigel Foster. You'd better get down here! There's been a frightful bloody accident – '

Foster. Nigel Foster. He jumped out of bed, holding the telephone. The Silver Falcon's trainer.

'What's happened,' Tim shouted back. 'What's happened to the horse?'

'It's not the horse,' the voice crackled in his ear. 'I'm not going into details. You just get down here and bring Mrs Schriber with you. And don't delay a bloody minute!' The connection cut off, and Tim stood, still holding the receiver. Nigel Foster was not an hysterical type; he rarely raised his voice or lost control. He had sounded desperate. Accident. A most frightful bloody accident. . . . His first reaction was relief. Nothing had happened to the Silver Falcon. A dozen different nightmare possibilities had rushed through his mind when Foster first spoke. The horse was dead. Colic. Cast in the box with a broken leg. A heart attack. An accident on the gallops. . . . For all its speed and strength, the thoroughbred was amazingly fragile. But whatever had happened, the horse was not involved. Good racing man that he was, Tim rated the safety of the Silver Falcon first; but there was no doubt about the shock in Nigel Foster's voice, or the frantic instruction. Get down here and bring Mrs Schriber with you. Tim banged the phone down and dialled reception.

'Get me Mrs Schriber, suite 206,' he said.

Ryan had rented a car for them; it waited outside the Strand entrance and as he followed Isabel into the back he gave instructions to the driver. 'Kresswell House, Lambourn. It's straight through Lambourn and on the left on the Ashbourn Road. And go like hell – we're in a hurry.'

'What is it?' Isabel said. 'What on earth could have happened – why didn't he tell you instead of just leaving it in the air like that? You should have rung back.'

'I told you – he said he wouldn't go into details. And when Nigel says he's not going to do something, he bloody well means it. I just don't know what sort of an accident. Christ, look at this traffic!'

'It must be very serious,' Isabel said. 'I wish we knew – '

'Try not to worry. Whatever it is, we'll sort it out. Falcon's all right, that's the main thing.'

'Thank God for that,' she said.

An hour and fifteen minutes later they were sitting in Nigel Foster's office.

Nigel Foster was fifty-four years old; an ex-major in a cavalry regiment, he had begun training after the war, starting with a few jumpers sent to him by rich friends and supplemented by two point-to-pointers that he owned himself. He was a renowned horseman and an equally skilled horse-master. He had a phenomenal memory and the indefinable sixth sense in placing horses which marks out the genius from the merely successful trainer. He had won a Cheltenham Gold Cup and had two seconds in the Grand National when he changed from National Hunt racing to the Flat. He liked explaining the transition. 'Jumping is for gentlemen. The Flat is for pros. As I took out a licence I thought I'd better do it properly.' He was a handsome man in a lean and angular way; extremely tall and thin with a deceptively quiet manner. He had won every Classic since the war, and he had trained all Charles Schriber's horses in England.

Now he faced Isabel, grey-faced and grim.

'We won't know till they've X-rayed and done all the rest of it, but there's a bloody good chance the lad will be a cripple for life. That is if he doesn't die.'

'And nobody knows how it happened,' Isabel said. 'It seems incredible.' Tim Ryan had said very little since Foster started talking.

'He was found in the Falcon's box this morning,' Foster said. 'My head lad went in to feed him and he saw the boy lying there. He thought he was dead.'

'They're certain his back's broken?' Tim asked quietly.

'Looks like it; that's what the hospital said when we brought him in.'

'But what was he doing in the box,' Isabel said. 'It doesn't make sense – surely every box is locked up at night – '

Nigel Foster didn't answer immediately. There was a bottle of vodka on his desk and he helped himself to a drink. Neither Isabel nor Tim had joined him. He looked as if he needed it.

'There's a man on permanent duty during the night, Mrs Schriber. We don't take any chances in this yard. We've got horses worth a fortune here apart from yours. He swears he didn't see or hear Dave Long go near that box, or anybody else. But the fact remains that however he got in to the horse, he was kicked and his back was broken. He didn't recover consciousness enough to call for help so he wasn't found till the morning. The point is, Mrs Schriber, we've got to consider the position. We don't want the press getting hold of this. I've put a total shut-down on the yard this morning. Anyone leaving the area, going to the pub or phoning in home will get sacked. I've made that clear. For now we can keep it quiet and the hospital isn't going to say anything. They don't know which horse it was and it probably wouldn't mean anything to them if they did.'

'When will we know about the lad?' Isabel asked. She was

trying not to think of what it meant to lie in a stable with a broken back, paralysa and unable to call for help. She shivered. 'I'd like to ring the hospital myself.'

'No,' Tim said gently. 'They wouldn't tell you anything. Leave it to Nigel.' He spoke to the trainer.

'Mrs Schriber will pay all expenses for Long,' he said. 'What about family – is he married?'

Foster shook his head. 'No. He lived in quarters here. Parents are up in Newcastle. The hospital are letting them know.'

'I'll do anything,' Isabel said. 'Anything at all. Get the very best medical advice and treatment for him. What a dreadful thing to happen. I feel quite sick.'

Foster stood up. 'The best thing would be to go up to the house and have a cup of coffee with Sally; she's expecting you. We hope you'll both stay to lunch. I'll walk up with you; Tim and I can go over a few details while you talk to Sally. It'll take your mind off it.'

The Fosters lived in a pleasant farmhouse some fifty yards away from the stables; Sally Foster was from the same background as her husband; hunting and eventing had brought them together. She was his second wife and ten years younger. His first marriage had ended in divorce.

Sally Foster came and kissed Isabel. She looked distressed.

'Come in,' she said. 'So nice to see you; what a dreadful thing – I've got some coffee ready.' Her husband laid a hand on Tim Ryan's arm as a signal not to go with Isabel. The sitting-room door closed on the two women and he jerked his head to the right.

'In my office.'

It was a small, rather dark room, its old-fashioned oak desk a mass of papers and reference books. There were two telephones, with a direct line to the yard. Foster dropped into a shabby stuffed chair.

'All right,' Tim Ryan said. 'Now tell me the truth. What really happened?'

'The bastard went in to do him over,' Foster said. 'We

found an iron bar in the straw. I got the story out of the watchman. Long came back from the pub about ten thirty; the other lads went to bed and he found the watchman and told him some cock about being worried about the Falcon. Said he wanted to make sure he was all right. The bloody fool opened the box up. Long said he'd see everything was secure and give the key back. He didn't, and the watchman admits he forgot about it. Sod probably went to sleep.'

'Christ,' Tim muttered. 'Christ Almighty. An iron bar. You're sure he didn't get at him?'

Foster gave a short unpleasant laugh.

'I don't think he got within feet of the horse,' he said. 'The Falcon went for him. He hasn't just got a broken back from one kick. He's been trampled and savaged. The bugger tried to kill him.'

'Serves him bloody well right!' Tim said. 'I wish it'd happen to more like him – but why, Nigel – why would Long try to do a thing like that! Had he got a grudge against you – or was it just the horse?'

'I don't know,' Foster admitted. 'My own feeling is it wasn't directed at me, or even at the Falcon. He's never had to do anything for him. I knew he was a dangerous bugger so I gave him to Phil to do. He can manage anything; no, I think this was a job from outside. Someone got at Long and paid him to fix the horse good and proper.'

'Who?' Tim asked. 'Have you any idea?' He lit a cigarette.

'Not the bookies,' Foster answered. 'There's not enough on him ante-post to get the wind up their skirts. Most of the money's been going on Rocket Man.'

'So I've noticed,' Tim said. He turned his cigarette over. 'You think there might be a connection there?' He was seeing Patsy Farrant sitting up in bed, displaying her breasts and talking about her husband's disappointment. Disappointment that Isabel hadn't drowned. It wouldn't exactly bother him to have a horse maimed. . . . But he wasn't going to say it. Not yet.

'I don't know,' Foster said. 'I don't like this sort of caper, I can tell you. It's never happened in my yard before. I shan't get a bloody wink of sleep from now on. If somebody's after the Falcon they'll try again. And there's another thing. If Long dies there'll be an inquest. The whole story will come out. I tell you something, Tim,' he leaned forward, scowling at the floor. 'If he wasn't the best colt I've seen in my life I wouldn't have him another night in the yard. He's got the killer instinct. And now he's got the taste for it. If this gets round, there won't be a lad who'll do him, not even old Phil. And public opinion will force Mrs Schriber to withdraw him from racing if Long dies.'

'Well, we just have to hope he doesn't,' Ryan said. Foster glanced at him quickly. Whoever said the Irish weren't cold-blooded bastards didn't know much about them.

'In the meantime, how are you going to stop the rumours? Everyone in Lambourn knows Long got kicked and taken to hospital by now, whatever you told your lad about keeping quiet. And who found the iron bar?'

'Phil,' Nigel Foster answered. 'He won't say anything. He's been with me since I started. He knows we've got the Derby winner and he won't breathe a word. Nor will that bloody watchman. He's got to stick to his story about not knowing how Long got there or get the sack without a reference, and he knows it. They'll keep quiet. As for the others, well, I'll get Phil to put it round the pubs that Long came back pissed and went into the wrong box. Luckily the fellow he does is right next door. But if he dies we're sunk. I think Isabel will have to shell out to him if he doesn't, just to stop any yammer from the family.'

'Oh, she'll do that all right,' Tim said. 'She'll be too bloody generous, if anything. She mustn't know a word of this – she'd pull the Falcon out if she had any idea. I used to make a joke of his temper, but this isn't funny. You'd lose your Derby colt. And I'd lose a bit besides.'

'You've backed him?' Foster asked.

'No,' Tim said. 'Not this time. The old man left me a present if he wins. I'd like to collect it. So fingers and legs crossed that that little shit doesn't blow the whistle on himself.' He looked at

95

Foster. 'Let's get down to business,' he said. 'What's the news on the horse?'

'As I said,' Foster remarked. 'He's the best colt I've ever seen, let alone trained. I know he was a bloody good two-year-old, but you know as well as I do, how easy it is for them to over the top and stay there. If I had a quid for all the good two-year-olds who didn't train on, I'd be a rich man. But this one's better than I dared to hope. He's just what you said. He's still growing, and he's the toughest horse in the yard. And as for speed – I sent him out on the Downs yesterday, with Adam's Rib and Precipice.' Tim nodded. Both the horses mentioned were experienced tough milers. Precipice had won the Prix Lupin the previous year and been second in the Two Thousand Guineas. Adam's Rib was a four-year-old with an impressive list of middle-distance wins behind him.

'Go on,' Tim said.

'He didn't fancy staying behind Precipice,' Foster said. 'He doesn't fancy being second to anything much. He took off with Phil on board. He was twenty lengths ahead at a half-speed gallop with Phil trying to pull him up, inside a furlong. And the other two were trying to pull after him. Christ knows what he'll do when we really ask him to gallop.'

'So it looks like the Two Thousand Guineas then,' Tim said. 'Do we go for the Greenham first?'

'I don't think so,' Foster shook his head. 'My feeling about this one is that he was trained the right way in the States. Not too often and then only the best. I think he'll run at the top of his form when he's fresh. I don't want to waste him on a Guineas Trial. We go straight for the Two Thousand. He may not win because I feel he needs the mile and a half. But we've got a bloody good chance.'

'That'll cheer Isabel up,' Tim said. 'This business has shaken her.'

'I know it has,' Foster said. 'We don't want her to lose heart; women are unpredictable enough anyway without a mess like this Long business upsetting them.'

'Don't worry about her,' Tim said. 'She's doing it for the old man. She made him a deathbed promise and she'll keep it. Provided that little rat recovers and she doesn't find out what happened. But you're going to have to set a twenty-four-hour watch on the Falcon. My hunch is there'll be another try before the Two Thousand Guineas. And I've another hunch. Whoever's trying to get at him doesn't give a damn about anything but the Derby.'

'You've got an idea who's behind this, haven't you?' Foster looked at him. 'I think you ought to tell me. I'm responsible for the horse's safety. I want to know who we're up against.'

Tim shook his head. 'I said it was a hunch. I didn't say I was certain. All you've got to worry about is making sure that the David Longs don't get within a mile of him. And I think a couple of security guards added to your watchman wouldn't be a bad idea either. We mightn't be lucky a second time. Let's go and find the girls. I don't want Isabel ringing up that hospital or trying to go and see him.'

They didn't stay to lunch with the Fosters; Isabel hesitated, not wanting to seem ungracious when Sally Foster tried to press her, but Tim made the excuse that she had to look at rented houses later that morning.

Nigel Foster gave her the customary social kiss on the cheek; it was reserved for the wives of the richest owners.

'Don't worry,' he said. He seemed much calmer since Ryan had talked to him. 'Don't think about this business again. I'll let you know how Long gets on and what has to be done for him. I'm sure he'll be all right.'

He stood outside the front door, his arm linked with his wife's, and they waved the car out of sight. Sally Foster turned to him.

'You told Ryan what had happened?'

'Yes. He guessed there was something anyway. He's as sharp as a tack, that fellow. We've got to hire extra security for the Falcon. That's going to cause a lot of bloody comment too.' He went back inside, his wife following. They sat together on the sofa in his sitting room; she put her arm round him.

'I'm glad they didn't stay to lunch,' she said. 'She was very upset. If she had any idea of what that brute did to the lad she'd back out of the whole thing. I had to do some pretty fast talking, darling. Told all about my accidents, broken vertebrae – the lot. I think it helped.'

'I'm sure it did,' Foster said. 'You're marvellous with them; bloody owners! If only we didn't have to have them near the place. Just turn up on the racecourse, fill themselves with champagne when the horses won and then piss off – Christ, I wish we'd never taken the Falcon! Ryan says there'll be another attempt to get at him, and he thinks whoever is behind it wants to knock him out of the Derby. I'm certain he knows who it is, too.' He lit a cigarette, passed one to his wife. 'She's a reasonable woman, thank God,' he said. 'And she's got Ryan behind her. But it would have been easier if the old man was alive. He could have been told the truth.'

Sally Foster shook her head. 'You can be glad he isn't,' she said. 'Don't wish to have him back. He was a difficult, ruthless bastard. I kept thinking this morning, thank God we don't have to tell *him* about this!'

'Security guards, rumours flying round the place – and a killer in the yard. Sal, tell me honestly; wouldn't we be better without all this? Shouldn't I tell her to send the Falcon somewhere else and let them cope with him?'

She leaned over and squeezed him. He was a moody man, inclined to fits of depression and elation, which his owners never saw. He was far the more temperamental of the two.

'No darling,' she said. 'You shouldn't. You're a great trainer; Charles Schriber knew it, that's why he picked you. You can cope with the Silver Falcon; security guards aren't that much of a nuisance, and if the rumours get round that somebody's out to get the horse, it won't do you any harm. It's all publicity, and so long as it's good, it keeps your name in the headlines. Tell Phil to have a lad with him when he goes into the box; Falcon doesn't try anything when he's out. Two of them will manage him. All you've got to do is train the brute. Remember Golden Bird – he used to get down on the gallops and tear up the ground with his teeth – you won the St Leger with him – '

'He was mad,' Foster said. 'Nutty as a fruit cake. This one's not like that. He hates people. He's a wicked bastard. I saw what he did to Long.'

'Long asked for it,' she said. 'Maybe the horse knew what he was going to do. Anyway it won't happen again. If you send him away and he wins the Derby for someone like Shipley or O'Brien, you'll never forgive yourself. So don't be silly!'

He looked round at her and at last he grinned.

'I'd shoot my bloody self,' he said.

'All right then,' Sally Foster got up. 'I'm going to get us both a nice big vodka tonic while you go and phone up the Securicor people. And I'll call the hospital later to find out how Long is, and then I'll ring Isabel this evening. How's that?'

'You're marvellous,' he said.

The estate agents in Hanover Square had provided a list of six suitable houses; two in Berkshire, one on the Sussex border and three in Surrey. Richard had arranged to take Isabel to see them. When she got back to the hotel she found a message from him saying that he couldn't keep the date. He gave no explanation.

Tim was delighted. 'That's great,' he said. 'That gives me the excuse to cóme. It's a beautiful day, we'll keep the hire car and go driving round the countryside. There's a nice little hotel near Dewhurst, and I'll take you to lunch. And I love looking at houses.'

'You're the first man I've ever heard of who did,' Isabel said. 'Charles never rented anything when he came over; we spent three months in the Dorchester last time. I was longing for a garden.'

'You're not a city girl,' Ryan said gently. 'I've always known that.'

He was determined to make her forget about what had happened that morning. She had been silent on the way back from Lambourn, asking only one question. 'Do you think that boy will die?'

And Tim had said no, decisively. He just hoped to G d he was right.

They lunched in the hotel he had chosen; it was a small, seventeenth-century farmhouse which had been skilfully adapted as a restaurant, with a limited number of bedrooms, and an intimate bar with a huge fireplace, filled with copper pots and artifacts, with fresh flowers on the tables and potted plants in the windows.

'I'll have prawns and then Dover sole. On the bone.'

He smiled. 'Fish twice?'

'It's just what I feel like.'

'Then that's exactly what you shall have. With a bottle of Montrachet to go with it.'

All his life Tim had assessed situations in terms of risk. He was a natural calculator, and he didn't pretend to be otherwise. Being the eldest son of a family constantly embarrassed by lack of money, with an old name and a crumbling ancestral house that nobody wanted to buy, Tim had learnt very early on the necessity to think before he acted, and then to act with a profit in view.

He didn't believe in waiting on events, or that opportunities arose without assistance. His attraction to Isabel had been spontaneous; looking at her now, part of his mind was asking questions. How important was the money?

'You're very quiet, Tim – are you worrying about this morning?'

'No,' he said. 'I wasn't thinking about it.'

'I was,' she said slowly.

He could say yes to himself, of course it hasn't made a difference, and still not know. He was prepared to do many things for money, but never consciously to marry for it. He wouldn't live at peace with her or himself unless he could give himself an honest answer. If Silver Falcon won the Derby, under the terms of Schriber's will he would inherit a quarter of a million dollars. Then there would be no need for any questions.

'What were you thinking?' he asked her.

'That it was like a bad omen,' Isabel said.

Ryan laughed. 'I thought it was the Irish who were superstitious! Bad omen be damned – there's enough superstition in racing anyway without you thinking up a new one. If every lad who got kicked in the arse was an ill omen, there wouldn't be a runner left on the racecourses!' He leaned over and put his hand on hers.

'Stop thinking about it,' he said. 'Come on; let's decide which house we're going to see. Ancient or modern – which do you want? An architect's dream house complete with indoor swimming pool and sauna, electronic kitchen and a master suite with circular, electrically controlled push-button bed, with panoramic views over the Sussex downs – '

'God forbid,' Isabel said firmly. 'What's the "ancient"?'

'Coolbridge House. A gracious seventeenth-century brick manor house in twenty acres of grounds – '

'Let's go there. I've always wanted to be the lady of the manor.'

He was pleased to hear her laugh. 'Even if it is only for a few months. How far is it?'

'Coolbridge – about twenty miles from Epsom and thirty from here. The situation sounds just right. Let's have some coffee and we'll go.'

They drove round the Sussex lanes after leaving the main Dewhurst road and, escaping from the ugly river of traffic were forced into a slow pace by the bends and twists, under the low branches of trees budding with spring blossom, the hedgerows wild and green on either side, blocking the view of the fields. There was nothing like it in the States, this small disorder where nature held ungoverned sway against an occasional incursion from one old man with a billhook to clear the way. Isabel had forgotten how narrow the country roads in England could be; she was conditioned to the broad highways and the open dust roads of the States. She had forgotten the essential smell of greenery and earth, and the brightness of the wild flowers growing in the ditches. There was a pair of wrought-iron gates between red brick pillars; a small Victorian lodge on the right, inside the gates. The driver had the prospectus and directions. He slowed down and glanced back at Isabel. 'This looks like it, Madam.'

The drive was bordered by huge lime trees, and it turned at right angles so that they didn't see the house until they rounded the bend.

It was two storey, built in the soft red brick which fifty years later would have been plastered over and painted white; the front was gabled, in the Dutch style that became fashionable during the reign of Mary and William of Orange. It was not a very big house, and on the lawn in front of the gravelled entrance, there stood the biggest copper beech tree that Isabel had ever seen.

There was a housekeeper to show them round; she was a pleasant woman in her forties, dressed in a blue nylon overall, and she seemed anxious to let the property.

'Sir James and Lady Beaton are in South Africa,' she explained. 'Their daughter lives out there. This is the drawing room.'

Isabel followed her, Tim a little behind. The hall was cool and casual, with a big open fireplace, relic of an earlier age, and the walls were covered with dark pictures, most of them portraits and too ill-lit to see. The drawing room was panelled and painted white; it was full of colour, and Isabel stood for a minute looking round it. It had the same casual, family atmosphere as the hall. There were charming materials on the sofas and chairs in a design of birds and foliage, some very fine eighteenth-century walnut furniture with a superb black lacquer bureau bookcase at the end of the room, its doors held open to display an elaborate interior. There were photographs and personal belongings on the tables, and a stool covered in gross point that was obviously the work of the absent Lady Beaton. There were potted plants arranged in a big centre piece.

Sunshine poured in through the windows. It was the most welcoming room Isabel had ever been into.

She turned to the housekeeper.

'This is lovely,' she said. 'Isn't it, Tim?'

'It is,' he said. He was looking with an appraising eye at some of the furniture. 'They have beautiful things,' he said.

The housekeeper nodded.

'Oh yes, and they've managed to keep quite a lot of them. But things are very difficult for people like Sir James these days, you know. They've started selling some of the family pictures already.' Her mouth set angrily. 'It's a disgrace, that's what I call it. Come through, Mrs Schriber and I'll show you the dining room. It'll be a great help to them if they can let the house while they're away. It's very comfortable and warm; if you can afford the central heating, that is. This way.'

She had made up her mind to rent Coolbridge even before she went upstairs and saw the bedroom, with its Hepplewhite four-poster bed, and the collection of exquisite eighteenth-century needlework pictures which were its only decoration. There was a warm and soothing feel about the house which appealed to her even more than the charm and elegance of its furnishing. There was no swimming pool and the kitchen, though clean and modern, lacked the refinements of the very rich.

'I've been with them fifteen years,' the housekeeper said. 'I live at the lodge, and my husband does the garden. I'd be happy to help out, Mrs Schriber, if you don't want to bring your own staff. If you take the house, that is.'

'I'm going to take it,' Isabel said. 'And I'd be very pleased if you and your husband would like to work for me. I'm not the sort of person who needs staff. I shall be living here alone.'

The woman glanced at her, and then quickly at the good-looking Irishman. Alone, she said. That was a surprise.

'You won't need to be nervous,' she said. 'This is a very quiet place. And we're on the end of the telephone, down at the lodge.'

Isabel shook hands with her; Tim did the same. 'I want to

walk round the garden,' Isabel said. She took Tim's arm. 'I love the house, don't you? Hasn't it got the most happy atmosphere?'

'Yes,' he said. 'I think it's just right. A bit big, and maybe you should think of getting someone to live in with you. A maid, somebody to sleep in at nights.'

'Don't be silly,' Isabel said. 'Whatever for? Besides, you can come and stay with me. Look, I knew it – there's the most lovely rose garden! Just think what it will be like in June!'

Ryan smiled at her. 'Just think of the party you can have here on Derby day,' he said. 'After we've won.'

6

Barry Lawrence had enjoyed his trip to Barbados. He liked staying with the Farrants; his association with Roy Farrant went back a long time, longer than anybody knew. They had a bond in common which made it easy for Barry to relax, and normally he wasn't a man who felt happy with owners. As a species, he despised and disliked them; those who knew nothing about racing in general and their own horses in particular were one degree less of a nuisance than those who prided themselves on being experts.

Even when he was an apprentice and had all the way to make, he found it difficult to be polite to them. It gave him positive pleasure to get down off some pig-eyed no-hoper and tell the flustered owner that in his opinion it was absolutely useless. He had lost a lot of rides in the beginning by being truthful about bad horses. Now, he always lied. It was expected; he had a string of excuses ready. The ground didn't suit him, or her. The distance was too long or too short. We got knocked into coming into the straight and he or she lost their stride. He or she needed the race. Jesus Christ, Barry used to think while he produced that knock-kneed old cliché, what the bugger really needed was a bullet through the ear – he had perfected a charming manner with owners. It was his only concession to an individual style which was otherwise modelled to the smallest detail on his hero, the incomparable Lester Piggott. He drove a big Mercedes and smoked cigars; his favourite drink was champagne. As he became successful, he took a chance and went freelance, riding for any stable that would retain him; he rode two Classic winners in his first season on his own, and he was suddenly a big-name jockey, able to pick and choose his rides. And the owners liked him. There was an old racing dictum among jockeys. You can call a man a crook, sleep with his wife, tell him his daughter's a prize whore, but God help you if you say his horses aren't any good. And it was true. He kept the truth for the trainers. After that it was up to them. The only man he had never deceived about a horse's capabilities was Roy Farrant. And if Farrant wanted him to ride for him, Barry rode. And rode to win. Unless otherwise instructed. The holiday in Barbados was an annual trip; he expected to be asked, and to be supplied with booze and girls. It wasn't that Farrant patronized him; it was much more of a partnership. He was loyal to Roy, not only because he couldn't afford to be otherwise, but because he liked him. Loyal enough to send Patsy Farrant back to her own bed when she tried creeping into his one night, naked as a snake. He didn't like her for it, but he knew better than to mention it to Roy.

He was on his way to the Farrants' house in St John's Wood. They had invited him to dinner. Whenever he saw that house, three massive storeys of brick and stucco, with a car port for eight and a swimming pool under glass that was Olympic size, he kept thinking of the first time he met Roy in Barnsley, when he lived in two rooms above his first ironmonger's shop, and he, Barry, was a skinny, semi-literate apprentice jockey to a moderate Yorkshire trainer with a mixed yard of flat and jumpers. He hadn't got tuppence to put together in those days. He struck up a conversation with Farrant in the pub round the corner, during a holiday spent with his family, liking the look of the big fellow sitting with a pint at the counter. There was one thing Barry Lawrence had always known, although he couldn't have expressed it properly in words. He wasn't going to work behind some lousy counter or in some rotten factory, working his guts out to end up like his father. With nothing. He had a way with horses. His first year of apprenticeship had taught him that. And his governor was teaching him to ride. That clinched it. As soon as he got up on one of the big thoroughbreds, his ego swelled and a sense of profound self-confidence came over him. He was a different human being, perched on the horse's withers, flat cap tilted a little over one eye. He was Barry Lawrence, riding the favourite in the Derby, with a million people crammed into Epsom watching him. It was always the same dream, the Derby. He never wanted to be a National Hunt jockey. There was no money in it. Just broken bones and cracked heads, and fuck-all at the end of it. The fools could go jumping. He was small enough and light enough to ride the Flat horses. And he loved them. He loved the good ones, and genuinely hated the bad.

He had talked about horses to Roy Farrant that night in the pub, making his one half pint of bitter last and last, until Farrant insisted on buying him another. And that was the beginning. The beginning of their ill-assorted friendship and of Roy Farrant's interest in racing which culminated in buying Rocket Man as a yearling at the Hialeah Sales for 118000 guineas because his pedigree made him a Derby prospect. It was one hell of a giant's leap, from the ironmonger's shop in the dingy Barnsley street to Farrant Enterprises Ltd. But Barry Lawrence had helped him make it. He grinned as he drew into the sweeping drive in front of the house. Even if they didn't like each other, they could never afford to fall out. He parked alongside a big grey Rolls Corniche and went up to the house. His cigar was already in his mouth. It wasn't just part of his champion jockey act. It helped to reduce his appetite. He might be asked to lunch but he wouldn't eat more than a token. The Flat season had begun and he was in full training. Two glasses of champagne, a maximum of 500 calories in the meal, and no water. He had learned to cope with thirst, to take pills to make him pee to the point of dehydration, more pills to quell his hunger, to sit and sweat in steam baths till he was sick and dizzy. But if Lawrence was riding, he always made the weight. He was fit and on time, and had a cheering word for the owners and a joke for the press. He was a very popular figure with the public. His fellow jockeys didn't trust him and there were trainers who went into seizures at the mention of his name. Barry Lawrence. He walked into the crowded sitting room and everyone looked round. There must have been nearly twenty people there. He saw Patsy coming towards him, swaying in pink silk trousers and top, a ruby and diamond pendant as big as a coffee saucer bouncing round her navel. She kissed him, and he smelled her strong, expensive scent.

'Hello, Barry – nice to see you – ' She always said the same thing, giving her bright smile to everyone. She seemed genuinely pleased to see him; he wondered if it was real good nature or plumbless stupidity that didn't bear him any grudge for turning her away. Not that it mattered.

Farrant came up to him, slapped him on the back, put a glass of champagne in his hand. He knew most of the faces. Racing associates, a press lord, the inevitable fringe models, a man whose name he remembered seeing in last week's edition of *Private Eye* in connection with a dubious merchant bank. The usual group. The Garvins, Dick Shipley from Newmarket, who had been leading Flat trainer two years before. He had run Nigel Foster very close. They were the two best in the game. People often said they wondered why Roy didn't send his Derby hope to Shipley instead of the less experienced Garvin. But Barry knew. Shipley didn't play games. And he didn't take orders from anyone. He would tell an owner when to bet but that was all. Lawrence knew Shipley had expected to get Rocket Man; he was sharp enough to know why it had been sent to Garvin as a two-year-old. He had two Derby hopefuls in his yard, and Roy didn't want any competition. Garvin would break his neck to win the race. And he would look the other way when Shipley wouldn't. Barry paused. The man talking to Dick Shipley had turned round. He saw that it was Richard Schriber. The trainer was hailing him and he had to go over.

'Hello, Barry – saw you had a nice winner at Chantilly the other day.'

'Yes,' Lawrence answered. 'Nice filly. Went like a bird.'

'Hello Barry,' Richard Schriber said. He always made the jockey feel uncomfortable. He didn't really fit in with the Farrant clique, and Lawrence didn't know why. He was a heavy gambler, went strong on the booze and the birds, but there was something about him which set Lawrence's teeth on edge. He felt that Schriber was laughing at him and at all of them. Even Roy. He didn't like him; he saw one of the model girls smiling at him and gladly turned away.

Shipley glanced after him. 'The trouble with him is he gets better and better. And the little bugger knows it. Do you know he rang me up the other day and *told* me he was going to ride Askara in the Oaks? He'd fixed it with the owners!'

'And what did you say?' Richard asked.

'I told him I'd pick my own pilot, thank you, and I told the owners the same. They weren't best pleased but I'm damned if I'm going to have that little monkey going behind my back and booking himself on my horses. Pity is, I think he'd do her very well. He's got a great touch with difficult fillies and she's a right bitch.'

Richard smiled. 'Then I shouldn't be proud, pal. Winning is all in this game. Put him up. Excuse me – I have to grab Roy.'

Farrant walked into a corner of the living room with him. There were huge red velvet sofas round the walls. The room reminded Richard of a luxurious hotel lounge, with glaring incongruities like an exquisite Sisley painting over the fireplace, outraged by some of Patsy's forays into Harrods gift department on the mantelpiece. She had a weakness for winsome china.

'I'm glad you invited yourself over – ' Farrant said. 'What's the news?'

'About what?' Richard lit a cigarette.

'Don't play bloody games,' Farrant said angrily. 'You know what about – the Falcon! What's happening?'

'Nothing much so far as I know,' Richard answered. 'He's down with Nigel Foster and according to Isabel they're delighted with him. By the way – ' he stubbed out his cigarette and glanced up at Farrant. 'I saw something in the paper last night about a lad in Foster's yard getting injured by a horse. Just a paragraph. Have you heard anything about it?'

'No.' Roy's face was blank. Too blank. 'Not a word. Why should I?'

'The rumour is,' Richard went on, still very casual, 'that the lad was trying to cripple a horse when he got kicked. And that horse was the Silver Falcon. You wouldn't be taking things into your own hands by any chance?'

Farrant's face turned red. He swung round towards Richard. 'I haven't seen anything coming from you! You gave me a lot of stuff in Barbados about stopping that horse running in the Derby, and he's been here a month, training on, with nothing but reports about how good he is, coming out. There was a whole column about him in the *Life* yesterday! What have you done, Richard – nothing!'

'And that's exactly what I will do, unless you lay off. All you've done is get Foster's yard crawling with security guards and dogs.'

'You've got the perfect set-up,' Farrant said. 'You're her stepson, you can go anywhere. If I give you some stuff, you could get at that horse. . . .'

Richard stood up. 'Nothing,' he said slowly, 'is going to happen to the horse.'

Farrant started to say something, and then changed his mind.

'I'm not staying,' Richard said. 'I just dropped by to tell you that either you let me handle this my way or you can count me out. One more bullyboy trick and you're on your own!' He turned and walked away.

There were three dozen red roses delivered to Isabel's suite that afternoon. She had tried to call Richard the evening before to tell him about Coolbridge, but there had been no reply, and she had accepted an invitation from friends of Charles to dine with them. The next morning she drove down to Oxford to lunch with her parents; it was a duty visit, and it depressed her. She had said goodbye to them with relief and known it was mutual.

The sitting room was full of the flowers; the card was on a silver salver on the table.

'Sorry about the house hunting. Money has its disadvantages, I had to see my accountant. I'll call for you at eight tonight. Richard.'

She put the card on the mantelpiece instead of tearing it up. She felt suddenly confident again; the uneasiness associated with her visit to her parents disappeared. She had missed seeing Richard for the past two days. If she had had another date for dinner that evening, she would have cancelled it.

He took her to dinner at Marks, the most exclusive and fashionable dining club in London. Isabel had chosen a new dress to wear; she liked the simplicity of Yves St Laurent clothes and she was slim enough to wear them. She felt guilty about buying so expensively, but now, irrationally she was glad. She chose a long cream dress in wild silk, and she was ready ten minutes before he was due to arrive. They didn't say much. Richard kissed her on the cheek and took her arm going down in the lift. He helped her into a red BMW which the Savoy doorman was watching over, and drove her to Charles Street.

'I hope no one's taken you here,' he said. 'I want this to be my surprise. It's the best place to eat in London.'

They drank champagne in the first-floor room in front of an open fire which was burning against a slight spring chill in the evening, surrounded by nineteenth-century pictures and bronzes, assembled with impeccable taste. The effect was deliberately casual; it was a splendid country house room, where at any moment the host would walk in.

'Do you like it?' Richard asked her. They were side by side on a sprawling deep sofa.

'Yes,' she looked at him. 'It's perfect. I want to tell you about my new house, Richard. I'm moving in the day after tomorrow.'

'Where is it? Not too far from London, I hope. You know what Dr Johnson said – he who is tired of London is tired of Life – '

'I am getting tired of it,' she admitted. 'This is a lovely place; and it's not far, about an hour I think. William and Mary with a gorgeous old-fashioned garden. Tim said we could give a fabulous party there after the Derby.'

'Good old Tim. He keeps his eye on the main chance, doesn't he – I suppose it's next door to Epsom?'

'Well,' Isabel said, 'it's very close.'

He laughed. 'I missed you,' he said.

Isabel looked at him. 'I missed you too,' she said. He reached across and took her hand. She wore Charles's engagement ring; it was a big pear-shaped diamond, surrounded by baguette sapphires.

'You have beautiful hands,' he said. 'That's too big and vulgar; it doesn't suit you.' Isabel didn't answer; he went on holding her hand. She couldn't draw it away. The head-waiter Luigi approached them; he was an urbane and charming Italian, who knew every member by name. He gave Isabel an admiring look; he seemed to know Richard very well. He advised them what to choose. The room had filled up since their arrival; there was a group of older men with beautifully dressed women in their early forties, a young couple sitting *tête à tête* in a corner near the window, and a man with a smart brunette drinking bourbon sours, and saying very little to each other. He was undistinguished-looking, with slicked-down brown hair and glasses, wearing a light-weight American suit. The woman with him was English and looked bored. Richard signalled Manuel, the barman, from the outside bar.

'We'll have another drink,' he said. 'Then we'll go down-stairs. I've asked Luigi for a table in the end room. I hope you're hungry?'

'Fairly.' Isabel withdrew her hand and laid it on her lap. The huge ring flashed in the soft lighting. Vulgar. He was right, but she wished he hadn't said it. The remark was like a signal, something for which she had been waiting.

'Richard,' she said quietly. 'Tell me something.' Manuel set down two glasses in front of them; whisky for him and champagne for her. Richard picked up his glass.

'Yes,' he said. 'Go ahead.'

'Why do you hate your father so much?'

He didn't answer; he sipped his drink, put it down, offered her a cigarette and lit one for himself. Then he smiled.

'I shouldn't have said that about the ring. I'm sorry.'

'I want to know,' Isabel persisted. 'Charles wouldn't discuss it; he wouldn't talk about you or your mother. I didn't want to pry. The ring is typical, and it keeps coming up in one form or another. Every time I mention his name I can feel it. Please Richard, tell me what happened.'

He turned round to her till they were face to face. Blue eyes, she thought suddenly, can be very cold.

'You really want to know all about us? You want to know about Charles Schriber and my mother and me – all right Isabel. But don't blame me if you don't like it. Let's go downstairs. They'll send the drinks to the table.'

The dining room was restful, decorated in a William Morris pattern paper, all soft greens and blues; the walls were hung with pictures and drawings of superb quality. He didn't mention his father during the meal, and Isabel didn't press him. They talked about her house, and he seemed relaxed and in a teasing mood. She noticed how the women in the room were looking at him. It was a splendidly handsome face, almost classical in its regularity, but with a firm, sexual mouth. The food and wine were excellent, the whole atmosphere luxurious and seductive. He leaned close to her and their bodies touched. The coffee came.

'Richard,' she reminded him with an effort. She didn't want him to press against her, and yet she hadn't moved away. 'Tell me about Charles.'

'You're a determined lady, aren't you? I said that to you in Barbados, when we went sailing, and you nearly drowned yourself. All right. Why do I hate my father?'

He was looking ahead of him, his hands cradled round a brandy glass. The skin round his eyes was drawn tight.

'He wasn't my father,' he said. 'I'm a bastard.' Isabel breathed sharply, audibly, with shock. He didn't move. He went on, talking in the same quiet tone, not looking at her. 'He told me that when I was fourteen. Up to then I thought he just hated boys. I wouldn't admit he hated me. I remember when it happened; it's not a scene I've been able to forget. He was bullying my mother and she was crying. As usual. I was a big kid for my age and I squared up to him. I called him a bastard. He used to beat the hell out of me when I was small; he hit me then, right across the face. "You're the bastard! You hear me – you're the bastard! You're no son of mine – " '

'Oh my God,' Isabel said. He didn't seem to hear.

'My mother tried to explain it to me, right there, with him standing over both of us. She was so scared, she hardly made sense. Something about making a mistake with someone and doing this terrible wrong to my father. She called him that. I put my arm round her; I remember feeling her tremble. I took her out of the room and upstairs.'

'I can't believe it,' Isabel said slowly. 'I can't believe he could have been so cruel. It's just not the Charles I knew – it's not the same person!'

'You never did know him,' Richard said. 'And you never hurt his pride. You came into his life when he was an old man and you gave him the ego-boost he needed. He didn't have to pretend with you. You walked into the set-up ready-made. Big Charles Schriber, the great sportsman, the popular millionaire, respected by all. He wasn't like that when my mother married him. She had the money. He used it to make himself a success. And he used her to make the social scene. The Ducketts were an old Carolina family; he was the son of a German immigrant, self-made all the way. Christ knows why she ever married him, but she must have thought she was in love. Her family never accepted him; she was cut off there too. And then she slipped up and had me, and he had her on her knees from then on. He was sterile, you see. That was the irony. So there couldn't be a real Schriber to make up for me.'

'He could have divorced her,' Isabel said at last. 'She could have left him, taken you with her.'

'He wouldn't let my mother go in a million years,' he said. 'He wouldn't stand before his little world at Freemont and admit he wasn't up to keeping a beautiful young wife happy. He'd have killed her before he let anyone know the truth. But there was nothing he could do about me. Nothing.'

'I don't know what to say,' she said slowly. 'Oh, Richard, how horrible. How cruel – cruel on all of you. And I feel so sorry for your mother – He must have suffered too, to behave like that.'

'I hope so,' he said slowly. 'Not because of how he treated me, but because of what he did to her. You saw that portrait. She looked just like that. She was quite beautiful, sweet and kind with it. She could have been so happy with a different man. Even with him if he'd ever forgiven her. But he never did. So let's cut the family saga short and just say that when she died I took my inheritance and left for Europe. Where I've had one hell of a ball ever since.'

'You blame him for her suicide,' Isabel said. 'That's really why you hate him.'

'Yes,' the tight little smile was back again. 'Yes, I think you could say that.' He turned and the smile became warm.

'Tears in the eyes,' he said. 'I shouldn't have told you. What good does it do? Come on,' his tone was gentle. 'Forget it. I'm going to sign the bill and take you over the road to Annabel's. I haven't danced with you yet. It would be good for both of us.'

The night club, under the same ownership as the drinking club, was smart but less exclusive. It was very dark and the noise was brutal. She hadn't wanted to go with him; she felt shaken and miserable. He took her straight onto the small, dark dance floor and held her in his arms.

The rock beat changed to a slow rhythm. He was pressing her very close against him, and he whispered to her. 'Stop thinking about him. Just relax with me, Isabel. He's gone. You don't belong to him any more.'

She closed her eyes and put her arms round his neck. She didn't notice that the man with the slicked-down hair and the American clothes who had been at Marks Club, had taken a table at the back wall, facing the dance floor. He had put his glasses away. There weren't any lenses in them anyway. The brunette, hired for the evening from an escort agency, sipped a whisky and tried not to yawn. She kept wondering what the hell this particular dummy wanted company for. He hardly talked and he didn't dance. She supposed, wearily, that the inevitable proposition would follow when they went home. MacNeil paid her no attention. Following Isabel was easy; bluffing his way into that exclusive club had been extremely difficult. Luckily he had London contacts and they had supplied him with a list of members of all the best places. He had got in by saying he was meeting a man on the club's list for drinks. The same ruse worked with the night club. The name he mentioned was very well known. He watched Richard and Isabel circling the floor. They weren't dancing. If he was going to follow them back he had to get rid of the woman. He paid her, added a handsome tip, and sent her off to find a taxi home. Then he settled back into the dark corner, ordered himself another Scotch, and waited.

There was an hour to spare before Andrew Graham's evening surgery began. He had done his afternoon round of patients, most of them old friends, spent the usual twenty minutes examining, chatting and prescribing and accepted a drink towards the end. He was tired. Medicine bored him; he sometimes wondered whether some of his patients, like Agnes Hilton for instance, fiftyish and hypochondriac, had any idea what it cost him in nervous tension to listen to their symptoms and commiserate over their non-existent ailments. But he couldn't afford to retire. He had three children, the last two still at college and the youngest starting high school. Joan and he had made a mistake in planning their family late. He was tied to his practice for another five years at least. Not that the Grahams were poor; although his wife liked to talk as if they were. He had a little private money, and a savings account of which she knew nothing, the result of careful betting and inside tips from friends. It was paying for the services of MacNeil at that moment. No, they weren't poor, but there was an element of frugality about their lives which didn't accord with their social status. As a young student he had been full of zeal for medicine; his father's gambling hadn't seemed to matter so much then. It was in the later years, when his practice was becoming a routine and much of his initial fervour had been dissipated in late-night calls and trivial illnesses, that he started regretting the money that had been lost on horses, cards and the backgammon table.

He had dropped his bag on a chair in his inner surgery, and asked his receptionist to bring him coffee from the dispenser outside. It was a beautiful sunny afternoon and he wished he was at home, wandering round the garden. He sipped his coffee, and flipped the page of his appointment book. Agnes Hilton's name sprang at him and he groaned. He leaned back in his chair and closed his eyes. The telephone on his desk rang. It was his receptionist.

'There's a personal call for you from England, Doctor. Will you take it?' He was instantly alert. He swung up straight in his chair.

'Yes – yes, put it through.'

He heard MacNeil's voice on the other end of the line. It was not very clear and there was a maddening echo that boomed across, repeating every word. He kept his voice low, he didn't want the receptionist to hear. . . .

He let MacNeil talk. 'It's only a matter of time,' he heard MacNeil say. He didn't answer for a moment, and the detective started to shout down the line, thinking they were cut off. The echo doubled everything.

'I'm here,' he said hastily. 'Just hold on a minute. What makes you so sure?'

'Why don't you come over and see for yourself?' was the answer. 'It'll make the gossip columns at this rate. I've got a suggestion to make,' the detective went on. 'Why don't you take a trip over – we could have a meaningful discussion.'

'Just a minute – ' Graham said. 'I haven't money to throw around like that. What good would it do?' Now the pause came from MacNeil.

'I think you should come,' he said. He sounded slow, decisive, as if he wanted to impress his view on Andrew Graham. 'I think you should make some excuse back home and take the trip. I think things are moving over here. Take down my number and think it over. Let me know.'

The echo repeated it. Let me know. He wrote down a telephone number.

'You got that?' MacNeil checked the figure again. 'Okay. Be in touch.' The connection went clear. Andrew stayed very still. It's only a matter of time. It'll make the gossip columns next. . . . He was surprised by the surge of his own anger. His hand shook as he reached for the coffee cup and put it down again. The coffee was tepid and bitter. Isabel had fooled them all. Including Charles. She wasn't content with grabbing everything, getting a dying man to change his will and leave her every cent. She had to add this final insult to the injury she did her husband's memory. . . .

His buzzer nagged at him from the desk. He snapped the switch and the receptionist's metallic voice announced that Mrs Agnes Hilton was waiting outside in reception. Andrew swore under his breath.

He said to send her in.

When Mrs Hilton, suffering from a dizzy feeling and a backache, walked into the surgery he was on his feet, ready to shake hands. Smiling and reassuring. So kind. He knew she wasn't in the best of health. But she did notice, in spite of her absorption in her symptoms, that he looked quite sallow in the face, and when they shook hands, he was trembling. She hoped the doctor himself wasn't going to be ill.

7

MacNeil was wrong when he reported to Andrew Graham that Isabel and Richard were lovers. They drove back to the Savoy, and Richard asked her if he could come up.

They had hardly spoken in the night club; they spent most of the time dancing on the dark, crowded little floor. In the car he had put his arm round her; 'I want to talk to you, Isabel. Let's get things straight between us.' She had brought him up to the suite with her, and MacNeil had seen them go.

Isabel hadn't known what was going to happen when they walked into the sitting room together; she only knew that ever since she met him, she had been relying on the barrier of his relationship to Charles. Now that had gone. She was face to face with Richard Schriber as a man, not as a stepson. A man who had been making love to her to music. And at the core of it all was a sense of sickness, of pity and shame and confusion because of what he had told her. She had hidden from it in his arms, but it was with her now.

'When I left Beaumont after the funeral,' Richard said, 'I came back here. I put the place behind me. And I'll be honest with you, Isabel, I tried to put you behind me too. It didn't work. For the first time in my life I really missed a woman. There were plenty around, but they didn't help. You don't want me to say this, do you?'

'No,' she said. 'I'd rather you didn't.'

'Because you want to run away,' he said. 'And I'm damned if I'm going to let you.'

Isabel sat down. 'I'm fond of you,' she began. 'But it's no more than that. . . .'

'Don't lie to yourself,' he said. 'I've held you in my arms; I know. I want to go to bed with you, Isabel. I want to wipe the memory of him right out of your mind; I told you before, he's got his hooks into you, even from the grave. And there's a part of you that knows it and wants to run away. And not to someone like Tim Ryan either. To me. And now you can, because there isn't any blood relationship. What would you feel if I said I was in love with you?'

He came to her and she got up; she couldn't stop herself going into his arms, and when he kissed her she resisted for only a moment.

'Love me,' he whispered. 'Break free of him. Don't you see – leaving you the money and the horses was just his way of holding on to you after he'd gone. . . .'

It was seductive and insistent; his lips were brushing her eyes, her mouth, her forehead, his hand smoothing her breast.

'Stop all this Derby nonsense,' he murmured. 'Send the Falcon back to Beaumont, sell him, do what you like. But cut the cord with Charles. It's the only way you'll belong to yourself.'

Her eyes were closed; he was holding her very close; he kissed her again. She had a sudden memory flash, as if she were back in the bedroom at Beaumont, listening to Charles's warning before he died. . . .

'And then come away with me,' he said. 'We can travel. Take three months just seeing places. I've never been to India. . . . You can have all the time in the world to make up your mind.'

And the dying man holding her hand, fighting for breath. 'Richard will try to stop you . . . don't ever trust him. . . .'

She freed herself from him. There was nothing in his face but passion and tenderness. There was no reason for suspicion. Everything he said made sense. Cut the cord, belong to yourself. But it wasn't the reason and she knew it.

'Will it matter all that much to you,' she said slowly, 'if I rob Charles of what he wanted most?'

He didn't falter or deny it. But the arms holding her were tense and the fingers on her shoulder were rigid. Their grip hurt.

'I can't ask you to do it for me. But I'd feel a lot better to see him lose for once. It's not a valid promise you gave; the whole thing is just a monument to his vanity. Winning from the grave. It's obscene. You know it is.'

'It didn't seem so,' she said quietly. 'I wish you didn't hate him so much. If you can't cut loose from him, how can I hope to?'

'We can do it by going away together,' he said. 'By getting out of his world. So long as you stay in racing, you're part of the Schriber myth. Ryan is part of it too; get rid of him. Send him home. Cancel the lease on this place at Coolbridge. You don't want a furnished house; you only took it because it's near Epsom. The whole thing is crazy – ' he said. 'I love you – and I know you love me.'

Isabel got up; he held on to her hand and she gently drew it away. He stood and put his hands on her shoulders.

'Think about it,' he said. 'I won't try to rush you. But get it in perspective. We could have everything together. I've lived my life in a certain way and I'm sick of it. I'm sick of the tramps and the booze and the whole set-up. I want to be with you. We can kick the past in the teeth and start again. Just think about it.'

He kissed her again, and this time it wasn't gentle. Then he left her.

She hardly slept that night. Images chased each other in the darkness, adding to the profound confusion in her mind and feelings. Charles, loving, strong, generous-hearted, had been presented to her in a hideous guise. A savage bully, obsessed with pride, punishing his unhappy wife for her one mistake, hating the innocent child who had been born as a result. Richard's words kept ringing through her head.

'He hit me across the face. You're the bastard – ' She could see him as a boy, all of fourteen, however he described himself as big enough to stand up for his mother, staggering back under the blow. It was unbelievable that the man she had lived with for three years could be capable of such an act.

And now Frances Schriber was very much alive; the wistful

figure in the portrait had been flashed out by her son, into a frightened, bullied human being who had succumbed at last and taken her own life. And still Charles's hatred had followed her. Her son had been driven out of the house, and all trace of her existence removed.

It was horrible and it was completely at variance with everything she knew about her husband. And then there was that other revelation. Richard hadn't known its significance to her. Charles had been sterile; his refusal to have children was a lie, concocted to hide his own shortcoming. And yet she could understand it; she had only to think of him, so vigorously male, to know what an agonizing blow to his self-respect that discovery must have been. It wasn't all on one side; there was no excuse in Richard's eyes, but he must have suffered too. And some people reacted to pain by being cruel and unforgiving.

She found herself crying, without being sure whether it was for Richard and his mother or for Charles, his memory tarnished, his pride in ruins.

She tried very hard to keep herself and Richard in perspective. When he accused her of wanting to go away with him, he had been right. Part of her longed to abandon everything and give herself completely to this new relationship. But it wasn't the strongest part. The other self refused, holding back from a final commitment, reluctant to cast off from the responsibilities her husband had entrusted to her. And if she dared to admit that she was falling in love with Richard Schriber, then where did her first loyalty lie . . .

In the morning, the issues were no clearer. The hotel bedroom was claustrophobic, the prospect of spending more time in London seemed unbearable. She phoned through to the estate agents and asked if she could take immediate possession of Coolbridge House if she paid the full rental in advance. It didn't take too long for the agents to decide. Money expedited everything.

There were two messages from Richard, taken by reception while she was with the agents. She telephoned him back, and a manservant answered. She was leaving for Coolbridge the next morning; he could contact her there. She suggested that he might come down on Sunday and spend the day.

That evening Tim Ryan came down to dinner. Mrs Jennings had prepared the meal; she had quickly decided that she liked working for Isabel. She was considerate and friendly, and her appreciation of the house pleased the housekeeper. They had drinks on the terrace; it was a lovely cool May evening. Isabel wore trousers and a silk shirt; Tim Ryan watched her. She looked relaxed and rested; much of the tension he had noticed since she came to England had gone.

'You're happy here, aren't you?'

'I love it,' she said. 'I feel as if I've lived here for years. I went shopping in the village this morning. You know, I've forgotten how easy country life is in England. People are friendly and helpful – I hope you've noticed my flowers?'

Tim had noticed. There were huge vases of lilacs in the drawing room and the big hall. The gardens at Coolbridge were full of flowering shrubs to give colour and variety before the roses came in June.

'What does Richard think of it?' he asked her.

'He hasn't been down yet,' Isabel said. He thought she had hesitated.

'I wanted to get settled first,' she said. They were sitting outside the drawing room on a flagged terrace; the rose garden, enclosed by dwarf hedges, stretched in front of them. It was a scene of soothing beauty. She hadn't wanted Richard to come immediately. She wanted to shelve everything, just for a few days, and indulge her fantasy that in a strange way she had found a home. That idea shocked her too. It showed how far she had moved from Beaumont in the few months since Charles died. Or how superficial its grip upon her had been without him. She was deeply glad to see Tim.

'Can you bear to talk business for a minute?' he said. 'Horse business, that is.' He noticed a look of strain that just as quickly disappeared.

'Yes, of course.'

'Foster wants to run the Falcon in the Prix Lupin. He doesn't fancy the Two Thousand Guineas after all. He wants to give the horse his Derby trial in France. What do you think?'

'Why has he changed his mind about the Two Thousand?'

'He doesn't want to give him more than one race. The Lupin is worth sixty grand, and he thinks the track at Longchamp will suit Falcon perfectly. He likes a bit of give in the ground and it's on the firm side here. What do you feel about it?'

'I don't know. Do you think it's a good idea?'

'Yes,' Tim said. 'As a matter of fact, I do. Nigel's delighted with the way he's been working. He's getting himself fit with the minimum trouble and the timing for the Lupin is just about right. If he wins that, he's got three weeks before the Derby. The race will put him right at the top of his form. I'd go ahead and send him. It'd be fun for us too.'

And much less dangerous to the horse than running him at Newmarket in the cavalry charge of the Two Thousand Guineas. There were at least three jockeys riding hopeless horses who might have been prevailed upon to crowd in and put him on the ground. Just one clever collision with a horse galloping at thirty miles an hour, and there would be no Derby.

'I've had some news about the lad who was injured,' he said. 'But I'm afraid the outlook is pretty bleak. He's going to be in a wheelchair.'

'If he's crippled,' she said slowly, 'I want to make arrangements to keep him comfortably for life. I'd also like to see him.'

'I talked that over with Nigel,' Tim said. 'If you come in on it, Long might get the idea he could sue for damages. And we don't want that. We don't want any adverse publicity for the Falcon before the Derby.'

The Derby. Suddenly the illusion she had fostered round herself was gone. The peaceful garden with its mellow brick walls and the ancient house behind them was no real protection. The decision hadn't been made; she had been running away from it. She couldn't go on letting Tim and Nigel Foster make their plans, without saying anything. She couldn't let the issue drift until it was too late to do anything about it. That was the coward's way.

And the last person in the world to listen to her with sympathy was Tim Ryan. Devoted to Charles, a professional with a great Derby prospect waiting to go for his first big contest as a three-year-old. She could imagine his reaction when she suggested withdrawing the colt. But she had to try and clarify her own feelings and it had proved impossible to do alone.

'Tim,' she said. 'There's something I've got to discuss with you. It's about the Falcon.'

There was a long silence when Isabel had finished. Mrs Jennings came to announce dinner, and they went into the dining room. It was a beautiful room, panelled in eighteenth-century pine: there was a fine Alan Ramsay portrait of a woman and two children over the fireplace.

'Help yourself, Tim,' she said. There were gulls' eggs and lobster salad. He ate very little; she could see how upset he was, and she didn't know how to cope with it. It seemed more than the disappointment of a racing manager. In the end she couldn't bear the awkwardness. The simple, delicious food tasted of nothing; he was drinking the wine as though it were whisky.

'I know what you feel,' she said at last. They had coffee in the drawing room; the curtains were drawn and it was just beginning to get dark. Mrs Jennings had lit the fire, because the evening had turned suddenly cool. It was a scene of elegance and serenity, and Isabel had seldom felt more miserable. 'Tim,' she said. 'Please, talk to me about it.'

He shrugged. 'How can I? You tell me you've decided not to run the horse because Richard hated his father and doesn't want to have him win the race. What can I say to that?'

'I didn't say that,' she said. 'I told you I felt perhaps that was the right thing to do. It's so difficult for me to know.'

He put the cup down. 'It isn't really difficult, Isabel,' he said slowly. 'You promised Charles, and now you're letting Richard talk you out of it. I can't argue about whether he's got the right to do this or not; his relationship with Charles is none of my business. They didn't get on, and everyone knew that. But to persuade you to withdraw the Falcon – out of personal spite against his father – that's unforgivable!'

'He has his reasons,' Isabel said. 'I can't explain them to you, but I promise you I can understand how he feels. There's so much I can't tell you because it wouldn't be fair. To him or to Charles. Please, Tim, you've always been such a friend to me – we've never had a quarrel – don't let's fall out about this!'

He got up and she thought he was going to leave. At that precise moment she was right. Everything on which he had based his hopes for the future was being destroyed. And then he saw the distress on her face, and his anger subsided. He chided himself bitterly. What a fool to lose his head and his temper – to walk away leaving the field clear for the man who was trying to spoil everything for him. He had never given way to outbursts of Irish temperament in his life; at this, the most important juncture in it, he was about to break that rule. He sat down again, beside her this time.

'I'm so sorry Isabel,' he said. 'I've been rude and thoughtless to you over this. And you're right. I ought to help you think it through instead of going up like a bloody rocket. Can I get us both a drink?'

She was glad to see him smile. There had never been friction between them before and she found it disturbing. 'Yes please. Brandy – it's on the table over there.'

They sat together. He lit a cigarette.

'Let's put Richard and his attitude aside,' he said. He felt calm now, ready to fight on any level. 'Let's think of Charles for a minute. He bred that horse; we saw it foaled together; we talked about it the night he died, remember?' She nodded, not speaking.

He went on, remorselessly reminding her. 'You asked me to help you run the stud and carry on the racing. Most of all you wanted to win the Derby for him. You told me it was his dying wish. We both know that he only held out against the cancer as long as he did in case he could get through till June. Isn't this true?'

'Yes,' she said. 'It is.'

'He trusted you,' Tim said. 'He put everything into your hands because he knew you'd take care of the horses and keep it all going. Richard hates the set-up; he's never pretended anything different. He hasn't any sentiment for Beaumont or what it means.'

'It isn't only that,' Isabel said. 'He feels Charles did it deliberately, to keep a hold on me. He says I'll never be free of him and able to find myself till I've got rid of all the associations with Beaumont and racing. And the trouble is, there's a lot of truth in it. Charles didn't give me any choice. Maybe I am in his shadow – perhaps he's right – '

'He's wrong,' Tim said. 'The only way you'll get free of Charles if you feel you have to – is when you've carried out your obligation to him. Run his horse, Isabel. Try and win for him. And then you can close the door on it all, if you want to. A lot of people are depending on you over this. There's Nigel; he's going to suffer professionally if you withdraw the Falcon – you know what a thing like that could do to his reputation. God knows how many people have backed it – they'll lose their money too. And then there's me. I've spilt my guts watching over the Falcon, planning for him, pointing him to that race. And if he wins I get a quarter of a million dollars under Charles's will. I'm being honest with you; my personal future depends on the Falcon. If you pull him out you've wrecked everything for me, too.'

'I hadn't thought of that,' Isabel said slowly. 'I wouldn't let you lose by it, Tim. You'd have the money. He shouldn't have made it a conditional bequest anyway.'

'No, thank you,' he said quickly. 'I don't take money that I haven't earned. That's why Charles left it in that way. If Falcon wins I've earned it. And that's the only way I'll take it. Not as a sop to your conscience. I'm not being a bastard, Isabel, I'm just telling the truth. You can't back off this just to please Richard Schriber or even yourself. And I don't think you'll ever forgive yourself if you do.'

She didn't speak for a while. She sipped the brandy, watching the fire flickering round the logs. Cold, common sense, plainly put by a man she respected and trusted, a man she couldn't bear to walk away from her in anger. She had never realized until that moment how close she had grown to him since Charles had died. Not like Richard; there was no sense of being swept relentlessly towards the reefs of a love affair. It was a different feeling; Tim was a man who would never lie to her or let her lie to herself.

'You're right,' she said at last. 'Richard will have to understand. It can't be done. I'm only surprised at myself for thinking it was possible. I'm sorry, Tim. I've got myself into an emotional tangle, that's all. Forget I ever mentioned it. Tell me, when do we go to Longchamp?'

'May 16th,' he said. He drew a long breath. 'Christ,' he said, 'you gave me a fright.' He laughed then, and suddenly Isabel felt the tension had gone. Everything was right; the room was warm and full of scent from the flowers she had arranged. It was as if time had gone into reverse, as if Richard had never told her about his father, never faced her with loving him. Tim had brought her back. Back to the safe world of Beaumont and the accepted pattern of her life as Charles's widow. She had been wrong to doubt her husband's motives. If only, she found herself thinking suddenly, if only it had been Tim instead. . . .

'I've got a suggestion to make,' he interrupted her. The idea had come to him soon after he arrived, when they were sitting on the terrace.

'There's a two-year-old colt over in Kildare we ought to see. I got a call from Brian Martin yesterday. It got the virus and wasn't ready for the Sales. He's seen it and he thinks it's great. It's by Monkstown, out of a winning mare by Never Bend. Fly over to Kilgallion tomorrow and look at it with me?'

'I haven't been to Ireland for two years,' she said. 'It would be fun to go. Nice to see Brian again too. All right, why not? How much do they want for the colt – or don't you dare tell me – '

Ryan grinned. 'I don't,' he admitted. 'I don't even dare tell myself till I've seen it. With that breeding, if it looks right, and Brian says it does, you're going to have to win the bloody Derby to pay for it!'

'Tim,' Isabel said, 'you're impossible. You'd better stay the night.' She reached up and gave him a grateful, affectionate kiss. He had another brandy, put through two calls to Ireland, one to Brian Martin asking him to meet them at lunchtime, and another to the owner of Kilgallion stud, saying they were coming to see the Monkstown colt. Once in Ireland they could linger until it was time to hurry back to England and then go on to Paris for the Prix Lupin. Richard Schriber wouldn't have a chance to upset her again. And there was something about the way she kissed him when she invited him to stay, that made Tim Ryan quietly confident. Richard had not won yet.

David Long was in a plaster cast from the waist down. His chest and shoulder were swathed in bandages. Heavy elastoplast supported his rib cage. He looked at the visitor with eyes full of suspicion. He had never seen the man before, but he had a good idea who had sent him. And about bloody time, he thought bitterly. Not a word from them since the accident. Not a penny either. He hadn't been too surprised; it was natural they wouldn't want to know when the plan went wrong. And wrong was hardly the word for it. Crippled for life; he wasn't fooled by the doctors. When they started talking about wheelchairs he knew what that meant. Useless. He cried a lot when he was alone, but he wasn't a coward. He had wanted to be a top jockey and he had the nerve all right, but not the skill. He had wasted away to a skeleton to make the weight for his first ride as an apprentice. Nigel Foster had given him the chance, and it had been disastrous. Long took the news that he couldn't expect to rise above a stable lad without saying much. He was a surly boy and seldom expressed his feelings except in four-letter words. He went back to work in the yard and knew he would never put on the silks again. So he decided to make a bit of money for himself instead. He had got away with a couple of jobs without anybody knowing. Nothing spectacular, just a horse in a seven-furlong race at Redcar that the bookies didn't want to win. A bucket of water half an hour before the race had settled him. He picked up a couple of hundred pounds for that. The second time he lamed one of Foster's two-year-olds with a well-timed kick when he was doing it in the box, and nobody suspected anything. She was heavily backed for a good race and he got five hundred for that. When he was approached over the Silver Falcon, it was in the bar at Newbury, on his day off. The amount of money was commensurate with what he had to do. He didn't hesitate; it was a fortune to him. They even supplied the iron bar.

'Who the hell are you?' he said to the man. He was a small, wizened figure, with a sad monkey face. Long knew the type. Another down-at-heel ex-jockey bumming drinks off the lads on the course, hanging round the training pubs, hoping for a hand-out or a casual job. They would send a little scut like him. . . .

'My name's Downs,' the man said, which was a lie, and which Long didn't believe for a moment. 'You stood me a pint or two at the Black Cock – I heard what had happened, so I thought I'd pop along and see how you were getting on.'

Long turned his head away. 'If that's it, then piss off,' he said. Downs didn't move.

'A friend of yours sent me,' he said. 'He wants to know what happened.' Long turned his head again and looked at him.

'He took his fuckin' time,' he said. 'I'm broke up. Tell him that. The bleeder broke my spine. I never got no chance with him.'

Downs leaned forward. 'How come?' he whispered. He had seen enough of Long's injuries to know that more than a single kick was involved. The upper half of his body was bandaged to the neck.

Long's face twisted, whether with pain or hatred it was difficult to tell until he answered.

'That bastard,' he spat out under his breath. 'That bleedin' bastard – he tried to kill me! He came at me as soon as I got in the box, laid one on me and when I was down, he nearly murdered me – '

'Christamighty,' Downs said. 'Savaged you, did he? Nobody said nothin' about that – '

'They wouldn't,' Long said. 'It wouldn't look good, running a bloody killer horse. Everything was hushed up all right. But I tell you, and you tell them, don't send anyone else in after him; he'll do for them like he did me. I've got teeth marks on me like something out of bleedin' *Jaws*.'

Downs screwed up his eyes. 'Christamighty,' he said again.

'What're they going to do for me?' Long demanded. It was worth a try, but he didn't have much hope. They only paid on results, and it wasn't possible to blackmail them. He would only lose out if he told the real reason why he had gone into the Falcon's box. And after Nigel Foster's visit the day before, he didn't want to take any chances.

The best medical treatment available would be provided for him, and enough money settled on him by Mrs Schriber to keep him in comfort for the rest of his life. Not comfort; luxury. His parents were being compensated too, and that had really earned his gratitude. They had a hard life, especially his mother. The money would make all the difference. He could go and live with them when he left Stoke Mandeville. But the price, and Nigel Foster had made this clear, was no press interviews, no publicity. He worried for a moment about having talked to Downs.

'Do for you?' Downs looked stupid, which Long felt wasn't difficult for him. 'I dunno; nobody said nothing to me. Just wanted to know how you was.' He got up quickly, patted Long on the shoulder.

'Glad you're not too bad,' he said. 'Keep smilin', lad. Accidents will 'appen.' He hurried out of the ward. Long raised his head and said something obscene at his back view.

Downs came out of the hospital entrance, looked round him, and then walked over to the hospital car park. He needed a drink, and the nearest pub was a good twenty minutes away. He slipped between the cars until he came to a blue Ford

Cortina. The passenger door opened as he approached and he got in. The man in the driver's seat wore a felt hat and dark glasses. Downs cleared his throat nervously; he felt sandpaper-dry in the throat. Thirty years ago, when he was a promising jockey with a retainer to a good stable, he started getting that same feeling. Drink had ruined his career and his life.

'Well Guv,' the words came out in a rush. 'I've talked 'im round – 'e won't give no trouble – '

Five minutes later he came out of the car park. There were four five-pound notes in his greasy inside pocket. He hurried towards the pub in the High Street as fast as his short legs could cover the ground. The blue Ford Cortina passed him on the way. The window was up and the man in the hat and dark glasses didn't look at him. The car turned off at the sign to the motorway and London.

The announcement that the Silver Falcon was to run in the Prix Lupin was made from Dublin. Nigel Foster had joined Isabel and Tim Ryan; he had heard about the Monkstown colt and, being a man who seized opportunities, flew out on a pretext of looking at something else. If anyone was going to train the colt that season, he was determined it should be himself. Tim had booked himself and Isabel into the Hibernian. He knew it well and liked its old-fashioned service and homely charm. Isabel hadn't been there before, because Charles had usually stayed at the Shelbourne or with friends when he visited Ireland.

Tim had driven her out to the Kilgallion stud the day after they arrived. He was in a buoyant mood, teasing her about having a hangover; they had spent the evening dining with Brian Martin, who had been a scout for Charles during the last ten years. He was a huge, jolly man, hard-drinking and over-fond of women, but with a faultless eye for a horse. He didn't always buy the most expensive either. His dictum was always the same. First look at the breeding and then look at the horse. They had spent a long, uproarious evening in Snaffles, a small dining club near Merrion Square, where the food was excellent. Isabel had never experienced Ireland with the Irish before; she didn't realize until she and Tim and Brian were all strolling back through the streets, arm in arm, with the big man rolling slightly, how Charles had dominated everything they did together. He moved on a princely circuit; nobody walked because there was always a vast sleek car in waiting. He overawed his guests a little; even Brian was subdued, though that wasn't saying much by normal standards. That night Tim showed her the city and himself as she had never seen them before. Driving down to Kildare along the two-lane highway out of Dublin the morning after that party, she did feel slightly hung over, but she couldn't remember having ever enjoyed herself more. Nigel Foster had telephoned them, full of disarming talk about co-incidences, which had amused Tim very much, and invited himself down to Kilgallion to look at the two-year-old with them.

The stud was one of the most famous in Ireland, standing in twelve hundred acres of prime pasture, with the Liffey river running through it; the house was approached by an impressive avenue of beech trees. She hadn't visited it before, and she was intrigued by the meeting with the owner. Mrs Muriel Bartlett Brown was a well-known Irish folk figure; revered, or detested, she had established herself as one of the most successful breeders in the world. Widowed at thirty-seven with four children and very little money, she had begun with two brood mares, purchased with money borrowed from friends, and ended as a millionairess owning Kilgallion and with many of the great Classic winners among her progeny. She referred to her bloodstock as my children, and had been known to send a buyer off the property if she didn't like his looks or manner, irrespective of how much he could pay. The house was a big Georgian rectangle, painted shell-pink, with creepers and wisteria trained up its walls. The lawns surrounding it were barbered and as green as the rolling paddocks on all sides. As the car turned into the gravelled courtyard, a horde of Border terriers came streaking out of the front door, barking furiously. The tall, thin figure of Mrs Bartlett Brown followed them. She had untidy grey hair, a grey, granite textured face, with bright blue eyes; she was dressed in a similar shade of pale pink to the walls of her house.

They were invited inside, and offered a choice between whisky and champagne. It was just before eleven o'clock in the morning. Tim and she talked most of the time; Isabel was happy to sit and listen to them, and to look at the sitting room. The curtains were pink and the chintz had the same predominant colour – obviously Mrs Bartlett Brown's favourite. There were photographs everywhere, of horses winning races all over the world. She seemed a woman of intelligence and charm, obviously an expert who knew her own mind, and either the reports were exaggerated, or else she had taken a fancy to them. They waited for Nigel Foster to arrive.

'No point in taking you out to see the little fellow, without him being here,' she said to Isabel. 'I imagine that if you do buy him, you'll send him to Nigel?' It wasn't so much a question as a statement. Tim winked at Isabel.

'Let's see him win the Derby with Silver Falcon first, Muriel. But I'll tell him you were working for him, anyway.'

She gave a loud, masculine laugh. 'I wouldn't if I didn't think he was the best. As English trainers go; I'd like to see my little fellow trained over here, but Nigel will do. That's him now; shut up, dogs! Shut up!'

They walked down to the paddock together where the colts were separated into groups of four, and the head groom went in with a head collar and rope to catch him. He trotted up to the call, a beautiful, compact, chestnut colt, with a white blaze down his face. He was brought out for them to see, walked up and down the enclosed yard, and at Tim's request trotted up and back a couple of times. Then the examination began, with Tim and Nigel walking round him. He fretted a little, and the groom soothed him, patting his neck.

'He's not been done up at all,' his owner said. There was a look of loving pride on her face, as if she were watching an actual child of her own. 'You're seeing him in the rough. It's the best way, I always think. Look at that movement,' she spoke to Isabel; the colt was trotting round for them. The rhythm was perfect, the action as light as a ballet dancer's. Tim came back to them.

'Pity he's a chestnut,' he remarked.

Mrs Bartlett Brown literally snorted through her nose.

'Don't tell me you take that rubbish seriously! What the hell colour were Secretariat and Grundy, may I ask?' The bright blue eyes sparkled angrily at him. Her cheeks were red.

'It's not a colour I like,' he insisted. There was a deep-rooted superstition about chestnuts; they had the reputation of being cowardly. The addition of four white socks made them virtually unsaleable to many people. 'If he had more than one white sock I wouldn't let Mrs Schriber even look at him,' Tim said flatly, apparently unaware that he was about to be expelled from the place. Isabel thought Mrs Bartlett Brown was going to explode. 'But as it is,' he went on coolly, 'he's a very nice fellow. Very nice indeed. Don't you think so, Nigel?'

'I do,' the trainer agreed. He was thanking God he had flown over and got in on the prospective sale at the beginning. It was the most impressive two-year-old he had seen in a very long time. And with that breeding there was no doubt about his Classic potential. He had run a temperature just before the December Sales – the virus had lasted for weeks. He was slow to recover, and this was why he hadn't been sold. Mrs Bartlett Brown insisted on waiting till the colt was a hundred per cent fit. He said to Isabel, 'If I were you, I'd snap him up. Muriel won't have him long.'

Isabel looked at the chestnut. He had a fine head with a big eye full of intelligence. Beautifully bred, he had that indefinable quality known in the horse world as presence. In human beings it was usually described as star quality. She stepped up to him and stroked the velvet nose. He nuzzled against her gently. There was no vice in him, no hatred for mankind. At the same age the Falcon had been savage and unapproachable. She stroked his neck and turned to Mrs Bartlett Brown. For three years she had lived with horses, the spectator among the experts. Charles had left her the Falcon, but he still belonged to him. She felt a curious affinity with the colt.

'He's beautiful,' she said. 'I'd like to buy him.'

Some of the angry colour faded from Mrs Bartlett Brown's cheeks.

'You've got better judgement than your racing manager, Mrs Schriber,' she said. 'Let's go back to the house. All right, Joe – put him back with the others.' She glared at Tim. 'Chestnut and white socks – good God I thought you were a sensible man!' She led the way back at a furious walk.

By the end of the morning they had agreed on a price, which was less than the 130000 dollars she had asked originally. A bottle of champagne was opened, and she shook hands with Isabel. 'It's a deal then,' she said. 'And for God's sake choose a proper name for the fellow – I sold a filly once to some bloody oaf from England and she was the most exquisite thing you ever saw – d'you know what he called her? "Mum's the Word"! I nearly killed him when I saw him at Ascot . . . she won three good races for him too – '

They were invited to stay for lunch; she chatted to Isabel and roared her loud laugh at Nigel Foster's funny stories, but her eye was baleful when she looked at Tim. She hadn't forgiven him for criticizing the colt's colour, and she managed to avoid shaking hands with him when they left.

The announcement about the Falcon running in France was timed for five o'clock and the press had been invited round for drinks at the hotel. Nigel put his head through the window and grinned at Tim before they drove back to Dublin in convoy. 'Congratulations,' he said to Isabel. 'He's a smashing chap – and she liked the way you made up your mind. As for you Ryan – Jesus, I thought she was going to brain you! *Nobody* tells her they don't like something about her horses and gets out alive!'

'Maybe not, but it got the price down,' Tim laughed. 'She puts on a bit of an act; playing the holy terror eccentric is all part of it. She knows damned well that a lot of people don't like the colour; she also knows there's something in it. It doesn't usually go with guts. But that's a gorgeous animal – did you see

136

the eye on him? Bold as a lion – that's what I go on. And he moves like Monkstown. I bet the old cat is on the phone to all the sporting papers, letting them know about the sale.'

On the way back to Dublin Tim turned to Isabel.

'That was a quick decision,' he said. 'Absolutely right too.'

He had been surprised by it, expecting her to wait for him to give the final judgement. 'What was it you liked so specially?'

'The expression in his eye,' she said. 'It was so genuine; bold and interested and yet gentle. I liked him immediately.'

'That's the only way to buy,' he said.

She smiled at him. 'But it's a very funny feeling; it's the first time I've bought a horse on my own initiative. I wonder what Charles would have thought – '

'Yesterday,' he said, 'you were telling me how you needed to get out of racing to escape from his influence. You're doing that all the time. He wouldn't have bought that colt today because he was riddled with superstition. But you did. You're making the decisions for yourself. You tell that to Richard next time he starts some bloody nonsense. And tomorrow, I'm going to take you down to Riverstown to meet my father. And to see my home.'

'I'd love that,' Isabel said. And then she remembered it was Sunday, and the day Richard was supposed to come to Coolbridge to see her. A feeling of unease came over her. She had done exactly the opposite of what he had asked. Far from getting out of racing and breaking her association with Charles's way of life, she had bought another Classic potential for a massive price. And she wouldn't be there to see him and tell him. She glanced at Tim; he looked carefree and he was humming as he drove. But she knew at that moment that he was fighting Richard Schriber for her. And he wasn't a man who usually lost.

Richard lived in a flat in Park Street in an exclusive block on the corner. When he bought it he had been too busy to decorate it; busy travelling and feeding the gossip columns. It was his only occupation and its object was to enrage and embarrass his father. That pillar of the Kentuckian community. The great sportsman and owner breeder. The glib catchphrase, beloved of journalists, had always nauseated Richard. It only pleased him when it was used in connection with some ugly exploit of his own. But that was a year or so ago; longer perhaps if he were honest.

He had no living-in servant; it didn't suit his life style to have people prying. A woman came and cleaned and an ex-valet looked after his clothes and prepared dinner or lunch if he was needed. Richard found Isabel's message when he came back on Saturday evening. He was going out to dinner and on to the Claremont Club with some friends who had flown in from Italy. It had been suggested that there was a beautiful Italian model in the company who might be of interest to him. He was more interested in the gaming tables than the model. He came in, picked up the message and took it into his bedroom as if it were a letter that needed re-reading. She couldn't see him at Coolbridge tomorrow; she was not coming back from Dublin until Monday. Or Tuesday. He threw the piece of paper into a corner. Then he undressed. He went under the shower and ran the water first hot, then icy cold. He came out, rubbing himself dry, his red hair wet and dark. Why had she gone to Ireland without telling him? Why hadn't she come back, or asked him to join her? She was slipping away. . . . Ryan, of course. Ryan had taken her over there, foxed her with Irish charm and blarney, brought his cronies into it to fill the days with Irish talk and whisky and never mind about tomorrow. The bastard. The cunning, quick-thinking bastard.

He went into the bedroom and put through a call to the Hibernian Hotel. Mrs Schriber was not in her room. Or in the bar. She was out. With Ryan, or with some horse-loving Irish crook who knew how much money she had and that Charles Schriber was dead, and she could be easily taken. . . . Richard dressed slowly. He drank whisky as he did so; the idea of going to dinner with the Farellis and listening to some high-class whore talking banalities before she made herself available, appealed to him less and less.

He had made a grave mistake with Isabel. He shouldn't have let her put him off; he should have moved her into the dream manor house, gone along with the fantasy, kept beside her every minute. Ryan had moved very quickly. By now he would have undermined his influence. He had so much on his side, not least the shade of Charles Schriber and everything he represented in her immediate past. He carried his glass and the whisky bottle into the small sitting room. He had bought a fine Lowry for the fireplace wall, as a focal point for the room. He had taken it down, and the portrait of his mother from Beaumont hung in its place.

The blue background clashed with the coffee linen walls; the style screamed in contrast to the drawings and modern lithographs. It was prominent and grotesquely out of place. The pale, pointed face, with its wistful, apprehensive expression, the stylized pose, framed in chiffon round the shoulders. Richard looked up at it.

'He's not going to win,' he said out loud. 'I promise you.' He poured himself another whisky, drank half of it, and then dialled a number. 'Peter? Hullo there – it's Richard Schriber. Yes, fine thanks. It is a long time.' He leaned back, holding the phone in his right hand, tipping the whisky back and forth in his glass with the other. 'Yes, no headlines is good headlines, or so they say – sure. Listen, I may have a story for you – yes, it is; in fact I'm the hero – I'm going to be in the bar at Les A. in twenty minutes. Meeting some old friends at eight thirty. We can have a drink together before they come. Okay, fine. See you then.' He hung up, finished his whisky.

Peter Partridge was the by-line under which the paper's gossip column appeared; in fact there were half a dozen reporters who covered the stories of fashionable love affairs, divorces and the odd financial scandal. The items had become increasingly salacious and bitter; it was a sign of the times that the debutante was as dead as the proverbial duck, while the doings of whores and homosexuals titillated the public fancy. Richard had featured on the page often enough. Escorting this and that, no longer living with, etc. Big gambling losses were noticed. Even, and this had amused Richard more than the rest, a photograph of him sitting on the ground, after a furious fellow guest had punched him outside a night club. He made certain a friend sent that one to Beaumont.

Richard checked his money and keys, switched out the lights and left the flat; it was a few minutes walk to Les Ambassadeurs Club in Hamilton Place. He arrived there and sat at a small table, ordering a whisky. Not long afterwards the original Peter Partridge appeared, hailed him silently from the entrance hall and then joined him.

He stayed long enough to sink three double martinis, and slapped Richard lightly on the back as he left. There was a hint of effeminacy in the gesture. He wrote in a particularly waspish style that was widely copied. But this story had to be printed straight. He had given Richard a promise, and he was too good a newspaperman to spoil such a useful contact by breaking his word. It might be possible to slip in a little thorn among the roses, but nothing more than a tiny prick. . . . People he had injured explained him as a nasty queer. In fact he was a vigorous womanizer who just happened to be a natural bitch. He saw Richard Schriber get up to greet a group of friends who were obviously not English. Among them was an outstandingly beautiful girl. He had to remind himself not to mention that in the morning's piece. . . .

8

MacNeil had booked himself into an hotel in South Kensington; it was widely used by Americans on business trips to England and by groups of tourists. He wasn't interested in making extra money by crooking on expenses; he insisted that a tired man in poor work conditions was not a good detective.

He woke that morning feeling refreshed and looking forward to an easy day. Isabel Schriber was in Ireland. There was no point in following Isabel alone. It was her association with Schriber he had been paid to watch. The morning papers were left outside his bedroom door; he got up and brought them in before ringing for coffee, rolls and orange juice. He opened the first of the newspapers and began to read. It took him ten minutes to reach the Peter Partridge column. He said, 'Christ!' out loud and threw back the bedclothes; he read the item again with his feet on the floor. It was the lead story and there were headlines in half-inch type above it. He shut the paper up and reached for a cigarette. He needed to think. He knew a lot more about Andrew Graham than most people in Freemont did. He wasn't all human goodness and concern for the widow of his best friend. Not by a long, long way. He looked at his watch. It was three o'clock in the morning in Kentucky. Too bad. Doctors were used to being woken in the middle of the night. Graham wouldn't want to miss out on this one. If anything was going to bring him over to England, the column and a half in the big-circulation daily paper was the one thing to do it. He lifted the bedside phone and put through the call.

Patsy Farrant saw the same news item. She was also sitting up in bed, with Roy beside her. He never ate breakfast and she only drank coffee, out of an unnecessary regard for her perfect figure. She didn't read anything about politics or world affairs; she liked the film reviews and the fashion articles; she was an eager reader of Peter Partridge because Roy had featured in it, and so had many of their friends.

She read the lead story and gave a little gasp.

'Roy – just listen to this!'

He was reading *The Times*; he had a catholic taste and the tabloids were sent in with the prestige papers. He liked to know what was going on everywhere and from all points of view. He glanced at Patsy irritably. 'Listen to what, for Christ's sake!'

She allowed herself to smile. It wasn't often she got the better of him. He'd just hit the roof when he heard. . . .

She began to read out loud. He didn't wait for her to finish. He grabbed the paper out of her hands and read it for himself. Then he threw it on the floor and looked at her.

'The clever bastard,' he said slowly. 'So that's what he's up to – '

'I don't see,' Patsy ventured, 'how it will help us. Over the horse, I mean . . .' She tailed off because of the expression on his face.

'I don't either,' he said. 'The bastard,' he said again. 'I believe he's been playing me along – keeping me from doing anything about it. . . .'

'You shouldn't have trusted him,' Patsy said. 'I never did. Of all your friends, Roy, he's the only one I never . . .'

'Shut up,' he said. 'Just shut up.' She shrugged and rescued the newspaper. She didn't like Richard and that was true. There was something closed and distant about Richard which worried her, and her instinct, unhindered by intellectual processes, decided he was better left alone.

She couldn't have explained it to Roy, who wouldn't have listened anyway, but there was something about Richard Schriber which actually frightened her. She watched her husband get up and bang into the bathroom. He was in a very bad mood indeed. She was thankful that it wasn't a weekend. He could take out his temper on his secretary. She read the story for a second time. No wonder Roy was angry. It looked like a nasty trick to play on his old friend. . . .

Riverstown House was in Meath; Isabel drove down with Tim to have lunch with his father. It was a warm, wet day, interspersed with sudden breaks of brilliant sunshine. The press conference had gone off very well. When asked if fears that the horse might be interfered with had prompted so much extra security at the Lambourn yard, Nigel Foster shrugged the question off. Falcon was second favourite in the ante-post betting; he had a duty to protect the public's money. They dined in the hotel afterwards and Nigel congratulated her again on buying the two-year-old. It would grow on into a magnificent three-year-old. He wouldn't dream of trying to pressure her – Ryan wouldn't let him anyway – but he hoped she was going to have it trained in England.

It gave Isabel real pleasure to tell him that she intended sending it direct from Kilgallion to Lambourn. And it wasn't till she'd said it, and been warmly kissed on the cheek by the delighted trainer, that she realized she was already thinking of staying on at Coolbridge after June. They didn't talk much on the drive; the way out of Dublin was through poor and dingy streets, they passed the airport and an Aer Lingus jet pelted upwards over their heads. She hadn't been to Meath before. It was a beautiful county, less spectacular than Kildare with the Wicklow mountains in the background and the elegant studs, but green and gently rural. Tim turned the car off the Slane road and down towards Dunsany. He pointed out the Gothic towers of Dunsany Castle. 'I used to go there as a child; it's a wonderful place. The old Lord Dunsany and my grandfather were great friends. They were fascinated by ghosts. There was supposed to be a haunted room at Riverstown but I never saw anything. Haunted by debt collectors, more likely!'

They went up a long drive with some fine elm trees lining the road, but the surface was rutted and broken and the grasslands untended. And then she saw the house. The size and grandeur of its façade surprised her; Tim seldom talked about his home or referred to his family. She had no idea the Ryans had lived in such style. It was a square, three-storeyed Georgian mansion, with a fine pillared entrance and the long sash windows of the period. There was a crescent-shaped drive in front of it. It was cracked and overgrown with weeds. When he stopped the car and they got out, she could see the house hadn't been painted for years.

'I asked my father to open it up,' he said. 'We can have a quick look at it inside and then I'll take you home for lunch. He's very excited about meeting you.' He took her arm going up the flight of stone steps. 'It'll be a bit musty,' he said. 'It's been empty since my mother died and we've been trying to sell it. But no one wants these big old places now. They cost too much to keep up.'

There was a circular hall with a beautiful plasterwork ceiling, and a fine Regency staircase that wound upwards. They stood looking round for a moment. There was a damp, airless smell, and the atmosphere of slow decline that creeps over a house left empty too long.

'I'll show you the drawing room,' he said. She could tell that he was both proud and unhappy; the paint was peeling from the window frames and there was a blank space like a wound, where the fireplace had been ripped out in the hall. The drawing room was shuttered; she waited by the door while he opened them.

'Oh, Tim,' she said. 'It's lovely!'

The room was a perfect double cube, and the ceiling above them was beautifully painted in the classical eighteenth-century style, with elaborately gilded and plastered cornices and a superb Adam fireplace, from which the ornamental grate had been removed. 'It's a period gem,' she said. 'Who was the architect?'

'James Cleave,' he answered. 'He built the house in 1773;

this room is supposed to be his finest creation. It's quite famous among Irish houses.' He said it casually, but she could see by his face how much he cared.

They walked through the ground floor; the library, its empty grilled bookcases stretching to the ceiling, a huge dining room with another fine fireplace and magnificent mahogany double doors, the small study which he told her was his mother's sitting room.

'She loved the place,' he said. 'My father kept it going until she died because he knew it would break her heart to have to leave it. But it was just too much for us by then. I won't take you upstairs, or we'll be late. I'd better close the shutters. Maybe someone'll come and buy it one day; if they don't it'll fall down.'

'And if the Falcon wins?' Isabel asked him. He closed the front door, and locked it.

'If that happens, I'll be able to move my father back in. Most of the furniture's in store; he insisted on keeping it for me. I can put the house to rights and we can live here again. But I won't let myself count on it. And don't say anything to my father. He's too old to be disappointed.'

'I won't,' Isabel promised. She put her hand on his arm before they drove away. 'Thank you for showing it to me,' she said. 'I want him to win more than ever now. And I believe he will. I think you'll take Riverstown off the market and have the workmen in by the end of June.'

Tim smiled at her. He had never wanted to kiss her so much. It wouldn't be just Riverstown he'd claim back. He'd lost her once to Charles Schriber. Showing her the house where he was born and spent most of his life had brought them closer. 'I hope to God you're right,' he said.

His father lived in a small modern brick-built house half a mile away from Riverstown. It was a depressing contrast with the elegance and grandeur of the old home; the inside was furnished with taste and there were many fine pieces and some pictures which she recognized were of good quality. Living with Charles's collection had moulded her taste in the direction of sporting pictures. Frederick Ryan was a white-haired version of his son; he entertained her with the unique blend of warmth and informality which was peculiar to the Irish. The food was simple, but the wine had come from a very good cellar. Frederick Ryan and his eldest sister, very frail and rather deaf, were obviously devoted to Tim. His father talked enthusiastically of his prowess as an amateur jockey, and then said how sorry he was to hear of Charles's death.

'I believe he was a grand man,' he said. 'Tim wrote us a lot about him. And about you, Mrs Schriber. You were both very good to him. I only hope he's looking after the horses properly for you. Will you excuse him, if he runs upstairs and looks in on my wife's mother? She's got very old and she doesn't get up these days. I don't say she'll recognize you, Tim, but she might. Ninety-eight, she is, and as difficult an old devil as the day I married her daughter!'

The afternoon passed pleasantly; Isabel felt herself relaxing more and more; it was the first time in her life she hadn't felt guilty about wasting a day just sitting and talking. And the quality of the talk was stimulating. Tim's father had known many different kinds of people, from the literary groups who gathered at Dunsany Castle to the great racing figures of pre-war days. He roared with laughter at Tim's encounter with Mrs Bartlett Brown.

'She was the prettiest girl in Kildare – and a dream on a horse. I used to squire her round in the old days, but there was always a crowd round her. She was as sweet as buttermilk – never a cross word, never a sign of temper. But, by God, the moment she married poor old Willy Bartlett Brown, the mask came off! She's a holy terror – I'd give a lot to have been there when Tim talked back at her – nobody's done it for twenty years!'

They drank strong tea and ate home-made sponge cake. There was a cheerful middle-aged woman, referred to by the family as a 'girl', who cooked and cared for them. Isabel understood more and more where a lot of Tim's salary went. They drove back to Dublin; they were scheduled to fly back to

England the next morning. The Prix Lupin took place four days later and she could feel her excitement rising. If the Falcon won as easily as Tim and Nigel Foster seemed to think, then his prospects for the Derby were stronger than ever. And now that she had seen Riverstown and had met Tim's family, it was even more important that he should triumph at Epsom.

She and Tim were having dinner alone that evening and she was looking forward to it. He seemed very happy and in high spirits as they said goodbye to his father and drove back to Dublin.

'It's been a lovely day,' she said. 'Thank you for taking me. I must send a note to your father. It was sweet of him and your aunt to take so much trouble.'

'It was a pleasure for them,' he said. 'They live very quietly and meeting you was an event. They fell in love with you, you know – ' he glanced at her. 'My father said you were a beauty, and he doesn't pay that kind of compliment unless he means it. And you were very sweet to them. I'm glad you enjoyed it.'

'I feel as if I'd never been to Ireland before,' Isabel said. 'It was so different, coming with Charles. We always moved so fast – rushing from one stud to the next, dinner every night and never a moment to relax. I never seemed to *see* the country or really talk to anyone. That's why I've loved it so much this time.'

'He was that kind of man,' Tim said. 'Couldn't sit still. It's the American disease. They think they've got to be earning a living twenty-four hours a day.' He grinned at her. 'It's not something we Irish suffer from.'

'You suffer from it more than you think,' Isabel retorted. 'I've seen the way you work – you don't sit still!'

'No, but I've an object in view,' he said. 'I needed to make money and I was ready to work for it. I wanted to take good care of my family and at the back of my mind I had the crazy idea of rescuing Riverstown. If you want something badly enough, you'll do anything to get it.'

They went into the Hibernian, and he couldn't resist taking

her arm in a proprietary way. The receptionist looked up and smiled at them.

'Good evening, Mrs Schriber, Mr Ryan. There's a gentleman waiting in the lounge for you, Mrs Schriber.'

She turned to Tim; 'I'm not expecting anybody – who do you think it is?'

He shrugged. 'Some journalist, probably. I'll see him off. You've given the interview. Go on up and I'll get rid of him.'

'Excuse me,' the receptionist had overheard them. She spoke to Isabel. 'It's not a newspaperman, Mrs Schriber. This gentleman came about an hour ago. He's booked into the hotel. He said he was your stepson.'

'I wanted to show it to you first,' Richard said. 'So I flew over.' They were alone in Isabel's suite. She had the newspaper in her hand. She had read Peter Partridge's gossip column. In the Irish edition there was a photograph of her. 'WEDDING FOR CHARLES SCHRIBER'S WIDOW?' That was the headline. 'No comment,' says Richard Schriber. It was a long piece, fluffed out with ambiguities. Mutual friends of the couple have noticed romance blossoming. A reference to the similarity in their ages. Seen dining and dancing at London's smart night spots, millionaire's widow and her playboy stepson. Richard Schriber refused to confirm that he was going to marry his stepmother. It went on in the same vein. By comparison with most of the items printed under Peter Partridge's by-line, it was positively sentimental. An announcement, it ended unctuously, could be expected soon.

'I rang them and tried to find out how it happened, but they wouldn't say anything. I'm sorry, Isabel. I know you must feel pretty mad, but I don't want you to be mad at me. That's why I came over.'

She shook her head. 'It's not your fault, Richard. How could I blame you? I suppose we've been seen together – they must have touts who send in stuff like this. It says you didn't comment. Did they approach you?'

'Didn't comment means I wasn't asked – I know these bastards, they're clever enough not to put words into someone's mouth.'

He had been friendly to Tim, but she detected hostility on both sides. He had asked her, pointedly, to see him alone, and there was nothing she could do but bring him up to her suite. He took the newspaper away from her and threw it into the corner. His eyes were narrow and very blue; she felt her pulse race, stupidly and without excuse, as he came near to her. He put his hands on her shoulders and she felt him move closer to her. Tim and the afternoon, full of Irish ease and casual pleasure, faded out of focus. He bent and touched her mouth. Lightly at first and then insistently, demanding.

'Why did you go without telling me?' he said. His hand stroked the back of her neck; she could feel his thigh muscles pressing against her. 'Why didn't you ask me to come – ' He kissed her and she couldn't answer.

'That bloody newspaper,' he murmured. It was an extraordinary feeling; it reminded her suddenly of the panic that engulfed her when she was swimming under water in Barbados, with the hull of the boat above her and no air to breathe. But this was different; it was the panic of desire that wants fulfilment and will not count the cost, the urgent cry for love that longs to be swept away and drown and sink. . . .

'I love you,' he said. His hands were moving on her, unfastening her dress. There was no clumsiness; he knew how to open women's clothes.

'I love you.' It was like an incantation. Repeated, accompanied by the powerful sexual stimulus of his kisses and his touch. She could feel a tremor in his body; it wasn't only his desire that dominated. And then the question.

'You love me, Isabel – you love me, don't you?'

She didn't know the answer. Her body cried yes, yes, take me, hold me, take me to bed. But something resisted. Something held back as the pull under water increased. Charles, from the grave. Don't trust him. Don't ever, ever trust him. . . . She drew away from him.

'Richard – we've got to stop. Before we make fools of ourselves.'

He looked down at her; she pulled her dress into place.

'You can't get away, can you?' he said. 'You can't trust yourself; he owns you, Isabel. Stamped and labelled. Charles Schriber's property; don't touch. I want to marry you. What do you say to that?'

'I asked you for time,' she said slowly.

'All right,' he said. 'But how much time – how long do you need to make up your mind to live your own life?'

She felt shaken and confused. Marriage. It was the last thing she had thought of; surely the last thing in the world he had in mind. . . .

'Is it Ryan?' the question was asked quietly; she had turned away from him.

'No,' Isabel answered. 'It's nothing to do with Tim. Or anyone else. I want to be sure what I'm doing.'

She heard him move behind her; he kissed the side of her neck.

'How much time?' he repeated. 'I'm not good at waiting.'

'After the Derby,' she said. 'After I've kept my promise to Charles.' She was expecting a reaction. None came and she couldn't see his face.

'You've decided to run the horse then?' He sounded quite unmoved. His hands had been caressing her shoulders; they were still but that was all. She turned and faced him; she felt suddenly distressed.

'I'm sorry,' she said. 'I couldn't pull out of it. Charles left Tim a lot of money if the horse won. I've met his family and seen his home; it's up for sale – they desperately need the money. And there's Nigel too. It wouldn't be fair to either of them. Apart from Charles. I know you feel so hurt and bitter, Richard, and I wish I could have done what you asked. But it wouldn't have been right.'

He showed no disappointment and he didn't try to argue. He smiled at her and kissed her lightly. 'A woman of determined character and strong moral principles. I'm going to have a hell of a life with you, I can see that!'

She was suddenly so relieved at his acceptance that she slid her arms round his neck and kissed him on the mouth. It lasted a long time. 'If crossing me up has this effect on you,' he murmured, 'you'd better make a habit of it – '

They had dinner together in her suite; it was as if some inner tension between them had been finally broken. Richard didn't mention the Falcon again; she told him, hesitantly and with a little defiance, that she had bought the chestnut colt. He laughed at her; she had never seen him in such a happy mood.

'You're a hopeless case. I bet they robbed you blind; Ryan took his share, and passed some on to Foster, and you paid about 15000 over the odds. You should have taken me with you!'

'It's a beautiful colt,' she said. 'I really fell in love with it. And afterwards I kept thinking how you'd feel about it. I thought you'd accuse me of living in Charles's shadow, and all the other charming things you say to me.'

'But it didn't stop you,' he remarked.

'No. I made up my own mind. There was something about the little colt – not so little either – but it was like a beautiful child. And very gentle. I just had to have him. Just for myself. Tim said he was a very good buy and all the rest of it, but even if he hadn't liked him, I wouldn't have changed my mind. I feel he's really mine.'

'I can see the signs,' he mocked her. 'You're getting the bug in a big way. Not only am I going to be bullied into moral reformation, but I'm going to have to live with horses.' He leaned across and kissed her.

'I feel closer to you than I've ever done,' Isabel said suddenly. 'What's happened to us?'

'We've come to terms with each other,' he said. 'There's been a battle going on between us. Now, somehow, it's over. I wanted you to do something for reasons very personal to me. You wouldn't do it and I've accepted that. End of the battle.'

Isabel looked up at him. 'Does that mean I've won?'

He shook his head. He took the coffee cup out of her hand

and put it on the side table. Then he pushed the table away. He put his arms round her firmly.

'No, Isabel,' he said. 'It means you've lost.'

When Isabel woke it was with a sense of panic. She had been dreaming, a confused and anxious journey into the past, with Charles alive again and changing into her own father, accusing her of something which she hadn't done. She thought she was at Beaumont in the bedroom they shared together when she first opened her eyes; her heart was beating fast and she felt out of breath as if she had been running. And she had, running with feet that were weighted down, from something or someone whose steps were coming closer all the time. She sat up, frightened for a few seconds at the unfamiliar room. It was semi-dark with the curtains badly drawn and she didn't recognize the hotel bedroom. It wasn't Beaumont; it wasn't the handsome room with the big windows and the view over the paddocks where Charles's mares and foals were grazing in the summer months. It was a hired room in a hotel three thousand miles away from her home in Kentucky, and the man who had spent the night in it with her had gone.

She sat back against the pillows; the bed was cold. He must have left her very early. When at last she slept it had been very deep. The sleep of emotional and physical exhaustion; there were moments during the night when she had cried, whether from happiness or the intensity of their experience, she didn't know. She only knew, waking in the impersonal room, that Richard had indeed won the battle. If this was love then she had never known even the imitation of it with Charles Schriber. He had been virile and experienced, but the underlying egotism of their sex life was impossible to ignore now that she had made love to Richard. She wished that he had waited; it chilled her to find the bed empty, the covers smoothed into place. It was almost as if he had been a figment of her own imagination. Women were supposed to wake in a state of cat-like sensuality after such a night; instead every nerve ending was alive, and the sense of apprehension characterized by the anxiety dream was still with her. She had committed herself to him, and now there was no going back. No refuge with Tim, no hiding place in her life with Charles. Her own instinct had been so strong; delay, wait, try to see clearly. But it hadn't stopped her. Now they were lovers, and the word marriage hung in the air. A total commitment. It would have been easier if she had found him beside her, if he had been there to confirm with tenderness what he had expressed in passion. She got up and pulled back the curtains. It was a grey, cloudy Dublin day, cold and unwelcoming. The room was centrally heated but she shivered. Then the telephone rang. It was past eight o'clock. She sat on the bed, reached for the receiver and prayed that she wouldn't hear Tim's friendly voice.

'Get up, darling,' Richard said. 'It's raining and I want to go for a walk.'

She leaned against the pillows. 'Give me fifteen minutes.' She looked at the window and smiled. In Ireland, nobody worried about the rain. With their genius for dignifying the drab, they called it angel's tears.

'I'll knock on the door,' he said. 'But you'd better be dressed or we won't do much walking.'

MacNeil had booked Andrew Graham into his hotel. He had arrived after a night flight and gone straight to bed; he found the time change difficult and prescribed himself a sleeping pill and slept through the jet lag. MacNeil could wait. He needed to be fully alert when he saw him. He needed the detective's advice on what should be done. He had brought sufficient clothes to last him for a couple of weeks' stay.

Sixteen hours later he woke up, ordered himself a breakfast of ham and eggs and coffee, and rang through to MacNeil. He was put through to reception. A woman's voice, shrill and staccato to his Southern ears, informed him that Mr MacNeil had left a message for any caller, that he had gone to Dublin for a few days and could be contacted at a Dublin telephone number. Graham swore, and asked for the number. In the process of being reconnected to the switchboard, he was cut off. As he was dialling again, his breakfast arrived. They had forgotten the orange juice. The eggs looked up at him reproachfully from a mean sliver of ham. He cursed again, at himself this time, for not going to a first-class hotel; then he remembered how much the trip was costing. How much MacNeil was costing. He ate the breakfast, sipped the coffee, which was tepid and too strong, and put through a call to MacNeil on the Dublin number. It was a hotel, and it took fully five minutes while the time signal pipped in his ear, to discover that MacNeil had checked out a few minutes ago. But, yes, he had left a message. If a Doctor Graham called, he would be in London and would join him for lunch. Andrew put the breakfast tray on the dressing table, looked out at the traffic pouring down below through Kensington High Street and decided to spend the morning walking through the park opposite.

By twelve thirty he was sitting in the hotel lounge waiting for MacNeil.

'Tim knows,' Richard said. They were sitting together in the Aer Lingus jet; Ryan and Nigel Foster were two rows in front of them.

'How can he?' Isabel asked.

Richard grinned at her. 'You've got a certain look about you, Mrs Schriber. He's no fool.'

'Stop being so pleased with yourself,' she said. She dug her elbow into his side. 'I think you're imagining it.'

'I'm not imagining the way he glares at me,' Richard retorted. 'He's lost out and knows it. He must be kicking himself – rushing you over to Ireland, taking you round the old family home and introducing you to the folks – he must have thought he'd got it made! You never told me – did he make a pass?'

'No,' Isabel said. 'He didn't. Stop crowing, Richard. I'm very fond of him.'

'I feel like crowing. No wonder the old bastard was so crazy about you. It's a very rare gift, darling, to make a man feel this good! When are you going to marry me?'

'I haven't said anything about marrying anyone,' Isabel said. 'I think you'd make a rotten husband. I like you as you are.'

'I'd make a jealous husband,' he said. 'Very jealous. There won't be any Tim Ryans sniffing around. I've thought of something to do while you're in France. What sort of a ring do you want – diamonds or a coloured stone?'

'Neither,' Isabel said. 'Stop rushing me. Why don't you come to Paris and see the Falcon run?'

'Because I'd rather look for something nice for you,' he said. 'Racing bores hell out of me. I might have an off-course bet on him. Just to show you I'm not prejudiced. Take that wedding ring off and give it to me; I need it for the ring size.' He held her hand and started working the ring over her knuckle. Isabel tried to clench her finger. The ring was a little loose and he had slipped it off before she could stop him. He held it and looked at it for a moment. There was a slight smile on his lips but his eyes were half closed as if he were concentrating on something.

'Richard, give it back,' she said. 'Please. I don't want an engagement ring or anything like that. Give me my ring.'

'Is it inscribed?' he said. 'I can't see.'

'No,' Isabel said. She held out her hand. 'Please,' she said again. He put it on her palm; it was a plain platinum band.

'My mother's was gold,' he said. He pressed the button for the steward. 'I think I'll have a Scotch.'

'Don't,' Isabel said. 'It's only a few minutes till we land.' She put the ring on, and then slipped her hand through his arm. 'Come to Paris with me,' she said. 'It's only a couple of days.' He turned and smiled at her.

'Do you know what I'd really like?' he said. 'Something that may surprise you.'

'Tell me.' He had taken her hand and was holding it.

'I'd like to borrow your house for the two days,' he said. 'I've never seen it, and I'd like to get out of the flat. Would you lend it to me?'

'Oh, Richard, of course – I'd love you to go there! It's so

beautiful, and so peaceful. I feel so much at home there I can't believe it's only rented. I'm going to try and keep it on after June. I'll tell Mrs Jennings to get a room ready for you; she'll cook and look after you till I come back. If you want to have friends down – '

'No friends,' he said. 'I just want to take a break. And see what you like so much about the place. It must be very special.'

'It is,' she said.

'Nicer than Beaumont?' He was teasing her, but kindly.

'Yes,' she said suddenly. 'Yes, it's even nicer than Beaumont. When do you want to go down?'

'Tonight. I'll be lonely after you've gone.'

'You could drive down with me; we could spend the afternoon together. I'm not leaving till about seven. Why don't you do that?'

He shook his head. 'I can't; I've got some business in London. And I'm going to have a look in Cartiers, whatever you say.'

The announcement came over the intercom that they were soon to land. At the airport they separated. Nigel and Tim went off to Lambourn to supervise the Falcon's departure by plane for Paris; Isabel took a hired car to Coolbridge; she was meeting Ryan and the trainer at the airport at seven that evening and the three were flying over together. Richard kissed her goodbye. A man carrying a canvas overnight bag stood on the kerb a few feet away; he wore dark glasses and seemed to be waiting for a taxi. He didn't appear to glance at them, or to watch as Richard helped her into the car and waved it off. Richard went to the No. 1 car park to collect his car, and the man with the canvas bag was allotted a taxi by the warden on duty at the rank. He gave the address of the hotel where Andrew Graham was staying. He looked at his watch. It was 11.58. If the traffic was bad into London, he was going to be late for lunch.

'He's looking really well,' Tim Ryan said. He and Nigel and Sally Foster were standing at the door of the Silver Falcon's box. Phil, who did the horse, was standing at his head. He was tethered by the usual length of string to a chain attached to the wall; Phil had his fingers hooked into the head collar just the same. He was a man who had grown up with horses on his father's Yorkshire farm. He had a gift for managing the difficult ones; he believed in gentleness, in gaining confidence through patient handling, and he used his voice a lot. The Falcon's ears were flat against his head. A little white showed round his eye as he looked from Phil to the people in the doorway. Phil murmured to him, and patted his neck with his free hand. He had never been afraid of a horse in his life. But he didn't argue when Nigel Foster forbade him to go into the box alone at any time. He always took a young lad with him, and the lad carried a pitchfork pole. He was pleased to hear the racing manager's compliment. It meant he'd be given a handsome tip. Mrs Schriber was a generous owner; the yard knew how well she'd looked after David Long. Not that the little bugger deserved anything after what he'd tried to do. The horse did look well. His iron-grey coat was gleaming with health and there wasn't a spare ounce of fat on him. He got himself fit very easily, and there was never any trouble with his appetite. He licked his manger clean at every feed. He was an ideal horse to train, and they had all put their wages on him to win the big French race. Nigel Foster said, 'He's in great form. I worked him over a mile last Tuesday; he just eats the ground without being asked any kind of a question. He'll murder them on Sunday.'

'I'd say so,' Ryan agreed. He spoke to Phil. 'How's his temper these days? Taken any lumps out of you?'

Phil shook his head. 'Oh no, sir. Quiet as a lamb he is now – no trouble at all.' The colt rolled his eye at them and tried to swing his quarters. The grip on his headcollar tightened and checked him.

'Right,' Tim turned away. His manner was unusually curt. Nigel had noticed a difference in him the last couple of days in Dublin. He seemed moody and reserved. There was tension between him and Richard Schriber. Nigel hadn't had the chance to tell Sally about it, but he was sure that Tim had expectations in Isabel's direction and something had gone wrong. She had seemed very intimate with her stepson. Nigel wasn't by any means a prude, but he didn't think much of the idea. And Richard Schriber wasn't his type. Sally would be fascinated. He had already told her about the two-year-old on the phone. She was just as excited as he was.

He glanced at her and smiled. He felt very conscious of his own good fortune. A super wife, some of the best horses in the world, luck running his way, and a probable Derby winner in the yard.

'Get him rugged up, Phil,' he said. 'I'll see him boxed up and on his way. You get your stuff together.'

Phil was travelling with the horse; the box was waiting in the yard to take them to London airport and there he would be loaded on a special charter flight to take them to Longchamp. A security man was going with them, as well as the second lad who helped out. The group was in charge of the travelling head lad, whose sole responsibility was transporting the horses from the stables to the racecourse and back.

'You and Sally go on up,' Nigel suggested. 'I'll follow on and we'll have some lunch.'

'Fine,' Tim said. He stepped into the box, and thrust some notes into Phil's hand. 'Look after him,' he said. For a moment he paused and patted the colt's neck. He saw the murder in the eye and the tension in the quarters. They were very slightly quivering. He had known a soft answer when he heard one. 'Quiet as a lamb.' He looked at Phil. 'Watch yourself,' he said. Then he went out with Sally Foster up to the house.

Roy Farrant had called a meeting with Gerry Garvin and Barry Lawrence.

They came to the Hampstead house at six o'clock that evening; the Farrants' Filipino butler showed them into his study and the door was closed. He handed out drinks and cigars and sat down, facing his trainer and the jockey. He had a look about him which Barry recognized. He was after something or someone. Lawrence had been summoned to these meetings before.

It would be interesting to see how Gerry Garvin took it. He sucked on his cigar and waited. Roy Farrant looked at Garvin first.

'We've got a problem,' he said. 'And I think you both know what it is. Rocket Man didn't win the Two Thousand. Okay, Gerry, I'm not complaining. We've been through it all before – you tell me he needs the extra distance and I believe you. But I've looked at that film every night since the bloody race, and I can't see that he had all that much in hand.'

'He's improved,' Gerry said. He felt uncomfortable and on the defensive. The horse had been beaten by a length; the victor was one of the less-fancied Derby runners, and Roy had needed a lot of explanations. Personally he was satisfied with the result. The horse needed the race and had enjoyed himself; he was in top condition and ready to go. He had refused Farrant's suggestion to run him in France in the Prix Lupin because he believed the horse might just go over the top before the Derby.

'He'll be that much better for the race,' Barry Lawrence said. 'And never mind about watching the film, Roy. I rode the bloody horse and I'm telling you, he could've gone on if I'd pushed him. But Gerry here said not to give him a hard race. You wanted to win the Two Thousand. I could have given him a hiding and he'd have done it. But you might've lost the Derby. You can't have it both ways.'

'I don't think we're going to have it any way,' Roy Farrant said. 'That's what I meant by a problem. Answer me this, Barry. Are we going to beat Silver Falcon?'

Lawrence shrugged. 'I haven't seen him run. All we have is a load of talk from Lambourn and a lot of press crap. I don't know why you go on about it, Roy. He could be the biggest flop since Crowned Prince!'

'We'll know after the Lupin,' Gerry Garvin said. 'If he doesn't come good – we've nothing to worry about. If he wins in a canter – ' he didn't finish the sentence.

Roy took a long swallow at his drink. It was a very dark Scotch. 'I don't think it's crap,' he said. 'I've had some pretty first-hand information about that horse, and I think he'll walk the bloody Lupin. If he does that, whatever you say about Rocket Man, he'll do us at Epsom. And I'm not going to be bloody well done!'

'I thought,' Gerry Garvin said, 'you had some kind of deal going with Schriber. What's happened to it?'

'The same thing that happened to the deal with Long,' Farrant snapped. 'Nothing. He promised me the horse wouldn't run. I didn't ask how and I didn't want to know. I had one crack at it which went sour, and then I left it with him. The next thing I read is some shit about him getting married to Isabel. So he's out for himself and he's been kidding me along. If we want to stop that horse, we've got to do it ourselves. And I say, don't wait for the Derby. Get him on Sunday!'

Gerry Garvin was holding his drink. He put it down. There was a slight flush round the edge of his collar and the red was creeping up his neck.

'You were responsible for what happened to Long?'

Farrant glared at him; he made a gesture of contempt. 'Don't pretend you didn't know. The bloody fool messed it up and got himself clobbered. All right, it was a clumsy job and it went wrong. So forget it. We've got another chance this weekend. I say take it. Stop him.'

Garvin got up. 'You can count me out,' he said. 'What you fixed up with Richard Schriber was something depending on his influence with Isabel. Sending a stable lad in to break down a horse and getting him half killed is something else. If you're suggesting anything like that, I'm not having any part of it.'

There was a moment's pause. Barry Lawrence was glancing up at Garvin; his usually impassive face showed interest. Farrant brought his right hand up and waved it slowly, up and down.

'Sit down, Gerry. Put your bloody moral indignation away; we all know you're a straight man. You don't have to prove it. Just sit down and listen.' Farrant got up and picked up Garvin's glass. 'I'll fill you up.' He didn't wait for an answer. He turned to the drinks cabinet set into the panelling and poured a large vodka and tonic.

Garvin hesitated; he stared at Farrant's broad back, and Barry Lawrence said very quietly. 'Sit down. You want to win as much as he does.'

The moment to go was then and not a moment later; Gerry Garvin knew it. What he had just heard meant that he should tell Farrant to remove his horses and walk out. He had promised Susan he wouldn't fall into the trap, no matter what the bait. He had a good name and it was never regained once the rumours got out. He didn't need Farrant's horses; he was successful and very rich in his own right. It wasn't the end of the world if he didn't win the Derby. He sat down and took his glass back from Farrant.

'Thanks, Roy,' he said. Barry Lawrence got up and helped himself to another cigar. He wasn't eating or drinking anything that night. The following morning he was flying to France to ride one of the French horses in the Prix Lupin.

'They've got Pierre Jean-Martin riding,' Farrant said. 'That means they're out to win it; this isn't any training gallop. The security at Longchamp is so tight you couldn't get a mouse in. So it's got to be done on the track. And that's where you come in Gerry.'

Garvin had lost and he didn't try to pretend otherwise.

'How?' he said. He took refuge in the vodka. He had a hollow feeling in his stomach. 'I won't do anything unethical. . . .'

'All you've got to do is jock off Simpson on your runner and put up Barry instead. Your horse isn't going to win it anyway. So what's the difference.'

'Mine has a chance,' Barry said. 'I could lose quite a bit.'

'You'll lose bloody nothing,' Farrant snarled at him, suddenly angry. He couldn't resist squeezing a stone to see if there was a drop left, greedy little swine. 'I'll see you all right. I always do. Just take the ride with Garvin. Fuck the French trainer. I'll double what you might have got *if* you'd won. Which you wouldn't!'

'Fair enough,' Barry said. 'I'm on. I'll take Gerry's ride.'

'That's all *you* have to do,' Farrant said to the trainer. 'Nothing unethical.' There was no attempt to hide his contempt. 'Just put up Barry. And he'll do the rest. Your owners will be delighted if they think he's picked their horse, and they won't lose anything because they weren't going to win anyway. Okay?'

'Okay,' Gerry Garvin said. He had decided he was not going home to Newmarket to face his wife. And he wasn't staying to have dinner in that house. He was going to spend the night in London and get very drunk.

'Not too much of a burden on your conscience?' Farrant jeered.

'No,' Garvin said. He stood up. 'I think I'd better get off home,' he said. 'I won't stay for dinner, Roy. I'll get back and phone the owners and get through to Simpson. He won't be very pleased about it but I'll try and square him. See you at the races, Barry.' He went out. Neither Farrant nor the jockey said anything until they heard the front door close. Lawrence stretched his short legs.

'Queasy bugger,' he said. 'I thought he was going to walk off for a minute.'

'Never,' Farrant jeered. 'Lot of bloody hooey all that ethical stuff. You find me a crooked gent, and he's the worst of the lot! There's always a first time; he'll do what he's told from now on. We won't have any more trouble with him. I've got some champagne on ice; sure you won't have a glass?'

'Just a half,' Barry said. He waited while Farrant went out of the room. Champagne wouldn't sweeten him, but money would. And if Roy wanted him to take on the Falcon with Jean-Martin up, then he was going to have to pay. He thought back to their first business association. He preferred to use those terms to describe the founding of Farrant's fortune and the first major payment into his own bank account. Twelve years ago. He was a young jockey, making a name for himself but with all the way still to go. He'd never been in trouble, never been up before the stewards or done any dirty riding. Until that night when Farrant met him in the same Barnsley pub; they had been friends for two years and both were prospering. But Farrant needed capital to expand. He had sold his ironmonger's shop and bought three more. He was being pressed by the bank to repay their loan. He had talked it out with Lawrence who was sympathetic. And then he made the proposition. The horse he was riding at Lingfield two days later was said to be a sure thing. Farrant said very simply to Barry that all he wanted was for that horse to *lose*. There would be a thousand pounds in it for him if it did. It sounded very easy. Just pull the horse. Any experienced jockey knew how to keep the reins at the crucial moment instead of letting them out a couple of inches as a signal to the horse to cruise ahead. And a sprint was so fast and over so quickly that it would be very difficult indeed to see anything from the stands. All he had to do was check his horse's stride and he'd never get it back in time to hit the front. He hadn't asked questions. He'd just said, 'Okay, leave it to me.' Next day he came in fourth, and told the trainer and the disappointed owner that the horse hadn't seemed to like the ground. Farrant paid him a thousand pounds in cash two days later. They both got drunk, and that was when Farrant told him about the friend. An Italian who owned a laundry business. A lunatic, ready to gamble his shirt. And Roy had given him Lawrence's horse as a certainty. He'd been going to Italy the day before the race and there was no ante-post betting. He'd given Roy 10000 pounds to bet on the horse for him. And all Roy had done was put the money in his own pocket. It was so simple it was genius. Barry had gazed at him in awe. Ten grand, just for doing nothing. Nothing but have the horse stopped. And there was nothing the Italian could do about it. The bet had gone sour. That was the end of it. But it wasn't the end. Four days later Barry saw an item in the *Sporting Life*. It reported the suicide of a certain Pietro Lambarzini; owner of a chain of laundries in Barnsley, he had been a heavy punter and sometime owner. He had left a note saying he'd plunged on a favourite to extricate himself from serious financial difficulties and the horse had lost. He had shot himself.

Farrant had never mentioned the incident again; neither had

Barry. But it hung between them, bonding them together. It was a long time ago, but Barry sometimes thought of it. He was glad he had remembered it then. It was going to put his price up.

9

MacNeil had eaten a good lunch; his client had no appetite. When he picked up his water glass the detective noticed that his hand was trembling.

'You think she's really going to marry him?' It was the second or third time Graham had asked the question. MacNeil gave the same answer.

'They're lovers; I found that out in Dublin. He spent the last two nights in her suite before they came back. I watched them at the airport. I'd say she was crazy about him.'

'The bastard,' Graham said slowly. 'He'd stoop to anything. It's my fault; I should have told her the truth right at the beginning. The day he walked back into Beaumont I should have told her.'

'Why didn't you?' MacNeil asked. He buttered a biscuit and spread it lavishly with cheese. The English cheeses were very good.

'I didn't want to let my old friend down,' Andrew Graham said. 'We'd covered it all for so long. He was a very proud man. He didn't want anyone to know about Richard. What his wife did was bad enough.'

'Funny,' MacNeil said, with his mouth full. 'A rich man like him; and so full of troubles.'

Andrew sighed. 'He was the best man I ever knew. Generous, loyal to his friends, a helluva good sportsman. And he had the lousiest luck in his private life. And he worshipped Isabel. Now I see this. Shacking up with his son. There are times, MacNeil, when I feel inclined to let her get married to him first and find out for herself!' He shook his head. 'But I can't,' he said. 'I owe it to Charles.'

'You better go and see her then,' MacNeil said. 'Take the papers along with you. That ought to do it. She'll run a mile.'

'I hope so,' Graham said. 'I've been trying to think how to handle it. We fell out about him last time; she forbade me the house. What do I do if she won't even listen – ' he wasn't asking MacNeil, he was thinking aloud. 'If he's living with her I won't get a chance – '

'He's not with her in Paris,' MacNeil said. 'I was sitting right behind them on the plane. I heard her asking him to come and he said no. As a matter of fact, he's going to be at her house in the country tonight.'

Graham looked up at him. 'Without her? What for?'

'Good question,' MacNeil said. 'I can't figure it out. Why don't you fly to France and see her there?'

'I think I will,' Andrew Graham said. 'And you'd better see what the hell Schriber's doing. I don't like it, MacNeil. I don't like him going down there alone.'

'No,' MacNeil agreed. 'You never know with guys like that – ' He finished his coffee. 'You're sure,' he said, 'that this is what's behind it all?'

'I'm certain,' Andrew said slowly. 'It all fits into the pattern. And that's what I've got to make her see. You don't know where she's staying in Paris?'

'Call the trainer – he'll know. And don't try to cover. Say who you are. I'll get myself into some pub near the house at Epsom and take it from there.'

MacNeil signed for the bill and Graham went up to his room. He called Nigel Foster and explained who he was. He wanted to contact Isabel in Paris. Nigel was having his coffee with Tim Ryan and Sally. He covered the mouthpiece and said to Tim, 'Someone called Andrew Graham asking for Isabel's hotel – says he's an old friend – '

Tim got up and reached for the phone. 'I'll talk to him,' he said.

'Andrew? How are you – it's Tim.'

On the other end, Andrew sighed with relief. 'Thank God –

listen, I've got to see Isabel. I can't go into too many details, but it's about Richard.'

Tim's voice changed. 'What about him?' he said.

'She's got to be told something. She won't like it, but I'd be grateful for your help. We've got to get her away from him. I can trust you, Tim, I know that. Charles always trusted you. He must be turning in his grave right now.'

'All right,' Tim said quickly. 'You can count on me. We're staying at the Ritz. We're taking the seven o'clock plane; you come up to the suite at about nine o'clock. I'll be there and I'll make sure Isabel is too.'

'That's fine,' Graham sounded relieved. 'I'll be there. Nine o'clock.' He hung up. Tim Ryan was an unexpected bonus. He'd be a powerful ally. Very powerful. He was going to tell him the same story and show him the same papers. That ought to clinch everything. He started packing his bag with pyjamas, shaving gear and a change of shirt. His hands were quite steady now. Then he put through a call and booked himself onto the six o'clock flight to Charles de Gaulle.

Mrs Jennings was waiting for Richard when he arrived at Coolbridge House. He drove down from London, taking his time; it was a hot evening and the traffic had moved sluggishly on the way out of the city. He had spent the afternoon, not at Cartiers as he told Isabel, but in a meeting with his solicitor. They had been discussing certain clauses in the multi-million-dollar trust his mother had set up for him. He drove slowly round the leafy lanes which had so delighted Isabel on her first visit; occasionally he blasted his horn at a blind corner, and then he passed the Victorian lodge and through the gates up the driveway. The house came upon him, richly glowing in the evening sunlight, a seventeenth-century red-brick jewel in a setting of great trees and lushly stocked gardens.

The housekeeper showed him inside and took his suitcase. He looked round the hall, which Isabel had so often described. Dark and cool, with the faint smell of must that comes with ancient brick and panelling. He followed Mrs Jennings up the stairs and she took him into a room at the end of the corridor. Richard looked round him.

'This is very nice,' he said. 'Mrs Schriber's been telling me how beautiful the house is – I'm looking forward to seeing it.'

'She's been very happy here,' Mrs Jennings said. 'I must say, sir, she's a charming lady. I don't mind telling you I was ever so worried about the sort of people we might have here, when Sir James decided they'd have to let. But Mrs Schriber looks after it like it was her own home. And there's a note over there, sir. The drawing room's at the bottom of the stairs on the right. I'll put some ice out for you with the drinks tray. And dinner'll be ready at eight fifteen, if that's all right.'

Richard smiled at her. 'That will be just perfect, thank you.' He picked up the envelope. 'Richard.' It was one sheet of paper and only two lines, obviously scribbled in a hurry.

'Darling – I hope you like it. Mrs J. will do everything for you. Wish us luck for tomorrow. I'll ring you after the race. All my love. I.'

The window was open and there was a soft breeze carrying garden scents. It was the sort of house she would fall in love with. He went down the stairs and in to the white and yellow drawing room. He poured himself a Scotch, filled it with ice and sat down in one of the deep armchairs.

There was no sound anywhere. It was the sort of house his mother would have loved. Peaceful, dignified, not vulgarized in any way by new wealth. His real father must have lived in a house like it. She had described him one day, her eyes full of tears, her voice guiltily low. They were alone together in her room at Beaumont. After she and Charles had been married for three years, Richard's real father had come to the house. He came to visit the stud; he was tall and blond, with a gentle manner, and from a similar background in England as her own in Carolina. He had been so nice, she whispered to Richard. So kind. And neither of them had meant to fall in love so quickly. In the space of a week. And then he went away. Back to

England. She had never heard from him again. When she found herself pregnant she hadn't known if he or Charles were the father. She hadn't known and neither had Charles until, two and a half years after Richard was born, Andrew Graham had examined Charles for a minor ailment, and the discovery was made that he was sterile. And always had been. She didn't tell Richard what happened. But there wasn't any need. He could imagine. The look was in her eyes. Fear. Physical and mental fear. He sat in the dying sunlight, with the evening shadows creeping through the garden and thought of his mother, with her nervous smile and broken spirit, and the hand holding his glass tightened and tightened. There was a sudden crack and the glass broke. Ice and whisky spilled on him, and blood mingled with it. He had cut himself. He got up, cleared the splinters and the ice away, wrapped his hand in a handkerchief. She was so close to him that night, closer than for a long time. He could almost feel her there. She had believed in life after death; remnants of her early Catholic upbringing clung to her. She had a hope of forgiveness and a trust in a loving God. God the Father. It wasn't a symbol that Richard could accept. Life was a brief excursion into the light, followed by everlasting darkness. There was no Heaven where Frances Schriber could find reward for her unhappy life on earth. There was no Divine justice, nothing but human vengeance if a debt was going to be repaid. He went in to dinner, apologizing to Mrs Jennings for the accident. She stayed behind to wipe up the spilt whisky and search for more glass.

After dinner he began to explore the house. He went upstairs and looked through all the rooms. He found Isabel's bedroom and lingered in it; her presence was in it, as strong as his mother's had been downstairs, he opened the drawers and touched her clothes. And the bed. Large and draped, piled with embroidered cushions. He could visualize her in it, dark hair against white pillows, slender arms linked above her head, smooth breasts. Then down to the hall and through to the kitchens. Old-fashioned. Stone-floored. A range of larders and a game room. Boot cupboards, racks for fishing rods. A row of mackintosh coats, wellington boots. A game bag. And the cellars. He switched on the light and started down the steps.

'Tim, you'd no right to do this. I'm not going to see him!'

Isabel faced Ryan angrily. They'd travelled over on the plane with Nigel Foster; Tim had been silent and unlike his easy self. Nigel was staying at Longchamp to be near the horse, he left them at De Gaulle airport in high spirits, predicting a decisive win the next day. Isabel and Tim checked into the Ritz; both were well known there. Charles always stayed in the same suite whenever he came to Paris, and he had insisted on Tim having a room in the hotel. Isabel didn't have time to unpack before Tim came to the sitting room. And then he told her about Andrew Graham. Her reaction was what he expected. She was surprised and then angry. He stayed calm.

'Why won't you see him?' he asked. 'He's Charles's oldest friend, and you went through it all together. What are you afraid of, Isabel?'

She swung round; for a moment she nearly ordered him out of the suite. Then she too controlled herself. There was an unpleasant sensation, as if her pulse was running too fast. The word afraid had stung.

'I'm not afraid of anything he can tell me,' she said. 'He hates Richard, just because Charles hated him. And I'm not going to be influenced. He's heard about the newspaper story and that's what's brought him running over here. He ought to have something better to do than interfere in my life now. It's none of his business, and I'm going to tell him so!'

'All right – but don't get so uptight about it. For God's sake just listen to him. That's all I ask you.' He abandoned his impersonal pose and came up to her, putting his hands on her shoulders. 'I may be your racing manager,' he said quietly, 'and you can sack me tonight if you like. But I also love you. And that's why I told Andrew to come here. Okay, you've chosen Richard and not me. I can accept that. But I want to be sure he's right for you. And if you're not frightened of hearing something that might prove he's not, then you'll see Andrew and listen to what he's got to say.' He let her go and turned away.

'I also love you.' She had known it ever since she came to Beaumont. Taken it for granted when she was married, and come closer than she realized during those days in Ireland before Richard came. She came up beside him and touched his arm.

'Oh, Tim,' she said. 'I'm so sorry. I'd no right to speak to you like that. I'm not frightened of seeing Andrew. It just seems unfair, when Richard can't defend himself.'

Before he could say anything, Andrew Graham's arrival in the lobby was announced. When he came into the sitting room Isabel came to meet him. She held out her hand. Her voice was calm and cool.

'How nice to see you, Andrew. Come and sit down. What would you like to drink?' He shook hands with Tim and took a chair. She thought he had aged in the months since she had last seen him. Out of his own environment, he looked smaller, uncertain.

And he was nervous; he kept wiping his hands on his trouser knees and glancing from her to Tim, as if looking for support. He asked for bourbon; until it arrived with Perrier water and ice, they made awkward conversation. She asked him about Joan and his children; he mentioned mutual friends in Freemont, and asked about the plans for the Falcon. Tim said he should back him in the race the next day; he looked to be a certainty. Graham said how pleased Charles would be if he could see it.

Graham drank his bourbon and coughed. Then he looked at Isabel. Some of his old authority had returned. He was Andrew Graham again, best friend of Freemont's most powerful and respected citizen.

'I don't know if Tim's told you why I'm here,' he said. 'But I ask you to believe that I wouldn't fly four thousand miles unless it was for a damned good reason. I've brought something to show you. But before I do, I'd like to tell you about Charles and Frances. I know he never talked about it, and looking back, it was a great mistake. I wish I didn't have to do it.' He waited, and Isabel hesitated.

'Before you say anything,' she said slowly. 'I know quite a bit about that marriage. And about Richard's childhood. He's told me everything. So it won't come as a surprise.'

Andrew Graham raised his brows. 'If you say so, Isabel,' he said. 'But I don't think you'll find the accounts match. Firstly, I'm here because I heard reports that you were going to marry Richard. If there's no truth in it, if you and he aren't involved with each other, I shan't say another word. I've had this family secret on my mind for a very long time; I'd rather go on keeping it. But in fairness to you, and because Charles loved you the way he did, I can't.'

'Go on,' Tim said. 'Tell her. Whatever it is.'

Andrew leaned back a little and sighed.

'The first thing you've got to believe, Isabel, is I've no personal motive in this. You accused me once of hating Richard. That's not true. I hate what he did to his father and how he treated him, right up to the end, but I don't hate Richard. I'm sorry for him. Just like I was sorry for his mother. You know she killed herself?'

'Yes,' Isabel said. 'Yes, I know she did. Poor thing.'

'That's not a bad description,' Andrew said. 'A poor thing; unstable all her life, unfaithful to the best husband a woman could have had, a hopeless neurotic who couldn't control herself and couldn't face the consequences. He lived a life of misery with her. Covering up for her breakdowns, for the illegitimate child she had, which he pretended was his own. And seeing that child grow up to be just like her. I know; I looked after him from the time he was born. And there was always something wrong. Charles knew it too. We both pretended it wasn't serious; just a difficult kid. Going through a phase. You know the lies people tell each other when they don't want to face the truth.'

The room was absolutely quiet while he talked. There was

no sound through the double-glazed windows of the traffic pouring through the Place Vendôme below them. Isabel was sitting rigid, her hands clasped in her lap. She could see Tim Ryan leaning forward, staring at Andrew Graham.

'He had a totally neurotic relationship with both his parents. He hated and resented Charles; he was insanely jealous of him because he was completely mother-fixated. He worshipped her. When he was a little boy it was cute; by the time he got to adolescence it was plain sinister. He followed her everywhere; if she had an argument with Charles the boy went berserk, yelling at his father, trying to fight him. I don't say she encouraged it. She probably didn't know what she was doing; she was so vain, so shallow emotionally. She had to have someone in love with her. Even if it was her own son.'

'I don't believe you,' Isabel heard herself saying. It sounded very clear. 'He told Richard he was a bastard when the boy was fourteen years old. He blamed and bullied both of them; she was terrified of him and so was Richard. He was the abnormal one, hating a child and punishing a woman for one mistake for all those years. I'd like you to go, Andrew. I don't want to hear any more.' She was on her feet.

'Isabel – ' Tim said. 'Isabel, for God's sake – listen to him!'

'I thought he'd tell you a load of lies,' Graham said sadly. 'That was another thing. He twisted everything. He doesn't know what the truth is. He's a psychopathic personality, Isabel. What he told you is exactly how he sees what happened. But it's all distorted. He hated his father so he makes out it was Charles who hated him. And when his mother took that overdose it wasn't the first time; she'd done so half a dozen times before. Not serious suicidal attempts, just trying to gain notice, frighten Charles. And of course get the boy's sympathy. But that night she went too far. By the time Charles found her she was dead. And Richard Schriber went clean off his head.' He bent down and took up a small briefcase. He opened it, and handed Isabel a plastic folder.

'If you won't believe *me*,' he said. 'Read this.'

She didn't move to take it. She stayed on her feet; she

wanted to tell him it was lies, to order him out. But she felt frozen, paralysed with the remorseless logic; the only thing Richard wanted from Beaumont had been his mother's picture. His obsessive hatred of Charles. . . .

'I'd like to see him lose just once.'

She didn't take the folder but Tim Ryan did. He read through it in silence. Andrew Graham looked very tired. He finished his bourbon. Then Tim looked up at Isabel.

'He was committed to the Graneways Mental Nursing Home for nine months after his mother died,' Tim said slowly. 'Two specialists diagnosed a severe personality disorder. Endemic schizophrenia. You'd better read it for yourself. And sit down. I'll get you a drink.'

She read through the typed pages, the doctors' reports. Paranoid delusions, a tendency to violence. And that final dreadful prognosis. A psychopathic personality with schizoid tendencies. Unlikely to respond to treatment. He had been released into the guardianship of his Duckett grandmother. She closed the folder and handed it back to Tim. She felt physically sick.

'I'm sorry,' Andrew Graham said. 'I'm really sorry. I know you won't tell anybody anything; for Charles's sake. I'd better take that back. And I'll be going now. Get rid of him, Isabel. He's not only unbalanced, but in my opinion, since his father died, he's potentially a dangerous man.'

She heard him leave the suite; Tim saw him out to the door; she could hear them talking quietly. She looked at the drink Tim had given her and sipped it again. It was brandy. Nine months in a mental home. A tendency to violence. Schizoid. Paranoid delusions. He had held her in his arms, made love to her, taken her on a crazy walk through Dublin streets in the early morning rain, with his arm round her waist, laughing as they got wetter.

He wasn't what they said. Living in a world of fantasy, seeing his mother and his life through a mirror of emotional distortion. That wasn't Richard. Tim had come back. He came and sat beside her and put his arms round her.

'You've got to believe it, Isabel,' he said. 'The evidence was all there. Thank God you found out in time. Andrew was talking to me just now. He reminded me of that swimming accident in Barbados. He thinks you could be in real danger if you go on seeing Richard. And so do I.'

'I don't believe him,' Isabel said slowly. 'I've known Richard long enough to judge for myself. Even if it *was* true – if he did go over the edge when his mother committed suicide, there's nothing wrong with him now. I love him. I'd know if there was. As for what happened in Barbados – I did that myself. I panicked and went wild under water. Richard saved my life. You ought to remember that when you say such things.'

'Don't cry,' Tim said quietly. 'He can't help it. It's not his fault.'

'Go away, please,' she whispered. 'Just go away and leave me alone. I know you mean well, but I don't want to hear any more. Please, go away.'

'All right,' Tim got up. He was reluctant to leave her, but she wasn't hysterical; he had never seen a woman cry so quietly, without any sound or ugliness.

He went out, and she heard the door close softly.

It had all been so factual, so low key. There was none of the heat which had characterized that early confrontation between Richard and Graham after the funeral. He had been so cool that evening, so determined to be impartial. 'I don't hate Richard. I feel sorry for him.' If Richard was lying, so then was Andrew Graham when he said that. He hated Richard just as Charles had hated him. If he had been sick and disturbed as a child, broken down as a young man after his mother's suicide, was that any reason to blame him – to keep him away from his home and his stepmother, away from the funeral of the man who was supposed to have loved and protected him in spite of not being his own. It was hypocrisy, and she could see right through it. She had lived in that tight little community, so insular and suspicious of anyone who broke its rules. Maybe Richard was everything they said; perhaps his mother was vain and empty and her love affair was an amoral tumble in the hay, dignified by her unhappy son into a single error. The way Graham spoke of her, it sounded like constant infidelity. Maybe it was all true, and Richard had been permanently scarred. It didn't mean he had to be abandoned, driven away, like the sick in primitive societies for fear they would pass on their devils to the healthy. Overlying the clinical terms, the cruel, impersonal terminology with which his suffering was described, there lay the pathetic image of the boy growing up at Beaumont. Unwanted, unloved, except by someone, herself, far too weak to help him. She went into the bedroom, picked up the telephone and asked for the number of Coolbridge. She made a great effort to sound calm when he answered.

'Richard?'

He sounded surprised and then pleased. It had taken a long time before he answered the phone.

'I just wanted to find out if you liked the house.'

'I think it's lovely. No wonder you took root down here.'

'Are you comfortable – did Mrs Jennings look after you?'

It was a silly conversation, banal questions, but it kept them talking, and she needed that. She needed to hear his voice, to hear it sounding normal and even gay. He was teasing her about Coolbridge; she didn't really listen. 'Lady of the manor,' he was saying. 'I liked your bedroom. That's one hell of a regal bed. I'll have to make an appointment – ' His laughter was so natural. She could imagine him at Coolbridge. Sitting in the yellow drawing room, with his leg slung over the arm of the chair. Drinking, of course. He drank too much. It couldn't help him.

'Where are you? What part of the house?'

'I'm in the hall. I've been exploring, that's why it took so long to answer. They've got a good cellar. How's the Ritz?'

'Just the same. I miss you.'

'I miss you too,' he said. 'I'm glad you called.'

'So am I,' she said. 'I just wanted to tell you I loved you.' There was a pause. 'Richard? I thought we'd got cut off.'

'No, darling,' his voice was louder as if he had moved the

receiver close to his mouth. 'No way. You might call back in five minutes and say it again. I rather like it.'

'I meant it,' she said. 'Take care of yourself. Call me after the races tomorrow.' She hung up and lay back on the pillows.

She fell asleep without realizing it, worn out with emotional strain and woke up with a cry of fear that echoed from her dream. A dark, confused and tortured dream in which she had been drowning, anchored under water by a chain which turned out to be an arm, gripping remorselessly, until her lungs burst and filled with water. The face floating so near to her, twisted in a murderous grimace, was Richard's, and the arm that imprisoned her under the suffocating seas belonged to him.

If there was one thing Roy Farrant didn't criticize about his wife, it was the way she dressed. She had a natural sense of what suited her, and the years when she modelled had given her a flair for line and colour.

Patsy had chosen white to wear at Longchamp, a crisp silk suit with a black and white spotted blouse, a straw hat trimmed with the same material. She looked magnificent that day and he was very proud of her; heads were turning as they walked round the members' enclosure. 'You look very good,' he said grudgingly. 'I like that outfit.'

She smiled with real pleasure. 'I'm glad you think it's nice. I went to this new shop in Knightsbridge – ' Farrant cut off, not listening. It was a brilliant day, mercifully cool with a pleasant breeze that fluttered the brims of the large hats. Farrant loved racing in France; he liked the elegance, the banks of flowers, the sensation of exclusivity which made every meeting an occasion like Royal Ascot. It didn't bother him that the doyens of French racing barely acknowledged him. He didn't speak French and he didn't give a damn about whether he was snubbed or not.

He, Roy Farrant from Barnsley, born in one of those grim terraced houses they showed on TV in documentaries about the twenties, was as rich as any of them and more successful than most. He had a beautiful wife on his arm and a string of winners to his credit. But at that moment he was looking out for Isabel Schriber. He had decided to come to the meeting after he and Barry had worked out their plan. He wanted to be there to see the Silver Falcon. The idea of that grey colt obsessed and tormented him more and more. He wouldn't rest until he'd watched the race and seen Barry Lawrence do his stuff. The draw favoured them; that was a piece of luck. Garvin's horse was a front runner who faded, that helped too; it meant Falcon wouldn't outdistance them to start with if Jean-Martin had been told to go on ahead, and if he was riding a waiting race, then Lawrence could hold his mount back and keep right with him.

'I'm going down to the paddock,' Farrant said. 'They'll be coming in any minute.'

'I'm coming,' she said. 'I'm dying to see the Silver Falcon, aren't you?'

'Yeh – ' he said, heavily sarcastic. 'Dying is the right word.'

The paddock was very green; in spite of the warm weather French racecourses were extensively watered, producing the smooth springy turf that so often confounded the firm-ground horses. They took up a position by the entrance for owners and trainers, perching on the little stools. There were three horses in the ring already, walking serenely round and round, led by their stable lads. Paddock cloths were bright, the coats of the three thoroughbreds, one chestnut and two dark bays, gleamed like oilskin. They stepped proudly, daintily, their eyes examining the scene. Farrant looked them up in the race card. He saw Garvin's horse Happy Hero come in, a strongly built bright bay, with a fine head; his looks belied his lack of stamina. Garvin always turned his horses out beautifully. This particular no-hoper looked a perfect picture of health and fitness. Farrant looked at the closed-circuit TV screen which showed the money going on each horse and noted that there was a fair bit on Happy Hero. Barry Lawrence's change of mount had been noted in the papers, and criticized as usual, but it brought the punters in.

A very dark bay horse, almost black, although superstition forbade anyone to mention the colour on a racecourse, walked into the ring.

'That's nice,' Patsy murmured. Farrant looked it up. 'Prince of Padua,' he said. 'Lester's riding it. Should have a chance.' It was a handsome horse with a fine action; its form was not too impressive.

Farrant thought for a moment he might have some money on, and then Patsy nudged him.

'Look! Look – there he is!'

There was a definite movement among the crowd gathered round the paddock. Farrant drew in his breath. The grey colt came into the ring like a monarch. His walk was long and arrogant, the man holding him was having his work cut out to keep up, the head was held boldly on a proud crested neck, the dark dappled coat was shining like metal in the sunlight, and the eye flashed an imperious challenge at the people and the other horses.

'Jesus,' Farrant said. 'That's some horse!'

Patsy didn't say anything. She was going to say soothingly he wasn't as nice as Rocket Man and thought better of it. There just wasn't a comparison between the grey and any other animal. She had never seen Roy look so sick for a moment. Then he turned quickly beside her and she heard him say heartily, 'Hullo, Isabel! Good luck today!'

Isabel, accompanied by Tim and Nigel Foster, was on her way to the paddock. She stopped, hearing her name, and Roy Farrant was beside her, smiling warmly, holding out his hand. She shook it and thanked him.

'Great looking horse, your Falcon,' he said. 'Knocks spots off everything here. But we're still going to beat you on June 5th!'

'We'll have to see,' Isabel said.

'Richard not with you?' Roy asked.

'No, he wouldn't come,' Isobel said. 'I was very disappointed. But he keeps saying he hates racing. So there it is.'

'You'll have to change that,' Farrant said gaily. 'Tell me – '

he had his hand on her arm, detaining her. 'Are congratulations in order yet? I read my Peter Partridge, you know.'

'Not yet,' Isabel said.

Tim Ryan caught her by the arm. 'Come on,' he said curtly, ignoring Farrant. 'The jockeys are coming in.' She smiled at Farrant and passed on.

'There's Barry,' Patsy said. Farrant could see him. He was standing in the centre of the paddock, with Gerry Garvin and three people talking in the earnest way that owners have before a race. They didn't know they hadn't got a chance. Barry Lawrence was standing with his short legs astride; he was very small, and he had to strain to look up at the others; his arms were folded, with the whip tucked under the left one. It was a jockey's stance, duplicated in other groups; the colours of the silks were like splashes from a spilt paintbox. The bell rang. The jockeys were put up and the horses began to leave the paddock, led by the great Lester Piggott, impassive and impervious as usual, perched as lightly as a feather on the back of his mount. Farrant wished again that he'd had a bet. Lawrence passed them high up on Happy Hero. He didn't look to right or left; his expression was relaxed.

'Come on,' Farrant said urgently. He began striding away towards the members' stands, his raceglasses swinging. Patsy, tottering on high heels, was left some way behind him.

Isabel, Tim, Nigel Foster and Sally were standing in a little group half way up the stand just short of the winning post.

'Nervous?' Tim asked her. 'You needn't be. I'd put my shirt on him today.'

'I *have* put my shirt on him,' Nigel muttered.

Tim grinned. 'I've had a few pounds on myself,' he said.

'I think he'll win,' Isabel said quietly.

'I heard Farrant wishing you luck,' Nigel said. 'I'd take that with a packet of salt, if I were you. I bet he came over here just to have a look at him.' He was watching Tim as he spoke. He had his suspicions about who had sent the unlucky David Long into the horse's box.

'He can look,' Tim said grimly. 'All he or his rotten horse will ever see of the Falcon will be his backside! They're under orders – ' he gripped Isabel's arm. 'They're off!'

The French jockey had been told to settle the Falcon, to let him come out of the stalls and get away behind the leaders and stay there for the first five furlongs. After that it was up to him to judge when to make the run for home. A lot would depend upon how hard the colt was fighting for his head. At all costs he wasn't to be given a hard race; the whip was not to be used, even to win. In Nigel's view it wouldn't be needed. If the Falcon's aggressive competitive spirit on the home gallops was anything to go by, then the real problem would be holding him back for the first part of the race.

Barry Lawrence came out of the stalls well. His horse had taken a strong hold and was fighting to overtake the three horses in front; it needed all Barry's extraordinary strength to keep him back without completely upsetting him. The grey colt was to the right, the masterly French jockey balanced on top; by the way he was sitting Lawrence could see that the Falcon was pulling his arms out in the effort to blaze away and pass the others. Lawrence held on, keeping as close as he could. After the five-furlong marker the course bends to the right and the field begins to run round the curve of the rails.

The Falcon was just ahead of him; there was a little bunch of horses in front, with Lester Piggott's mount well up among them. If daylight showed, Barry judged that the Falcon would streak through it. His jockey wasn't moving on him, just keeping him in check, not flickering a hand to change the rhythm of that hungry stride. The moment was coming; Barry wasn't frightened. He had done it once or twice before and he had the advantage of being the aggressor. He began to move inexorably towards the right-hand side of the course, easing the reins a fraction to let his horse come within striking distance of the Falcon.

On the stands, Roy Farrant, glasses tight against his eyes, saw the move begin; he started to whisper under his breath. 'Go on . . . go on, you bastard . . . get him, get him – '

And Tim saw it too, watching the Falcon racing on the right

hand, near the curve of the rail, ears flat back, fighting to get ahead the moment a gap appeared in front of him. He saw Barry Lawrence and Happy Hero moving up and hanging right.

'Christ!' he said it aloud, 'Christ, he's going to bump him! He'll put him into the rails. . . .'

Lawrence was up by the Falcon's quarters. He saw Jean-Martin glance sharply to the left as he began to draw level and to come closer, forcing his horse to hang inwards, edging the Falcon nearer and nearer to the spinning line of white railing. He saw Jean-Martin raise his whip and guessed that the blow was coming at him; he crouched lower and belted his horse with his own whip on the left shoulder to bring him in to the right. Another few seconds and both horses would strike into each other, and at that speed of forty miles an hour, the horse on the outside would crash sideways into the rails like an express train. Lawrence tensed himself for the impact and made ready to pull Happy Hero away to the left the moment after-wards.

But it was at that precise second, when the collision was only a mere two feet off, when a blow from Jean-Martin's whip actually cut into Barry Lawrence's shoulders and his furious curse in French was torn away on the wind, it was exactly then that the horses in front of them were separated by the lay of the ground and the Falcon saw the gap he had been waiting for. There was no time for his jockey to give any signal; it was like launching a rocket. He lengthened his stride and catapulted forward through the gap. Jean-Martin gave him his head; his whip had gone in the brief flurry trying to beat off his attacker. It was Happy Hero, swerving right-handed towards a buffer that had shot past him, who lost his balance and went crashing into the rails.

The death of Barry Lawrence made headlines. Happy Hero had to be destroyed on the course; he had a broken cannon bone on the off fore. The Silver Falcon won the race by three lengths. Isabel had hardly seen the accident; she had been too engrossed in the fantastic burst of speed that carried the grey colt away through the rest of the field and out in front. She heard the huge gasp from the crowd and exclamations from all sides of her, but the race-glasses were shaking in her hands with excitement; all she saw was the Silver Falcon eating the ground with every stride, passing the winning post with contemptuous ease. At the same moment the hooter blared, signifying a Stewards' Enquiry.

Tim and Nigel had grabbed her by the arms and hurried her down to the winner's enclosure. There was a burst of applause as the grey came through the crowd; Nigel ran to meet him and was hurrying alongside, patting the horse's neck and talking up to Jean-Martin. People were congratulating Isabel. The jockey had dismounted; he slipped off the saddle, shook hands with her, and said briefly in French, 'A marvellous horse, Madame. Nothing came near him.'

She patted the Falcon's neck; a light steam was rising from him and her hand was wet with his sweat. There were photographers crowding round them; the Falcon stood while a blue sweat rug was thrown over him and then the great quarters bunched and he let fly a savage kick which scattered everyone behind him.

'My God,' Tim Ryan kept saying, over and over in his excitement. 'What a race – did you see that finishing speed?'

'We'll murder them at Epsom,' Nigel Foster exulted. He wasn't a man who made extravagant claims to the press but he said it loud enough for anyone to quote.

And then they heard the howl of the ambulance as it raced down the course; the veterinary ambulance was following more slowly. And the first rumours, whispered among the crowd surrounding them.

'There was a terrible accident – Barry Lawrence – the horse crashed through the rails.'

One of the Stewards of the French Jockey Club approached them in the unsaddling enclosure. He took his hat off to Isabel. 'Congratulations, Madame Schriber. A superb performance. You must be looking forward to the Derby with some confidence – such a pity that this terrible accident happened. I hear that the jockey Lawrence was killed outright.'

When he went on his way, Tim and Nigel Foster looked at each other and then at Isabel. She had turned very white.

It was Nigel who spoke first. 'Don't let it upset you,' he said. 'Tim and I saw what happened; so did a hell of a lot of other people. He was trying to put the Falcon into the rails; it could have been Jean-Martin with his neck broken for all he cared. He got what he deserved.'

'He was put up to do it,' Tim said flatly. 'I should have known when he changed to Garvin's horse. It was all fixed by Farrant. He went out there to kill or maim the Falcon, and the Falcon bloody well did him instead.'

'That's the second time,' Isabel said. 'That stable lad David Long – '

'Went into the stable with an iron bar,' Tim said brutally. 'Paid by the same person. If the Falcon hadn't gone for him, he'd have broken that colt's front legs and left him there. I didn't want to upset you by telling you all this, but it's time you stopped seeing omens – there've been two attempts to kill or cripple the Falcon and he's just looked after himself, that's all. And I reckon we'll find he's broken the course record today.' He went to the bar and came back with another bottle of champagne. His expression was grim.

Nigel found seats for them and Tim opened the bottle and filled three glasses.

'Let's drink a toast,' he said. 'To the Falcon. And to Charles Schriber. He bred a horse that won't be beaten!'

Before Isabel could answer someone had come up behind her, full of congratulations and there were others rapidly approaching. There was a look on Tim's face that surprised Isabel. A look of hard determination, a look that said he didn't give a damn for Long or Lawrence or anyone else who tried to get in the way of his horse. And he expected her to match him. Two attempts on the horse; paid for by Roy Farrant who wanted his horse to win. The genial host in Barbados, lavishing hospitality upon them. Making a point of wishing her luck only minutes before the race, congratulating her about Richard as if he were pleased for them both. Knowing that he had arranged a hideous accident which could have killed the Falcon's jockey. As it had killed Barry Lawrence. She looked into Tim Ryan's face and deliberately raised her glass.

'Here's to the Falcon,' she said. 'And to the Derby.'

They took a party of thirty people to Maxim's that night to celebrate the win. The chef had prepared a special dessert for them, a mountain of meringue and chestnuts and cream, topped by a galloping silver horse. A telegram was delivered to Isabel at the table. It was from Richard.

'Congratulations, darling. Hurry home. Richard.'

Tim hadn't told her the truth about Long's attempt; there had been a general conspiracy to keep her ignorant. She leaned across to Tim and said quietly, 'Tomorrow morning, before we leave for England, I want to see you and Nigel in my suite.'

It was not an interview that Ryan or Nigel Foster enjoyed. 'Sit down, please.' She dismissed their attempts to be jocular; when Tim complained about a hangover she didn't respond. 'I asked you both to come and see me because I felt there'd been a misunderstanding,' Isabel said. 'Charles left me Beaumont and his horses. When he did so, he was perfectly confident in my ability to know exactly what was going on. I'm surprised and rather angry that you, Tim, especially, should have lied to me over David Long. You'd no right to keep me in the dark. Nor had you, Nigel.'

'We did it from the best motives,' Tim protested. 'You'd just lost Charles, you weren't in a fit state for any more shocks. If you'd known that Long had been injured trying to maim the Falcon, you might have decided to pull out altogether.'

'And that wouldn't have suited you,' Isabel said. 'Either of you.'

'No,' Tim Ryan said. 'It wouldn't. But that isn't why we kept quiet. We genuinely didn't want to worry you. It was our responsibility to protect the colt. Nobody could anticipate what happened yesterday.'

'I ran him in the Lupin rather than the Two Thousand

Guineas to avoid any attempt at interference on the course,' Nigel Foster said. 'I'm sorry if you're annoyed, Isabel, but as Tim says, we did it for the best.'

'I'm sure you did,' Isabel stood up. 'But please – don't do anything like it again. We'd better hurry now. I'll meet you downstairs.'

Outside the suite Nigel looked at Tim.

'Christ,' he muttered. 'I've always said women shouldn't be allowed in this game! If you tell them anything they throw a fit and if you don't they yell bloody murder. For a moment I thought we were going to get our marching orders.'

He was surprised to see Tim Ryan grin. 'So did I,' he said. 'And I like her all the better for it. You'd better smile sweetly on the way home, or you could lose that Monkstown colt!'

'Oh Christ,' Nigel said again. He sat in the car on the way to the airport with an air of deep gloom. He had no talent for soothing angry women and he hated atmospheres. He couldn't think what the Irishman found so admirable about Isabel Schriber wanting to read the small print. It was just going to make training for her more difficult.

Tim took the seat beside her on the plane.

'Are you still mad with me?'

'No,' Isabel said. 'But I wasn't joking.'

'I didn't think you were,' he said. 'I'm really sorry. It was a great evening last night. I didn't get a chance to tell you this morning, but the Falcon's in grand shape. He ate his manger clean and looked as if he'd been out for a hack yesterday. That race was just what he needs. Next time we'll be at Epsom with him.'

'Yes,' Isabel said. 'Whatever happens now, we're going to run and I believe we're going to win.'

'Richard, why didn't you tell me yourself?'

He was propped up in the bed beside her, smoking. He hadn't turned round to look at her while she talked. He had been at the airport to meet her, and driven her straight back to

Coolbridge. He had made love to her with furious urgency; the wine and the cold food laid out for lunch was untouched. He took her to bed and kept her there. Lying in his arms Isabel gave herself up to him with pity and tenderness as well as passion. She felt that behind the intense sexuality there was a need for reassurance. And this was only natural; insecurity was the cornerstone on which his life had been built. She kept seeing him as Andrew Graham had described, and far from turning her against him, it added a deeper significance to her love for him.

'Why didn't I tell you – ' he repeated the question. There was no expression on his face. 'Tell you what, Isabel? The true version of what happened, or Graham's pack of bloody lies? Which would you believe?'

'Darling – ' she said. 'If you were ill after your mother died, there wasn't any need to hide it. There's nothing to be ashamed of – '

To her surprise he laughed out loud.

'Ashamed? Of being locked up as a nut for nine months – what was that diagnosis he gave you – schizoid tendencies, paranoia? For Christ's sake, Isabel! I wonder you're not scared being alone with me – aren't you just a little worried I might turn peculiar?'

'Please, Richard, don't take this attitude. It doesn't make the slightest difference to me. If anything,' she said it slowly, 'I think it's made me love you more.'

'Pity is akin,' he quoted. 'No thanks, darling. I can do without that.' He threw the covers aside and got up.

He began to dress without looking at her. Isabel watched him, helpless and unhappy; he turned at the bedroom door.

'If you loved me,' he said harshly, 'you wouldn't have bloody well listened to him!' Then he went out and the door crashed behind him. Isabel dressed slowly. The change from passionate tenderness to anger and reproach had been dramatic. She had been very gentle in her approach; it hadn't diminished his reaction. He hadn't defended himself, he hadn't explained anything or even really denied it. The door had slammed so hard that it shook the pictures on the walls. Isabel went down-stairs; Mrs Jennings went home in the afternoon and they were alone in the house. She called him.

'Richard! Richard, where are you?'

He came into the hall as she ran down the stairs. He had a whisky in his hand. It reminded her painfully of the first time she had seen him at Beaumont, drinking before breakfast.

'Oh, darling, don't be angry – don't be upset – ' She came and put her arms around him. 'I love you so much – '

'In spite of my mental history?' It was said with such bitterness that she stepped away from him.

'Are you sure you're not just sorry for me? Poor Richard, he went into a nut house after his mother killed herself. No thanks, darling. You want to believe Andrew, go ahead. You might try a little loyalty next time.'

She saw him drain the glass. 'You know something – ' he was moving to the front door as he spoke. 'I haven't been properly drunk in weeks. I'll call you, Isabel.'

'I wish you wouldn't go like this,' she said. 'Please, Richard – '

He stopped and faced her. They were standing apart like strangers. He looked white and tense.

'I've been trying to rush you, and you were the one who wanted time. Now I want you to have it. I want you to think very carefully before you commit yourself to me. You've touched a very sore spot, Isabel; maybe I'm over-reacting, but I can't help it. I'll be in touch.'

He didn't come near to kiss her; he put his empty glass down on the table and walked out. She went to the window and saw him get into the car; there was violence in the way he wrenched the door shut, and the car shot forward, skidding on the gravel and sending a shower of little stones to either side. The house was very silent then. A grandfather clock in the hall struck four. She turned and went back upstairs. She was angry with herself because in some way she had behaved with less tact than honesty, but honesty was what was needed, if they were going to make a life together. There could be no question marks, no grey areas which couldn't be discussed. And his reaction had been out of all proportion. She had never seen him so close to losing control. It was a disturbing sensation. She went upstairs slowly, borne down in spirit; the loving reunion, the aftermath to her triumph at Longchamp had gone awry. She felt nervous and depression was creeping over her.

She had a bath and changed her clothes. When she came down again Mrs Jennings came hurrying to meet her.

'I read about the race, Madam,' she said. 'Terrible that jockey getting killed like that – congratulations on your win, though. Lots of us had a little bet on your Falcon . . .' She followed Isabel into the drawing room still talking. She had liked Mr Schriber. He'd been so interested in the house. Went round the grounds and into all the rooms . . . the kitchen and the pantries. And there was a bit of a bloodstain on the drawing room carpet where he'd cut himself, but she'd get it out in time. . . . Isabel wasn't listening. She longed for the woman to go away. She had a headache and a sense of desolate anticlimax as the result of their quarrel. Alone at last, she tried again to rationalize his anger.

Male pride was an obvious reason; she had made the stupid mistake of showing that she pitied him. She blamed herself for insensitivity. The aftermath of his long, eager love-making was the worst moment in which to remind him of an episode in his life which he had hidden from her out of shame. She had been thoughtless and crude. Fool, she called herself, fool to have hurt him, driven him to defend himself.

She picked up the telephone and dialled his number.

There was a car driving slowly up the leafy lanes leading to Coolbridge House; although it was now quite dark, the car showed only sidelights. There was nothing else on the road at that hour of the evening. The lodge and the white gates showed up on the right-hand side, dimly in the darkness, picked out for a second as the headlights flashed on and then cut out. The car slowed abruptly; it drew into the side of the lane and turned up a cart track where it stopped. Engine and lights were switched off. The driver was alone; he sat very still in the parked car, with the darkness and silence of the sleeping countryside around him. He looked at the luminous dial on his watch. It showed a few minutes to ten. He took off the watch, laid it in the glove pocket, and began to struggle out of his jacket. His shirt and tie followed; it was difficult to strip within the confined space but after some minutes he was completely naked. He opened the car door and slipped outside. Rain had begun to spatter down. He waited, listening, watching for some beam of light along the road. There was no noise, and no penetration of the darkness by a distant headlight. He went round, stepping carefully on the rutted ground, and opened the boot of the car. A dim light showed as he lifted the lid. He took out a parcel wrapped in newspaper, and unrolled it. There was a pair of cotton gloves, and an industrial spanner, about a foot long and made of steel. The end had been bound round with adhesive tape, forming a handle. He put on the gloves and took up the spanner. The car boot snapped shut and the little blur of light was extinguished. The naked figure came to the end of the cart track and onto the road. It crossed over to the gates of Coolbridge House and lifting the latch, opened them wide enough to slip inside. There was light showing in the lodge, behind transparent curtains, and a faint murmur from a television set was the only sound. The man shifted the spanner in his right hand for a moment; it was very heavy. Then he bent low and crept past the lodge and began to move up the drive in the shelter of the trees.

It had begun to rain heavily.

IO

There had been no reply from Richard's flat. The delay till the morning wouldn't make her apology more convincing. It would look as if she had thought it out and planned what to say. The advantage of true spontaneity was lost. Where had he gone – to friends, to gamble – to a woman? She felt an ugly pang of jealousy. Pride had made him leave, and pride had made her let him go instead of resolving the misunderstanding.

And she knew without any doubt that she loved him enough to face anything; even if Graham's warning were the truth, then what he most needed was her love and help. She went into the drawing room, and after dinner Mrs Jennings brought her coffee.

'I've put a little brandy on the tray,' she said. 'There's nothing like it if you're feeling a bit tired. You can see that bloodstain there, Madam, just by the armchair. It was lucky Mr Schriber didn't cut himself badly; broken glass is such a nasty thing – '

There was a small mark on the yellow carpet; it was difficult to see how he could have cut himself if he had knocked over the glass.

'How did he do it? Was he picking up the pieces?'

'I don't think so,' Mrs Jennings said. 'He told me the glass just shattered in his hand. Funny thing really; I suppose there must have been a crack in it.'

Isabel didn't answer. The incident was unimportant, yet it worried her. He must have put considerable pressure on the heavy whisky glass to break it, even if there was a flaw in the glass. She had noticed the dressing on his palm when they were together that afternoon. He had laughed, saying he'd nicked himself. The glass had burst in his hand. . . . There was a suggestion of unnatural force that was disturbing. What had been in his mind to make him grip and grip, without realizing?

'I'll unpack your things,' the housekeeper said. 'Don't you bother tonight. I'm not in any hurry.'

Isabel sipped the brandy and lit a cigarette. There was an odd atmosphere in the house, which she felt sure was being created by her own disquiet of mind. Richard seemed very close to her; she couldn't get the picture of him into focus because it kept blurring.

There was something about him which didn't equate; an inner rage – she stubbed out the cigarette quickly, alarmed by the accuracy of the description. There had always been a quality of enigma about him; even in their most intimate relationship there was a sense that part of him was hidden. And that was what she had felt, without being clear enough to isolate it. Rage; a force concealed and controlled within him. And if Andrew Graham called him dangerous, it was because of this. Isabel shivered; the fire had burnt low and the room was unnaturally still.

Mrs Jennings had forgotten to draw the curtains. She had a feeling of being watched; silly and irrational, but strong enough to make her get up and cover the windows. She looked at her watch; it was getting late, and sitting alone, letting her imagination run away with her was quite atypical. If she didn't take hold of herself she would begin to be frightened of staying in the house when Mrs Jennings had gone. Which she must have done by now. Isabel opened the drawing room door. The hall was dimly lit by picture lights; her voice echoed as she called out.

'Mrs Jennings? Are you upstairs?'

There was a pause; then the housekeeper appeared at the top of the staircase.

'Yes, Madam. I've just turned down your bed. I'll turn the lights off for you.'

She came down, and Isabel walked towards her. 'Good

night,' she said. 'It's raining hard – listen to it! Have you got a coat?'

'Yes, thank you. Breakfast upstairs tomorrow? Nine o'clock. Good night then.'

Isabel went up the stairs to her bedroom. Here the curtains were drawn, the cover taken off the four-poster bed and a nightdress laid out. The two bedside lights were on; she closed the door and felt suddenly secure. Only then did she admit that she had been cold with fear as she sat in the room downstairs. It was entirely her own fault. The darkness and the hiss of rain outside had exaggerated the feeling of loneliness. And the ridiculous sensation that there was someone outside watching her. . . . She was tired and overwrought, the victim of her own nerves. If she went on imagining such things she couldn't live alone at Coolbridge. She undressed, slipped the silk nightdress over her head, and sat on the edge of the bed. She found herself looking at the door. There was no key. She could have asked the housekeeper to stay; she could ring down to the lodge at that moment and say she felt nervous and would Mr Jennings mind if his wife came back and stayed the night – but it was inconsiderate and hysterical. She got into bed, chiding herself.

Then she switched out the light.

He had seen her quite clearly through the window; the big room was well lit and there were no net curtains. She was sitting on the sofa, drinking coffee. He was crouched under a tree, his body glistening with the rain, the heavy spanner in his left hand; the cotton gloves were sticking to him.

He waited quietly, watching as she smoked a cigarette, finished her coffee. When she got up he flattened against the tree trunk; the light was behind her as she came to the window. Her silhouette was totally black, with the yellow and white room behind her. Then the curtains slid across, shutting her out of view.

He saw her appear at the second and third window, and pull the curtains until there was no light, except a few cracks where the material didn't quite meet.

He didn't mind about not seeing her. He knew where she was.

He came out from the shelter of the tree and the rain lashed his skin. He crept to the grass verge round the side of the house, making his way to the back. There was a door, with glass panels and a large dustbin outside it. The window was in darkness; he could see through the glass that there wasn't a light anywhere inside. He tried the handle. If it was locked, he could break the panel, put his gloved hand inside and turn the key. . . . The back door was far enough from the main rooms; she wouldn't hear any noise. But there was no need to do anything more than turn the handle. The door hadn't been locked. He opened it carefully and stepped inside.

Isabel had switched her telephone off. Mrs Jennings, checking the fire in the drawing room picked it up. It was her husband.

'It's getting late, Em – you coming back soon? I'll walk up and fetch you if you like; it's raining cats and dogs.'

'I'm on my way,' she said. 'I've got an umbrella, don't you worry. Put the kettle on in five minutes.' She put the receiver down, and turned back to pull the iron screen across the dying fire. Then she switched out the table lamps one by one and went to the door; she had already turned off the lights in the hall. She didn't need them, she knew every inch of the house. She'd left her coat and umbrella on a chair by the front entrance. She wasn't going to leave by the back and take that much longer to walk through the downpour. She opened the drawing room door and stepped out into the hall. She gave one cry of terror as the dim, nude figure rose up in front of her and the first blows of the spanner fell.

Nigel Foster loved watching television; Sally had cooked them an excellent dinner, accompanied by some of Nigel's best claret, and Tim and he settled down in the sitting room while she made coffee. Nigel was in a mood of glowing confidence, assisted by the wine and inroads into a bottle of vintage port.

Normally they lived quite frugally when they were not entertaining, but the evening was a continued celebration of the Falcon's victory.

He looked across at Tim and grinned.

'I don't want to sound too much like a smug old sod, but I think we've got that race in the bag. I can't wait to see the video tape of the race!'

'He walked through them,' Tim said. 'And he wasn't asked a single question. I think you do sound like a smug old sod, but I think you're entitled to!'

Nigel laughed. Sally appeared with the tray of coffee. He got up to take it from her. 'Come and sit down, darling. I'll pour it out. Lovely dinner – ' He pecked at her cheek. 'There's a damned good programme on the box tonight.'

He said the same thing every evening; it was part of his routine and Tim was quite accustomed to it. He and Sally gossiped while Nigel settled in front of the set. Whatever he was watching, whether it was comedy, documentary or an old film, he was fast asleep within ten minutes. Sally had taken some needlework out of a bag and was sewing peacefully. Both of them prayed that from the hour of eight o'clock onwards, their owners would leave them to enjoy their evening in peace.

'I meant to tell you,' Nigel said, 'I heard on the grapevine last night that Gerry Garvin has told Farrant to take his horses away.'

'About time – you can't have owners like Farrant without getting dirty yourself in the end. I wonder where he'll send Rocket Man?'

'I don't know and I don't care,' Nigel announced. 'He won't get within spitting distance of our fellow.' He got up and switched on the television. 'Ah, Benny Hill – I like his programmes. Bloody funny. . . .'

Tim watched his head droop to one side; within a few minutes his breathing was loud and slightly hoarse.

'It's so good for him,' Sally said. 'He gets terribly strung up, though you'd never think it. He was having a fit all night before the Lupin; couldn't sleep, bouncing in and out of bed – I nearly go mad with him before a big race. I dread the Derby!'

'You needn't,' Tim said. 'I think we're going to win.'

'It'll make a big difference to you, won't it ? Nigel told me about that codicil in Charles's will.'

'I'll be set up for good,' Tim said.

'We all will,' she said, bending over the square of tapestry work. 'It's three years since we won a Derby. There's a South American we're trying to get interested. He's so disgustingly rich it's a crime. If we pull this off with the Falcon, he'll give us a commission for a dozen yearlings next year – just for a start!'

'It means a hell of a lot to all of us,' Tim said. He lit a cigarette. The television screen flickered, showing the comedian's moon face in close-up. Nigel was still fast asleep.

'How much does it really mean to Isabel?' Sally asked him. 'I can't make up my mind about it.'

'I don't really know myself,' Tim said. 'She wanted to carry out Charles's wishes. I don't think she would have done it except for that. Now, I rather think she's got the bug herself. She bought that Monkstown colt entirely on her own, you know. Didn't ask me, or Nigel. Just made up her own mind.'

'I'm dying to see it,' Sally said. 'Nigel's mad about it. He's talking about Epsom next year!'

'What about Epsom?' Her husband had woken up.

'Nothing, darling,' Sally said. 'Go back to sleep.'

'Sleep? I haven't been asleep – I was watching the programme. What were you talking about?'

'Running Isabel's new colt next year,' Tim said.

'Hmm,' Nigel pushed himself up in the chair. 'I'm looking forward to that. But I don't know what'll happen if she marries Richard Schriber. He hates racing – wouldn't even come to Longchamp to watch the Falcon. A husband like that could turn her off completely.'

Tim said nothing. Sally Foster looked up. 'You don't think she'll marry him, do you? I know you said they were pretty thick in Dublin but I didn't know it was that serious.'

'The newspapers said so,' Nigel pointed out. 'You never

know. What do you think, Tim? Would she go that far, do you think?'

'I don't know,' Tim said slowly. 'I bloody well hope not. I think I'll go to bed,' he said.

'Good idea,' Nigel agreed. 'We all will. Tomorrow is another day. Come on, Sal – it's past ten o'clock.'

Tim Ryan didn't sleep. Pretty thick in Dublin. So even Nigel had noticed it, and he wasn't a man who concerned himself with people's private lives. He kept seeing Isabel in tears in the Ritz the night before the race. And her words. 'I love him. There's nothing wrong, I'd know if there was.' An affair was bad enough; he couldn't bear to think of her in Richard's bed. But marriage to the man described in that dossier Andrew Graham had shown them – that was unthinkable. But Richard had met her and she had driven away with him. It looked as if she had disregarded Andrew's warning. And that was his damned fault, Tim thought furiously. He didn't know why he'd made a mess of that interview but he had. He hadn't frightened Isabel away; he'd merely added the lethal quality of compassion to her feelings for Richard Schriber. There was nothing about Richard to suggest that he was not exactly what he seemed. Yet cunning was a recognized ingredient of psychopathic disorder. An appearance of perfect normality could be assumed and maintained for years, provided nothing happened to disturb it and set the irrational impulses in motion. And you didn't grow out of schizoid tendencies; Isabel was wrong. You might subdue them, but they never disappeared. Andrew had talked of danger. His reaction when she left him at the airport and went away in Richard's car, had certainly been one of hurt and jealousy. But there was an extra element in it, which was growing as he lay awake. He had been worried. Not just jealous, but terribly uneasy, seeing her go off alone with her stepson. She must be with him now; either at Coolbridge or in Richard's flat. He turned on his light and looked at his watch. It was nearly one o'clock. He gave up trying to sleep; there were few books in the bedroom, and all of them connected with racing. There was a book written about the great steeplechaser Red

Rum which was more a work of literature than the life story of a National winner. He lit a cigarette and started to read it. It was an hour later when the telephone in the Fosters' hall began to ring and ring.

There was a tremendous amount of blood. It had spurted everywhere, on the walls and the floor. He was standing in a pool of it. There was a sickly smell and a sticky wetness on his naked skin. He looked down in the dimness at the body of the woman. She had given just the one cry, high-pitched with terror, and then the first blow had silenced her, followed so quickly by the second and the third. He had struck and struck at her as she staggered in the darkness. He crouched down beside her and found a slack, bloodied arm. There was no pulse. There was no need to switch on the lights, to make sure. The big hall windows were uncurtained. It might attract attention. She was dead. He dropped the spanner on the floor, quite close to her body. It clanged on the stone flags. He turned and padded away towards the kitchen; his feet were wet and sticky. In the kitchen he switched on the lights; the windows faced to the back, no one would see anything. He filled the sink with warm water. It didn't take him long to wash himself; he filled a bucket with the water and sluiced his body; he washed his hair under the sink tap. Water was running everywhere over the floor, coloured red. He turned off the lights and opened the kitchen door. He stepped out into the rain. He ran back down the drive, keeping in the shadow of the line of trees. The windows of the lodge were still illuminated. He sprinted past, bending double. At the gates he paused; the road was in pitch darkness, sheeted in rain. He was shivering with cold and he still wore the reddened, sopping gloves. He peeled them off, wrung them dry of water, opened the boot of the car and threw them inside. From the recess at the back he brought out a towel. He opened the back door of the car, spread the towel over the seat and got inside. Within five minutes he had dried himself and dressed. He slicked his hair back with a comb, checked himself briefly in the driving mirror, and then doused the inside light. He started the engine and began to back out of the track and onto the main road. He had a feeling of elation, of a destiny fulfilled. What had happened seemed to be inevitable. There could be no guilt where events were predestined. What he had done was justified and he felt only satisfaction. Life was a pattern in which the design only became clear at the end. He had completed a cycle which had begun long ago. He picked up speed and drove on to the main London road. It was exactly a quarter to eleven.

Tim and Nigel Foster drove down to Coolbridge. Isabel, fully dressed and with the local doctor beside her, was sitting in her room upstairs; she was very white and there was a glazed look on her face. She had been given a strong sedative, the doctor explained. Luckily the solid construction of the house had prevented her hearing the murder and coming down to investigate.

It was Mrs Jennings's husband, alarmed when she failed to come home, who went into the house through the open back door and discovered his wife's body. The first thing Mrs Schriber knew of the tragedy was when the police came up and woke her. She was suffering from shock, and the police had given permission for her to leave the house. She had answered their questions, and the sooner she could be got away and into a hotel where she could go to sleep, the better. The doctor looked sick and shaken himself as he talked to the two men. He had seen Mrs Jennings's body. 'A maniac,' he said. 'I've never seen such a sight – the place is like a slaughterhouse. Only a maniac would have gone on and on. . . .' He had turned away and lit a cigarette; his hands were trembling.

Nigel drove her to Lambourn; she hardly spoke in the car. Tim Ryan stayed behind to talk to the detective inspector who had been called in to take charge of the case. He had wrapped Isabel up in a fur coat, supported her down the back stairs and quickly through the staff quarters and out through the kitchen.

The kitchen was full of police. There was water all over the floor by the sink; a small pool had collected in an indentation at the base, and in the bright fluorescent lighting it had a pinkish tinge. Ryan put her into Nigel's car and held her hands. They were freezing and limp.

'It's all right,' he said, slowly and distinctly, repeating it. 'It's all right, Isabel. You're going home with Nigel. He and Sally will look after you. I'll be down later. You're not to worry any more. You've had a bad shock. You'll be all right now.'

She had looked at him, and answered slowly, forcing out the words.

'Mrs Jennings . . . I fell asleep. He's given me something – I'm so deadened, I can't feel anything.'

'Just as well,' Nigel answered. 'I'm getting you home and into bed. I'll wait for you, Tim.' He had whispered through the driving window to Ryan before he drove away.

'Christ Almighty. If he'd disturbed them instead of the housekeeper . . .'

'Get her home,' Ryan said. 'I'll sort everything out with the police and get down as soon as I can. She should never, never have stayed in that house alone!'

'Thought Richard would have been with her,' Nigel muttered.

'So did I,' Ryan said. He went back into the house and Nigel drove down the drive towards the lodge and the gates. It was no longer raining; he could see the house in his driving mirror, blazing with lights like a beacon in the darkness. He had seen enough action in the war to be immune to horror, but the scene in the hall at Coolbridge would remain in his mind for the rest of his life. The most horrible and vivid memory was of a trail of imprints on the polished stone floor of a naked, bloody foot. He shuddered, glancing at the silent woman beside him. She was leaning against the head-rest, and her eyes were closed.

By the mercy of God she had gone to bed before the intruder broke in. The distraught husband of the murdered woman had repeated over and over again that his wife normally came home an hour earlier. Just that evening she had chosen to stay late. . . .

Nigel put his foot down as soon as he had left the narrow country lanes and drove towards Lambourn at top speed.

The headlines were staring at Andrew Graham.

'Murder at Millionairess's Rented Mansion. Housekeeper Beaten to Death.' He was sitting up in his hotel bedroom with a tray of coffee and the papers. He gave a gasping exclamation of shock. The housekeeper had disturbed an intruder and had been brutally battered to death, while the wealthy racehorse owner and widow of the American multi-millionaire Charles Schriber, slept upstairs, unaware of the horror taking place on the ground floor. Andrew put the paper down. He reached for the telephone and called through to MacNeil's room. His voice was muffled and hoarse with shock.

'It's Graham. Have you seen the papers – '

'Yeah,' the detective's voice sounded metallic. 'Attempted robbery is what it says. Pretty brutal murder.'

'I've got to talk to you,' Andrew said. 'Come up to my room. It says Isabel's staying with her trainer. I'm going to put a call through at once!'

MacNeil was sitting by his bed, fully dressed. He picked a cigarette out of a packet with one hand, cradled the telephone under his chin while he lit it. 'I'll be right up,' he said.

He found Andrew Graham shaving; the buzz of the electric razor hummed for a few minutes before he came out of the bathroom. MacNeil sat on the rumpled bed and read the newspaper. It was not the tabloid which he ordered for himself; it catered for a more select, yet equally sensation-seeking public. The account dwelt on the ferocity of the attack, the miraculous escape of Isabel, and the strange theory, borne out by footprints, that the thief had been barefooted. Robbery was obviously the motive, and the unfortunate housekeeper had disturbed the intruder as he was going through the house. There was a picture, taken from a snapshot, of Coolbridge House, and an inset of Isabel, smiling at Longchamp after the Falcon's victory. The police were mounting a nationwide hunt for the killer. MacNeil grimaced at the cliché. The attack was described as maniacal in its fury. He re-read that line.

He looked up as Graham came out of the bathroom. The doctor looked tired and grim. 'I rang through to Foster,' he said. 'They wouldn't let me speak to Isabel. She's under their own doctor and he says she's to have complete rest. I guess that's the best thing.'

He came and stood close to MacNeil, looking down at him.

'I've got to see her,' he said. 'However long it takes, I've got to talk to her again. Do you believe that was a robbery?'

MacNeil sucked on the end of his cigarette. 'No,' he said. He stubbed it out in the metal ashtray by the bedside. 'I don't see this as any burglary. This guy went berserk. I don't think it was a robbery.'

'Where was Schriber?' Andrew Graham asked him. 'Last night – where was he?'

'I don't know,' MacNeil admitted. 'I only trail him when he's with her. You didn't tell me she was back – I thought she was in France.'

He looked up at Andrew Graham.

'You tell me,' he said. 'What do you think?'

Graham turned suddenly and sat down; he passed a hand over his face and back over his sparse sandy hair.

'I think that what I've been afraid of all along has finally happened,' he said. 'And the terrible thing is, that an innocent woman has been butchered because nobody would listen to me. And so long as they keep on calling this a robbery, nobody *will* listen to me. I think Richard Schriber broke into that house to kill Isabel. Just as he tried to kill her in Barbados. Somehow, the housekeeper got in the way. That's what I think. It's come to the crisis point for him; his father's death triggered off the first attempt. Now the Derby's getting close. That's another flashpoint in his mind. So he goes down there and gets into the house to murder Isabel and make it look like a robbery.'

'You're the expert on this kind of thing – you really think he did it?' MacNeil asked.

'I do,' Andrew said. 'And you can be sure he'll try again. It follows the pattern; he wants to rob his father of the final triumph and revenge his mother at the same time. He'll kill Isabel to stop the horse from running, and to punish her for taking his mother's place. But he'll protect himself. He'll try to make it look an accident. He's cunning, mad cunning, don't forget that. And he's just made a very bad mistake. He'll be extra careful next time. Jesus, what can I do to stop him?' He covered his face with his hands for a moment.

MacNeil lit a cigarette. He didn't say anything.

'He's living with her,' Andrew went on. 'We can't stop something happening when they're alone. There's no way to protect her if she won't protect herself!'

'Then you'll have to try again,' MacNeil said. 'She's safe so long as she stays with the Fosters. He can't get at her there. Meantime I'll keep him in sight twenty-four hours a day. How about this guy Ryan?'

'I think he'll believe me,' Andrew said. 'And that may be her best protection. He can stick close to Schriber; and to her.'

MacNeil nodded. 'Fine, that way Schriber will be watched around the clock.'

He went out, leaving Andrew Graham alone.

'He's gone,' Patsy Farrant said. She stood in the doorway of the principal guest room in the Hampstead house; Roy Farrant was behind her. The bed was stripped back to the bottom sheet, its covers hurled to the floor. The curtains hadn't been drawn, and the overhead reading light was still on.

Roy pushed past her into the room.

'Bloody fool,' he said. He went in and pressed a switch; the curtains hissed and drew back, flooding the room with bright morning sunlight. He looked haggard, and there was a shrink-age about his face and jowls which hadn't been there on the morning of the Prix Lupin. Patsy came in after him. It was only two days since the death of Barry Lawrence and he hadn't sworn at her or lost his temper since.

'He was in such a state,' Patsy said. 'I thought he'd sleep through till lunch. Where do you think he's gone?'

'Christ only knows,' Farrant said. 'He must have heard about the murder. Maybe he woke up this morning and tried to phone her.'

'He's come to you before when he's been in trouble,' Patsy said. 'I think it was very generous of you to take him in last night at that hour, considering how he let you down over . . .'

'Shut up,' Farrant said. 'Just shut up, and don't ever mention anything about it. Ever.'

'All right.' Her shoulders lifted under the expensive satin dressing gown. His rebuke was comparatively mild. She had no idea he had felt so deeply about Barry Lawrence. To Patsy he was just another crooked jockey that was mixed up with Roy, and their association had gone on a long time. Lawrence's death had really upset him. And when Richard Schriber had turned up drunk the night before, he had simply taken him upstairs and put him to bed without a word. He was a funny man; she would never, ever understand him, however hard she tried. She went over to the bed and stopped.

'Oh hell,' she said, forgetting herself. 'He's bloodied my sheet – look at that!' Roy turned and glanced down; there was an ugly stain on the crumpled top sheet. He looked at her briefly, and his face was blank. 'Buy a new one,' he said. 'I'll ring his flat – maybe he's gone there. Bloody fool,' he said again, lower this time, talking to himself. 'I'd have gone with him.'

He went out of the bedroom, leaving Patsy fingering the sheet with the bloodstain. He had been astounded to find Richard Schriber on his doorstep at two in the morning. They hadn't seen or spoken to each other since the story about his proposed marriage had appeared in Partridge's gossip column. Farrant had sworn never to forgive him, to pay him back one day no matter how long it took. And he had meant it. If Barry Lawrence hadn't been lying in a French mortuary, he would have kicked Richard Schriber in the groin and left him lying there. But something had happened to Roy since Lawrence's body was brought back from the racecourse. Something he couldn't understand in himself. Ruthless, ambitious, tough, with one man's death on his conscience, he had suddenly weakened when Barry was killed.

There was a curious affinity between them, an emotional tie which had its origins and its strength in the shared guilt of that first crooked alliance which had ended in the victim's suicide. Roy could and did argue in the beginning that he hadn't known how desperate the Italian Lambarzini's financial situation was; it looked to him like a rich man's gamble which he could well afford to lose. But sharing the guilt had helped them both. They buried it and built on it further, with a multitude of dubious deals, culminating in the final disaster at Longchamp. Now, suddenly, the steel in Farrant cracked. He had paid the price and the price was too high. When an old friend turned up and needed help, he didn't think about revenge. He was glad of the chance to take him in. He didn't know it, but it was a subconscious longing to make amends.

He had seen the report of the murder at Isabel's house, and gone upstairs with Patsy to wake Richard and tell him. He would have welcomed the chance to drive him down there, help in any way he could. But Richard had gone. Almost too drunk to stand the night before, with the look of desperation about him that Roy had seen only when alcohol had totally disarmed him, Richard was in no fit state to be alone. He had homed in on his former friend, acting from blind instinct. Roy understood this, and accepted it. And Patsy had been intuitive enough for once not to argue with him. Even his constant irritation with her had suffered a diminution. He kept seeing Barry, smoking his big cigars, sipping champagne, in every corner of the house.

Sally Foster was doing the accounts; she was better at figures than Nigel, who had given up trying to make up the bills years ago, because he considered it a waste of time. Sally didn't argue with him: she merely took over the financial side of the business without any fuss. She had a bright little sitting room with files and a telephone on the desk with an outside line. Difficult owners were often switched through there when her husband didn't want to talk to them. Sally combined charm with brevity; the most persistent talkers found themselves cut short without a feeling of dissatisfaction.

She hadn't slept much the previous night. It was three in the morning before Nigel returned with Isabel; Sally had their spare room ready, with the electric blanket on and some hot milk and brandy in a flask. She was very good at looking after people, and she took charge of Isabel, putting her to bed. She gave her the milk and settled her down to sleep. She looked dazed and sick; Sally knew a lot about the effects of shock, and she came back and woke up her own doctor to explain the situation and ask him to make Isabel his first call in the morning. His diagnosis had been what she expected; complete rest for twenty-four hours. It was very lucky, from what he had read in the papers, that his patient hadn't seen the body of the housekeeper. The press was making a meal of the bloodstained horror in the manor house; the word maniac was being widely used to describe the attacker. One of the more sensational tabloids screamed about the barefoot slayer.

Sally, practical and unimaginative, couldn't begin to visualize the scene. She felt very sorry for Isabel Schriber, and fought off all press enquiries ruthlessly. When her daily woman reported that there were newspapermen in the yard asking for Nigel, she marched out stony-faced, to meet them and with the authority that came from being an upper-class English woman whose father was a General, told them to clear off before she called the police. The gates into the yard were locked, and she stamped back angrily into the house. She felt for a moment that it was just too damned unfair on Nigel, with a horse being readied for the Derby, to have this dirty mess thrown at him. Owners, she thought furiously; always some bloody trouble with them – and immediately she was sorry, thinking of Isabel that morning, white-faced and hollow-cheeked, sitting up in bed. Sally was a genuinely kind person, but her first love and primary consideration was for her husband.

She picked up the shrilling telephone for the umpteenth time, and it was Richard Schriber.

'Oh, thank God it's you,' she said. 'I've been going mad, fobbing off the bloody press all morning. Yes. She's here, with us. Nigel went down and got her last night. What a ghastly thing to happen!'

'I'm at Coolbridge,' he said. 'I phoned her this morning and got the police. I drove here. They wouldn't let me in at first till I proved who I was; then they told me she was staying with you.' His voice sounded unsteady. 'I'll come straight down.'

'She's not supposed to see anyone,' Sally said. 'Doctor Graham phoned and I wouldn't let him come. Richard – are you there? Hullo – oh, good. I thought we'd been cut off – Is it very bad down there – the papers have been too horrible. . . .'

'It's unbelievable,' he said. 'Nothing's been touched; they're going through the house, photographing and looking for finger-prints. God Almighty, when I think what might have happened – I'll be with you as soon as I can. Tell her I'm coming. Is she very shaken?'

'Yes, rather,' Sally Foster said. 'I think she'll be perfectly all right by tomorrow. It'll do her good to see you. We'll give you some lunch.' She had no sooner hung up than the phone went again.

It was a reporter from a large provincial newspaper. Sally cut right through his conversation. 'No comment. Sorry.' She put the telephone down. After a moment's thought, she took it off the cradle. Nigel had done his morning telephoning; owners wanting to natter about their horses would just have to wait till the evening.

She went in to see if Isabel was awake, and to tell her Richard was on his way. Personally she didn't dislike Richard; he wasn't in the least like his father, and to her that was a recommendation. She had never got on with Charles Schriber; Nigel had liked him and spoke of him as a good sportsman and a great authority on bloodstock, which was true. But it went with an autocratic, ruthless personality which aroused Sally's antagonism. She wasn't impressed by his charm, and she was always on the defensive with him, guarding her husband's interests. She had hidden her feelings, because as a trainer's wife, she was bound to entertain his owners and keep the social ball in the air. It was easy with Isabel, whom she thought very nice, and if she had moved on to her stepson, that was really none of their business. She sat on the bed, a cup of coffee in her hand. Isabel looked less pale.

'I'm so sorry about this, Sally,' she said. 'I'm quite able to get up. I know how busy you are here, and I told the doctor I should go to a hotel.'

'Certainly not – ' Sally patted her hand. 'You've had a very nasty experience, and the rest will do you good. You're staying with us till the end of the week and that's decided. Nigel would be terribly hurt if you moved out and so would I. After all, we've got your horse to think about, and that'll take your mind off things. So no more arguments, please!'

'All right,' Isabel said. She felt a continuous tremor in her limbs, too slight to be noticed, but evidence that she was far less recovered than she tried to pretend. The room was warm and comfortable and the practical approach of Sally Foster encouraged her to relax and let her nervous system settle.

And Richard was coming. That, more than anything, had helped her fight off the sickened, shivering reaction to the night before. If she allowed herself to think of Mrs Jennings she began to cry. If she remembered, against her will, that nightmare moment when her bedroom door burst open and she woke to see the figures of police come crowding in, then the tremor in her body became uncontrollable.

'You're not supposed to have visitors,' Sally was saying, 'but I didn't think that would apply to him. Your friend Andrew Graham wanted to speak to you, but I fobbed him off till tomorrow.'

Isabel looked up quickly. 'Thanks, Sally. I don't want to talk to him. Oh, I shall be so glad to see Richard!'

'He sounded very upset,' Sally said. 'He's certainly fond of you – '

'Yes,' Isabel said quietly. 'I know he is.'

Sally Foster glanced at her. 'I thought it was going to be Tim,' she said.

'I'm afraid Tim thought so too,' she answered. 'Where is he – out with Nigel?'

'They'll both be in for a drink before lunch; he'll be in to see you then. And you're staying where you are – no nonsense about getting up today! We can come in and drink round your bedside.'

When Richard came into the room neither of them spoke. He came and took her in his arms and held her for some moments. She felt his hand stroking her hair, and she found herself crying and crying, as the pent-up shock was finally released. He sat on the bed and let her exhaust herself, murmuring quietly to her, soothing her gently till it was over and she was calm.

'It's all right, darling,' he said, repeating Tim's words of the night before. 'It's out now, and you don't have to talk about it again. Just say you forgive me for being such a selfish bloody fool and leaving you alone. Just say that, please.'

He was holding both her hands and his head was bent, so that his face was partly hidden from her. His grip was so tight it was painful. She saw a thick dressing round his right palm and over the back of the hand itself. And she remembered the shattered whisky glass.

She freed herself. 'Your hand is worse,' she said. She turned it palm upward and there was a stain on the dressing.

'It keeps on bleeding,' he said. 'I was drunk last night; I haven't been so drunk for years. I woke up in Roy Farrant's house; I don't know what I did, but I've opened the cut again. I don't even remember going to Hampstead, or seeing him or anything.'

'Why did you do that?' she asked him. He raised his head; his eyes were bloodshot and heavily ringed.

'Because I thought I'd lost you,' he said. 'I thought Graham had won. You pitied me, Isabel, and that meant you believed him.'

'I love you,' Isabel said. 'And that's all that matters. And I don't care what Andrew Graham said. I shall never think of it again.'

'I want to tell you something,' Richard said slowly. 'But not now and not here. It's going to take time. When can you come home with me?'

She put her arms around his neck.

'In a few days.'

'Why not tomorrow – you'll be up by tomorrow. You don't have to stay here; you can move into my flat.'

'I can't,' Isabel said. 'The Fosters would be very hurt if I just walked out. I said I'd stay till the end of the week. They've been marvellous, Richard. I'll come with you at the weekend – Sunday.'

He kissed her suddenly, urgently.

'It's a long time to wait. Let me talk to Nigel: he won't mind.'

For a moment she hesitated. She wanted to go with him. But deep inside her there was a residue of fear, left over from that last evening at Coolbridge, when unease had crept over her in the drawing room and the sensation of hidden eyes watching from the darkness had brought her close to panic. Panic that had lasted, and proved to be horribly intuitive. There had been a watcher outside; waiting to break in and steal, prepared to murder if he was disturbed. And no ordinary thief. She knew enough from the police questioning to guess that it was a ferocious crime, and at the back of her mind, hazy with the injection of the tranquillizer she had been given, the word 'slaughterhouse' floated in the doctor's shocked voice, whispering to Tim. Richard's arms were round her, his mouth was pressing kisses on her lips, her cheeks, the side of her neck, his voice was murmuring to her, urging her to come and stay with him, to let him take care of her.

The fear was growing; the trembling had begun again and the sense of nightmare was creeping back. She was safe with the

Fosters, safe in this cheerful bedroom, with Sally and Nigel, and all the bustle of preparation for the Derby. Outside there was menace, danger which she couldn't see. The arrow that flies by night; the watcher in the trees.

It was a nervous reaction and she told herself so, angrily. But it won. 'I'm not up to going yet,' she said. 'I need the few days here. I'll come back with you on Sunday.'

He kissed her gently, signifying his agreement.

'All right, darling. I was just being possessive. I'll take a room somewhere near. I'll even put up with the non-stop horse talk, as long as I can see you.'

She felt intense relief. And then disquiet again.

'Why did you go to Roy Farrant's – I tried to ring you several times last night. I was so unhappy the way we'd left each other – why did you go to him?'

'I don't know,' he said. 'I went out on the town. I went to the Claremont and played backgammon and I lost. Then I went on somewhere else; I can't remember where. I was just drinking; I didn't want to think or feel anything, and I suppose I got myself to Roy because I used to go there sometimes. Couple of years ago I was in a bad way and I stayed with him.'

'Tim says he bribed Barry Lawrence to put the Falcon into the rails at Longchamp,' she said slowly. 'I didn't mention it to you when I got home because we had that stupid misunderstanding and I was too upset – he got that jockey killed – and Tim says he bribed that wretched stable lad to try and maim the Falcon in his box. Did you know he was like that?'

Richard Schriber looked down at her.

'Yes,' he said. 'It doesn't come as a surprise. Racing is a rough and dirty business. But you choose to stay in it, so you mustn't complain. You want to win the Derby, darling. So does he. So did Charles, and I promise you, he would have done exactly what Roy did and more, if it helped to get him past the post first.'

She didn't answer because there was a knock at the door and Nigel Foster put his head round. He looked at them both and his face creased into a wide grin. He came round the door, with a bottle of champagne in his hand. Tim and Sally were behind him.

'We've come to see the patient,' he announced. 'Sally ₤. .ys we can come in if we're very quiet and don't stay long. Your Monkstown colt has just arrived, Isabel. I've got us a bottle of Dom Perignon '64 to celebrate.'

The following day the detective in charge of the murder case drove down to Lambourn to see Isabel. Nigel tried to stop him, but he insisted with a firmness that was only just polite. He quite understood that Mrs Schriber was recovering from a nasty shock, and he would do his best not to upset her, but there were a few more questions he felt she might be able to answer. It was hardly necessary, the brisk voice said into Nigel's ear, to remind them that an innocent woman had been brutally murdered.

Nigel showed the detective inspector, accompanied by a sergeant, into the sitting room. The two men were scrupulously polite. They wiped their shoes as they came into the entrance hall, put their hats on the table, and called Tim sir. The senior officer was a man in his late forties, stocky and blue-jowled, with glasses, neatly dressed in a grey suit and striped tie. The younger was a slight man, with thick fair hair brushed back, wearing a tweed sports jacket and casual trousers. He carried a black briefcase.

There was nothing about either of them to suggest that they were policemen, except that air of cool authority which knows it doesn't need a uniform.

'Mrs Schriber's inside,' Tim said. 'I must emphasize that she's been under the doctor. I hope you won't stay too long.'

'We'll do our best, sir,' Inspector Lewis said. 'Thank you.'

Isabel shook hands with them both. They took seats in the two armchairs facing her, asked if she smoked or minded if they did, and the junior officer opened his briefcase, handed his superior a file, and prepared a pad on which to take notes.

Isabel felt nervous in the beginning; but the two men were calm and reassuring, the senior was particularly gentle in his manner. The first questions were prefaced by an apology; he wanted to check back on her earlier statement on the night of the murder. It was just routine and to make sure he hadn't overlooked anything. Isabel found her hands gripping together as she listened to the young sergeant read her own words back to her. Her evening spent at Coolbridge, dining alone, taking coffee in the drawing room; Mrs Jennings offering to stay later than usual and unpack. As she listened her mind was racing backwards, reliving that evening, the memory of that hour spent in the drawing room was bringing back the sense of blind unreasoning fear.

'What's the matter, Mrs Schriber – is something upsetting you?' The voice recalled her. The young man had stopped reading. They were both watching her, expectantly.

'I was terrified,' Isabel said slowly. 'I was alone in the drawing room after dinner and the curtains weren't drawn. I had the strongest feeling that I was being watched. It was a dreadful night, raining hard and pitch dark. I knew it was just nerves, but I got up and pulled the curtains. I had the same feeling when I went upstairs to my bedroom. I remember looking at the door and realizing for the first time that there wasn't a key. It was quite irrational; I'd spent weeks alone down there and never been frightened before. But I was then.'

'You didn't see or hear anything when you were downstairs?' Inspector Lewis asked her quietly. 'Nothing to make you think there was an intruder hiding outside? You'd never had telephone calls when the person just hung up when you answered? No callers or travelling salesmen? Nothing at all to account for this instinct of yours?'

'No,' Isabel said. 'Nothing like that. Mrs Jennings did mention someone had come round while I was away. They had heard the house was for rent. But it was nothing sinister. It was just a nervous feeling on my part.'

'It was more than that,' he said. 'It was very intuitive. You were dead right, Mrs Schriber. There was someone outside those windows, hiding under the trees, watching you.'

The room was quite silent; neither of the officers moved or said anything. Isabel looked at the detective.

'How do you know?'

'Because we found footmarks in the earth round the trees,' he said. 'Bare feet, like the prints in the house. Whoever killed your housekeeper was lurking out there in the darkness, waiting to break in. Mrs Jennings usually left around nine, didn't she?'

'Yes. She stayed late that night as a favour.'

'So her husband said. He rang up to ask if she wanted him to come and fetch her as it was raining. She said no, she'd be home in a few minutes. If he'd gone to get her, Mrs Schriber, she'd have been alive today.'

'I'd like a cigarette,' Isabel said. He sprang up immediately, offered her one of his, lit it for her, holding the flame longer than usual.

'Mrs Schriber,' he said. 'I don't like doing this, believe me. I know it's very unpleasant for you, and I promised your friend Mr Ryan I'd be as quick as I could. But this is a terrible murder. Not just a robbery with violence, but a really horrible murder. Your housekeeper was literally beaten to death. Her head and face were smashed to pulp with a two-foot spanner. And I am beginning to think that the man who did it was not just an ordinary thief who was surprised in the hall, about to nick the silver.'

He sat down again and waited. Years of dealing with criminals of all varieties had completely hardened his sensibilities. He could see that Isabel Schriber was feeling sick and he didn't want her to cave in until he'd got everything he could out of her. And to do that he was going to shock her even more.

'This was no ordinary thief,' he said. 'I'll admit, we took the view that it was an attempted burglary because you're a rich woman and it was a big country house where jewellery and valuables would be found. But no professional thief takes off his shoes. He might wear tennis shoes, to creep about, or rubbers, but he doesn't go barefoot. And he doesn't slosh bucketfuls of water round, just to wash his feet.'

He paused. 'It was a very messy killing,' he said. 'I've seen a number of murders, Mrs Schriber, but I've never seen so much blood before. It was everywhere in that hall. Over the walls and the drawing room door, pools of it on the floor. Whoever killed Mrs Jennings must have been spattered from head to foot. He couldn't have travelled a yard in that state. And he used a car because we found tyre marks in a field outside the gates. So I reckon he wasn't just barefoot. He was naked, Mrs Schriber. Stark naked, but wearing gloves. And that means he went in there to commit murder. He washed himself clean in your kitchen.'

'I don't believe it.' She heard her own voice from a distance. She couldn't take her eyes off that square face, with the blue shadows round the chin, and the hard little eyes behind the glasses.

He had conjured up an image of such horror that she couldn't accept it. A naked, bloodstained figure, wielding a heavy spanner, while all around the blood flew, drenching the walls and the floor. And then padding away in the darkness, to wash the reek and stain away. She had left the house through the kitchen. She remembered that floor, slippery with water, and the pinkish colour under the strip lighting.

'You said it was burglary.'

'I know we did,' he agreed. 'At first sight. But we think differently now. We think someone went into that house to murder the woman he saw in the drawing room. A woman he knew to be living there alone, sleeping alone. We have a maniac on our hands. A homicidal murderer. He must have watched that house because he knew your habits and your housekeeper's. And he knew his way about. It's a horrible thing to say, Mrs Schriber, but if he hadn't chanced on Mrs Jennings you'd have woken up to find him standing by your bed.'

It was a warm afternoon, with sunshine flooding through the open windows. Isabel was freezing cold.

'Is there anyone,' his voice said, slightly confidential in a lower tone, 'anyone at all who might want to kill you?'

'No,' Isabel said. 'No. You can't believe a thing like that. . . .'

'We're trying to find a reason,' he explained. 'Otherwise we've just got to look for a madman. And he'll do it again. There'll be another woman in a lonely house or a flat. I want you to think of anything, anything, however trivial or unrelated it may seem, and tell me, because it just might be a clue. Like that feeling of being watched. You didn't mention that when I first saw you. You were too shaken up. But things come back. People remember. That's what I want you to do, Mrs Schriber. Think back from the time you moved into that house. Mr Jennings also said there *was* a man who called there one afternoon when you were in London. His wife told him about it; he said he'd heard the house was for sale. It's probably nothing. But we've got to follow up everything, every clue. We've got to catch this man. I'm going to leave you in peace now. But just try and think back, and if you remember anything – anything at all . . . let me know.' He was holding his hand out to her, and the pressure was surprisingly limp for such a decisive person. She got up as the two men went out.

'Good afternoon,' they said and closed the door. She heard Tim's voice outside, with other voices.

She found a cigarette in her handbag and lit it. Her hands were quite steady. There was a second door, leading out into the back corridor. She didn't want to see Tim or Nigel or anyone. She opened the door and went through into the passage; there was a door at the end, leading to the Fosters' swimming pool and garden. She walked out quickly, closing it, and stood for a moment in the sunshine. There were chairs and a swing seat, and a portable barbecue by the changing rooms. Isabel walked towards the swing seat; the sun was quite hot, the air very still.

The sense of inner chill was still with her. She sat on the sofa seat and swung herself to and fro, her face turned up towards the sun.

Cold with fear. The basis of most clichés was solid truth. She was shivering in a temperature of close on seventy degrees, because her nervous system was reacting to the stimulus of fear and horror.

Coolbridge, the lovely manor house set in its splendid gardens, had symbolized her search for security and identity after Charles's death. It was her first step towards breaking the links his personality had forged around her. She had sometimes described the house as having a dream-like atmosphere; so still and peaceful with the serenity of great age. Now it was a dream transformed into a nightmare, a place where evil had stalked naked and red, and the victim could so easily have been herself. Did anyone want to kill her? She remembered that question, asked so deceptively as if it weren't really important. And her own answer. No. An answer that came from utter conviction. No. She had been sitting with her eyes closed. Now they opened, and the glare of the sun stung them to tears. No one had any reason to kill her any more than the unfortunate housekeeper whose kindness in staying late had made her the victim. If that tough, smug policeman was right, then a lunatic, possessed with a desire to kill, had wandered into the district and fastened on Coolbridge and its lonely occupant as the object of his mania. It was an idea of sickening horror, but it ended there.

She was feeling warmer. There was nothing more to remember, no point in playing back the details of that night. It was time she took up responsibility for herself, and repaid the Fosters for their kindness, Tim for his solicitude, by putting what had happened where it belonged. As a dreadful incident in her life which was best forgotten. She was not going to hide by the swimming pool, indulging herself with fears. She was going to walk round the yard and see the colt she had bought in Ireland, which had arrived yesterday. She was going to talk about that at dinner and forbid anyone to mention the police. And on Sunday, as she had promised, she was going back with Richard. Ten days later, on Wednesday 5 June, she would be at the Derby to see the Silver Falcon win.

II

The voices Isabel had heard did not belong to the police. Nigel Foster was irritated to find Tim and a strange man waiting in the hallway. Tim had introduced them.

'Nigel, this is Dr Graham. An old friend of Charles. He's driven down to see Isabel.' Foster glanced from Tim to the older man. 'Was she expecting you? She's only got up today. Her doctor said . . .'

'I can appreciate that,' Andrew interrupted. 'Believe me, I would not impose myself on you unless it was really very urgent. All I want is a chance to see Isabel for a few minutes.'

Nigel went on being irritated.

'She's just been visited by the police. I shouldn't think she'll feel much like seeing anyone else straight away. I'll go and ask her.' He went into the sitting room, shutting the door on Tim and Andrew.

Andrew didn't say anything. 'I can't find her,' Nigel was back immediately. 'She must have gone out in the yard. Excuse me, Doctor. I'm a bit pushed at this hour of the day.' He stamped off, leaving them.

'Don't mind him,' Tim said. 'It's just pre-Derby nerves. He's been snapping at everyone this morning. We'll go and look for her.'

One of the lads had taken Isabel to see the two-year-old colt. It was the start of evening stables and the yard was full of activity. There was a brisk, cheerful atmosphere. People grinned at her; it was an overspill from the victory at Long-champ and excitement was building steadily about the great

218

day on 5 June. The day after he had won the Prix Lupin, the Falcon's odds had shortened to four to one with the leading bookmakers; every lad in the yard had backed him to win, and the rumours were flying round the pubs about his fitness and improvement since the race. The boy guiding Isabel was seventeen, a round-faced, cheery apprentice, with a strong midlands accent. He had been promised a ride that season, and been given the new colt to 'do'. He brought Isabel to the box and stood aside to let her go in.

'Luvly lad this one, Madam. Manners like a real gennlmun. Not like your other one – can't get too near 'im! C'm on now, there's a good lad – ' The chestnut colt was standing near his haynet; he turned to watch as Isabel came towards him. The beautiful intelligent eye regarded her with interest. The lad had come to his head and slipped on a head collar. He patted him on the neck, and offered him a hand to lick and nibble to keep him occupied.

'Don't even really bite,' he said. 'Big baby, aren't ye – '

Isabel came close and stroked him; his neck was silky, the skin soft and warm to the touch. The affinity she had felt for him in Ireland was even stronger. There was immense dignity and pride in the way he held himself and a true alertness in the splendid eye. But no vice, no stallion savagery looking for the chance to lash out at the human enemy.

There were many emotions contingent upon owning a race-horse, and Isabel had seen most of them. Pride, greed, sentiment, gross commercialism, ambition; and very rarely love and understanding of the animal concerned. Charles had loved his horses and she knew this to be exceptional. But this tenderness towards his mares and foals had never prevented him from getting rid of the unsatisfactory or the barren. Equally his pride in his stallions was in a way an extension of himself. She did something she had never done in her life before at Beaumont. She kissed the colt lightly on his satin nose. There was a faint lipstick smudge on its white muzzle. 'For luck,' she said to the lad. 'I'm delighted with him. Has he travelled well?'

The lad hesitated; the colt hadn't eaten up the night before, and left part of his morning feed. The journey had upset him. But it didn't do to worry owners. He had learnt that much.

'Not a bother on 'um,' he said. 'Never turned an 'air, Madam. Did ye, old lad?'

'Isabel.'

Tim was standing in the doorway, and there was another figure with him, not quite so tall. He moved into clear view and she saw that it was Andrew Graham.

'We've been looking everywhere for you,' Tim said. 'I went to the Falcon's box first. Andrew wants to see you for a few minutes.'

Isabel turned to the stable lad. 'Thanks,' she said. 'I'll see you tomorrow.' The boy saluted, sure of a tip the next day. She was a generous owner, not like some of them. One bugger with three top-class horses never gave more than a pound to the lads who 'did' them. He was lucky to have Mrs Schriber. Never less than a fiver there.

Isabel went out of the box into the evening sunlight. Her heart was beating very fast. 'Hullo, Andrew.' He held out his hand and she took it.

'I'm so sorry about what you've been through,' he said gently. 'I called yesterday to say so. You weren't up to taking the call so I came down. I hear the police were here today – how did it go?'

They were walking slowly back towards the house.

'It was very unpleasant,' Isabel said. 'Horrible. I don't want to talk about it.'

'Do they think they'll catch the killer?' She looked at him and shook her head. 'Do they have any clues?'

'They didn't mention anything. But they don't think it's a burglar.'

'No,' Andrew Graham said. 'I don't think it is either. That's why I came down to see you. I have to see you, Isabel. And I'm sure you know why.'

They had come round the back of the house; they were close to the garden and the swimming pool. Isabel stopped and faced him. She saw that Tim was ranged alongside him and knew that before they found her in the yard, he had been saying to Tim Ryan what he was now trying to say to her. 'I don't know why, Andrew,' she said. 'If it's to talk about what happened, I've already told you, I don't want to discuss it. It's a horrible nightmare, and I want to forget it. I want to forget the whole thing.'

'You wouldn't listen in Paris,' Andrew said. 'For God's sake, Isabel, for your own safety, you've got to listen now.'

'How dare you say that!' Her pulse was racing now. 'Just because this ghastly thing happened, you start bringing up that business about Richard's illness – it was ten years ago and it's got nothing to do with our lives now. I'm going inside.'

She turned and hurried through the garden into the house. They heard the back door bang shut.

'She won't face it,' Andrew said. 'Deep inside she knows, and she won't face it. That's why she had to run away just now. Before I put it into words.'

Tim was very white-faced. 'I'm going to the police,' he said. 'I'll drive up and see Inspector Lewis tonight.'

'No,' Andrew said. 'I'm the one who has to do that. I should have done it yesterday, but I hesitated. Now I know I was wrong. I have the medical record. They'll listen to me.'

'I'll talk to her,' Tim said fiercely. 'I'll bloody well make her listen – '

'Don't,' he advised. 'You might push her into doing something foolish. If she tells him he's suspected anything could happen. He mustn't know. And he won't try anything while she's here. We have a day or two. You leave the police to me. I'll go now; you've got the hotel number. Call me tomorrow.' He turned and walked away; his shoulders were slightly bowed. He looked like a man who had finally lost a long, sad battle which was none of his making.

MacNeil was asleep when the telephone rang. He always slept well, and his subconscious was seldom troublesome. He was one of those people who will insist that in defiance of medical evidence, they never dream. His meal lay heavy in his stomach; a yearning for home had sent him to the German Centre, where he could at least escape the tepid roast meat, sliced paper thin, and neutral vegetables of the hotel cuisine. He liked German food; it had a bite to it and it was very satisfying to a hungry man. He didn't enjoy being in England. Richard Schriber was staying in a pub that called itself a hotel in Lambourn, and Isabel was safe with her trainer and his wife. Andrew Graham had promised to keep him posted about her plans to move out. He was in constant touch with the racing manager. MacNeil had spent the afternoon in the movies watching a grotesquely violent film about the Mafia, come back to his hotel, bathed and gone round to the Centre for dinner. Then he had decided on an early night. When the phone rang beside his bed, his watch showed it was ten minutes to midnight. He switched on the light and grabbed the phone. Only New York would be calling at that time. Unless it was Andrew and something had gone wrong. . . .

It was New York. The voice of his operative Bert Todd came through clearly. Bert was one of his best men; he had worked for the agency for five years, and MacNeil had put him in charge of investigating the background to the Schriber case. He had been gathering information round Freemont, since his return from Barbados. He sent MacNeil regular photocopies of his reports. The originals were on file in the New York office.

'Hi,' MacNeil said. 'I was asleep. How's it going?'

'Hold on to your hat,' Todd answered. 'I've just got back from Freemont. I got an item of news I thought needed looking at, so I went ahead and looked.'

MacNeil sat higher up in the bed, dragged a cigarette out of the packet by his bedside and lit it, cradling the telephone under his jaw. 'Yeah? So let's hear it.' He sat still, drawing on the cigarette. 'You went along to the hospital?'

'Just on a hunch,' Todd was saying. 'You know the kind of thing – something feels wrong. And here's what I turned up.' MacNeil listened for some minutes.

'Jesus!' He exhaled cigarette smoke and the word at the same time. 'This is really beginning to figure – You keep playing those hunches, Bert – '

'What're you going to do?'

MacNeil stubbed out the cigarette. 'I'm going to watch the bastard till he makes another move. And he will. He killed that old woman by mistake. So he'll try again. And I'll be right there with him. Jesus,' he said again. 'Was Mrs Schriber lucky! . . . Okay, Bert – hey, do me a favour, will you – call Alice for me – tell her a big kiss and I'll be in touch but I'm pretty hot on something right now. Okay, thanks.' He put the phone back. He got up and took a notebook out of his briefcase and, with the pillows piled behind him, he began to write.

There was nothing Tim Ryan could do to stop Isabel leaving on Sunday with Richard. He had telephoned Andrew in desperation, and received the same advice. Do nothing; the police were in possession of the medical reports. There was no more anyone could do for the moment; it was vital that Richard shouldn't be alerted. From his reading of the reaction of a psychopath in this situation, he was unlikely to try and harm Isabel until just before the Derby. That was the time to get her away from him. Tim hadn't been satisfied and he said so. And on Sunday morning, as she was packing to leave, he came up to the room to see her.

'Don't go with him,' he said. Isabel was facing him; she had turned pale and he could see that she was making herself angry. As angry as she had been when she walked away from Andrew Graham. And he knew that the motive was the same. She was afraid, and she wouldn't admit to her fear. He had never loved her more than at that moment when she showed how deep, albeit foolish, was her capacity for loyalty to the man she loved. 'Stay here with Sally and Nigel. There's only ten days to go before the race. Why does he want to take you away from here?'

'Wouldn't you, if you were in his place?' she countered. 'He loves me, Tim. He says he wants to take care of me himself.

And I believe him. I'm going with him because I want to.'

He came so very close to telling her the truth, to making her admit there was a hideous question mark over that night at Coolbridge, and until it was answered she should stay where she was safe.

It was a gamble he dared not take; if she rejected his warning, as she had done when Andrew came to see her, and told Richard. . . . He came up and took her hand.

'Nigel wants you to come back and stay here before the race; he wants you to see the Falcon given his final piece of work. You've got to promise that. They're fixing a pre-race party and you've got to be there.'

'I will,' she said. Her hand was tense, and her smile strained. 'We'll both be here. I promise.'

She turned and went out. Nigel and Sally were in the yard, seeing them off. There was a lot of waving and kissing goodbye, in which he took no part. He felt sick and helpless; the sense of premonition came over him so strongly that he couldn't move when Isabel waved to him from the front seat.

Richard sat beside her, smooth and smiling, setting the car in motion. He heard Sally Foster say behind him, 'Isn't it nice to see two people so happy?' Then the car had gone through their white gates and was out of sight. Tim didn't say anything. He turned and walked away from Nigel and his wife and down to the yard. He couldn't rationalize his feelings, but he felt that Andrew Graham was wrong. And he had made a terrible mistake in taking his advice.

MacNeil parked his car on the stretch of road that lies at the junction between Wantage and Hungerford. It was a deserted area, without a house in sight. Ahead stretched the rolling Berkshire downs; the sun had barely risen and there was a dull grey in the sky, shot through with pink and yellow. It was too early for the first strings of horses to be out on the gallops for their morning's work; he had sat in his car smoking, waiting until it was light, and nothing had passed him on the road. It was a very isolated spot, and the place he was walking towards was sheltered by thick-growing hedgerows and a clump of elder trees. MacNeil stepped over the grass; it was wet with the early dew and his shoes glistened. He wore a waterproof coat, buttoned to the neck against the chill of the early morning. Inside the circle of the trees he stopped, and bent down, looking carefully at the ground. It was soft earth, grassy and weed-covered, its surface friable with old leaf mould. At the foot of one of the smaller trees he stopped. He took a trowel out of his pocket and, crouching on his haunches, he began to dig. It didn't take long; the trowel lifted a clod of damp earth and what MacNeil was looking for lay underneath it.

He picked out the little sodden, ball shape, black with soil, and slowly pulled it apart. Two misshapen cotton gloves lay on the ground. He took a small plastic bag out of his other pocket, held it open and dropped the gloves in, holding each one by the fingertips. The plastic bag went into his pocket; he kicked the trowel aside. Then he made his way back to the car, walking slowly, his head bent against an early drizzle of rain which had sprung up. This was the bonus that suddenly made his profession exciting. The hunter's instinct was in full play; he had the quarry cornered and there was nowhere for him to run. He got into the driver's seat and felt in his glove compartment for a cigarette. The bastard; the cunning, crazy bastard. He felt a sense of personal hatred directed at him and all his kind. He wouldn't get the gas chamber in England; more was the pity. They had abolished the death penalty, at the behest of the usual crowd of left-wing commie liberals. He felt, rather than heard, the man rising up from the back seat; he had begun to turn his head when the blow caught him. It was delivered with tremendous force and it broke his neck. The weapon was a heavy stone, wrapped in the newspaper MacNeil had been reading during his early vigil waiting for the dawn. He was a heavy man, but his attacker was very strong; he shifted the dead man into the passenger seat, took his place and started the engine. He drove steadily, making for the top of the downs where the ground fell away in one of the loveliest panoramic views in that part of England. He pulled up on the edge of the road. The sun was fully up and the little rain storm had stopped. He leaned across MacNeil and searched his pockets; he took the plastic bag out of his raincoat. He held it for a moment and then put it in his own coat. Then he dragged the dead man back into position behind the wheel. He paused to look up and down the road; he could see for miles in both directions and there wasn't a car in sight. He switched on the engine, engaged the automatic gear and took off the handbrake. Then he slammed the door shut and stepped back as the car began to move, nose forward across the grass verge and onto the lip of the slope.

Seconds later it was hurtling down into the valley. He watched it bounce and somersault its way, shedding parts of itself, the stillness punctuated by the crash and shatter of metal and glass. And then, as he had been hoping, there was an ugly boom as the petrol tank ignited and the car rolled on down to rest among the distant trees, a mass of flames and acrid smoke. He turned and began the long walk back to where his own car was hidden, parked in a private drive some half a mile from where MacNeil had stopped. He got in, reversed quickly onto the main road and drove off towards London.

'I'm going out for a few minutes,' Richard said. 'You unpack, darling and make yourself at home. I won't be long. I'm going to surprise you!'

He caught hold of Isabel and kissed her. 'Sunday is a hell of a day to shop – ' He had brought her case into his bedroom; she heard him close the flat door, and she turned to look around her. There was plenty of space for her clothes; the room was geared for two people, by the size of the bed and the amount of cupboards. And yet it was a very masculine room, without a sign of female occupation. However many women had stayed there, not one had left a trace. She saw a big bowl of hot-house roses on the chest, and guessed they had been ordered for her.

He had sent her roses that day at the Savoy. It was a smart room, decorated in shades of yellow, with a striking abstract on the wall facing the bed. Yet it was wholly impersonal. There were no photographs, no trivia scattered about. Everything was neat and functional as if a decorator had arranged the room before she came. Her case lay open on the bed; it was full of clothes he had collected from Coolbridge. She didn't want to unpack them. The flat was totally noiseless; its windows double-glazed against the traffic outside. It was like being encapsulated. She went to the door quickly and opened it wide. He had pointed out the drawing room as they came in. She opened that door too and went inside. She hardly noticed the expensive, elegant décor. The first thing she saw was the portrait over the fireplace. Isabel went across the room and stood, looking up at it. The only time she had seen it was in the attic at Beaumont. The oval face, framed in red hair, seemed sadder, more vulnerable; there was a droop about the shoulders, artificially swathed in chiffon. How old was the girl when that was painted – in her early twenties –

Andrew Graham's words came back to her. 'Completely mother-fixated. He worshipped her.' The painted face was innocent, idealized, a boy could look at it and dream, playing out adolescent fantasies in which the lovely image was the heroine. As a middle-aged woman Frances Schriber would have retained that romantic quality; a frightened woman, bullied by her husband, bound to her only child by the guilt of his birth. Frequent suicide attempts, so Andrew said. A hopeless neurotic, feeding on the adoration of her son. And the son growing up to hate his father, so possessive of his mother and so jealous of their relationship that his whole view of life was mentally distorted.

'She doesn't go in this room,' Richard said behind her. 'But I like to have her there.'

Isabel turned slowly round to meet him. He was smiling at her. He came and slipped his arm around her, and they stood and looked at his mother's portrait together.

'She would have loved you,' he said. 'You're just her kind of person.' His face was in profile to Isabel, she glanced up at him. There was a slight smile on his lips; his expression was tender. Their hair was exactly the same shade of red.

He turned away suddenly; his mood had changed completely. It was excited and passionate. He kissed her hard, holding her painfully tight.

'At last I've got you to myself,' he said. 'I'm going to cook lunch for us, and then maybe we'll go to bed – '

She had a sense of unreality; part of her was trying to respond to him. But another part was chilled and apprehensive, taut with nervousness, the part that kept beating at the door of her mind, trying to ask questions. . . .

He stepped back and let her go abruptly.

'Isabel – ' he said slowly. 'There's something wrong. What is it?'

'Nothing,' she denied it quickly. 'Nothing's wrong, don't be silly. Let's have a drink, shall we – '

'You never needed drink with me before,' he said. He shrugged. 'If that's what you want, darling – sit down and I'll open the bottle I bought to celebrate.'

It was Saran Nature, which she didn't want, because it was chilled, and she was cold already. They had drunk it on the boat in Barbados. Just before she nearly drowned. He sat on the big sofa beside her, and after a few moments he gently took her hand.

'What is it? What's the matter, darling. You're not yourself.'

'I'm still shaken by what happened,' she said. 'I can't get it out of mind.'

His arm came round her, cradling her against him. Her body was stiff, resisting him. He felt it, and took his arm away.

'I thought you'd want to be here,' he said. 'I shouldn't have forced you to come. You obviously felt happier with the Fosters.'

'That's not true,' she said. 'I can't stop thinking about that night at Coolbridge. I feel frozen by it. It wasn't even a burglar – it was a homicidal maniac. The police think he'd been watching the house; that he knew I lived there alone and broke in to kill me.' He got up and went to the fireplace; he turned and faced her, standing under the portrait of his mother.

'There's no need to be frightened now,' he said. 'He's hiding somewhere, but they'll get him. You're safe, darling. Safe with me.'

Isabel didn't answer. She sipped the cold wine. She tried to smile at him but her lips were stiff and it felt like a grimace.

The second self was winning. The self that quoted Andrew Graham and Tim: *Don't go with him. For God's sake, for your own safety you've got to listen.* . . . And the policeman, with his quiet voice asking, 'Is there anyone who'd want to kill you?' The killer had known his way around the house. Known what time the housekeeper left, watched her through the uncurtained window, while he crouched naked in the rain. No thief but a madman, crazed with hatred, wielding a heavy spanner. A man possessed by violence which was finally unleashed. A glass, held with such force that it had shattered in his hand, leaving a deep cut. A cut that had been reopened and was bleeding badly. A night that was lost in drink, where he remembered nothing but the homing instinct that took him to Farrant's house in the small hours. The pieces were flying together, like fragments of metal to a magnet, fitting and forming a picture. That sudden request to stay at Coolbridge while she went to Paris. 'He explored all over the house, even the kitchen and the pantries.' Poor dead Mrs Jennings, saying it so innocently. And his reaction when she told him about Andrew's visit to her in Paris. He had gone away that night, leaving her alone in the house.

A psychopathic personality, schizoid tendencies. Fear rushed up and overwhelmed her; she sat immobilized, looking up at him.

He didn't move, he was standing watching her, his glass in his hand.

There was a curious lack of expression on his face. She mustn't let him know; she mustn't arouse his suspicions. If she could get out into the hall and get to the front door. She leaned back on the sofa and prayed to God that nothing of her feelings showed.

'I'm sorry, darling,' she said. 'My nerves have gone to pieces. Could I have a brandy instead of this? I'll be all right then. What are you going to cook for lunch – I didn't know you cooked – ' It sounded forced and insincere; she was trying too hard.

'Bœuf Stroganoff,' he said. 'It's my speciality. They'd forgotten to send the cream and the courgettes. That's what I went out to buy just now. I'll make lunch early and we can have a quiet afternoon. You'll feel more relaxed tomorrow, darling.' His voice was reassuring.

He took the glass of wine away and brought her a balloon with brandy in it. He sat beside her, and to her relief, he didn't touch her. But this was alarming too. He always touched her; he either held her hand or put his arm round her, or sat with his body in close contact. Now there was a deliberate gap between them. He was smiling and concerned but there was something wary about him. She drank some of the brandy.

'That's lovely,' she said. 'Thank you, darling. I'm quite hungry.'

He didn't take the hint. He lit a cigarette. 'Nerves can be hell,' he said. 'No wonder you're so uptight with me. For a moment I was worried. I thought all those lies Andrew told you had come between us. You haven't stopped loving me, have you?'

'No,' Isabel said. 'No, of course not. You mustn't think that. . . . I'm just nervy. . . .'

'You're sure?' he asked her.

'Of course,' she said again. He leaned slowly towards her; he didn't put his hands on her, he just closed his lips on her mouth and kissed her. It lasted a long time. Then he drew back. He touched her face lightly with his index finger.

'That's a good girl,' he said. 'You finish your drink and I'll make lunch for us.' Isabel sat back, sipping the brandy as he went out. He left the door open and she could hear him moving round the kitchen. She stood up. The floor was thickly carpeted and she made no sound. She put the glass down, very gently, moving with exaggerated care; she was trembling, watching the open door. The sense of fear was almost paralysing, it inhibited her power to move quickly. She felt as the dreamer does in the middle of a nightmare, leaden limbed and unable to flee.

'You all right, darling?' His voice made her freeze in the angle of the doorway.

'Yes,' she called out. 'Fine.'

The kitchen was at right angles down a short corridor; the door was wide open and she shrank back as she saw him cross the kitchen and then disappear. The front door was to her left, only a few yards away. She heard a clatter as if he were taking pans out of a cupboard. She fled the short distance to the entrance, wrenched at the catch and dragged the door open. Seconds later she was running down the stairs to the street level, and behind her the door swung back on its hinge and slammed loudly.

She was in the street and it was lunchtime on a Sunday and there was nobody about, no taxis and only the back of a solitary car vanishing down Mount Street. Her heart was drumming so fast that it was difficult to breathe. She had no money, her handbag was left behind in the bedroom. She began to run down the street towards Park Lane; several times she glanced behind her, but there was no one following. He hadn't come after her. She had a terrible feeling that he was watching her flight from the window. At the entrance to Park Lane she saw a cruising taxi and ran towards it, waving. It pulled in and she jumped inside.

'Where to, lady?'

Isabel hadn't thought where she was going. She sank back into the seat, gasping her breath. 'Will you take me to Lambourn,' she said. 'I'll pay double fare. . . .' The driver turned right round in his seat.

'Lambourn – in Berks.? Sorry dear, no way on a Sunday. I'm going home in half an hour.' He leaned out and opened the passenger door for her to get out. Then she remembered where she could go; where she was known. She slammed the door shut quickly.

'Never mind,' she said. 'Take me to the Savoy.'

They gave her a room on the second floor. She shut and locked the door, lay on the bed and after a time she cried. It was more than just a reaction from the dreadful panic of the last hour. She cried for Richard and for herself; for what they had both lost. The rift in his personality was too deep, the balance between sanity and psychosis too precarious. And she herself was responsible for releasing the violent schizoid into full control. She had told him what Andrew Graham had said in Paris.

His reaction was to try and kill her. There was no doubt in her mind now but that he had driven down to Coolbridge, and broken in expecting to find her coming out of the drawing room in the darkness.

Something had to be done, and she couldn't escape that. For his sake as much as to protect herself. She thought of Tim and decided against him. He would have only one solution. The police. Richard didn't need to be arrested, tried, shut up in prison for the rest of his life, or confined in those bleak terms reserved for the insane. 'During Her Majesty's pleasure.' He needed hospital treatment, sympathetic care. There was only one person she could turn to; the man whose advice and help she had rejected. She asked for a call to his hotel. It took some time to find him. He was in the dining room when they paged him.

'It's Isabel,' she said. She wiped her eyes as she spoke. 'Andrew, listen – I'm at the Savoy. I've got to see you. Please come round. It's about Richard.'

She heard his voice change in tone.

'What about him – what's happened?'

'Nothing's happened,' she said slowly. 'But you were right. He needs help, Andrew. Please come over.'

'I'll be with you in half an hour,' he said. 'You're all right? Thank God for that. Just wait for me.'

'I don't know what we *can* do,' Andrew said. He smoothed his thin hair across his scalp. He shook his head, looking at Isabel.

'Not unless he can be made to face the truth. If we could prove to him what he'd done. . . . But he's forgotten it, Isabel. Don't you see? If he killed that poor woman in mistake for you, he's buried it completely from his conscious mind. He has to. Why are you so sure of it now? Did he say or do anything – '

'No,' Isabel said slowly. 'But the moment I let myself think it through I knew. He disappeared that night. He turned up dead drunk at Roy Farrant's house in the middle of the night, not knowing where he'd been or what he'd done. He told me that himself. He'd cut his hand a few days before; when he came down to Lambourn to see me, the cut was reopened and bleeding right through a thick dressing. Hitting someone with a heavy spanner would have opened it up like that. And the police said it was someone who knew his way round that house. Richard had been staying there. It all fits, Andrew; and now I believe it was because I'd told him I knew about his illness.'

'He denied it, of course,' Andrew said quietly. 'I could have told you he would. It was all lies, a conspiracy thought up by Charles and me. Part of him had hated you from the beginning. You took his mother's place. But another part, the normal side of him, fell in love with you. I believe that's true. It kept the schizoid impulses at bay for a time, until you opened the Pandora's box and told him the truth about himself. He had to kill you after that.'

He lit a cigarette. 'Your instinct saved you today,' he said. 'You're a very lucky woman.'

'I want to help him,' Isabel said slowly. 'I want him looked after. Medical science is always discovering new cures. Maybe in a few years something could be done for him – '

'Maybe,' he admitted. 'But I doubt it. I don't see there's anything you can do unless he agrees to commit himself. I could find you a specialist in the States who would take care of him. If you could persuade him to go. Otherwise we'd better go to the police.'

'No,' Isabel said. 'No. I must give him the chance.'

'You still love him, don't you?' Andrew said. He shook his head. 'You won't thank me for saying this, Isabel, but there are many kinds of mental illness. I know insane people who are like saints. Richard is evil. And I believe in evil. There's an old tradition that the people in the Bible who were possessed of the devil were schizophrenics . . .'

Isabel got up. 'I'm going to try and help him,' she said. 'I won't take any risks, but I'll see if I can get through to him. I wish you could pity him, Andrew. But I suppose you can't.'

'The best possible solution for him,' Andrew Graham said quietly, 'would be to go out of this world before he does any more damage. Talk to him, Isabel, but don't ever be alone with him. I'll go now. Call me when you've thought about it.' He got up, and Isabel helped him into his coat. He fumbled for his cigarettes again, stuffed them into his pocket.

'Goodbye,' he said. 'Take very great care.'

'I will,' Isabel said. She watched him button his coat; it was a warm June day, and he didn't really need one.

'Andrew,' she said. 'You've dropped something. Here.'

He turned at the door. 'Oh – yes. Thanks.' He took the plastic bag from her, with the stained and muddied cotton gloves inside and rammed it back in his pocket.

12

Isabel saw him come through the doorway and walk down the short flight of steps into the main lounge bar. Several women turned to look after him as he passed. He came up to the table where she was waiting for him, and she got up. She held out her hand to him.

'Richard – I'm so glad you came.' He looked at her, and the expression was the one she had seen on his face the first time she met him in the study at Beaumont, the morning of Charles's funeral. Cynical and appraising.

He sat down opposite to her.

'It was nice of you to call,' he said. 'I guess you must be feeling better than you were on Sunday. What would you like to drink?'

'Nothing,' Isabel said. 'I wanted to talk to you. To try and explain.' Richard smiled, not really looking at her. He signalled a waiter and ordered himself a double Scotch on the rocks.

'You don't need to explain anything,' he said. 'All of a sudden you were alone with Andrew's psychopathic patient, and you were scared stiff. I quite understand. In fact,' he took a large swallow of the drink, 'I half expected you to run out on me.'

'I'm sorry,' Isabel said slowly. 'I didn't mean to hurt you. Before we say any more, I want you to believe something.'

'Try me,' he said. He finished the drink. 'I'm in a gullible mood.'

'I love you,' Isabel said. 'Nothing has changed that. Nothing ever will.'

He still didn't look at her.

She hesitated; tears were in her eyes. 'Where did you go on Monday night. Before you went to Farrant?'

Richard turned round and stared at her. 'Monday night – I told you – I went to the Claremont and lost money. Then I got drunk. Why Monday night?'

'Richard,' Isabel was almost whispering. 'Richard, darling, didn't you go somewhere else? Didn't you take the car and come back to Coolbridge?'

There was a total silence between them then; the sounds of the busy Savoy bar grew to a crescendo of talk and the subtle clink of glasses became loud. Somebody quite close to them broke into laughter.

Richard leaned a little forward, facing her.

'Let's get this quite straight. You're saying that I went to Coolbridge that Monday night – the night of the murder?'

'Didn't you?' Isabel said. 'Didn't you go down there and didn't something awful happen?' Suddenly she reached out and caught hold of his hand. The tears overflowed. 'Oh, darling, darling, don't you see it wasn't your fault – you couldn't help it – you're not well. . . . I love you and I only want to help you. . . .'

He stared at her; his eyes narrowed and suddenly went wide. Then to her astonishment he laughed.

'Good Christ,' he said. 'You think I murdered that poor old woman!'

'Please trust me,' she begged. 'I won't tell anybody. I just want to help you. Tell me, darling – tell me the truth – '

He didn't speak for a moment. He finished the whisky. 'Tell you I did it? Say I had some kind of brainstorm and beat old Mrs Jennings to death? Is that what you want me to say?'

He picked up the empty glass again and held it in both hands, staring into it. His voice was low.

'And if it was true,' he said. 'If I admitted it – what would you do, Isabel?'

'Take you back to the States with me,' she said. 'Get the best doctors – anything in the world. . . .'

'Well,' he said at last. 'You do love me don't you – that's something, anyway.'

She looked at him. 'Richard – please – '

'It so happens,' he said, 'that after the Claremont, where I was playing backgammon in front of a room full of people, I went on to Tramps, where I got very drunk and started swinging a chair at the manager when he asked me to go home. That I know because I got a bill for the damage yesterday and a nice little note saying they hoped I would resign my membership. I didn't actually have time to kill anyone last Monday.'

She couldn't believe it; she stared at him, and she couldn't find words. 'I have the bill and the letter on me,' he said. He put them in front of her, and beckoned the waiter. 'Go on,' he said. 'Read them.'

'Richard,' Isabel said at last. 'Oh God, what have I done?'

'Proved that I should have told you the truth a long time ago,' he said. He leaned across and took her hand. 'So that's why you ran away on Sunday – you thought I'd killed Mrs Jennings. And you've been staying here trying to figure out how to get me doctored up and cured. . . .' He shook his head. 'Like I said, you really do love me, don't you?'

She nodded. 'I don't know what to say to you,' Isabel said at last. 'Except to ask you to forgive me.'

His expression was grave. 'I think I can manage that,' he said. 'Tell me, darling, how did you work this out – who put this lovely idea into your mind?'

'I'm not sure,' she said. 'Andrew kept hinting . . . he kept saying you were dangerous, that I had to be careful – Mrs Jennings told me you went all over the house, into every room – the police said whoever killed her knew his way about. You disappeared that night, nobody could find you – your hand was opened up again and you couldn't remember where you'd been – oh darling, it all seems so flimsy and ridiculous when I put it into words – '

'So Andrew started it,' he said. 'That figures. Let's take it point by point. You were shown a medical file in Paris, saying

I had a history of mental illness – right? Potentially dangerous – ' Isabel nodded. She felt shamed and numb. 'So the doubt was there. And that bastard played on it. We'll come to him in a minute. Sure I went through every room in Coolbridge. I was planning to buy it for you as a wedding present. I'd already cabled the owners in South Africa. As for my hand – swinging the chair around at Tramps opened that up; I bled over their carpet and they're billing me for that too.'

'I don't understand,' Isabel said. 'Why would Andrew try to make me think it was you? Even if you were ill, it was years ago. . . .'

'For the same reason he and my father got me shut up,' Richard said quietly. 'To protect themselves. To make sure nobody would believe me if I told the truth.' He took out two cigarettes and lit them, handing one to Isabel.

'My mother took an overdose, that's true. I was out the night it happened, but she'd left a note for me in my room. She'd decided to leave Charles. She'd been contacted by my real father. His wife was dead and he was in the States. She tried to tell Charles, and there was a terrible scene. He threatened to kill the other man. She could never stand up to him, and she just went to pieces, I guess. She asked me to forgive her for what she was going to do.' Isabel said nothing; his hand was gripping hers so tightly that it hurt.

'When I went into her room she was still alive,' he said. 'I ran down, yelling for Charles. He was in the study with Andrew. They were sitting there, drinking. I'll never forget it. He got in front of the telephone and wouldn't let me call an ambulance. He looked me in the eye, and told me she was dead. And I knew what they were doing. They were leaving her there to die. I went berserk. I hadn't a chance against the two of them. Andrew jabbed me full of dope. There was nothing I could do, Isabel. They timed it just right. She died on her way to the hospital. Next morning I walked into Freemont police headquarters and accused them both of murder.'

The waiter approached, asking if they needed any more to

drink. A famous television personality walked past their table, a phallic cigar in his mouth.

'You can guess how much sympathy I got. They called up Beaumont and Charles came down with Andrew and they explained I'd blown a fuse when I found my mother dead. I was driven to Graneways nursing home in a police car. And I went wild. It was exactly what they wanted; Andrew got two doctors he knew to examine me, and I played right into his hands. I accused him and Charles of murder, I threatened to kill them, I was violent as hell. Andrew's friends signed the certificates and I found myself in a padded room. I was nine months in that place.'

'Oh my God,' Isabel whispered. He wasn't over-dramatizing; his voice was calm, unemotional. But the words were making pictures in her imagination; that charming, panelled study at Beaumont, so closely associated with Charles – she had often remembered him there, sitting in his favourite leather chair. She wondered if he was sitting in it that night, when he deliberately left his wife to die. The big bedroom with its magnificent views over the paddocks, where he had been nursed and comforted right to the end. Richard's mother had died there too, but alone and by murderous design. And the lies, the conspiracy of lies surrounding Richard. She shuddered, and Richard felt the tremor.

'If it hadn't been for my Duckett grandmother,' he said, 'I'd never have gotten out. But she hated Charles and she got a court order releasing me. By that time I knew I had to play it very cool. I didn't repeat the accusation. I made sure I was calm and reasonable, because I knew damned well that nobody would believe me if I tried to tell the truth. Not even her. And Charles knew it too. They had a medical file on me and I'd been nine months in a mental home. He didn't fight my grandmother; she took me away and I lived with her for a year. Then she died, and I took off for Europe. There was nothing I could do, Isabel. They'd killed my mother and gotten away with it. And they'd discredited me for ever. But even so, Charles took precautions. He didn't hide what had happened.

He made sure everyone knew what I'd told the police, and the whole neighbourhood was just so sorry for him. First his wife and then a son like me. It all helped the noble image; and he loved that. What he didn't like was the publicity I gave him. It wasn't much of a revenge but I took it. I smeared his name in every newspaper in the States. He knew why. But I was out of his reach and there was nothing he could do to stop it. Of course he had to make sure you didn't get anywhere near me.'

'The same for Andrew too,' she said slowly. 'How could I have lived with Charles for three years and actually loved him – without really knowing him at all. . . .'

'Because he'd convinced himself of his own legend,' Richard said quietly. 'He was an old man, and he'd won all the battles. He could afford to live up to the hero image. He probably loved you in his own way because you were a part of it. And you know something, darling? That really used to rile me – the thought of you loving him. It doesn't any more. I've lived with hate for too long. I'm sick of hating him. I came back to Beaumont because I was curious to see you and because I wanted to stand over him and gloat. He was dying of cancer and he wasn't going to see his Falcon win the Derby. And I made up my mind he wasn't going to win from the grave if I could help it. I didn't want the horse to run; I didn't want him to have his place in racing history because I knew it meant so goddamned much to him. And then I fell in love with you, and things started getting back into proportion. I saw what I was doing didn't make sense. You can't frustrate the dead. Any more than you can raise them. I'd never loved any woman except my mother until I met you. That wasn't easy to face. I'd made a shrine to her in my mind and all of a sudden the image was fading. You'd taken her place. Do me a favour, Isabel. Take off that ring of his.'

She looked down at the diamond on her hand. 'Yes,' she said. 'I will. I'll never wear it again.'

'Try this instead. I bought it when you were staying at Lambourn. It was going to be my surprise for you on Sunday.'

It was a simple ring, set in gold. Two hearts, a ruby and an emerald, surrounded by small diamonds. It was exquisitely made by a nineteenth-century craftsman.

'I hope you like it,' he said. 'It seemed your style. Now that you know I don't go round killing people, when are you going to marry me? After the Derby?'

'Whenever you like,' she said quietly. 'What about Andrew – Isn't there anything you can do – '

'No. Forget about him,' Richard said. 'He's failed, and he'll find out soon enough. He'll creep back to the States and maybe he won't sleep too well for a while. To hell with him. To hell with everything about Beaumont and Charles and everyone but ourselves.'

Isabel had moved into the flat with Richard. When they went to bed, she found herself too nervous to respond to him properly. The shock of what she had discovered was taking toll; Richard sensed it and made no demands upon her.

She went over what Richard had told her, again and again, in the early hours while he slept. Murder, coldly premeditated on a helpless woman, motivated by insane pride and jealousy. Charles wouldn't let her go, because it would damage his image, reduce him in status before his admiring world at Freemont. And Andrew had helped him kill her. The good friend, the family doctor; always advising her in his slow way on how to do this and that in the way her husband liked it. . . .

She shivered physically, remembering. He was dominated by Charles, mesmerized by his money and his power. And then to certify Richard! Nine months in a mental home. He had spoken of a padded room. And his necessity to suppress the truth, in order to achieve his freedom; unable even to confide in his own grandmother, because his credibility had been destroyed. She found herself in tears. Andrew had spread the poison well. She had actually believed the man she loved was guilty of an atrocious murder, and fled from him in terror of her own life. Even when the police questioned her, the doubt was in the depth of her mind, suppressed but growing, that the maniac they talked about was really Richard Schriber. And whoever it was, some madman with a lust to kill, still wandered undetected. . . .

Richard woke to find the bed empty, and instantly he leaped out and went to look for her. He found Isabel in the kitchen, sitting at the table drinking coffee.

'I couldn't sleep,' she said. 'I'm sorry, darling, my mind is going round and round. I didn't mean to wake you.'

Richard put his arm around her.

'It's not surprising,' he said gently. 'Drinking that stuff won't help – people take it to keep awake – I'll make you some milk.'

They didn't talk, he sat smoking and watching her while she sipped the hot drink. 'It's just been a bit too much for you, all at once,' he said.

'I started thinking about the murder at Coolbridge,' Isabel said. 'They haven't found that man yet. I'm just being hysterical, I suppose, but it really got on my nerves, lying there in the dark; and thinking about your mother and what happened to you.'

'Don't think about it,' Richard said firmly. 'I told you, darling, it's all over. Charles is dead, Andrew is just a paper tiger now you know the truth – let the past lie. We've got everything to look forward to; forget what happened. And don't worry about that business at Coolbridge. It was a madman, and they'll get him. You must put that right out of your mind. Promise me?'

'I'll try,' she said.

He kissed her. 'Come back to bed,' he said. 'You'll be asleep in a few minutes. We'll stay quiet here for the next couple of days, give you time to settle down. After all, you'd better get used to living with me properly.'

On the evening of the second day they telephoned Nigel Foster, and Isabel spoke to Tim. 'Everything has been sorted out,' she said. 'I can't explain over the phone, but I'm going to marry Richard.' There was a long pause, and Ryan said nothing. 'Tim? Listen, I promise to tell you the whole story. After the Derby, yes. Tell Nigel, will you – Oh, all right, wait a minute.' She turned to Richard. 'They're giving the Falcon his work over a mile and a quarter on Saturday. Nigel wants us to come down – there's a party in the evening.'

'That's fine,' he said. 'Tell Tim to book us into the hotel on Friday night if Sally can't put us up. I know those early-morning work-outs in the middle of the night!'

'What time is he going out?' Isabel asked, watching Richard. She nodded at him and smiled. 'Around seven in the morning – yes, yes I was going to ask – tell Sally thanks, we'd love to stay. See you on Friday.'

She came and put her arms round Richard. 'I couldn't get you near a racing stable a few weeks ago. You sounded almost enthusiastic just now.'

'I'm a changed man,' Richard said lightly. 'Changed, note, not reformed. As far as I'm concerned, you own the Falcon and I want him to win as much as you do. You're looking better, you know that? You've got your colour back. I was worried about you the last two days.'

'You needn't be,' Isabel said. She leaned her head against his cheek, holding him. 'I've been thinking so much about it all and everything is making sense at last. I love you, Richard. I think we're going to be very happy.'

'I know we are,' he said.

Andrew Graham put down the telephone; he looked at it for a moment as if it were alive, his forehead puckered, his mouth drawn into a grimace. His right hand was sweating all over the palm; there was a dewy mark on the black surface of the receiver set. He had just finished speaking to Tim Ryan at Lambourn.

He had been waiting two days to hear from Isabel. He hadn't telephoned her; it seemed wiser to let the initiative come from her. Then he could suggest a meeting, make a plan. And a plan which wouldn't go wrong like the other one. The trouble was, the housekeeper had been about the same height and the hall at Coolbridge was dark. . . . He went backwards from the telephone and suddenly the hotel room was unbearably stuffy and confined. He had a sensation near to claustrophobia. He grabbed his room keys from the bedside table and hurried out. He went quickly through the reception hall; people had got used to him coming and going, and several had spoken to him. He had heard one elderly woman remark to her husband what a charming man the American doctor was. So full of Southern courtesy. He didn't want to speak to anyone. He wanted to get outside, somewhere where there was space. He went to Kensington Gardens, just as he had the first day he arrived. He walked quickly, brushing against people. He found a seat at the edge of the Round Pond, which was said to be famous, though he couldn't see why. He sat down, and crossed one leg over the other. His foot trembled. Isabel was going to marry Richard Schriber. That was what Tim Ryan had told him. He had hardly listened to the Irishman's exclamations of alarm. She sounded confident and happy. He remembered a single phrase. *One day Tim would know the whole story.* That was her promise and it could only mean one thing. She knew. Richard had told her the truth and she had believed him. The façade he had so cleverly built around Richard had collapsed. He closed his eyes for a moment; it was a very sunny day and the light reflected from the water was strong. Two little girls were at the edge, throwing bread to some excited ducks. She was going to marry him. And that meant he would never inherit the money. He could recall his wife complaining about the will and his own defence of Charles. You don't equate friendship in terms of money. He had tried hard to convince her that he meant it. But he had expected gratitude for letting Frances Schriber die. He had expected money to be left to him. A strange man, Charles. A great man, of course, with a powerful personality that dominated. But even so his wife had slipped away with someone else and borne that lover a child. And had rejected Andrew. He opened his eyes again; he had a tendency to drift lately, to confuse things like time and place. It was the strain of the past few days. It had been a tremendous strain, even for someone as tough and resilient as himself. He had been quite handsome when he was young; he rode well to hounds and he had a good figure. A lot of women had found him attractive. And he had sensed very quickly that Charles's young wife was unhappy. He hadn't rushed anything either. He came to Beaumont with Joan, and they made up parties for bridge and talked horses with Charles, while he watched Frances Schriber and longed and hoped. It was a summer evening when he made his move; it was carefully planned to coincide with Charles taking a trip to the Sales at Keenland. Frances had been alone in the house when he called. Remembering that night caused him so much humiliation that even now, sitting by the lake in an English park, he winced. He had tried to make love to her, and she had refused him. With such scorn and anger; it made him realize that he had totally misjudged her friendliness. Her accusation of disloyalty to Charles, his great friend, frightened him, because Charles was so powerful and such a dangerous enemy. To save himself, Andrew had been humble, almost servile in his apology. She had kept her promise not to mention it to her husband, but her contempt for him was in her eyes every time they met. If he had been in love with her before, he grew to hate her from that moment. And when Charles came to him for a minor examination and he discovered his sterility, he hadn't been able to resist the chance to expose Frances and her child. It had been a long punishment for her acceptance of another man instead of him; Charles had made her suffer. And he was glad. Glad when her health began to break, when her spirit wilted. And he hated her son as much as Charles did; he was a symbol of failure to them both. And at the end, because it was the ultimate revenge, he had let her die. She wasn't going to leave Charles and go to someone else. When Charles poured out the whole story of his marriage, his loathing for her and for her bastard son, he had known what Charles wanted, what his appeal for help and friendship really meant. And he had said the words that Charles wanted to hear.

'She's beyond helping anyway. I guess we let her pass away in peace.' And he had put his arm round Charles's shoulders and seen the relief, and the gratitude in his eyes. They hadn't reckoned on Richard returning. It hadn't been too difficult; both of them acted quickly, and the boy, crazy with grief and suspicion, had made it so very easy for them. . . .

Andrew stared at the ducks on the water. The children had gone, and the birds circled, looking for food. Charles had never mentioned money.

But he had talked of his gratitude. What they had done was never put into words. He spoke of the way Andrew had cared for his wife, and his sick son, and Andrew played the game with him, shrugging it off as the least he could do for the family. It was almost as if the truth receded and its place was taken by the lies they told each other and the world. He made Andrew feel indispensable, his closest friend. And he was grateful. He made sure Andrew understood that. And then he married again.

An Englishwoman, twenty-seven years younger. An outsider. It had been easy to dislike and suspect her. More difficult to justify it as the marriage proved successful. He hated her. He was jealous. As jealous as a woman, whose lover has found someone else. His friend had shifted his allegiance. And she was a threat, a threat to the expectations which he had taken for granted. Charles was older than he was, godfather to one of their children. He owed Andrew a great deal. Even if he had remarried, carried away into folly by an old man's lust, he would remember that debt. But he hadn't. He had left the kind of will one might expect from a man with a clear conscience. Twenty millions to a woman who had given him three years. She didn't even lose a dollar of it if she married someone else. Only if she died in a specified time, unmarried. Then Andrew got what was rightfully his. And Charles himself had told him the terms of that will. A month before his death, sitting propped up in the bed where Frances had been left to die, he told Andrew that he had left everything to Isabel. Nothing to Andrew. Nothing to his godson. Not a red cent to anyone. It was that day, driving home to his own house, that Andrew had made up his mind to kill her. And again, he hadn't reckoned on Richard.

Richard coming back, raising his mother's ghost. And incredibly, pursuing his stepmother. If he married her, that would be the ultimate injustice. That Richard should be the instrument chosen by Fate to deprive him of the money. . . . They were going to be married, so Ryan had said. After the Derby. It had come so close to working out. Then he had made the first mistake and killed the housekeeper that night. Even that was not irretrievable. It had cast suspicion upon Richard; it had almost brought Isabel into his reach. MacNeil had been the greatest danger. It was pure chance that he discovered what MacNeil was doing. Driving down to Lambourn on his way to warn Isabel against Richard, he had noticed a black Ford Cortina following him along the road to Hungerford. He had decided to bury the gloves somewhere on the downs. It was too dangerous to try and dispose of them in the hotel, and they had stayed in the boot of the car. That worried him. If there was an accident, if anyone broke open the boot when it was parked in the street outside the hotel. He had decided to get rid of them early that morning. And he had found just the place. A secluded belt of trees, where nobody would notice him digging a shallow hole. There was no car behind him then. Nothing aroused his suspicion until he saw the same black Ford come out of a turning when he left Foster's yard. It hadn't appeared to follow him. He lost it quite soon, but the sight of it reappearing made him uneasy. And that night, putting his own car into the hotel car park, he had seen it there. It was the hall porter who told him it belonged to MacNeil. Then he knew MacNeil had seen him go into the little copse. That the detective, far from shadowing Richard, was following him.

So he had reversed the roles, and followed MacNeil. God knew how he had found out or how much he knew. Or what his motive was. Probably blackmail. But Andrew had killed him, so for the moment he was safe.

He found himself unable to think too far ahead. Too much had happened and was going to happen. The Derby, with Charles's horse bidding for the greatest racing prize in the world. Isabel, moving nearer to marriage – events were crowding him. The goal had seemed so near only an hour or so ago, until he spoke to Ryan. It would have been easy to kill her; he had planned it all so carefully. A meeting to discuss what could be done about Richard, a drink in her suite. Enough barbiturate in it to make her sleep – a tragic suicide, brought on by shock after the murder. . . .

But not now. She wouldn't let him get within a mile of her now. And there were only four days till the Derby. He felt in his pocket. The little plastic bag was there. Imagine dropping it in front of her – his mouth widened in a mirthless smile. If she had known what was inside it. . . . He clasped his hands together and then released them, flexing the fingers. They had all made a fool of him, in their different ways. Counting him for nothing. Charles, Frances, Isabel, even MacNeil.

But he wasn't going to be cheated. He was going to have what was rightly his. Charles had made use of him; he admitted that, bitterly. And let him down in the end. He wasn't going to get away with it.

None of them were. He had four days left. He got up slowly. Two women walking past him turned to stare. He didn't know it but he had been talking to himself. He began to walk away from the Round Pond towards the muffled frenzy of the London traffic.

Seven a.m. on Saturday 1 June and the horsebox carrying three horses from Nigel Foster's yard wound its way up to the Lambourn gallops.

It was a glorious morning, crisp and fresh, the green sweep of the downs sparkled with the early dew and the sun was raising a very light mist over the ground. Nigel, with Isabel, Tim and Richard, followed the box in a Range Rover.

'Here we are,' he said. 'I'll pull in here and see them unboxed, then we'll drive on ahead and get ourselves positioned before they come up.' He turned up a rough track, and the big horsebox was already stopped, its side ramp lowered, lads busy getting the saddles out, watched by the travelling head lad.

Minutes later a bright green TR7 shot up the road like an iridescent beetle, swung in behind the Range Rover, and a very small, wiry figure in jodhpurs and sweater climbed out, a tweed cap pulled at an angle on his head. 'Morning – ' he greeted Nigel, nodded to Tim, and shook hands with Isabel. 'Morning, Mrs Schriber.' Jimmy Carlton was a head shorter than she was; he had been Champion Jockey twice. He had always ridden Charles's horses in England, as the great Jean-Martin rode them in France. He had a wide, gap-toothed grin and bright brown eyes; he was known for speaking his mind to owners and trainers if he was given a bad horse. He was a superb horseman and famous for his stylish riding of a finish. He had agreed to come down and give the Silver Falcon his work over a mile and a quarter, before riding him in the Derby.

Two of the horses were out of the box, stamping and fretting while they were saddled up. Then the Falcon came down the ramp.

He didn't hurry; he stepped down and stood on the ground, glancing from right to left, the lad holding him at his head. A big bay colt who was to work with him moved sideways, and the Falcon's ears went back. His iron-grey coat was shining like gunmetal, and as he moved the muscles in his body showed taut under the skin.

'He looks well,' the jockey remarked.

'He's cherry ripe,' Nigel Foster said. 'All right, Harry, let's get him saddled up – '

It took two lads to hold him while the saddle was put on and the girth tightened. Isabel watched him, her arm linked through Richard's. The horse had a quality that generated excitement, fear and pride; the ownership of so much beauty, ferocity and power carried a sense of awe. She made no move towards him; there was no personal relationship possible between that horse and any human being except constant warfare on his part and vigilance on the other. He was man's enemy, and his servant. The other two horses were saddled up and mounted; they fretted and jigged, waiting to walk off down the road towards the gallops. The jockey was swung into the saddle by Nigel and gathered up the reins. The lad holding the Falcon backed away and the grey colt swung round, dancing with impatience, testing the skill of the man on his back. Carlton had beautiful hands, firm and yet gentle; they settled the colt into a swinging walk in the wake of the others, their hooves clattering along the empty road.

'By God that's some horse,' Tim Ryan said, almost to himself. He turned and went back to the Range Rover, holding the door open for Isabel. He didn't look at Richard as he climbed in beside her.

Ever since she had announced that she and Richard were getting married, his spirits had been at their lowest ebb. She was too happy, too confident in her decision to listen to anything except congratulations. And sensing that he was unenthusiastic, she had put her hand on his arm and repeated her promise that one day soon, she would tell him everything. Miserably anxious for her, and heartsick for himself, he had telephoned Andrew. Graham had said very little. To Tim's questions about the police, he had been negative, even defeatist. They weren't considering Richard seriously. There was nothing to be done. The great grey colt had raised his spirits for the first time in days. As a professional he couldn't hide his satisfaction, and as a true racing man he longed for the contest between the horse he had nursed and directed since it was a yearling, with this one race in view. With a quarter of a million dollars added if he won. . . .

They drove past the horses, keeping carefully to the far side of the road. Their heads turned to watch the grey as they drew away. He was leading the file, dancing as lightly as a silver leaf, the power and thrust of his compact body perfectly controlled by the rider. Nigel grinned, returning to his concentration on the road ahead.

'Won't even walk behind another horse,' he muttered.

Tension was growing in the yard as the hours ran into each other and the days before the great race shortened. So much depended upon how the horse worked over the mile and a quarter that morning. His performance would not only determine his chances, but whether he ran at all. A lack-lustre gallop, any indication that the horse was not in the peak of spirits and physical condition would put his fitness to race in doubt. And the thoroughbred, as highly tuned to pitch perfection as any racing machine constructed by man, was notoriously unpredictable. A change in blood condition, the presence of a sub-virus lurking in the system, an unsuspected strain in the fragile legs which were expected to carry their two-ton burden across the turf at a speed of forty miles an hour – any one of these imponderables could emerge during or after that gallop and change everything. It was not surprising that Nigel had shouted at his staff that morning and kept Sally up half the night going to the lavatory, switching on lights and generally expressing intolerable nervous tension. 'We'll pull in here,' he said to Isabel. 'Then we can walk across to the bushes at the final furlong. We can see them perfectly most of the way from there.'

The sun was higher and the early ground mist had evaporated. It was a perfect June morning and the panorama of the gallops unrolled before them as they walked to the edge of the line of little bushes, no more than eighteen inches high and spaced to mark the distances. The ground rolled and swelled to the right, coming up into a testing incline for the last three furlongs. Isabel had a feeling of tightness in her throat; Nigel and Tim were both silent, yet intently listening. The horses were approaching from a hidden angle. They would begin their work just below the dip, and out of sight for the first hundred and fifty yards. Richard gripped her arm. Nigel a flat tweed cap pulled low over his forehead, a husky waistcoat buttoned to his chin, stood with his legs astride, arms folded, tensely waiting. There wasn't a sound to be heard. Suddenly Tim thrust his head back.

'I can hear them!' Isabel, straining, couldn't distinguish anything. But from the sudden pressure on her arm she knew that Richard could. And then it came to them, borne in the ground under their feet before it was discernible to the ear. The thud of galloping horses; and then clearly below them, rounding the swell in the green turf which had hidden them, a group of three horses, closely bunched, with the head of the Falcon protruding like a prow just in front. Tim raised his field glasses, Nigel, clear-eyed as a hawk, was leaning slightly forward, hissing under his breath. It was not meant to be a race; its purpose was to demonstrate the horse's peak of fitness and to bring him to a physical pitch which would need a final six-furlong gallop the day before the Derby to complete his preparation. But it was becoming a race. The iron-grey head was stretching forward, the ears flattened against his skull. The Falcon was to be allowed to go ahead from three furlongs out, but not at full stretch. A lot depended upon the ease with which he cruised past his companions. The jockey sat on top of him, perched in perfect balance and control above his withers, not moving, holding him in check.

'Christ,' Nigel kept muttering, 'Christ, he's pulling like a train. . . .'

And then the three-furlong bush was in sight; the noise of the flashing hooves had become a furious drumming, and as they watched, the Falcon started to draw clear as if someone had released a spring. There was nothing smooth about the way the horse emerged from the middle of the group. It was the same rocket-like propulsion he had shown in the Prix Lupin, an enormous surge of energy and speed. He thundered past them, drawing lengths clear of the others, Carlton pulling him up.

'Fantastic! Bloody fantastic – ' Nigel and Tim were exulting together. Richard turned to her. There was a look of excitement in his face which had never been there before when watching a horse.

'I've never seen anything like him,' he said. 'He left the others standing. Come on, darling, they're coming back now.'

The horses had pulled up and were walking back, led by the Falcon. Nigel and Tim had run on ahead; they were talking to the jockey, who was leaning down, patting the colt's steaming neck.

'No problem,' he was saying. 'Soon as I let him have an

inch, away he went – he's got more acceleration than anything I've come across. He'll do the job all right on Wednesday!' The wide mouth split into a grin which included Isabel. 'You've got a nice horse here, Madam – ' Isabel came close to the colt's head. The eye showed a rim of white and the ears flattened. He was jigging about impatiently, his nostrils dilated and reddened inside, the tracery of veins in relief under his coat.

Nigel turned to Isabel. 'Look at that – ' he said. 'Not blowing hard enough to blow out a bloody candle!' He was patting the colt on the neck, ignoring the horse's evident resentment at being touched.

'All right,' Nigel said. 'You walk on back to the box. We'll go ahead and wait for you.' He linked his arm through Isabel's for a moment. He wasn't a man who was very demonstrative, except to Sally, but he was so pleased he couldn't contain himself.

'We're going to do them,' he said. 'We're going to murder the lot of them on Wednesday! There isn't anything to touch him!'

They drove back to the place where they had left the box. Isabel and Richard stayed behind in the Range Rover while Tim and Nigel got out to oversee the loading up of the horses.

'We're going to win,' Isabel said. 'I knew it after the Lupin. That horse is a freak – I've never seen anything pull out a turn of foot like that – '

Richard grinned at her. 'You sould like a seasoned campaigner,' he said. 'Remember what I said in Barbados – I didn't want you to end up knee deep in manure and married to Tim? I can see I'm the one who's going to need the wellington boots!'

'You're just as excited as I am,' Isabel reproved him. 'So don't pretend. It's a pity the Falcon hates people so much, but maybe that's what makes him want to win. Charles always said the great horses are the ones who would have led the herd in the wild state; you have to have the same aggressive spirit to beat the other horses on the track.'

'Darling,' Richard said gently. 'I grew up at Beaumont. I lived and breathed horses from the moment I was born. I do know what makes a great racehorse. And they don't all have to be bastards like Falcon.'

'I'm sorry,' Isabel said quickly. 'I'm just getting Derby fever that's all. Everything's turned out so wonderfully well for us – and I'm so happy!' Nigel, his horses safely loaded up and the box on its way, turned back to the Range Rover with Tim following. He stopped and caught his arm. Isabel and Richard were clearly visible.

'Uhm,' Nigel coughed. 'Time those two got married.' He didn't notice the expression on Tim's face or the fact that he didn't answer.

The party that Saturday night was held in the Fosters' garden. Sally Foster was an accomplished hostess; she didn't particularly like entertaining, but she did it as efficiently as she did her husband's accounts. There were sixty people invited, including all the leading trainers in the Lambourn area and their wives, some of them with horses running against the Falcon in the Derby. The party was in Isabel's honour and about half-way through, Nigel called for silence and announced his owner's engagement to Richard. Somebody raised a cheer, and immediately they were both surrounded. One flamboyantly pretty blonde, eyes bright with Moët and Chandon, kissed Isabel, who had never seen her before. They stood together, in a group of well-wishers that eddied and flowed around them in the Fosters' pleasant garden, the sun dipping behind the line of trees, radiating happiness. Tim stood a little apart, watching them. Somebody touched him on the arm; it was one of the Fosters' small daughters. There was a telephone call for him. He was glad to escape into the house, to leave Isabel and Richard, arms linked, laughing and holding court. It all looked so marvellous, and yet he couldn't rid himself of the most unhappy premonition. A feeling of coming disaster that was quite separate from his own jealousy. He took the call in Nigel's office. It was Andrew Graham.

There was only one incident that shadowed a very gay weekend. Inspector Lewis telephoned, asking for an appointment to see Isabel in London. She agreed to meet him on Monday afternoon, giving him Richard's address. He tried to be brief on the telephone, unwilling to be drawn, but she managed to elicit one answer. There were no further clues as to the identity of the man who had killed her housekeeper. Nothing fresh had turned up. Which was one of the reasons he wanted to talk to her. She might have remembered something else; like last time – Isabel saw Tim waiting for her as she came out of Nigel's office.

'Any news,' he said. He looked strained and awkward. 'Have they found anything – '

'No,' Isabel said. 'Nothing. They want to see me again in case I've got anything new to tell them.'

Tim hesitated. 'You're sure they don't think whoever it was might try again – '

Isabel stood still. 'No,' she said. 'It wasn't directed at me; I convinced them of that last time. I told you, the Inspector didn't mention anything new. They've run out of clues.' She turned and walked away, leaving Tim Ryan standing in the hall. Exactly as Andrew Graham had said. The police hadn't turned up anything and they hadn't taken his proposition seriously. And Isabel wouldn't listen. . . . That's why he, Tim, was her last hope.

The hotel receptionist called out to Andrew Graham as he walked across the hotel lobby. 'Dr Graham – could you spare me a moment?'

He nodded. 'Of course. What can I do for you?'

'It's about one of our guests. A Mr MacNeil.' The half-smile of enquiry on Andrew's face went a little stiff.

'Yes?' he said mildly. The woman looked uncomfortable.

'He seems to have disappeared,' she said. 'He hasn't checked out and his luggage is all there. I've seen you talking together and I wondered whether you knew where he'd gone . . . he didn't say he was going away or anything. I can't understand it.'

'That's odd,' Andrew said. 'I thought he would have told you . . . he's gone to France, and he didn't want to take all that baggage with him. He asked me to take care of things, and we're going to meet up in Paris at the end of next week. Maybe he expected me to say something – I must have gotten it confused. But that's how it is; there's nothing to worry about. Did he settle the bill – otherwise I can do it. . . .'

'Well,' she hesitated. Being owed money, and having a room which couldn't be let, outweighed the doubts about letting the other American take charge. They were friends; it must be all right. Anyway if he'd had the manners to tell her before going off. . . . A nasty, brusque type, typical Yank. She leaned over the counter and smiled at Andrew. 'Thank you very much, Dr Graham. I'll make up his bill along with yours. Just make sure he pays you – what about the luggage?'

'Just send someone up with me and I'll take it all into my room. And I'll be leaving myself around ten o'clock on Wednesday morning. I'll settle both the bills then.'

'Sorry to lose you,' she said. 'I hope you've enjoyed your stay in London. Maybe we'll see you again?'

'I hope so,' Andrew said. 'I've been very comfortable. Next time I'll bring my wife.'

As Andrew had suspected, MacNeil had made notes. He sat in his room surrounded by MacNeil's cases, and prised open the black briefcase which he had found in a drawer. He adjusted his glasses and sat down to read. He had been puzzled by MacNeil's discovery of him. He couldn't think what had made him suspicious in the first place. He was also surprised at the amount of investigation that had been undertaken behind his back, home in Beaumont. There were pages of photocopied reports which had come in from the States. He read through them slowly. Frances Schriber's suicide. The accusation of murder made by Richard, and his subsequent certification. Gossip gleaned from servants, interviews with friends. All gained by a clever ruse. The investigator had posed as a journalist writing an article on Charles for one of the major news magazines. People had fallen over themselves to talk. And in Mac-Neil's own handwriting, he read of the doubt which started it all. He had looked up the terms of Charles's will, and seen the clause there which nobody else appeared to have noticed. If Isabel died unmarried within two years, Andrew would inherit everything. It was the mind trained to detect crime, a mentality warped by years of dealing in human venality that saw the crooked in preference to the straight. He had asked himself the simple question, and underlined it. *'If Isabel S. marries anyone, Andrew G. loses the lot. Time factor of two years. Does this connect with Andrew G.'s attitude to relationship with stepson? If stepson really attempted homicide, Andrew G.'s prospects of inheriting twenty million look bright. Why would he stop him? There ain't nobody that noble.'* It went on for page after page, tearing Andrew's stories to pieces. MacNeil had been very fair. He had tried to trust his client, and it wasn't until almost the last two pages of the notebook, that Andrew found what had given him away.

It was a report of a telephone call from MacNeil's agent, the bogus journalist, who had come back from Freemont. It was there, ringed around and standing out. One of the maids at Beaumont had been taken to hospital after an overdose of sleeping pills. The journalist had decided to visit her when he heard it was Mrs Schriber's personal maid Ellie.

His interview with Ellie had been illuminating. The girl had talked her head off; reading it, Andrew called her obscene names under his breath. She had been a junior maid at Beaumont when the first Mrs Schriber was alive. She talked about the night she died, and here MacNeil had scored heavily with a pen. It seemed a long time to her between the time when she saw Master Richard go into his mother's room and come out again, rushing downstairs and shouting for his father, till Dr Graham called an ambulance. She was only a girl in her teens and nobody paid any attention to her, but she was certain it was something like five hours from the time Richard discovered his mother unconscious before help was summoned to the house. She didn't say anything, it wasn't her place to comment, but she hadn't forgotten. And then after Mrs Frances Schriber died, Mr Charles had cleared out all the medicine cupboards and thrown every single thing away. He had forbidden the prescription of barbiturates to any member of the staff. Here the investigator added his own comment. Almost as if he had something on his conscience concerning drugs. It was all the more worrying for Ellie, when Dr Graham came and told her to put two sleeping pills in a hot drink and give it to Mrs Isabel, after the master died. He had sounded as if he wanted to help her, but Ellie didn't hold with putting something into a drink without the person knowing, so she didn't do it. Andrew swore out loud. He had made a terrible mistake, trying to trust that stupid black bitch.

After Mrs Isabel left for England, Ellie had found the pills in her bedroom. Dr Graham had calmed her scruples about giving them to her mistress by telling her they were a special kind that gave sweet dreams to a sad person. Ellie's young man had gone off with another girl in Freemont, and she was feeling mighty sad. So she took the pills herself. Out of ignorance she had overdosed and nearly died. MacNeil's man had taken what was left of the pills and had them analysed. They were the strongest and most addictive of the barbiturates, and their prescription was very rare because of the danger of rapid dependence. Anyone taking them unwittingly over a short period in that strength, would have become addicted. MacNeil had written his comments at the end of the page. 'No doctor would administer such a drug without his patient's knowledge, unless his motive was sinister. Looks to me as if he and the old man let the first wife die, and then A.G. was setting up the second one for a fake suicide. Certain now that my original hunch was the right one. They framed the son to cover themselves, and A.G. expected to get the money. If Isabel S. is in danger of her life it's always been from Dr Graham, with twenty million bucks to gain. Has he an alibi for the night that housekeeper was murdered. . . .'

Andrew dropped the folder. It all stemmed from that one attempt to hurry; to get Isabel hooked on the sleeping pills, to establish that she was taking them. And then it would have

been so easy to put enough in a drink to be fatal. A tragic
suicide, brought on by grief after her husband's death. All
neatly tidied up. His second mistake had been to over-react to
Richard's reappearance. Getting himself banned from the
house, so she was out of reach. And then she went to England.
That was why he had employed MacNeil; to keep him informed of what was happening, so that if there was any truth
in his wife's spiteful allegation, and Isabel and Richard were
lovers, he could fly over and take action. He knew that the
accident in Barbados was just that; but it gave him the excuse
to employ the detective and set the scene in which Richard was
to play the villain. And if there was the slightest danger of remarriage, he would know at once through MacNeil. He put the
notebook away. He didn't need to read any more. That explained why MacNeil had followed him instead of Richard.
Down to Lambourn that day in the black Ford, and again in
the early morning when he went to bury the gloves. He had a
moment of palpitating shock, and hustled through the final
entry in the notebook. There were no records of a telephone
call to New York, or any written or cabled communication.
There hadn't been time. What the operative in New York
knew about the sleeping pills presented quite a different problem. The kind of problem that twenty million dollars would
help to solve quite easily. Andrew would go and visit the operative whose name had been conveniently written down in the
notebook. He didn't need to be too worried by that.

It could have been so easy if his original plan had worked.
A tragic suicide after Charles's death. So easy. But things had
never come to him without a struggle. And twenty million
dollars was worth fighting for. He gave a little chuckle. MacNeil
had written about him, the evening before he himself was
murdered. 'Probably killed the first wife . . . could be a real
psychopath. . . .' He chuckled again. There was nothing mad
about him. He knew exactly what he was doing; MacNeil had
found that out. He wanted the money, because it was due to him.
He might not be rich, like Charles, because his father had been
a damned fool gambler, but he was more of a gentleman than

any uppity German immigrant. . . . He was respected and admired by everyone. He'd fronted for Charles for all those years, and he was *owed* every cent of that money. He closed the notebook. That would have to be destroyed. Leaf by leaf. He took it into the bathroom, and began tearing out the pages, one by one, and setting them alight. He dropped the twisted ashes into the lavatory, flushing them away at intervals. Then he went back into his room and searched through MacNeil's belongings. He found the gun, as he expected, with MacNeil's identity card and gun licence. There were two clips of ammunition. All legitimate. And so convenient. He had wondered how to get hold of a gun when he first formulated his plan. It would be possible; he was certain that enquiries in the sleazier districts of London night life, accompanied by enough dollars, would get one for him. Now he didn't have to worry about it. He tested the weapon; it was a Luger automatic. He had been a very good pistol and rifle shot from the time he was a boy. He locked up MacNeil's suitcases and pushed them under the bed. He hid the gun under a heap of clothes in his own chest of drawers. Then he went down to the restaurant for dinner. He felt very hungry, and in a mood to celebrate. Everything was falling into place.

'Well,' Inspector Lewis said, 'that was a bloody waste of time.' He paused on the pavement outside Richard Schriber's block of flats. His assistant opened the rear door of the car, and stepped back to let him go in first. They settled themselves in the back seat and the car moved off towards Park Lane. 'Bloody useless,' Lewis repeated. 'She didn't want to know about it.'

'I don't know,' the younger man said, 'I don't think she had anything more to tell us. And there's all that stuff in the paper this morning about a man confessing – '

'We've had half a dozen cranks trying to claim they did it,' the Inspector said angrily. 'You always get the nutters coming out with a nasty case like this. Just fogs up the issue.'

'We'll have to go and see this one, won't we? Kent police seemed to think he might be a possible. Vagrant with a record of petty break-ins – '

'We'll go,' Lewis said irritably, 'because we can't afford not to; but it's a waste of time. The man that went into that house went in to kill, not to steal. And we're nowhere near catching him yet.'

'She gave me her horse for the Derby,' the assistant said. 'Seemed very confident. No kind of a price though; I might have a couple of quid on him.'

The inspector grunted. He didn't understand racing and he never bet. 'Bloody Kent,' he grumbled. 'Waste of time. We'll have the papers yelling if we don't turn up something soon. There's been something about the murder nearly every day.'

'It caught the public's imagination,' the other man said.

'It would,' Lewis sneered. 'Anything with a bit of horror and they lap it up. Nothing like a good murder to keep them happy. Christ, I think human beings stink!' He leaned forward to the driver.

'Call through to my office and tell 'em I'm going direct down to Maidstone to see this joker they've got there. And tell the press the same if they come sniffing round. Bloody waste of time.' He sat back, chin down on his chest, discouraging conversation for the rest of the journey.

The racecourse at Epsom was deserted on a Sunday. It was a warm sunny morning when Andrew drove up and parked his car by the side of the grandstand. The famous turf was smooth and richly green; there was a group of model-plane enthusiasts flying their machines on the downs across the track, and two riders, out for a morning hack, cantered along the grass in the distance. Andrew had never been to Epsom; twice Charles had invited him to France to see one of his runners at Longchamp, but not to England. He got out of the car and looked round. The pace was impressive; photographs and television coverage of the Derby gave no indication of how open and rural Epsom was. On the day of the great race it was a seething mass of people, a Martian invasion of cars, and decorated buses, with private helicopters buzzing overhead. A brilliant backdrop for the most prestigious race in the world. But that morning it was ghostly; the huge stands gaped at him, the little sward of turf reserved for the first three horses, the Royal Box above it, looked insignificant. The banks of flowers had not been put in place around the semi-circle. The Members' Enclosure, with its lawn and seats, was safe behind its gates and rails, the space reserved for the élite. It seemed sadly isolated. Andrew ducked under the white rail and began to walk along the course, down past the winning post to the final furlong marker, past the stands. There were notices forbidding people to walk across the sacred turf, soon to be raced over by the world's most valuable bloodstock. Andrew ignored them and walked on; he noticed a little group of Sunday idlers, obediently keeping the other side of the rails. The English were a law-abiding people. They took notices more seriously than anyone in the States. He could feel their disapproval as he passed them.

One side of his mind noted the sharp fall in the ground on the rail side, and the steep incline of that final run in after Tattenham Corner, deceptive even viewed from the other end. To a tired horse that combination of fall in the level and rising ground for the final hundred and fifty yards must make the post seem like the summit of a mountain still to climb. Easy to become unbalanced after the sharp turn from the back straight into that fearsome corner and then out again, on and up, assaulted by the unbelievable roar from the crowd on both sides of the course fighting for the stamina and speed to reach that little white circle on top of its post. . . . Everest indeed, for horse and jockey.

Andrew paused for a moment as he turned, facing towards the end of the course, the sun warm on his back. All his life he had loved racing and he had forgotten for a few moments his purpose in coming to the course. Charles's horse would face that test. Charles, his great friend, who had betrayed him and

used him. Tears stung in his eyes. He pushed his clenched hands
into his jacket pockets, dragging them down, and began to
walk slowly back. He searched the stands, looking upwards to
the tiers of private boxes, each named after horses which had
won the Derby. Hyperion; Alycidon, My Babu, Roberto, Mill
Reef. . . . Tim had said Isabel would be in the Mill Reef box,
on the first level. He paused to look up, straining his eyes. Too
far away, too high up. He ducked under the rails and began to
walk along the narrow path to the right, leading to the paddock. It was a long walk from the stands. There was a line of
loose boxes behind the railed paddock, saddling enclosures. A
veterinary box. Tiers of steps around the paddock itself, with
mushroom seats at the rails. She would walk down to the
paddock just before the race, and go in to see the Falcon
mounted up, with Tim and Nigel. And Richard, of course.
Andrew's mouth turned down in a grimace. Richard would be
there. If Charles Schriber could see that, wherever his spirit
roamed, that moment would almost be sufficient punishment
for the way he had treated his best friend. . . .

The paddock was always crowded. He knew that, because
the Queen was present at the Derby and her procession down
the course to the paddock was one of the highlights of the day.
He remembered reading an article in a sporting magazine in
the States, commenting on her vulnerability to assassination
from any terrorist in the crowd.

There would be police hidden among them, detectives placed
at vantage points along her route. Her security would envelop
the others in the centre of that big green ring. He couldn't do
anything there. He turned away and began walking back
towards the road at the back of the stands, there stood the
stables, where the horses waited before each race. Maximum
security. No admittance. Some came and stayed overnight;
others arrived that morning. Nobody was allowed into that
yard without a special pass and an identity card. Then only the
trainer, members of his staff, and the owner if signed in by him.
Everyone signed the book on entering. There were no loopholes
left for a potential doper. The gates were manned by racecourse

security guards; all winners were dope tested, in the Classic race itself all placed horses were examined.

It was shut tight against outsiders. So Tim had explained to him. He strolled across the empty road and stood looking up at the solid gates. Until after the last race. He took his hands out of his pockets, flexed the fingers. That was the moment. Flushed with triumph after her win, perhaps. . . . It would be all the more just. And of course he had an ally; someone who was co-operating with him, helping every step of the way. That was ironic too. He would have been helpless without Tim Ryan. He gave a little laugh and turned away, back to his car. He had to call his wife that evening. She had written to him twice and he'd fobbed her off with a couple of telephone calls. Now he could give her a date for his return. She could get everything ready to welcome him back. He got into the car, reversed into the road and turned back for London. He hummed a little tune as he drove.

13

Roy Farrant stood on Newmarket Heath; it was eight o'clock in the morning and he had seen his horse Rocket Man do his final six-furlong gallop the day before the Derby. He had always loved Newmarket; it was the centre of British racing, headquarters of the National Stud, populated by the top flat trainers, proud of the tradition that stretched back to Charles II's love of racing horses on the superb heathland. Royal patronage had given the town its birth and 250 years of racing had stamped it with indelible character.

Dick Shipley had taken Rocket Man and the others; he stood beside Farrant now, a short, stocky ex-jockey who had made the difficult transition from race riding to training with incredible success. He was a taciturn man, who didn't feel at ease with owners, and he had made it plain to Farrant that so far as the running of his horses was concerned, he wouldn't stand for any interference.

Roy turned to him; Rocket Man had finished his last work and was walking slowly back towards them.

'Well,' he said. 'What do you think?'

'I think he worked very well,' Shipley answered. 'He's fit and ready to run for his life. I can't say more than that.'

'You don't think he'll win,' Farrant said flatly. 'Why the hell don't you say so!'

'Because I'm not a bloody fortune teller,' Shipley was curt. 'I'm sending your horse to Epsom to win the race, and further than that I'm not prepared to go. He's second favourite; that ought to satisfy you.'

'Silver Falcon is five to four,' Farrant said. 'He's certain to be evens tomorrow. Everyone says he'll beat us.'

'More people have made mugs of themselves picking the winner at Epsom than any other race in the world,' Shipley said. 'Falcon can disappoint tomorrow, and your fellow can pull something out of the bag that no one knows he has. A complete outsider could come cruising up and do the lot of them. I'm keeping my fingers crossed and my knickers dry.' He didn't suggest in words that Farrant did the same, but the implication was there.

'I'll ring you tonight,' Roy said. 'Just for a last-minute check on him.' He began to walk back towards the place where his car was parked in a rough patch off the main road. There were other cars belonging to owners parked there. Shipley followed him, pausing to watch Rocket Man and the horse he had worked with, safely across the main road. He had never liked Roy Farrant; he'd lost a lot of his arrogance and bluster, but it wouldn't be long in coming back. Also he hated owners ringing up. That was his job. He got into his own small car, and waved briefly to Roy. He saw Patsy sitting in the back seat. Farrant opened the door and got into the driver's seat.

Patsy leaned forward.

'How did it go, darling? I wished you'd let me get out – I couldn't see anything – '

'He worked very well,' Farrant said. 'But not well enough. That little sod knew it, and started flannelling round saying you couldn't predict the outcome. . . . A lot of bullshit.'

'He might do it,' Patsy said comfortingly. 'Even if he came second it would be quite nice – '

He turned and glared at her.

'For Christ's sake, don't be such a stupid cow. I'm not going to come second. I'm going to win that bloody race. And I don't need Shipley to help me do it.' He started the engine and the big Rolls slid out towards the road. Patsy watched him silently from the back. She could see his face reflected in the mirror. It was flushed with temper, and the mouth was grim. He was more like his old self every day. The respite since Barry's death had been brief. His tout, Downs, had come in useful dealing with that stupid bugger Long. He was going to be useful again.

He drove back through the centre of Newmarket, cursing as they hit a traffic jam on the main road to London. He glanced at Patsy in the driving mirror.

'If he came second it would be quite nice. . . .' He growled at her under his breath, sitting there so incredibly beautiful, and two planks thick between the ears.

He wasn't going to be second. There were only two horses in the Derby that could beat Rocket Man. One was French bred, owned by a rich South American film star, who felt that it was good for his image to float through the international racing scene. The other was the Silver Falcon. He had squared the French jockey weeks ago. Now it was up to Roy to 'see to' the Falcon himself. And that was exactly what he intended doing. Breakfast was waiting for them at the rented house; and so was Downs.

Tim and the Fosters were also having breakfast. They had worked the Falcon very early, eluding bookies' touts who spied on the gallops, and Sally had cooked them a hearty meal of eggs and bacon and sausages. She didn't ask questions until they had finished eating and Nigel was mumbling about more coffee. He hadn't slept properly for some time, and he was grumpy in the mornings, inclined to snap if confronted with anything until he'd had his breakfast and relaxed. Tim looked at her and grinned.

'We're all set for tomorrow,' he said. 'Marvellous piece of work this morning. Wasn't it?' he turned to Nigel. Nigel nodded.

'He went super,' he said. There was no greater praise in racing parlance. 'He's like a tiger, so Phil says, just waiting to go. It's almost as if he knows that tomorrow is the big day.' He looked at his wife and grinned at her affectionately. 'If we win tomorrow, Sal, I'm going to take you up to London and you can have the shopping spree of your life!'

'I'd settle for a good night's sleep,' she laughed.

'And you'll be a rich man,' he said to Tim. 'Don't tell me

you're able to put your head down and drop off tonight, I won't believe you – '

'I'm not a temperamental Englishman like you,' Tim said. He had grown very fond of the Fosters; they were nicer as one got to know them, and he had never felt more at home than he did in their house. The relationship between them was ideal; their interests were identical, and their characters complementary.

Most of all, they truly loved each other, and this was what gave their house its warmth for outsiders. He didn't want to think about people being in love; he had submerged his own feelings about Isabel in the preparations for the race, but pain was near the surface, and jealousy tortured him when he saw her with Richard. He couldn't deny that Richard had changed. He was tender, protective, aggressively in love with her. Nigel and Sally talked about the marriage with enthusiasm.

'Charles was too old for her,' he remembered Sally saying. 'Much too dominating. I think they're just right for each other.' He hadn't said anything, because he couldn't. He had to pretend to accept it too. Tim's thoughts were far from his surroundings. Andrew Graham had met him for lunch in the Chequers Hotel at Newbury. He had looked thin and oddly pathetic; he seemed to have aged very quickly since Tim had seen him last. Andrew had talked to him. Talked quietly and at length, about things which Tim could hardly believe were the truth. And yet as he listened, they explained so much. Richard was not his father's son. Andrew had kept that secret to the last, hoping not to humiliate Charles; a foolish reason, founded in sentimentality, he admitted that, but he had no other excuse. This was what Isabel intended telling Tim, when she spoke of the whole story. But there was more to it than she knew. Much more.

He had tried to convince her that Richard was both unstable and unsuitable, without exposing the final fact that he was the bastard son of another man. A man who had died in a mental hospital just five years previously. From hopeless schizophrenia. Tim had been too shocked to speak for some moments. He would never forget the way Andrew Graham had slightly hung his head after he told him that. Or his words, spoken in a mumble. 'I blame myself for all of it. If I'd been honest with her in the beginning – this engagement wouldn't have happened. I'm not saying he murdered the housekeeper at Coolbridge – I'm not saying anything except she mustn't marry him. . . . You're the only one who can help me, Tim. . . .'

And Tim had known he was right. Right to try and protect Isabel in spite of herself. Admirable even more, because a less dedicated man and a less scrupulous doctor would have let her go her own way. She had rejected his advice, refused to speak to him, even refused Tim's suggestion that as her dead husband's closest friend, Andrew should be invited to the Derby. And so, in the dining room of the hotel, with a sullen waitress hovering close by, hoping to drive them out, Tim and Andrew Graham had sat on, working out a plan. It was Andrew's idea, and as he explained, his last hope of stopping the marriage. He had to return to the States immediately after the Derby; Joan wasn't well and insisting on his coming home. If he didn't see Isabel before he left, she would be Richard's wife by the end of that week.

'You're a long way away,' Nigel's voice sounded suddenly loud. Tim started; the trainer had folded up his *Sporting Life*, showing the big black headlines. 'Silver Falcon Set to Take the Prize Tomorrow.' 'Thinking about the quarter of a million you'll have in your pocket by tomorrow?'

'Yes,' Tim lied. 'But it's dollars, not pounds – '

'Don't be bloody greedy,' Nigel shouted cheerfully, as he went through the door. 'All I get is ten per cent of the stake!'

'And a thumping great present – ' Tim called back. He got up from the table, and paused to read the *Sporting Life* again. He and Nigel and Sally had already read every word written about the race and the Falcon. He was tipped by five out of the six newspapers quoted as a certainty to win the Derby. He was also quoted as evens in the betting. Rocket Man was second favourite at nine to four and the French colt Mexican Star was three to one. Only twenty-four hours to go. There was a security guard on duty outside the Falcon's box from that morning until he was loaded up to go to Epsom tomorrow morning; as he travelled well, Nigel decided not to make him stay a night away from home. The whole stable was keyed up to a frenzy of excitement; wages had been placed in advance with the bookmakers, and one of Nigel's lads was sporting a black eye after a fight in a Lambourn pub with a lad from a rival stable who had the temerity to suggest that the Silver Falcon had three back legs and was a useless bugger. . . .

Tim went into Nigel's office and settled down at his desk to go through the long cabled reports from Beaumont, giving details on the engagements and progress of the rest of Charles's horses, and the news that four of his mares had just foaled and a further two were expected to at any moment. It all seemed a very long way away.

Isabel gave a dinner party in the Star Hotel at Epsom that night. There were thirty people in a private room, including Tim, the Fosters, friends of Charles who had flown in from the States to see his horse run, and, incongruously, because they had accepted in order to meet Richard, Isabel's parents. Richard sat at the opposite end of the table; he thought she had never looked more beautiful. She seemed to burn from within, a mixture of excitement and personal happiness that gave her a magical quality. She was wearing a dark red dress, with Charles's lovely matched pearls, her hair very simply brushed back from her forehead, showing an unusual peak. A widow's peak, it used to be called.

She had an old friend of Charles on her right, a distinguished breeder and owner, whose wife glittering with diamonds, was seated next to Isabel's father. Isabel had been careful not to put any of the old Freemont coterie beside Richard. Her mother, an intense and determinedly dowdy intellectual, sat on his right and didn't attempt to make conversation. It was a noisy, lively group, absorbing the alien elements without difficulty by its own exuberance. The talk was limited to horses and racing, and returned inevitably, and with boisterous forecasts, to the great race the next day. Isabel glanced down at Richard and smiled, raising her glass. He lifted his, and they toasted each other. Nigel was getting a little drunk, and Tim Ryan, who should have been riding as high as any of them with his prospects if the Falcon won, was sober and restrained. Not long ago, Richard would have jeered at him. Now he was sorry for him. He must love Isabel very much to be so cast down. It was a pity; someone had to lose. And looking down towards her, Richard suddenly banged on the table. He stood up, and the faces turned towards him. He didn't see any of them. He was gazing at Isabel, and she was looking up at him and smiling.

'Let's drink a toast,' he said. 'To the Silver Falcon. And to Isabel.' He felt a tightness in the throat as everyone stood with him, leaving her sitting alone, suddenly isolated. 'The Silver Falcon! Isabel!' And then it had to happen; the silver-haired Kentuckian who had been on her right, remained on his feet and raised his glass in turn. 'And I give you a great sportsman, and a good friend. Charles Schriber. Tomorrow is as much his day!'

It was Isabel who hesitated, Richard who saved the situation from becoming noticeable. He spoke out clearly and firmly.

'To Charles,' he said. He went up to Isabel and kissed her on the cheek. 'I'm keeping her in the family,' he said. 'We're getting married on Saturday.'

There was another party in progress in a big mock-Tudor house two miles away from Epsom. The Farrants were staying there with friends; Patsy was astonishingly beautiful in emerald green, with an emerald and diamond necklace to match. Roy had suddenly produced it that morning. He didn't explain that it was because he had been particularly nasty to her during the last few days, but it seemed some kind of omen. He felt that spending 25 000 pounds on Patsy would bring him luck.

The dinner was a large buffet; there was a lot of champagne and a number of guests were getting drunk. Roy himself had never felt more sober. It was all set for tomorrow. His horse was going to win. His host, a furniture manufacturer who had made a fortune out of marketing a cheap line in ready-to-assemble units for the home, flung an arm round Roy's shoulders.

'Going to clean up tomorrow, eh? I've had a tidy little packet on your horse – got him ante-post at four to one.'

'I got him at sixes,' Roy said. He hated being pawed, and he shifted a little, hoping his friend would notice. The encircling arm slipped away. 'What'll he be worth, if he wins – a million?' The words were a little slurred, but the eyes searching his face were bright with greed.

'Two million, more like it,' Roy said. He knew how much his friend worshipped money. 'I've got three parts of a syndicate together. I'm keeping twenty per cent myself.'

'Any shares left?'

Roy hesitated. He had put the syndicate together in the last week, but there were two full shares unsold. He could gamble on winning tomorrow and getting double their value as it stood the night before the race. 'Come on,' his host said. 'What happens tomorrow if he loses? I'm willing to take a chance – ' Roy gave him a wide smile.

'He isn't going to lose,' he said. 'And I'm not selling till after the race.' He moved away. Downs had done a good job. It was all set up. He avoided a group composed of a major bookmaker with a chain of betting shops throughout east London and his girl friend, charitably described as a television dancer, and an ageing whizz kid, complete with trendy suit and rings, who looked after the furniture manufacturer's advertising account. Roy saw Patsy chatting to a youngish man, and turned away towards the bar. He would want her tonight. He would want that extraordinary sexual talent to take the knots out of his stomach and send him exhausted and sated into a deep sleep. He picked up a glass of champagne and sipped it. He didn't want to talk a lot of cock to the people there. He wanted to stay alone, until Patsy could take his mind off tomorrow. But he was going to win the Derby and he knew it. He also knew, that no matter what he did afterwards, whether he made millions more or lost everything, there would never again be this sense of anticipation so close to ecstasy that it was actual torment.

Downs was in the third pub on his progress through Epsom. He was drinking Guinness followed by chasers of whisky, and he was weaving slightly as he stood holding onto the bar. He had started out by himself, and soon found company. Farrant had treated him well. He had a wad of money and more to come. He talked about everything, about his old career as a jockey, boasting about the races he had won and the personalities he'd known. As he was buying the drinks, he had a captive audience. He watched them, focusing with difficulty; greedy bastards, sopping it up, thinking he didn't know they were codding him along while the drinks kept coming. He didn't mind paying. He liked a bit of company, and he liked talking about himself. There was no harm in that; he *had* ridden in the bloody Leger, and the Two Thousand Guineas, and won some decent races before the bottle started getting the better of him. Not that it mattered. Fuck-all difference it made in the end. So long as he talked about himself, and not about anything else. Not about the race tomorrow. Somebody asked him what he fancied and he mumbled about a couple of outsiders as long shots. Nothing else was worth backing. The odds were too short. He slid away from the subject of the Derby. One young lad, too cheeky for his own good, piped up and asked him if he'd ever ridden in the race.

Downs looked at him with contempt, seeing two peaked, jeering little faces instead of one. 'No,' he said. 'But I would have done. Drink was the ruination of me riding career.' When they laughed he didn't join them. A tear welled up in his eye. It was the truth. He was just a crooked little runner, doing the dirty work. . . . By Christ he'd done a bit of dirty work for Farrant in the last few days. . . . No wonder he'd given him a hundred quid on account and promised him five hundred after the race . . . no wonder. Six horses. Six bloody horses. That grey wouldn't stand a chance in hell. He put the thought out of his mind. Not to be thought about. Or spoken of. Never. Like what happened to David Long. What had happened to other horses, other jockeys.

Barry Lawrence got himself killed. .... He took a deep breath, tipped the last of the whisky down, and made his way out of the bar into the fresh air. There was another pub a couple of hundred yards further on. Nice little place. He'd find a new crowd there. He was drunk, but a long way from losing his legs or passing out. He wandered off towards his goal.

'Darling,' Isabel said. 'It was a very successful evening. And you were marvellous.' He stopped kissing her for a moment. They had taken rooms in the hotel; it was past midnight and the party had broken up.

Richard was holding her in his arms, watching the moon through the bedroom window, beginning the preliminaries of their love-making. She had been very proud of him that night; the moment when Charles's name was mentioned had frozen her. Richard's reaction had been symbolic. Watching him raise his glass proved that he had finally won the battle. He was free of Charles Schriber now, because for the first time he could be detached. Bitterness and frustrated revenge had warped his life; now it was becoming an episode, that for all its horror, belonged to the past. That was what she meant when she said he was marvellous and Richard understood that too.

'I love you, Isabel,' he said. 'I had such a strong feeling tonight – as if my whole life was beginning again. I made up my mind to something.'

'What?' she asked gently.

'I'm never going to mention what happened at Beaumont again. I'm not going to talk about it or think about it.'

They stood, holding each other, not moving or speaking. The window in front of them showed dark trees and a huge white moon with thin shreds of cloud fleeing across it, driven by a sharp wind.

The forecast for the next day was dry, with sunny intervals. Perfect Derby weather.

'You know, darling,' Isabel said quietly, 'I'm almost too

happy. Everything has gone so right so quickly. I thought tonight, tomorrow the race, and the Falcon wins. Then I marry Richard. It's too good to be true.' She gave a little nervous laugh. 'Something has to go wrong – '

'Nothing has to go wrong,' he said. 'When the luck's running nothing stops it. And our luck is running now. This is just a reaction; you've been keyed up for days and now it's only hours away you're getting nervous. Don't be silly, darling.'

'I thought,' Isabel said suddenly, 'just then: *something is going to happen to spoil it*. It just came into my mind. A horrible feeling – a premonition.' She stepped away from him and looked up at him. 'One moment I was up in the clouds and the next I feel frightened.'

He took her back in his arms and kissed her. 'Too much champagne and nervous tension,' he said firmly. The clouds which had threaded their way across the moon suddenly converged upon it in a sullen black mass, and the room became dark. He felt Isabel shiver.

'You stop all this nonsense,' he said. 'A good night's sleep is what you need.' He switched on the lights and pulled the curtains. Isabel watched him. It was a pleasant, chintzy room, less impersonal than most hotel bedrooms. Friends had sent flowers and telegrams, and the sight of them stacked on the chest of drawers cheered her.

She went up and put her arms around Richard. 'Get undressed,' he said. 'I'll tuck you in.'

'I'm all right now,' she said. 'It was just silly. Everything is going to be marvellous.'

He fell asleep before she did. She lay on her back, his arm protectively across her, her eyes closed against the total darkness in the bedroom. The feeling of unease had returned. It didn't take a rational form, it couldn't be expressed as anything more than a whisper in the mind, too faint to distinguish its message. Not so much a message as a warning. It seemed to be a long time before she drifted into sleep. When she awoke Richard had gone to his own room, her curtains were drawn back and the sun was flooding in.

She sat up, and threw the covers back. Tomorrow had become today.

Derby Day.

Crowds had been converging on Epsom since the early morning. The atmosphere was festive; for a million people it was one of the highlights of the year, a day when the greatest race in the English racing calendar was run, when families picnicked on the Downs, enjoyed the huge funfare that was traditional, and watched the Queen and the royal family walking within feet of them down the course before the Derby. There were hundreds of coaches, specially chartered, special trains teeming with racegoers, equipped with the usual complement of petty crooks, hundreds of thousands of cars of all shapes and sizes, packed into the car parks. Helicopters whirred like angry insects overhead, landing on the downs outside the main stands; there were expensive champagne picnics in the car parks, where the rich unpacked their hampers of smoked salmon and lunched off little tables; across the racecourse on the other side, the massive crowds were besieging the racecourse bars, eating sandwiches and sausage rolls, laughing and shouting, and jostling. There were tipsters, selling racing certainties for fifty pence a tip, pickpockets and bookies' touts, souvenir sellers, ice-cream vans, candy-floss stands and newspaper sellers, offering the *Sporting Life* and the early editions of the evening papers. Children and dogs abounded, push prams and querulous toddlers, roving groups of teenagers, gypsies, strategically placed outside the entrances to the stands, pestering passers-by with sprigs of lucky white heather. And holding court on the Downs, the traditional Cockney Pearly King and his Queen, magnificent in clothes shimmering with pearl buttons, sweeping ostrich feathers in the lady's hat. It was garish and bursting with vitality, colour and variety; there was a constant roar from a million voices concentrated on both sides of the white rails enclosing the course. And in the owners' car park, there were elaborate lunches being held; caterers served out cold salmon and sliced the finest Scotch beef, mixed vast salads and dispensed strawberries and cream. Champagne was spilling into hundreds of glasses, and the voices were as high as the hopes.

Rolls, Bentleys, Daimlers, huge and sleek, like giant cockroaches, sporting the horse and jockey mascot of their owners on the bonnet, were merely commonplace. A bright red Lamborghini stood out among the status symbols like a jewel.

In the Members' Enclosure across the road, railed in by white railings, women in elegant pastel colours and smart hats complemented the sombre elegance of the men in their black morning suits, and silk top hats, sometimes enlivened by a figure all in grey. The bars were full, and the figure of the Queen, dazzling in sunshine yellow, could be glimpsed briefly moving in the Royal Box. Flowers were banked round the magic enclosure for the winner and placed horses; the sward of grass running up and past the stands was lush and green, the winning post a white disc on a white stand, almost insignificant. The weather was perfect; the sun was shining and there was no breeze. Across the road from the stands, behind the tall green gates, guarded by security men, the horses waited in their stables. It was the racecourse security's boast that a mouse couldn't have got into the yard without a pass.

Outside the white railings, the bookmakers' stands blossomed, the well-known firms like Ladbrokes and Corals with rich account customers offered their services, their operatives in morning clothes; in Tattersalls and the Silver Ring, the bookmakers shouted the odds and balanced on their stepladders, taking money on the first race. The tictac men, perched above the heads of the crowd, signalled changes in the betting. There was a pervasive atmosphere of high holiday and growing excitement, which would reach its climax at the moment of three fifteen.

Isabel and her party were lunching in the members' restaurant. Richard stayed close to her, Tim was nervous and preoccupied, Nigel ate and drank very little and was visibly strung up. Sally looked quite different in a smart blue and white suit and a blue Stetson hat; Isabel hardly recognized her.

Without her uniform of sweater and jeans, and the ubiquitous anorak, she was a very attractive woman. Isabel had chosen dark green; her colours were green, with a light blue sash. Charles had given her a diamond brooch horse, with the tiny jockey set with emeralds and sapphires. She had decided not to wear it. She didn't need his luck that day. She didn't need or want anything to remind her of him. The Silver Falcon was carrying her colours. Charles was dead. This was her race, and if the Falcon won, it would be Richard who stood beside her to receive the golden trophy.

They went down to watch the first race, and suddenly the time, which had seemed not to move at all, began rushing past. The second race was a winner for Richard, who was betting seriously and with total concentration; Nigel fidgeting and finally disappearing, with the words, 'I'll meet you in the paddock – ' and then suddenly, Richard was beside her, they were in the middle of a crowd which was gathering by the exit from the Members', and it was a quarter to three. The horses would be walking round, displaying themselves before the television cameras and the massive crowds around the paddock. At any moment the Queen and her party would leave the Royal Box and begin to walk down the course to see them.

Roy Farrant had a lunch party in the owners' car park. There was a moment when he paused in the middle of it, listening to the babble of voices, with a pop of champagne corks going off like fireworks, and thought of Barry Lawrence. It was an eerie feeling, as if his friend had joined them, and was standing close. He would have been riding Rocket Man that day; they would have spent the night before in council together, as they had done before every race over the years, and before three previous Derbys when Roy had a runner and more hope than chance.

Barry had died trying to stop the Silver Falcon. He owed it to him to make sure the horse didn't win today. Patsy had been very good the night before. There were moments like this when he forgot how much she irritated him normally, and appreciated her good qualities. She had kept out of his way that morning, only appearing as they were due to leave for the race-course, looking breathtaking in his colours, yellow and white. She must have had it specially made, without saying anything. He came up and put his arms round her waist and squeezed her.

She smiled back at him with genuine pleasure because he was being nice. And she was good at the lunch party; she looked after his guests, introduced people, generally took the burden off him. The knot in his stomach had returned; it felt as if his whole gut was ravelled up in one writhing mass of nervous tension. He had drunk a great deal; it didn't matter if he got a bit high now, there was nothing more to do. There were six outsiders in the race. He knew their names off by heart. Four maidens, never having won a race, and two moderate animals whose owners wanted the kudos of having a runner in the world's greatest Flat race. Arthur's Boy. Snow Prince. Charley Barley. Fitters Mate. Mynah Bird. Jakestown. Four English jockeys, and two Australians. No chance, any of them. 100 to 1 outsiders. An outlay of 12000 pounds, two grand each. Downs had done his job properly. One of the six must get to the Falcon. There were eighteen runners in the field.

The fancied French horse was a colt bred in the States, sired by Nijinsky. A beautiful, sleek chestnut, its legs clean of white markings, named by its film star owner as Mexican Star. He had gone over to France himself to fix that one. No middle man could be trusted with that. It wasn't going to beat the Silver Falcon, but it was expected to run into a place, and its form was just as good as Rocket Man's over a mile. He had given Mexican Star's jockey 10000 pounds to pull his horse. Patsy came towards him; she had a glass of champagne in her hand, and he could tell by the expression on her face that she was slightly drunk.

'It's two thirty, darling,' she said. 'Hadn't we better give people their tickets?'

He brought out the badges from his inside pocket. Entrance to the boxes on the first tier. Alycidon and Airborne. Airborne was a grey; there hadn't been another grey among the Derby winners since the war. It looked like an omen. He had chosen to go into the box named after Alycidon himself. The great stallion was in Rocket Man's pedigree. Patsy linked her arm through his.

'I can't wait,' she said. 'I know we're going to win – '

'Yes,' Roy Farrant said. 'This time, we are. Come on.'

They led the way across the road to the course and joined the slow jostling crowd inside the pathway alongside the course rails. There was the sound of clapping. The Queen had come down from the Royal Box and was coming out onto the green track on her way to the paddock.

Andrew Graham went into Tattersalls. He wore an ordinary suit and a panama straw hat; he carried a race-glasses case slung over his shoulder. He had fought his way through at one of the crowded bars and given himself a double whisky and a ham sandwich. He felt very calm; he took an interest in the racing and placed a successful cash bet on the first two winners. He looked at his watch more than usual: at half past two, he pushed his way out and joined the crowd gathering on the rails to watch the Queen. He was mildly interested to see her.

She passed within a few feet of him, smiling and talking to the Senior Steward of the Jockey Club, a tall heavily built man, who had to stoop to answer her. Andrew was surprised at how good-looking the Queen of England was: her photographs gave no idea of her beautiful complexion and eyes, or the sweetness of her smile. The harsh bright yellow didn't please him; it made her stand out among the greys and blacks, and the paler pastels of her entourage and family. A perfect target. It seemed to him incredible that she should expose herself to such risks. He had based his own plan on the belief that the security surrounding her would protect anyone else in the vicinity. But he couldn't see anything out of the ordinary. There must be detectives among the group following her, but she stood out in front, walking alone with the one escort. Anyone standing as he was, by the rails, could have shot her dead. He turned away, pushing hard to get to the paddock.

It was a wide green circle, flanked by an open stand for spectators, with little mushroom seats at the rails, all fully occupied. Two huge marquees provided a backcloth to the downs. Television cameras probed from above, a helicopter chugged overhead. There was a dense coloured mass of people circling the green paddock, and inside it, walking by, came the best of the world's bloodstock, graceful, satin-coated, led by the gleaming dark dappled silver of the only grey colt, the Silver Falcon. Phil was leading him, dressed in his best brown suit, with a neat shirt and tie, the label bearing the horse's name and number, tied to his left arm. No. 5.

He walked out strongly, showing the horse's paces, murmuring to him, occasionally patting him quickly on the neck. The Falcon held his head high, looking suspiciously at the crowds; his grey tail swished angrily from side to side. There was a slight patch of sweat on his neck, a sign that he was fussing, as Phil described it. 'There, old son,' he muttered, 'there, steady on. Nothin' to worry about – '

Immediately behind him was Jakestown, bought for 1500 guineas as a yearling, a nice, handsome bay colt, with a deceptive presence about him, winner of two moderate two-year-old races and running only to please the vanity of his owner. Behind him walked Rocket Man. He looked superb; Dick Shipley had brought him to his peak. He glowed with fitness and there wasn't a sign of pre-race nerves. He seemed interested in the crowds without being in the least disturbed. The French horse Mexican Star was pulling around and jigging from side to side, visibly sweating up in alarm at his surroundings. Behind him, his almost black coat glowing like coal, came the horse which Lester Piggott had announced that he would ride just four days before the race. He had partnered it in the Prix Lupin, when it ran third to the Falcon, and it carried the hopes and the black and white colours of the well-known owner Charles St George, one of the most consistently successful figures in English racing, bidding for his first Derby. Prince of Padua, by Faberge out of a Sea Bird mare. Top-class Classic breeding, but lacking the turn of foot to beat the Falcon. He was drawn no. 2 on the inside. Money was going on him because he was Piggott's choice of mount, and Piggott had won the Derby seven times.

A big bay, very impressive, very calm, running for the first time that season, Snow Prince, half-brother to the '74 Derby winner Snow Knight, and without Snow Knight's excitable temperament. A good two-year-old, but an unproven three-year-old. Odds of eight to one were being offered.

Owners, their friends and the trainers were in the centre, making little knots of colour, talking anxiously. The Queen's distinctive yellow dress glowed. A stream of jockeys began to trickle through, splitting up towards their owners, bright as paint in their silks. On the television screens all over the country, and in Europe, people were watching the scene, as were the crowds massed in the bars and pubs, hearing the commentary.

'We're seeing the favourite now, the grey colt, Silver Falcon, by Silver Dancer – an impressive winner in the States as a two-year-old, and he won the Prix Lupin by three lengths from Just Fair, with Prince of Padua a length away third. A very impressive horse indeed, sweating up a bit though – he was bred by the late Charles Schriber expressly to win the Derby. It looks as if he can do the job today. Not quite so well drawn, he's no. 18 on the outside. Here's Mynah Bird, nice-looking sort but right out of his class, I'm afraid, and there's the second favourite, Rocket Man, looking really well. Dick Shipley always turns his horses out looking a picture and this one certainly impresses – ran very well in the Two Thousand Guineas, where he was second to Lightning Strike, probably do better for the longer trip. If anyone can worry the Silver Falcon it should be him – there's Jimmy Carlton, the Falcon's jockey, wearing Mrs Charles Schriber's green and blue colours – Lester Piggott, riding as usual for Mr Charles St George on Prince of Padua, very dark bay, almost black. There's Prince of Padua now; he's a calm sort, not bothered by all the crowds. Mexican Star in the picture, very sweated up, not liking it at all. He's a strong front runner this horse, but he may well be doing his chances in by getting himself so worked up.'

The bell rang, as Isabel shook hands with Jimmy Carlton. *Jockeys please mount.*

'Good luck,' she said. He grinned and nodded; the grin disappeared quickly as he strode away towards the grey colt, followed by Nigel and Tim. Nigel legged him up onto the horse, and immediately the Falcon fly-bucked. It took a minute or two to settle him, Carlton soothing him and Phil holding tight to the lead rope. The black patch of sweat on his neck had spread; there were white flecks of foam on it. Isabel watched anxiously. She turned to Richard.

'He's getting upset,' she said. 'That isn't like him.'

'He'll be all right,' Richard slipped his hand through her arm. He was watching the Falcon, and he didn't like what he saw, but he didn't want to worry her even more. The grey colt was bouncing and twisting, fighting the lead rope, trying to unseat his jockey. 'The sooner they get on with the parade the better,' Richard said. 'Come on, darling, let's get up to the box.' He led her out of the paddock; the horses were being led out onto the course for the ritual parade in front of the stands, going in alphabetical order. The unconsidered Arthur's Boy, carrying no. 1 on his saddle cloth, had the honour of leading the parade.

Roy Farrant had gone on ahead as soon as Rocket Man was mounted. He was almost sprinting, Patsy trying unsuccessfully to keep up as he shoved his way through. His horse looked a picture; he had never seen him in such marvellous condition, completely unconcerned by the people and the general atmosphere of excitement. A winner if ever he'd seen one. The knots in his stomach were unbearable, and his hands shook. He was out of the lift and hurrying along to the door marked Alycidon, while down below, Patsy found herself getting into a second lift with Richard and Isabel. She smiled at them and held out her hand.

Isabel took it. 'I can't wish you good luck,' Patsy said, 'because I do want Roy to win. But congratulations; I hear you're getting married.'

'Yes,' Isabel said. 'Thank you.' She felt stiff and awkward. But there was no guile in Patsy Farrant; her beautiful smile was genuine. Richard leaned over and kissed her lightly on the cheek.

'Thanks, Patsy. Give my best to Roy.'

'I will. Bye.' She drifted out of the lift ahead of them.

'Richard,' Isabel said, as they reached the box with Mill Reef's name above it – 'Richard I can hardly breathe I'm so excited – oh, what's happened!' There was a gasp from the crowd below them, and the voice of the commentator on the loudspeaker system came over clearly. 'Bit of trouble here – Silver Falcon's decanted Jimmy Carlton –' Isabel rushed to the front and looked down.

'Oh my God,' she said – 'oh, Richard, look at him!'

The rest of the eighteen horses had passed the grandstand; the grey colt, with Phil and another assistant at his head, was rearing and plunging in the middle of the track. He backed up dangerously close to the rails and fly-bucked viciously towards the crowd. Nigel and Tim were running towards him; the jockey stayed back, not attempting to remount. The other horses had reached the point where they wheeled round and cantered back down to the paddock and the long walk up to the mile and a half start. There was a road to cross and a passage through staring crowds to be endured before the stalls were reached. There was a saying that many a Derby had been lost on the way to the start.

'The bastard!' Richard said angrily. 'Look at him, lashing out – he'll crack himself against the rails in a minute –' Isabel just stood and watched, aware of murmurs behind her from Harry Grogan and his wife, and a silence from Sally Foster that was more expressive than any words.

'He won't even start at this rate,' she heard Grogan say, and suddenly she turned and snapped at him, her nerves breaking with tension. 'Don't be ridiculous! Of course he will –' And at that moment, they got him under control long enough for Tim to throw the jockey into the plate, and instantly, Phil, Nigel, Tim and the official helping them scattered out of the colt's way, as he half reared, feeling the man on his back, and then with Carlton hanging onto his head, he plunged forward in pursuit of the others, back the way he had come. Isabel was literally shaking. The huge crowd was growing quieter: in the bars the television commentator Peter O'Sullevan's voice came over again.

'Crossing the road now – Mexican Star really playing up, Rocket Man followed by Jakestown, and there's Prince of Padua, Snow Prince in the colours of Lady Beaverbrook – people are being asked to keep back behind the second rail – there's the favourite Silver Falcon, not liking it at all, sweating up a lot. Jimmy Carlton'll have a problem there – he's very much a horse who likes to go out in front, and he'll have to decide whether to go on so as not to be cut off at the initial elbow after one and a half to two furlongs, or drop him in behind. . . .'

They were completely out of sight for a time, their progress charted by the commentary, and then the little coloured dots appeared against the green backcloth of the downs, making their way steadily round the back to the starting stalls. Behind the stalls, the runners circled, waiting. Richard had his race-glasses up.

'He's all right now,' he said. 'Carlton's got him settled, he's walking round with the others quite calmly. Don't worry, darling – he's fine.' Sally Foster was standing beside them. She put a hand up and tugged at the brim of her smart blue hat. Isabel had never heard her swear before.

'Jesus God,' she said slowly. 'I think I've aged twenty years. I don't dare think what Nigel felt like – '

Isabel was watching through her glasses; she was finding it difficult to focus. 'My hand's shaking,' she said, 'I can't hold the damned things steady – Can you see him, Richard? What's happening?'

'They're going into the stalls,' Richard answered. He dropped his glasses; they swung from their strap round his neck. He turned, put his arm round Isabel and kissed her hard on the cheek. 'He's in,' he said. 'Went in like a lamb – no trouble at all!'

The voice over the loudspeaker again, 'All loaded up now bar Rocket Man and Snow Prince – Snow Prince in – Rocket Man giving a bit of trouble there – '

Roy Farrant began to swear under his breath; his glasses

were clamped tight against his eyes and he could see his horse, backing away from the starting stalls. His exultation when the Falcon misbehaved had turned in seconds to a crushing terror that somehow, by some crippling blow of fate, Rocket Man would do what he had never in his life done before, and refuse to go into the stalls. Sweat started on his forehead and sprang out over his hands till they were slippery. 'All in,' the disembodied voice said. There was a sudden, complete silence over the vast crowd; the barking of a dog sounded absurdly loud from the opposite side of the course.

'They're off!' There was a massive gasp of excitement and then silence again, with nothing but the loudspeaker commentary echoing out.

Down below in Tattersalls' stand, Andrew Graham stood on tiptoe, listening and watching the blur of colour moving in a mass round the back straight, led by the grey horse.

Carlton had decided not to hold the Falcon back; he had jumped out of the stalls, fighting every yard of the way to get in front, followed very closely by Jakestown, with Mynah Bird and Snow Prince pressing close behind him. Fitter's Mate began to move up on the outside; he was a strong front runner with no stamina; his bolt would be shot by the time they ran down the hill before they got to Tattenham Corner. His jockey had been given 2000 pounds to do a job and he was coming out to do it. So too was Mynah Bird. Both jockeys applied their whips; Charley Barley had got away from the stalls so badly that he was the back marker of the field. The pattern was changing as they ran up the hill. The commentator told the silent crowd, his own voice quickening with excitement, 'Running up on the hill now, Silver Falcon just in front, with Fitter's Mate coming up fast on the outside followed by Snow Prince and Mexican Star making good progress, running on now to the top of the hill, it's Fitter's Mate pressing Silver Falcon, and they're closely bunched now, with Rocket Man well placed in fifth and Prince of Padua on the inside going up to join the leaders, running on down the hill now, all very close together still, Mexican Star dropping back now, and Rocket Man going very well just in behind Snow Prince.'

Roy Farrant, race-glasses clamped to his eyes, let out a muffled exclamation, as he saw the challenge of Mexican Star disappear, and the bright chestnut head drop further and further back from the leaders. His money had been well spent. In that direction. Now everything depended upon the others. And the only horse in touch with the Silver Falcon was the outsider Fitter's Mate.

The jockey riding Fitter's Mate had judged it perfectly; he knew that in another twenty yards his horse would start to drop out. Carlton had made it difficult by running ahead instead of laying in behind where he could have been the target for the fixed horses.

Fitter's Mate had to take his ground now and get him off balance or the chance would be lost.

And Carlton saw him coming, with the instinct that senses more than mere pursuit. He turned his head a fraction and saw the big bay horse racing upsides, bearing left to throw the Falcon off balance. He shouted a furious obscenity and kicked on, but Fitter's Mate, tiring even more suddenly than his jockey anticipated, hung inwards and the Falcon's stride was checked. Isabel saw it happen, so did Richard and she heard Nigel Foster groan out loud. The commentary rose in pitch as the horses rounded the steep angle of Tattenham Corner, a turn acute enough to unbalance all but the best horses after that gruelling up-hill down-hill run.

'Silver Falcon losing ground now, being pressed by Rocket Man who's taken up the running, with Snow Prince coming right up now to join him. . . .'

'He's lost,' Isabel whispered it. 'He's dropping back. . . .'

Roy Farrant was leaning over the edge of the box, his race-glasses dangling, shouting to his horse, Patsy shrilling with excitement at his elbow. 'Come on – come on, boy – you've got it, you've got it!' He could see the bay horse in the lead, his yellow and white colours standing out; he began pounding the edge of the box with his fists, not able to get out coherent words as he saw his life's ambition within reach.

'Inside the two-furlong marker now and it's Rocket Man, with Snow Prince under pressure, and Silver Falcon coming back! Silver Falcon fighting to get on terms again. . . .' There was a great roar from the huge crowd, as the grey colt began eating the ground with every stride. 'Silver Falcon pressing Rocket Man now, with Snow Prince dropping back, and Prince of Padua making a run, a furlong left now, and it's Silver Falcon from Rocket Man, coming on up the straight and it's Silver Falcon and Rocket Man fighting it out and Prince of Padua making very good progress, Silver Falcon well in the lead now in the final hundred and twenty yards it's Silver Falcon. . . .'

The crowd was roaring, screaming with excitement, Isabel could hear herself crying out, with Richard shouting beside her as the grey stormed towards the winning post.

'It's Silver Falcon. . . . Silver Falcon leading, being challenged now by Prince of Padua, less than fifty yards to go it's Lester Piggott on Prince of Padua coming up, Silver Falcon, Prince of Padua, neck and neck, twenty-five yards to go – '

There was a wild tumult of cheering and shouting as the two horses swept up to the winning post.

'It's Prince of Padua, just heading him, Prince of Padua and Lester Piggott, Silver Falcon second, Rocket Man third.'

And the voice of Peter O'Sullevan from millions of television screens all over the country.

'Prince of Padua wins the Derby, with Silver Falcon the favourite beaten by half a length, and Rocket Man some six lengths away third and Snow Prince in fourth place. One of the greatest contests ever seen at Epsom.'

Isabel stood frozen, tears came into her eyes. She saw Nigel leave the box, followed by Sally, to go and meet the Falcon. She felt Richard take her arm.

'Never mind, darling, never mind. It was lousy luck. Come on down now. Nigel's bringing him in.'

The winner's enclosure was small, flower-banked, over-looked by steps where spectators crowded, with the stands and the Royal Box above.

Steam was rising from the horses in clouds; the winner was given an ovation as he walked in off the course, with the Falcon following.

Photographers converged on the black colt, Lester Piggott jumped off and removed the saddle, people all around were clapping. The delighted owner and his attractive wife were swallowed up by reporters.

Isabel, with Richard beside her, waited for the Falcon. His neck and flanks were black with sweat, his ribs heaved from the enormous heart-bursting effort of that final run. For the first time, the proud head was lowered as if he knew of his defeat. She felt a surge of pity for him, and of pride in the lion-like courage that had brought him storming back to fight for supremacy to the last. Isabel patted the sweat-soaked neck; his saddle was off and the jockey stood holding it, talking to Nigel and to her. Tim, white-faced and silent, stood a little apart. Isabel suddenly remembered what this defeat meant to him.

'He was hampered coming up the hill,' Jimmy Carlton said. 'He lost his stride round the corner; that's what beat us. If he hadn't been interfered with by that little sod, we'd have won by three lengths. . . . He's a great horse, Madam.' He was facing Isabel, his face puckered with disappointment. 'Don't let anyone say anything else. He shouldn't have got beat.' A sweat rug was thrown over the Falcon; he stood quietly, devoid of spirit, nostrils flaring, blowing hard. The racing press were coming over to them, Nigel and Tim stood beside her. Nigel shook his head.

'It's the rottenest luck I've ever seen on a racecourse. He was bloody magnificent.' He pressed her shoulder and turned aside for a second.

She caught Tim by the arm. 'Oh, Tim – I'm so sorry.'

He managed to smile. 'Never mind; I'm just as disappointed for you. It was bloody bad luck, that's all.'

'Come on,' Richard said quietly. 'Beaten by half a length – he put up a performance that will make racing history. Here come the press. Chin up, my darling – they love a good loser.'

Roy Farrant was standing by Rocket Man in third place. Dick Shipley was with him, and they were talking to the jockey. He too cradled the saddle as he paused, anxious to be gone and weigh in.

He was sour with disappointment and he didn't try to be tactful. He spoke directly to Roy Farrant. 'He had every chance,' he said bluntly. 'No excuses for him – he just didn't have the speed.' Then he turned and hurried away. Patsy watched her husband. His face had sagged; if it was possible to age in the two minutes while the race was run, then he had done so. He didn't touch the horse.

'Never mind,' Dick Shipley said crisply. He hadn't expected to win; those few moments when the Falcon fell behind and Rocket Man went in front had come as a complete surprise to him. He knew a bad loser and he was anxious to withdraw Farrant from the public eye. 'Never mind, he did his best. Come and I'll buy you a drink.'

Roy looked at him. 'He's a duck-hearted bastard,' he said thickly. 'He hit the front and he gave up. Don't try and kid me.' He turned and walked away. Patsy gave Shipley an apologetic smile.

'Don't take any notice,' she murmured. 'He's just upset. He was sure he was going to win. We'll just have to try again next year.' She slipped away to try to find her husband.

Andrew Graham had hurried into a bar. There were very few people inside and he ordered himself a second whisky. The Falcon had lost. He sipped the drink slowly. Charles Schriber had lost. He had seen Isabel for a brief moment, standing beside the Falcon. There was no triumph for her after all, no presentation, no cheers. The Schriber luck was out. He shifted the race-glasses against his shoulder. He hadn't opened the case once. He had an alarming thought; perhaps Tim Ryan wouldn't remember or even bother to keep to their arrangement. He had just lost a quarter of a million dollars under the terms of Charles's will.

Anxiety made him shake. He finished his drink and hurried out; people were flooding in again. The race following the Derby was an inevitable anti-climax. He could hear the comments, the praise for Lester Piggott, and the laments of punters whom Silver Falcon had disappointed. He pushed his way against them and reached the open air. The rails separated him from the Members' Enclosure, guarded by officials scrutinizing badges. Isabel and Richard would be in one of the bars, consoling themselves . . . but not Tim. Tim would have gone with Nigel Foster to see to the Falcon. Andrew almost ran to the exit; he had wasted time having that drink, Tim could have gone into the stables and returned to the Members'. . . . He rushed across the road, hooted at furiously by a driver who had to brake to miss him. The big green gates of the stable yard were guarded by two security men. He hesitated. Then he went up to one of them. 'Pardon me,' his Southern accent was disarming. 'Do you know if a Mr Ryan is inside? Mrs Schriber's racing manager – Silver Falcon?'

The man shook his head. 'Couldn't tell you, sir.' His look was discouraging. His companion was more forthcoming.

'I've just passed the horse's trainer in,' he said. 'He had a gentleman with him; he signed the book. Might have been the one you mentioned, sir. I'd wait outside for a bit; they shouldn't be too long. They're dope testing inside at the moment.'

'Thank you,' Andrew said. 'That's mighty kind of you.' He saw Nigel Foster before he or Tim saw him; both men were walking side by side, their heads slightly down. He half turned away, not wanting Nigel to see him, and then decided that it didn't matter. Nothing was more important than contacting Ryan. He came up to Tim, who stopped and looked startled. 'I'm so sorry about what happened,' Andrew said. 'He should have won.' Nigel hardly looked at him; he walked on, leaving Tim behind him. He had seen so many people that day, and heard the same thing said over and over again in the stable yard and the Members' Enclosure. He should have won. He put up a magnificent fight. Damned bad luck, if he hadn't got hampered coming into Tattenham Corner. It was all true and said with generosity, but nothing relieved the sick pangs of disappointment. He should have won, but he hadn't.

And coming second is never the same, however you could claim to have been cheated. He didn't take any notice of Andrew Graham or give him a thought. He crossed the road and disappeared back into the Members' to join up with Sally.

He would really have liked to get away from Isabel and Richard for a half an hour, and just stay with his wife.

Tim looked at Andrew. The older man's expression was sympathetic.

'I'm really sorry,' he said again. 'What a blow for you, too.'

'Can't be helped,' Tim said. He put his hand on Andrew's shoulder. 'Come and have a drink,' he said. Andrew accepted.

'You'll have to come slumming with me,' he said. 'I'm in Tattersalls.'

Tim said nothing, reminded that it was Isabel's hostility which denied him a Members' badge. He felt suddenly shamed at the thought of Charles's oldest friend standing the other side of the rail to watch the Falcon run. Shamed and angry. It was so unlike her to be mean spirited; it could only be Richard's influence. He talked to Andrew about the Falcon as they stood together in one corner of a large bar under the Stand.

'I've never seen him like it,' he said. 'Normally you can't get near him, but he just stood there while they did the dope test, with his head down. He broke his heart trying to win today. Nigel hasn't said anything but I know what he thinks. He's afraid he'll never be the same again.'

'And how is Isabel taking it?'

'Very well,' Tim said. 'Richard couldn't care bloody less. Full of good cheer, and think how marvellous it is to be second. . . .' He glared at Andrew, and most of his resentment was the ruin of all his hopes. There was no money to restore the house in Kildare, his father would die in the modest little cottage and he, Tim Ryan, would go on working for other rich men for the rest of his life. 'He's a mean bastard,' he said savagely. 'He never wanted that horse to run and I believe he's rotten enough to be glad it lost today – '

'And she doesn't see any of it,' Andrew said quietly. 'She takes everything at face value.' He shook his head. 'I've got to see her today. You're sure you can do it?'

'I'll make bloody certain,' Tim said. 'I'll get her there. Don't you worry. After the last race.'

'Yes,' Andrew said. 'It seems crazy to have to do it this way but it's our only hope.'

'She wouldn't see you otherwise,' Tim said bitterly. 'She's completely under his influence. You just be there and leave the rest to me. I'll go back and find them now.'

He went up the steps and out to the entrance to the Members'. He felt sick with anger, anger at the rotten fate which had robbed him of so much, anger with Isabel for behaving in a way that was obstinate and out of character, and real hatred for Richard Schriber. Richard had taken her from him; if it hadn't been for him, the Falcon might have lost the race, but he could well have been on the way to marrying Isabel. Not for her money, but because he loved her, because they had everything in common and together they could have made his dream into a reality which would have given her as much joy as himself. Richard had wrecked everything, with the cunning of his kind, turned her against Andrew Graham because he knew the truth about him, beguiled and dominated her sexually until she hadn't a mind of her own.

The subterfuge he and Andrew had to adopt to get her to speak to Charles's best friend was typical of how cleverly Richard had managed her. Lies and deceit were a necessity, if she was to learn the truth.

He didn't care if she sacked him afterwards. It would be worth anything to get her away from Richard before she was duped into marrying him. He placed a bet on a horse in the next race and then went in to find her. Luckily Nigel was of the same opinion as himself. The Falcon needed time in his box before the journey. He wouldn't be going home to Lambourn until after the last race.

14

'I feel so desperately sorry for Tim,' Isabel said. She was walking with Richard down to the paddock to see the horses before the last race. Her arm was through his, and they were able to pass through much more easily; some of the crowd had thinned out and only the enthusiasts were making the long trek down to the paddock at the end of the day. Isabel had wanted to get away from people and out of the stuffy champagne bar; the sense of frozen disappointment was changing to positive regret for Nigel and for Tim. 'He's lost that money Charles left him,' she said. 'It's a dreadful blow to him.'

'I'd forgotten about that,' Richard said. He squeezed her arm against his side. She had behaved with admirable restraint after the Falcon's defeat; there was no sign of low spirits when people commiserated. She had shown generosity and good sportsmanship, and without any prompting, had come up publicly to congratulate Charles St George, Prince of Padua's owner.

Such gestures are noted in the racing world; she and the Falcon would get a very good press the next day. Richard had never been more proud of her or admired her more. He had wanted the Falcon to win for her, but as he said, it was a defeat without disgrace. The horse had earned himself a place in the history of the great race, by a performance of breath-taking courage which had almost won him the crown.

'If you're worried about Tim,' he said, 'maybe we could do something.'

'He wouldn't take a penny,' Isabel said. 'I tried that before. He was going to restore the house and put his father back into it. It was so mean of Charles to have left the money like that – he should have given it to him!'

'Typical Charles,' Richard said. 'He would have called it an incentive. Don't worry, darling. We'll think of something. The house is for sale, isn't it?' She nodded. 'Well, maybe we could buy it. That would give him the money anyway. As my life is going to be one long trip from racecourse to racecourse, we might as well have somewhere in Ireland.'

Isabel stopped and looked up at him. 'Richard, that's a wonderful idea! Because there's something I've been meaning to say to you. I don't want to live at Beaumont.'

He walked her slowly forward; they came to the paddock rails and stopped. The horses walked past them.

'Neither do I,' he said slowly. 'I wondered how to suggest it to you. I never want to see the place again. We could transfer most of the horses to Ireland and sell off the stock we don't want. And get right out the States. Personally, I don't want to have a place there.'

The owners, trainers and jockeys were entering the ring. It was strangely muted, a pale copy of the high drama which had taken place earlier that afternoon.

'We'll talk to him about it,' Isabel said. She turned to Richard and smiled. 'I'm so relieved,' she said. 'I've wanted to get rid of Beaumont ever since Charles died, and I didn't know how to admit it. And we can help Tim and his family too – without hurting his pride. I'm sorry about the Falcon, but it isn't the end of the world. Either we'll go on running him as a four-year-old or he can retire to stud. We can bring the best of the brood mares and the stallions over and start breeding in Ireland – darling, you really are wonderful – are you sure you're not going to hate every minute of it?'

'Don't worry,' Richard said. 'I shall have my own interests. I shall drink and gamble and run after women; but maybe not for the first twenty years – let's go back and watch this race. I fancy no. 7. Nice-looking sort, rather like your chestnut. By the way, you haven't given him a name yet. . . .'

'You think of one,' Isabel said. 'And that scraggy animal isn't anything like him – you can lose your money on him if you like!'

They watched the race from the stands; it was won by Richard's choice. Isabel found Tim coming towards them. He smiled, but it was obviously an effort. 'I've been looking for you,' he said to her.

'Richard's just backed another winner,' she said. 'He's the only one who's had any luck today.'

'I'll go and collect it,' Richard said. 'Take care of Isabel for me; I'll meet you both in the owners' bar. We'll have a bottle together, and get Nigel and Sally to join us. They need cheering up.' He turned away, making for the Tote. Tim watched him go.

'Nigel wants you to come and see the Falcon,' he said. 'Phil and Harry would appreciate it. He'll be loaded up pretty soon now.' Isabel nodded. 'Of course I'll come. I'd like to see them and thank them. How is the Falcon?'

'I'm not sure,' Tim said slowly. 'It's certainly taken the stuffing out of him. Let's go this way, we can dodge some of the crowds coming out.'

He took her arm briefly, steering her to the exit nearest the stable entrance, guiding her through the cars which were beginning to stream out onto the road. She wouldn't thank him for what he was doing; she might even turn round and walk away when she saw Andrew Graham. He would probably lose his job when Richard heard what he had done. But he didn't care. He had lost everything himself, and seen his horse defeated. He thought of the Falcon as his, as much as anyone's: he had nurtured the foal through his first year of life, watched over him as a yearling, and planned his victorious two-year-old campaign. He had shared Charles Schriber's hopes every day for three years, seeing the dream come nearer to reality, seeing, in that codicil, a new life for himself and a bright future. Now there was only disillusion and disappointment left. From the time he was a boy, and he had realized that so much depended upon him, Tim Ryan had suppressed and disciplined his emotions. He had prided himself on being a cool, hard-headed

Irishman. Now his nature was in revolt; bitterness and frustration had overcome his caution and innate shrewdness when the Falcon lost the Derby, beaten by one he had so easily defeated when they met at Longchamp on equal terms.

And he had lost Isabel too. If she could somehow be dragged back from marrying Richard Schriber, then he could perhaps hope that one day. . . .

'Here we are,' he said. 'Last race, and they send the security boys home. We can just walk in.'

Andrew Graham had timed it perfectly. He too had crossed the road but earlier, loitering near enough to the stable gates to go through as soon as the guards went off duty. He walked through into the big yard, unchallenged by anyone. There were horseboxes inside, and a lot of bustle; horses were being loaded up, engines started to rev up and a giant blue-painted horsebox loomed in front of him, making for the open gateway. He stepped aside, bumping into a stable lad carrying a travelling rug. Andrew shouted at him.

'I'm looking for the Silver Falcon's box – you know where it is?'

The lad called back as he hurried away. 'Down on the right – '

Andrew quickened his pace; he asked again at the start of the row of loose boxes, some with their doors wide open, and someone pointed to a box at the very end of the line. He thanked him, but they had gone back inside their box, tending the horse hidden from view. Andrew was smiling. Right at the end of the line. He would have a perfect view of her when she came along. And of Ryan. There was so much activity about, and noise. It would be so easy – so quickly done, and then he could slip away – twenty million dollars, the house and the stud, the horses. . . .

He raised his left elbow and unfastened the race-glasses case. He had reached the end box; the door was closed, and he looked inside.

A man was crouching beside the Falcon, tying the ends of the last bandage on his foreleg. He straightened up as Andrew spoke to him.

Andrew had dealt with stablemen all his life. He had a natural authority.

'Your boss is looking for you,' he said. 'He wants you up at the main gate right away. Mrs Schriber's on her way over.'

The lower door opened and Phil came out. 'Thanks very much, sir.' He strode off in search of Nigel Foster. Andrew slipped off the race-glasses case and opened it. MacNeil's gun was inside, fully loaded. He turned aside slightly and slipped it into his right pocket; then he adjusted the empty case back on his shoulder. His heart had begun to beat faster, but not too fast. His hand was steady, and dry; he felt as he had done the night he waited outside the drawing room door at Coolbridge, with the spanner in his grasp. Calm, almost detached, possessed of unnatural strength and nerve. It would look as if someone with a racing grudge had killed them. Them. He couldn't let Ryan live, of course. Nobody would ever know of the arrangement they had made to bring Isabel to the stables. It would be a real mystery. His plane ticket was in his wallet; he would be on his way back to the States while they were still in the first stage of investigation. And with so much noise and activity, the sound of the two shots wouldn't be noticed. He would be out of the gates while everyone else was running towards Isabel and Ryan. . . . He looked up and then he saw Nigel Foster. The trainer was half turned away from him, talking to someone else. Andrew went stiff. Foster had seen him when he called at Kresswell House. And again that afternoon when he came up to Tim Ryan. He hadn't bothered to acknowledge him then, but if he saw him again, just before the killings, he would be certain to remember. If he turned fully round and saw him, his whole plan was at risk. Andrew didn't hesitate. He swung round, unbolted the Falcon's door and slipped inside.

Isabel and Tim came through the gates; they paused, as Andrew had done, stepping aside to let a transport through. Phil came up to them. 'Afternoon, Madam. Bad luck our feller didn't win – he ran a great race though – '

'Yes,' Isabel said. 'He did.' She opened her handbag and took out a clip of notes. Phil saw it coming and pretended not to; she pressed the tip into his hand, and he saluted.

'Thank you, Madam. Thank you very much. Have you seen the guvnor? He wants me – '

'No,' Tim spoke impatiently. 'He's sure to be here somewhere.' He took Isabel's arm and led her through and into the yard. He couldn't see Andrew anywhere, and it was just as well. He must be keeping in the background. They had planned exactly what to do. He would bring her to the Falcon's box, show her the horse, and Andrew would come up and speak to her. After that it was up to him to make her stay and listen to him. Tim would have played his part; he intended to slip away and leave them alone. Andrew said he had the copy of the death certificate, showing that Richard Schriber's father had died in the mental institution.

'This way,' Tim said to her. 'He's in the last box up here.'

The inside of the Falcon's box was dim. Andrew stood pressed against the side of the upper door, where he could see out. The grey horse hadn't moved. He was standing at the back, and Andrew had soothed him quietly as he came inside. His head had raised for a moment at the intruder and then lowered. Man, the enemy was close to him. But not too close. His quarters stung from the cuts of the whip and there was pain and stiffness in his body from the tremendous physical strain it had endured. Andrew glanced back at him briefly, and then looked sideways out of the open door. Isabel and Tim Ryan were walking directly towards him, Ryan a little in front of her on the nearside. Andrew took the gun out of his pocket, balanced his left arm on the edge of the door, rested his gun arm on it and took careful aim. One shot; he was aiming at her head, and he had been a first-class marksman with both a rifle and a pistol since he was a young man. Right through the middle of the forehead, so conveniently exposed by the close-fitting hat. And then Ryan. One. Two. Two seconds and it would all be over.

He slipped the safety catch.

It was pure chance that he killed Tim Ryan first. Pure chance that Nigel Foster broke off his conversation with a fellow trainer and called out to them as he saw them walking along the line of boxes.

'Isabel! Hang on a minute – ' She heard him and stopped, half turning as she did so. Tim Ryan swung round with her. In the split second when Andrew Graham squeezed the trigger, it was Tim who came into range. For the next two or three seconds his body masked Isabel, the bullet had hit him in the side of the head, his hat went spinning off, and he began to sag quite slowly. Andrew had lost the sighting necessary to get a lethal shot at Isabel. He heard her scream as Ryan collapsed; for a moment she stood upright, paralysed, and he steadied his wrist again to take aim.

There was a rustle behind him but he didn't hear it.

The noise of the gunshot had exploded in the Falcon's ear. Suddenly the lethargy, the instinct that knew he had been beaten, vanished with that sudden assault upon his nerves. His ears went flat; hate boiled up in him, imperious rage at the presence of the human enemy. He sensed danger, and his reaction was instantaneous. He reared up and launched himself. Andrew Graham fired a second time, but the bullet sang its way past Isabel, as she dropped to her knees by Tim Ryan.

There were people shouting, and running, converging on the stricken man and the woman trying to support him. The crowd hid them from view; a horse began to plunge and rear with fright on the end of its rope, refusing to go up the ramp of a waiting horsebox, infected by the panic in the yard. Somebody running towards the scene heard a terrible scream coming from one of the boxes, but only remembered it afterwards.

The full weight of the horse struck Andrew Graham from behind; the hooves crashed into his back, knocking him to his knees; he shrieked with pain and terror, and the Falcon, maddened with rage and panic by the noise, rose up and crashed down upon him again. It was the classic fight to the death in the colt's mind. He reared and trampled, reared and trampled as he would have done to a fallen contender to his title for leadership of the herd. With his teeth he savaged the crumpled body in the straw and turning contemptuously on it, lashed out with his hind feet. He sensed death and neighed in triumph. He had forgotten how his heart had burst in vain on the racecourse, forgotten the humiliation of spirit as he was passed by his rival, in spite of all his savage striving. He had killed the enemy. He stood still at last, trembling in the quarters and the forelegs, breathing hard. Then he turned away and pulled a few wisps from the hay in the rack above his head.

It was a long time before anybody opened the box.

It was an afternoon of sudden showers and brilliant sun; the sky was a patchwork of prussian blue and rolling rain clouds. Ireland in late summer, with the trees dropping water on the walkers underneath whenever the wind blew. The driveway was smooth, its edges clipped and the surface gleaming with new gravel; the house waited for Isabel and Richard at the end of it, framed in the clouds, with the sun striking off its grey slate roof and the unshuttered windows, splendid with glass. Richard drove slowly; it was the second time they had been to see it since Tim Ryan's funeral. His father was waiting there to welcome them. It was nearly three months since they had bought the house; he had taken her away on a honeymoon that was as far from recent places and events as his imagination could devise. They had got married after Tim Ryan was brought back to Ireland and buried in the cemetery near his home. And Richard had known that what Isabel needed was change and time. He took her to Sicily, and they wandered through the ruins of the Arab and Greek civilizations, and from there to North Africa until the heat drove them back to Europe, and finally he decided that the peace and beauty of the Loire valley would complete the process of healing before they came back to England. And then on to Ireland, where they were to make their home. Beaumont was sold in the high summer; he didn't even show her the cable telling her the record price it had fetched. They were in Taormina at the time, staying in a villa perched on a hill, where the flaring magnificence of Etna provided the backcloth to their nights.

It was she who decided when they should return. She put her arms round him one evening, when they had come back from a long, lazy stroll through the French countryside, and said quietly, 'Darling, I think it's time we went home.' Richard booked on a flight two days later.

He had bought the Ryans' family home and given it to her as a wedding present. And they had gone to see Tim's father together and asked him how he wanted the money to be distributed. He had taken some time to answer; his son's death had made him hesitant, the shock was too recent to be absorbed. He wanted very little for himself – Tim had two young nephews that he had been devoted to – it was such a lot of money. When Richard and Isabel asked if he would leave its disposition to them, he had merely nodded, anxious to avoid decisions. But time had healed him too; he had written to them reporting progress on the house, and asking if he might go there and meet them when they arrived from England. To welcome them, the letter said, on behalf of his son Timothy. And his grandsons, who'd been so handsomely endowed. As they stopped in front of the entrance, Richard held her hand. Her face was fuller, with a healthy colour from hot suns; being loved by him had made her beautiful, and there was no longer any shadow in her eyes. Instead there was a new serenity, a spirit strengthened by absolute trust and love. He thought suddenly how different she looked, and couldn't quite see why.

The crumbling plaster façade had been renewed; the walls were a soft pink, the stucco pillars splendidly white, and the steps led up to a handsome mahogany door. They walked up together, and for a moment he felt Isabel hesitate.

'I did exactly this with Tim,' she said. 'It was the same sort of day.' And then the door opened and Frederick Ryan was waiting for them. He took Isabel's hand, and she bent forward and kissed him.

'Welcome, my dear,' he said. 'Come in.'

The interior was light, with delicate Georgian colouring, and the beautiful double cube room, with its painted ceiling, was completely restored. There was no furniture, or carpets, just the smooth shell of the house, waiting to be made into a home.

Frederick Ryan paused. 'It's looking as beautiful as it did when I brought my wife here, forty years ago. I know you're going to be very happy.'

'We are,' Richard said. 'It's a new start for us, Mr Ryan. And we both need it.'

'You're young enough,' the old man said. 'You can overcome the evil in the world. I used to pray that my son's children would grow up here one day. Now it's your children I hope I shall see. And because of your generosity, my family has a chance to start again. My daughter's sons. . . . Tim would be so happy about what you've done for them.'

Isabel looked at him. 'He loved this house so much,' she said. 'And the horses. I felt he was quite near when we arrived.'

The old man smiled, 'You're sounding very Irish, Mrs Schriber,' he said. 'But why shouldn't you be right? He loved the house and he loved his horses. That grey colt of yours – and you. You don't mind me saying that, Mr Schriber – my son loved your wife very much. . . .'

'I know,' Richard said, 'and I don't mind.'

They walked through the rooms together; Frederick Ryan pointed out the view from the main bedroom on the first floor. 'I was born here,' he said. 'And my father and grandfather before that. And all my children. I have a few things in store which belong here. I would like you to have them.'

'Thank you,' Isabel said gently. 'We'd love to have them.'

They paused by the window; the view was magnificent, rolling green fields with a background of low hills, veiled in purple clouds.

'Your stallion boxes are all finished,' the old man said. 'And they're well ahead with the foaling boxes and the rest – it's looking splendid. I hope you'll invite me over to see the horses.'

'As soon as they arrive,' Richard promised.

'Will the Silver Falcon be standing here?' He turned to look at them. Isabel hesitated.

'He's killed one man, and nearly killed another. You can't pass that temperament on.'

Frederick Ryan looked at her and then at Richard. 'He saved your wife's life,' he said. 'He killed my son's murderer. Horses have more sense than men. Are you telling me he's dead?'

'No,' Isabel said. 'We were advised to do it, but I couldn't. . . . I wanted time before I made up my mind.'

'Race him, if he'll train on,' Tim's father said. 'That's what he's bred for. Let him fight his own kind on the racecourse.'

'Nigel wants to try for the Arc de Triomphe,' Richard said.

The old man nodded. 'He'll win it for you. Tim wrote to me once and said that he believed he could take that prize as well as the Derby. I'll leave you now, and let you wander round your new home by yourselves.

They shook hands and he kissed Isabel. 'Goodbye, my dear,' he said. 'And God bless you. Be happy.'

Richard put his arms round her; they stood together in silence for some moments. 'He's a wonderful old man,' Richard said. 'I'd forgotten there were people like that left.'

'I think we're going to love it here,' Isabel said. She looked round the bedroom; there was a magnificent marble fireplace, decorated with vines and flowers in different coloured marbles. The same decoration had been copied by the plasterers who moulded the cornices round the ceiling.

'I love this room,' she said. 'I think we'll carry on the tradition and have our first child here.' She saw the look of surprise on his face and she smiled.

'In about seven months' time,' she said.